# EXO

# Steven Gould

# EXO

WITHDRAWN

**TOR®**

A TOM DOHERTY ASSOCIATES BOOK

NEW YORK

EXO

Copyright © 2014 by Steven Gould

A Tor Book
Published by Tom Doherty Associates, LLC
175 Fifth Avenue
New York, NY 10010

www.tor-forge.com

Tor® is a registered trademark of Tom Doherty Associates, LLC.

Library of Congress Cataloging-in-Publication Data

Gould, Steven.
    Exo / Steven Gould. — 1st ed.
        p. cm.
    "A Tom Doherty Associates Book"
    ISBN 978-0-7653-3654-5 (hardcover)
    ISBN 978-1-4668-2848-3 (e-book)
    1. Teleportation—Fiction.   2. Science fiction.   I. Title.
    PS3557.O8947 E96 2014
    813'.54—dc23

                                        2014015849

Tor books may be purchased for educational, business, or promotional use. For information on bulk purchases, please contact Macmillan Corporate and Premium Sales Department at 1-800-221-7945, extension 5442, or write specialmarkets@macmillan.com.

First Edition: September 2014

Printed in the United States of America

0  9  8  7  6  5  4  3  2  1

For John Robert "Bob" Stahl

5 June 1952–19 December 2013

"What if . . ."

# EXO

# ONE

## Cent: Tell him about breaking the guy's jaw—he'll like that

I was breathing pure oxygen through a full face mask and the rest of my body was covered in heavily insulated hooded coveralls, gloves, and boots. The electronic thermometer strapped around my right sleeve read forty-five degrees below zero. The aviation GPS strapped to my left arm read forty-five thousand feet above sea level. I was three miles higher than Everest.

The curvature of the earth was pronounced, and though the sun was out, the sky was only blue at the horizon, fading to deep blue and then black overhead.

There were stars.

The air was thin.

I was dropping.

I reached two hundred miles per hour within seconds, but I didn't want to go down yet. I jumped back to forty-five thousand feet and loitered, falling and returning, never letting myself fall more than a few seconds. But then the mask fogged, then frosted, and I felt a stinging on my wrist and a wave of dizziness.

I jumped away, appearing twenty-five thousand feet lower, in warmer and thicker air. I let myself fall, working my jaw vigorously to equalize the pressure in my inner ears.

Jumping directly back to ground level would probably have burst my eardrums.

With the air pulling at my clothes and shrieking past my helmet, I watched the GPS's altimeter reading flash down through the numbers. When it blurred past ten thousand feet, I took a deep breath and jumped home to the cabin in the Yukon.

"Looks like frostbite," Mom said two days later.

I had a half-inch blister on the back of my right wrist and it was turning dark brown. "Will I lose my arm?"

Mom laughed. "I don't think so. What were you doing?"

I shrugged. "Stuff."

She stopped laughing. Mom could smell evasion at a hundred yards. "Antarctica?"

I thought about agreeing—it *was* winter down there, after all. "No, I was only nine miles away from the pit."

"West Texas? It has to be in the nineties there, if not warmer."

I pointed my finger up.

She looked at the ceiling, puzzled, then her mouth formed an "o" shape. "Nine miles. Straight up?"

"Well, nine miles above sea level."

Mom's mouth worked for a bit before she managed. "I trust you bundled up. Oxygen, too?"

"And I didn't talk to strangers."

She was not amused.

"How are your ears?"

"Fine. I jumped up *and* down in stages. Deep breaths. No embolisms. No bends."

Her eyes widened. "I didn't realize *bends* was an issue. I thought the bends were a diving thing."

Me and my big mouth.

"Uh, it can happen when you go to altitude."

She waved her hand in a "go on" sort of way.

"Nitrogen bubbles form in the bloodstream when you drop the pressure faster than it can be offloaded by the lungs. So, yeah, it happens when you scuba dive deep, absorbing lots of nitrogen, and then come up too fast. But it can also happen by ascending to high altitude with normal nitrogen in your bloodstream."

"How do you prevent it?"

"I prebreathe pure oxygen down on the ground, for forty-five minutes. It flushes out the nitrogen so it doesn't form bubbles. No decompression sickness."

I rubbed the skin around the blister. "But what I really need is a pressure suit."

"Like a spacesuit?"

"Yes."

*Very* like a spacesuit.


Dad showed up in my bedroom doorway before dinner.

"Are you trying to kill yourself?"

*Someone* (I'm looking at *you*, Mom) had clearly told him about the bit of frostbite on my wrist.

I raised my eyebrows.

He held up his hands and exhaled. After two breaths he said, "Starting over." He paused a beat. "What are you trying to accomplish?"

I hadn't talked about it, mainly because I knew Dad would wig out. But least he was making an effort. "For starters, LEO."

"Low Earth orbit." He took a deep breath and let it out. "I was afraid of that." He sounded more resigned than anything.

I stared hard at his face and said, "You can't say it's an unworthy goal."

He looked away, avoiding my eyes.

He was the one who'd jump me into the tall grass on the dunes, Cape Canaveral, at about T-minus-five minutes back when the shuttles were still operational. The night launches were my favorite.

His homeschool physics lessons used spacecraft velocities and accelerations. History work included manned space travel, and we worked the 1967 outer-space treaty into politics and law.

He helped me build and fire model rockets into the sky.

He sighed again. "I'd never say that," Dad agreed. "I just want you to *not die*."

Lately I wasn't as concerned with that.

It even had its attraction.

It had only been one-and-a-half years, but both of us had changed.

I was a bit taller, a bit wider in the hips and chest, and it looked like I'd seen my last outbreak of acne vulgaris. I was more experienced. I was far less confident.

New Prospect, on the other hand, was the same size, but it wore natty fall colors. The aspens above town were a glorious gold, and along the streets the maples and oaks and elms ranged from red to yellow. The raking had started and bags waited at the sidewalk's edge for the city compost pickup. I'd seen the town decked out before, but that was austere winter white, or the crusty grays of snow waiting too long for more snow or melting weather.

Main Street, though, hadn't changed enough to be strange. It was full of memories, and when I saw the coffee shop the whole thing blurred out of focus and ran down my cheeks.

I had to take a moment.

The barista was new, not one from my time, and she served me with a friendly, yet impersonal, smile. I kept the hood of my sweatshirt forward, shadowing my face. The place was half full. It was Saturday afternoon, and though some of the patrons were young, they looked more like they went to the community college rather than Beckwou th High. I didn't recognize any of them until I went up the stairs to the mezzanine.

I nearly jumped away.

*When the lemon gets squeezed it's hard on the lemon.*

Instead I went to the table and pulled out my old chair and sat across from her.

She'd been reading and her face, when she looked up, went from irritation, to wide-eyed surprise, then, *dammit*, tears.

I leaned forward and put my hand over hers. "Shhhhh."

Tara had also changed. When I'd first seen her, she bordered on anorexic, but the last time I saw her she was putting on healthy weight. Now she looked scary thin again, but it could be a growing spurt. She was taller than I remembered. At least she no longer hid herself beneath layers. She's Diné on her mother's side and Hispanic on her dad's, though she never talked about him other than to say he was well out of her life.

It was so good to see her.

"Sorry, Cent," she said after a moment.

I gestured toward the window with my free hand. "I just did the same thing on the sidewalk. I know why *I* did it. Why did *you*?"

It set her off again.

"Should you even be here?" she managed after a while.

I shrugged. "I missed the place."

"Where are you going to school now?"

I grimaced. "Back to homeschooling. Sort of. Most of what I'm doing lately has been online, or I'll audit a college course if the class size is big enough. I don't register. How are you doing at Beckwourth?"

She shrugged. "Coasting. I'm taking marketing design and women's studies at NPCC. That's where my real effort is." She tapped the book.

I read the chapter heading upside down, "The Social Construction of Gender."

"And Jade?"

"She's at Smith. Two thousand miles away."

I nodded. I'd heard that from Joe. "You guys still, uh, together?"

The corners of her mouth hooked down. "As together as we can be from that distance." She shook her head. "We text, we talk, we vid-chat on computer. We do homework together." She glanced at her phone, lying on the table. "My phone would've beeped six times already if she weren't in class. Her parents are taking her to Europe over Christmas break. I think her mother is doing it deliberately, so Jade will have less time with me."

"Really?"

She shook her head violently. "I'm probably just me being paranoid. It's the opportunity of a lifetime, you know? Jade swears that they're okay with us. Or at least they're resigned. But she's not coming home for Thanksgiving. They could afford it, but her mom arranged for her to spend the break with some East

Coast relatives—*distant* relatives. I won't see Jade until the third week in January."

*Ouch.*

"Enough about my shit," Tara said. "Are you seeing anybody?"

I had to look away. I felt the same expression on my face that I'd seen on hers. Then I told her what I hadn't even told my parents. "I was. No longer."

"Oh," she said, quietly. "Sorry." Then she quoted me, from the first day I'd met her: *"So I'm unsocialized and very likely to say the wrong thing. Just want you to know I was raised in a box, right? I'm not trying to be mean—I'm just stupid that way."*

It worked. I smiled. "I know. *Muy estúpido.*"

She hit me. "You want to talk about it?"

I shook my head. "A little too *fresh*, you know?"

She nodded. "Oh, yeah. I know." She gave me a moment, sipping at her drink. "So, are you going to be around? Or is this just a quick check-in, with you disappearing for another year or two?"

I hadn't thought about it. Mostly I just wanted to see the place. It was probably the breakup. It brought back memories of all those places where things had started, but I realized how good it was to see her.

"I missed you guys. I'd like to keep in contact, without being stupid. Remember what happened to you and Jade when you hung out with me before?"

*"You* didn't do that."

"Yeah, but if you hadn't been hanging with me—"

"I *wish* you could hang out with both of us. It would mean Jade and I were in the same place."

"Ah. Well, right." I said. "Maybe I can help with that."

I can't jump to someplace I've never been. The exception is jumping to a place I can see from where I am: to the other side of a windowed door; to a ledge up a cliff; to the other side of persons facing me. I've jumped as far as a half mile using binoculars to pick my destination.

But I'd never been to Northampton, Massachusetts, where

Smith College was. The closest I'd been was New York City or Boston. I could've jumped to one of those cities and taken a train or a bus. Or I could've flown into Bradley International near Hartford, Connecticut, but going into airports was something we avoided unless there was no choice.

I stepped out from between two trees against a wrought iron fence in Washington Square. I was overwarm even though the insulated overall I wore was off my shoulders, the arms tied around my waist and its hood was hanging down over my butt. It was only *slightly* cool here. People walked by in light jackets or pullovers. The leaves were starting to turn here, too, but it was the beginning of the change, with many trees still green and very few fallen leaves.

The sun had set twenty minutes before, but the sky was still lit, and, of course, it was New York City, so it never really got dark. One way or another, barring power outages, it would stay brightly lit until sunrise.

And that would never do for my next trick.

I caught a half-full, uptown A train at the West 4th Street station, and rode standing, a grip on the vertical stanchion near the door. I put my earphones in and pretended to listen to music, but, as usual, when I'm *en público*, I people watch, and the earphones make them think I'm not listening.

A man, olive-skinned, light, trimmed beard, early thirties, well dressed in slacks, silk shirt, and a leather jacket, stepped up to me. He gestured at his own ears and said loudly, "Watcha listenin' to?" He grabbed the same stanchion I was using, brushing against my hand.

I shifted my hand up the pole and leaned back. He was in my space. The subway car wasn't *that* full.

He grinned and repeated himself, increasing the volume.

I sighed and took one earphone out. "Pardon?"

"Whatcha listenin' to?"

"An audio book."

He raised his eyebrows, prepared, I guess, to have opinions about music, but thrown by literature.

"Oh? What book?"

I looked around. There was an empty seat at the other end of the car between two big black guys, but they were sitting with their legs apart and their knees nearly touched, despite the empty seat between them.

"Must be a good book, yeah?"

I said, "Yes."

"What's it called?"

"*Walden.*"

"Huh. What's it about?"

"It's about someone who wants to be left alone."

I put the earphone back in my ear.

He frowned, and then deliberately slid his hand up the stanchion. At the same time he swung around it, his free hand coming up behind me.

I let go and stepped away. "Hands to yourself!" I shouted. He flinched and the other passengers looked up.

"What the fuck are you talking about, girl?" he said.

"Get away from me!" I kept the volume up.

Mom told me that. *When someone is acting inappropriately, don't normalize it. Make it clear to* everyone *that you are not okay with the behavior.* I'd seen her demonstrate it, once, when she and I were shopping in Tokyo. A man grabbed for her breast on the train. We'd had a long talk about it.

The asshole held his hands up, palm outward, and said, "You're *crazy*, bitch."

I walked around him and went down the other end of the car, standing by the two black guys. He followed, muttering angrily. I wasn't worried about him. Worst-case scenario, I would just jump away, but he creeped me out.

The bigger of the two black men stood up and said, "Have a seat," then stepped suddenly past me, blocking my friend with the boundary issues.

I sank down into hard plastic seat, watching, fascinated.

No words were exchanged, but the man in the silk and leather backpedaled, two quick steps, before he turned away and went back to the other end of the car.

The black man turned around and grabbed the stanchion. "You okay?" he said.

I nodded. "Thanks."

He reached into his jacket and pulled out his phone. After going through a few menu choices he showed a photo to me. "My daughter. She's at Columbia. On my way up to visit her."

*Oh.* "Sophomore?" I said, smiling.

"Freshman. Engineering."

She was tall, like him, probably a year older than me. "Isn't it, like, *really hard* to get into Columbia?"

He nodded. The paternal pride was practically oozing out of his pores.

"She must be *very* smart."

I wasn't looking at the asshole directly, but I saw when he exited the car at Times Square.

I shook the hand of my protector when I got off at Columbus Circle, and this time, when I put my earphones on, I turned the music up.

By the time I'd wound my way into the middle of Central Park, dusk had gone to true night, and though there were some lights and the ever-present glow of the city all around, the woods gave patches of true darkness.

I was shrugging my way into the arms of my insulated overall when the man grabbed me from behind, one arm across my throat, the other hand pawing down my torso, starting at my breasts, then diving into the still unzipped front of the overall and trying to worm under the waistband of my jeans while he ground his hips against me.

I jumped in place, adding about thirty-feet-per-second velocity, straight up.

I instantly regretted it. As we shot into the air, the top of my head felt like I'd been struck with a two-by-four. I jumped back to the ground below.

My assailant kept going, briefly, topping out at around fifteen feet in the air before dropping again. *My* turn to backpedal. I took two quick steps away and felt his impact through the ground. He collapsed like a sack of potatoes, no flailing, no sound, and I wondered if I'd broken his neck when my head hit him.

I took out my cell phone and used the flashlight app to illuminate his face.

Olive-skinned, with a light, trimmed beard—the asshole from the train.

When he got off at Times Square, he must've stepped into a different car, then followed me from Columbus Circle.

I shook my head and turned off the damn music player. He'd never have gotten close if I hadn't been blocking the ambient noise with earplugs.

*Stupid!*

His eyes were closed and his mouth was open and bleeding slightly, but he was breathing. I didn't want to go too close, in case he was faking.

I rubbed the top of my head. There was a serious goose egg forming and it stung. When I examined my fingers with the light I saw a smear of blood on my fingertips.

I remembered his hand raking across my body and I had to resist the urge to kick him as he lay there.

He didn't look poor. As I remembered, he wore gleaming loafers, slacks, a silk shirt under a leather jacket. He was wearing a fancy watch and two gold rings.

I slipped on my gloves and searched him.

His wallet held a driver's license for one Vincent Daidone, four hundred dollars in cash, several credit cards in the same name, and three condoms. There was a baggy of white powder in his jacket pocket and an expensive phone in a silver protective case.

I looked at the picture and for a moment thought it couldn't belong to the man on the ground. Something wasn't right. Then I realized his face was swollen under his ears and his lower jaw was projecting forward, like a bad underbite.

*His jaw's dislocated*, I realized. *Or broken.* I touched the bump on my head again. Lucky I hadn't broken *my* neck.

I no longer felt like kicking him. I activated his phone. It was locked, but there was a button for calling an emergency number. I dialed 911.

"What is the nature of your emergency?"

"I've found an unconscious man, unresponsive, Central Park, in the trees behind the Dairy Visitor Center. He has some head trauma, but he is breathing and I'm not seeing any major bleeding. This is his phone. I'll leave it on."

"Who is speaking?"

I put the phone back in Mr. Daidone's jacket pocket, careful not to hang up. The battery indicator showed three-quarters charged. I could hear the operator still talking, trying to get me to respond.

Mr. Daidone didn't *look* like he had the financial need to rob, but perhaps that's how he paid for his nice clothes. Still, I thought that his thing was more likely sexual assault, pure and simple. *Not pure. Not simple.* I hoped the white powder was drugs, but I wasn't going to check any closer. I was still mad. I thought about taking the money, but instead I used my phone's camera to take a close-up of his driver's license, then put the wallet back in his pocket.

I walked away, to the Chess and Checkers House, jumping to the roof and crouching by the cupola in the center. It took the park police five minutes to respond, a car coming up East 65th. I watched their flashlights flickering through the trees for three minutes before they found him.

While I waited, I'd zipped up the coveralls, put on my goggles, and cinched the hood tight around my face. I'd only done this once before, in West Texas, as an experiment, but it had worked just fine.

I left the rooftop at 130 miles per hour, rising nearly a thousand feet before I slowed, then doing it again before I started changing the vector, adding horizontal velocity toward the northeast. I'd like to say that I shot into the air cleanly but, just like the first time I'd tried this, I tumbled wildly out of control the first few jumps.

At a 130 mph, the air feels like a wall, a palpable barrier that tears at you as you push your way though. It pulls at your clothes and snaps at your exposed skin. You want your shoes tied tight, and all your zippers secured. You want earplugs—or at least good flying music—because the air screams as it rips by.

Every time I tumbled, I jumped in place, changing my orientation, pointing my head to match the velocity vector. At these speeds the slightest movement of hand or leg, the crook of an elbow, the turn of the head, sends you spinning, and tumbling. You hold yourself semirigid. The more you relax, the more drag you have, but you can't stay stiff as a board for too long, it's exhausting.

You slow as you rise, but since you're not rising straight up, you don't come to a complete horizontal stop. There's a moment when you feel yourself hang at the top of the parabola and then you're falling again. At this time, I arch to a facedown free-fall position, then "cup" my arms and hands close to my body, steering. I'm tracking and, usually, I move a meter forward for every meter I fall.

I covered the length of the park in seconds, crossing the top of Manhattan, and then into the Bronx. I could see Long Island Sound to my right, a dark stretch between the lighted shores.

I had a GPS with a preset waypoint on my wrist and I would tweak the direction of my jumps. I was nervous about letting myself drop too far on the other end of the parabola, so I found myself rising higher and higher.

I knew I had to stay well above 854 feet, the highest hill anywhere near this route, but I soon found myself whistling along at five thousand feet and freezing my *tuchus* off.

It was exhilarating but tiring.

I'd checked the driving distance online, and between Manhattan and Northampton was 157 miles of highway, but as the crow flies (or the Cent plummets) it was 126. But I was getting cold and the roar of the wind wore at me.

I endured. After all, I'd only have to do it once—for this location anyway.

The Connecticut River Valley and the I-91 corridor were easy to make out, but the GPS told me I was a bit south and that the mass of lights I'd pinned my hopes on was Holyoke, not Northampton. I followed the highway north.

Three more jumps and I was over Northampton, adjusting my speed until I stopped dead five thousand feet above a cluster of athletic fields by Paradise Pond, my chosen waypoint.

Gravity took over and I fell, face down, my eyes flicking back and forth from the altimeter readout to the green grass below.

At a thousand feet I killed my downward velocity, then dropped again, never letting myself drop more than three seconds before stopping my downward velocity again.

At thirty feet, I jumped to the ground and fell over.

I thought I was just tired. The passage through the air had been like being pummeled with socks filled with dirt, and my body was stiff from the wind and stiff from holding low-drag positions for extended periods of time. Still, when I came down into the kitchen after returning to the cabin, Mom took one look at my face and said, "What happened?"

I blinked. "Huh?"

"You looked angry just then. Did your father do something?"

I shook my head. Angry?

Then I remembered the hand pawing across my front and the hips pushing at me.

"You *are* angry about something."

I nodded. "This guy grabbed me from behind in Central Park and groped me."

Mom's eyes widened and she looked closer at me, up and down. "Are you all right?"

I touched the top of my head. "Bit of a bump here."

"He hit you?"

I shook my head. "I jumped up, like I do. Took him fifteen feet in the air, but my head—" I bumped my own chin from below with my fist. "—hit his jaw."

"What happened to him?"

"Broke his jaw, or dislocated it. He was unconscious when

I left. I called the police on his phone and backed off until they found him."

"You could have just jumped away," Mom said. "The *other* kind of jump."

"He had his arm across my throat," I said. "He might have come with me." I sighed. "I didn't even think about it, really. Just happened. At least this way he's not likely to grab anyone else for a bit. Hopefully even longer than that. I think he had a Baggie of cocaine. At least he had a Baggie of white powder. Hopefully the police will bust him."

Now that Mom had assured herself I was okay, *she* was getting angry. "They might not search him at all. After all, as far as they know, *he's* a victim. Unless you told the police he'd attacked you."

I shook my head. "No. I just described his injury and his location."

"Did he just come out of the bushes or something?"

"He followed me. He tried to pick me up on the A train and when I was having none of it, he tried to grab my ass, but I yelled at him to keep his hands to himself. There were plenty of witnesses. I *thought* he got off the train at Times Square, but he must've gotten right back onto the next car. Then when I got off at Columbus Circle—" I shrugged. "It was my fault."

"What?" Mom sounded really angry suddenly. "Honey, it was *not* your fault."

I held up my hand. "Oh, no. Not my fault that he attacked me. I'm with you on that. He deserved everything he got, maybe more. It was careless of me, though. I put in my earphones and was listening to music. I don't think he could've snuck up on me otherwise."

Mom closed her eyes and took a deep breath, then let it out slowly. "Ah. I see. Yes, you should be careful. You know what your father would say it could've been—"

I finished the statement, making air quotes with my fingers, "—*them*."

Mom nodded. "Yes. It could've been a loop of wire and a hypodermic."

I nodded. "Yes. Believe me, I thought about that, too. I'll be more careful."

"You should tell your father about it."

I winced. "Do I *have* to? You know how he'll get."

She raised her eyebrows. "Keep it brief. You don't have to tell him about the earphones. Tell him about breaking the guy's jaw—he'll *like* that."

She was right. When I described being attacked, Dad's eyes narrowed and I could see his jaw muscles bunch as he ground his teeth together, but when I described the condition of the guy's jaw and his fifteen-foot drop, he smiled.

But he also asked me to Bluetooth the picture of Mr. Daidone's driver's license from my phone to his.

"Just want to check on his status. Find out if they busted him for the coke or not. Whether he has priors, especially for sexual assault."

"What are you going to do, Daddy, if he does have priors?"

"Not much. But I'll know he's probably not one of *them*."

"One of them wouldn't have *priors*?"

"If they did, they'd be made to go away, but really, *their* people don't get caught in the first place. Not usually."

"I thought you just wanted to make sure he paid, uh, for what he did."

His face went still but there was a tic by his right cheekbone.

"Oh. You *don't* approve of his behavior," I ventured.

His eyes narrowed and for a moment, he seemed like someone else—someone a little scary. He pointed at me. "Just be careful, okay?" Then his face relaxed and he was back. "Speaking of that, let me see your wrist."

I held up my left arm and he said, "Very funny," so I peeled the Band-Aid back on my right wrist. The blister had popped a few days before and in its place was a swollen scab.

"It's doing better," I said, though, to be truthful, it looked a little worse than the blister had.

Dad made a noise in the back of his throat, but didn't gainsay me. "So, what are you going to do? We could probably get a used Orlan suit on eBay, but it would probably be too big. Don't think we're gonna spend twelve million on a new NASA flight-rated EMU."

I shook my head. "I've been doing some research. There's a team at MIT doing lots of work toward a Mars EVA suit, and this other guy in New Haven who just lost his funding."

Dad rolled his eyes to the ceiling, then blew out through pursed lips. He glanced at my wrist again, and I covered the scab back up.

Finally he said, "Okay, give me the details."

Jade came out of Hatfield Hall, where, according to Tara, her accelerated elementary French 101 class met. She was in a cluster of other girls and they were talking up a storm, but not English.

Some of their accents were clearly American and some reminded me of the streets of Paris. I tagged along behind the group, waiting for my opportunity. They moved toward the Campus Center, a thoroughly modern silver building totally at odds with the red brick nineteenth-century buildings all around.

Well before they got there, Jade said, "*Au revoir,*" and split off toward Elm Street.

From studying the map, I knew that Northrop House, her dormitory, was on the other side. I caught up with her as she waited for the light and said, "*Comment allez-vous?*"

She glanced sideways at me, and then jerked back, nearly stepping out into traffic.

"Cent?"

"*Mais oui.*"

"Wow. What are you doing here? Tara told me she'd seen you, but that was back at Krakatoa." Unstated was the *two thousand miles away.*

I nodded. I hadn't told Tara what I had in mind. I wasn't sure it was a good idea myself, and I *knew* Dad wouldn't think so. "Yeah. Tara really misses you."

Jade sighed. "Yes."

"You've got a walk signal," I said, tilting my head toward the light.

"Oh. Right." She didn't say anything else until we'd crossed. "Are those people still after you, from before?"

I made a show of yawning. "Always."

"Does that have anything to do with why you're here at Smith?"

I shook my head. "No. I'm here for the same reason I saw Tara: to see how you're doing."

She reached out and touched my arm. "Okay—you really are here? Not my imagination?"

I hugged her and felt her stiffen, then clench me tightly. When I let go, her eyes were wet.

I smiled. "Maybe you have a really good imagination."

"Come on up to my room. My roommate's gone home to New Jersey for the weekend."

"Sure."

In her third-floor room, I sat on her desk chair and she sat cross-legged on her bed. The room wasn't huge, but it was cozy. Her roommate was a bit of a slob but the mess stopped midway across the room, where a line of masking tape ran across the floor.

I glanced down at the line, my eyebrows raised.

"Yeah, she's a bit of a pig, but she's really nice. She just doesn't care about, uh, being tidy. At the beginning of the semester we squabbled about it a little, but once I started moving her stuff back to her side of the room, *she* put the tape down and she's really good about keeping her stuff on that side.

"Still, next year I can have a single room. I'm really looking forward to that."

I asked her about her classes. It was only her first semester and she wouldn't have to declare before the end of her sophomore year, but she was seriously considering international affairs and public policy.

"So you like it here?"

She nodded and starting crying.

Damn.

"Homesick?"

She nodded. "They're different here. Everybody talks too

fast and interrupts each other and you really have to be pushy to be heard in group discussions. And the food is bland."

"Ah. No chile?"

"Not like home."

In my time in New Prospect I hadn't gotten *used* to the red and green chiles. Still, I understood.

"No friends?"

She shrugged. "My house is friendly enough, I guess."

I pushed a little, "No *special* friends?"

She frowned at me then said, "What? I'm with Tara!"

I blew out a deep breath. Relief, I guess.

"Sorry," I said. "Sometimes when people go away to college, they change. Long-distance relationships are really hard to maintain. Even when one person still wants the relationship, sometimes the other one . . ."

She was staring at me. "You aren't talking about Tara and me, are you?"

It was my turn to tear up a bit. Unable to talk I just flipped my hand over, palm up.

Her cell phone chirped and she glanced down at it, read the screen, then smiled.

"Tara?" I managed.

"Yeah. She just got to the coffee shop." There was a two hour time-zone difference. She lifted the phone again. "Wait until I tell her you're *here*."

I held up my hand, to keep her from texting.

"If I could bring Tara to you, right now, would you like to see her?"

"*Not* funny," she said.

I jumped across the room to the window seat.

It was a good thing she was seated on the bed. She would've fallen off the chair.

"What the fuck?!"

She looked scared. I smiled, though I didn't feel like it. "There's a reason those people were, and will probably always be, after me and my parents."

"What are you?!"

"Cent, remember?" I walked slowly back to the chair and sat down again. "I'm your *friend*. Just a girl who can do this *extra* thing."

Her eyes were wide still, but her breathing slowed.

"So I meant it, when I asked if you'd like to see Tara."

Tara was not surprised to see me but her eyes were wide when I walked up the stairs to the mezzanine of Krakatoa.

She held up her phone. "Jade just texted that I would see you in a moment. *She's* got your number and *I* don't?"

I shook my head. "She doesn't have my number. Come on."

"Come on? What's up? Where are we going?" She pulled her backpack closer and slid her notebook into it.

There was no one else on the mezzanine. I let her stand and sling her backpack over one shoulder before I did it.

Tara screamed when she appeared in Jade's room, and collapsed, but I was ready and eased her to the floor, and then Jade was there, clinging, and they were both crying.

I left the room the normal way and found the floor's communal bathroom.

I stared in the mirror. The expression on my face was bleak.

I'd jumped into a *different* dorm room three weeks before.

Joe and I had been seeing each other only on the weekends—so he could get into the college groove properly—but I'd wanted him bad that night and I figured he could make an exception.

Apparently so did he, 'cause he wasn't alone in his bed when I got there.

When I returned to Jade's dorm room, I tapped gently before pushing the door open.

They were both sitting on the bed, side by side, no space between them. Both of them looked at me with large eyes.

"All right?" I said.

They looked at each other and involuntarily smiled, but when they looked back at me, their smiles faded.

"And they *all* moved away from me on the Group W bench," I said. "Don't make me sing. You won't like me when I sing."

Tara giggled and some of the tension went out of Jade's posture.

"Let's go get something to eat. I hear Northampton has *great* restaurants."

They hesitated and I added, "Don't make me hungry. You won't like me when I'm hungry."

And they both laughed and they stood and it was all right.

# TWO

## Millie: Tell him to stay longer next time

*Assisted living.*

Until recently Millie's mother, Samantha Harrison, had lived in a nice apartment but wore a med-alert necklace to call for help. A health aid checked on her mornings and afternoons and a cleaning staff came through daily. She used a walker to go down to a group dining hall where she gossiped with friends, or to the activities lounge where she'd tutor people in the finer details of standard Stayman contract-bridge bidding. She'd play, too, but as a Gold Life Master, she had very little local competition.

Now she was in the attached nursing facility, bedridden.

Millie paired the two in her head. She couldn't help it.

*Assisted living and assisted dying.*

It was a death trap in other ways, too.

At 4 P.M. Millie grabbed a taxi at Wichita Mid-Continent Airport and took it to the retirement community near Buffalo Park, on the west side of the city. Wearing a wig and dark glasses and carrying flowers, she checked in with the front desk. She gave a false name for herself and said she was visiting Agnes Merriwether.

"You know the way, dear?" asked the receptionist.

Millie nodded solemnly. She didn't feel like smiling and she was pretty sure they were used to that here.

Agnes was an early onset dementia patient whose failing cognitive abilities were supported by an all-too-healthy body. She barely recognized her own immediate family and the staff was quite accustomed to her not recognizing more remote family and friends.

It was painful for Millie. There was less and less of an actual personality there, but Agnes still ate, keeping up a healthy weight, and she could move her limbs for the physical therapists. She would probably linger for years.

Exactly the opposite of her mother.

For cover, Millie spent fifteen minutes talking with Agnes, who responded with completely random nods and occasional shakes of the head and never took her eyes off the television. After a bit, Millie walked down the hall to the restroom then, on leaving it, walked into a different room down the hall.

"How are you today, Ms. Harrison?" she asked, forcing a smile.

The bed look oversized, but only because her mother was shrunken, with thin flesh draped over too-apparent bones and an incipient dowager's hump from osteoporosis. She was wearing an oxygen cannula and there was a saline drip in her arm. Another tube ran from the sheets' edge to a bag of yellow liquid on the end of the bed.

*Foley catheter.*

Her mother's eyes widened for a moment and she lifted her head, but then settled back against the pillow. "I'm fine . . . dear." Her voice was faint and Millie barely caught it.

Millie moved closer, pulled up a chair, and took her mother's hand. The return squeeze was pathetically weak. She searched her mother's eyes and her mother winked.

Millie wanted to gather her up in her arms and hold her, but Samantha was five days post-op from hip surgery. The first fall, two years before, had resulted in a hip replacement. The previous week's injury could not be fixed in the same way.

Her sister had filled her in: "Too much bone loss. They've put plates and screws and I don't know what else in there, but they don't think her pulmonary function is up to a full replacement. They said it won't be long before she'll need some kind of ventilator full time." Besides the bone loss, her mother had had bouts of polymyositis, a muscular inflammatory disease that was slowly depleting her overall strength and her ability to breathe.

The weak voice said, "How's that daughter of yours?"

*Thanks, Mom. Way to combine my two most pressing concerns!* "She's okay. She's got a new hobby." *Making me* insane *with worry.* "She says hello."

Cent *had* sent her love but they always assumed the room was bugged and probably had video cameras, too, another reason Millie wasn't too openly affectionate. Millie tried to make up for this with her eyes.

"And the rest of your family?"

Meaning Davy. "All good. Busy, busy, busy."

"I'd like to see them again," her mom said. "Before—"

An RN came in, holding a magazine and a pen. "Oh, excuse me, Sam. Didn't know you had a visitor." Her eyes scanned the drip bag, the oxygen settings, and glanced at the catheter bag. "I'll come back." She started to turn to leave but Millie's mother stayed her with a twitch of her fingers.

"This is Seeana," she said to Millie.

Seeana was a short black woman with her hair shaved close on the sides and straightened, spiked, and dyed blond on top. Seeana said, "I always come to Sam for help. We've got the rest of the puzzle but this clue doesn't make sense!"

Millie leaned back and raised her eyebrows and her mother flicked her fingers again.

Seeana said, "Nine letters. 'A line that goes to the North Pole.' "

"Longitude," said Millie.

"Yeah, that's what I thought, but all the horizontal words that run across it don't work. It needs to start with a *D* and end with an *A*. I tried a dictionary and even Google, but I'm *stumped.*"

Millie's mother looked up, briefly, to the ceiling, then said softly. "Try 'Dear Santa.' "

Seeana shook her head, not in disagreement, but in wonder. "That's it!"

Millie laughed and then nearly burst into tears. All that razor-sharp intellect trapped inside brittle bones and wasting muscle.

"Thanks, Sam. I *knew* I could count on you."

Millie's mother twitched her hand again and Seeana left.

"She seems nice," said Millie. It sounded inane, but anything to avoid what her mother *had* been saying before Seeana stuck her head in.

"She's great—she should be supervisor. I get to hear about her love life. She has a real fondness for guys that her mother hates."

Millie winced. "I suspect there are quite a few, then."

"The mean and median duration is about five weeks. You could chart it. She's in a rough place. When she doesn't have a boyfriend, her mother is all over her about that, too."

"Have you pointed this out to her?"

"She pointed it out to *me*. She's stuck, but self-aware. I'd really like to see her find someone worthy before I die."

They were back to it.

Millie said, "Remember our offer?"

"Yes." Samantha sighed. "I probably should have taken you up on it back then."

Even before the first hip fracture Millie had asked Samantha to come live with them, but back then Samantha still had an active social life. While she still lived in the facility, it was dangerous for Davy, Millie, and Cent to visit her. It wasn't that their enemies kept permanent employees in the retirement community—but they suspected electronic surveillance and Davy was convinced that some of the staff was on retainer to report all of Samantha's visitors.

Millie thought Davy paranoid, but she still followed most of his recommendations. She'd arrived by taxi because they might have installed a local gravimeter. Jumping opened a point between two different places and, for a tiny but measurable period, gravity readings from both sides of the jump registered if the jump was close enough.

"It's not too late," Millie said. "You can still—"

"Good afternoon," a cheery voice said. A white-jacketed man walked into the room, a stethoscope hanging from his neck, a file folder in his left hand, his right hanging down on the far side of his body.

Millie glanced at her mother's face and saw her brow furrow. *She doesn't know him.* She jerked her head back toward the man as he lifted the gun, pointing it not at Millie but at her mother.

"Do *anything* and I'll shoot *her.*"

Millie held perfectly still.

The man moved closer to the bed, the gun pointed at Samantha's chest. He threw the file folder onto the bed and reached into his left jacket pocket and pulled a different gun, yellow plastic with a square black muzzle.

*A Taser.*

"I mean it. You do *anything* and she's—"

He was gone.

Millie saw it, but then, she knew what to look for.

Like lightning, like a single frame of film in a projected movie. She couldn't even tell how Davy grabbed the "doctor." Did he grab the neck, the jacket, hook his arms around from behind?

Subliminal. Below the threshold of perception.

She stepped to the doorway and peeked both ways down the hall, but no one was waiting there. She didn't hear any sudden footsteps or distant commotion.

Not yet.

Samantha's eyes were wide when Millie returned to her bedside, but she said dryly, "Tell him to stay longer next time."

"Are you all right, Mom?" She should have avoided saying "Mom" but she wanted to hear the word—hear it out loud.

"I wasn't worried about *me* if that's what you mean." Samantha's face was oddly reflective. "Don't trade the years of your life for my fifteen minutes! Think about Cent."

Millie winced. "Come spend some of your time with *us.* With your granddaughter."

Samantha looked up into Millie's eyes, searching. "All right." Then she sighed. "But next week, after they get the staples out. When they know I haven't taken any infections."

Millie bent over and kissed her mother's cheek, then stroked her hair. "Okay. I'll prepare a space, and I'll start interviewing medical staff. We'll want a nurse and a couple of aids. A hospital bed. Do you want to stay on the catheter?"

"I'd rather wear diapers, frankly, but I can use a bedpan, once I can move my hip a little." She tilted her head. "Are you *sure*? It's a stinky, smelly business."

Millie nodded. "Yes. I'm sure."

Samantha clucked her tongue and gestured. "Closer." When Millie bent down, Samantha whispered, "You might give Seeana a try."

Millie raised her eyebrows. "Really?" She gestured toward file folder still lying on the bed.

Samantha whispered, "They don't pay her shit. Doubt if she's on the payroll of *them*, or she wouldn't still be living with her mother."

Millie straightened. In a normal voice she said, "Okay. We'll see."

*Now* she could hear steps running in the hall.

"How did Davy know to come then?"

Millie smiled and leaned close. "They're not the only ones who can install video cameras," she whispered, then kissed her mother's temple.

And jumped.

# THREE

## Cent: He keeps saying that

When I asked for directions, the department receptionist on the third floor of the engineering building gave me a room number and said, "That's down in purgatory."

At my blank look she added, "The basement? With the graduate-assistant cubbies? Are you an engineering student?"

"No, ma'am." I didn't add that I wasn't a student at the university either.

"Oh, sorry. Our kids all know what 'purgatory' means. Well, take the elevator all the way down and follow the hall around to zero five seven. He's not going to be there much longer, you know."

"I thought his office hours were until six?"

"They *were*, but he's no longer a professor at this university. His contract was terminated, so if you were going to talk to him about getting into one of his seminars, you're wasting your time."

I bobbed my head. "Thanks for the directions."

When I stepped off the elevator I saw immediately why they called it purgatory. There was an HVAC plant on this floor and some kind of machine shop, and they hadn't spent much on sound insulation. It got a little quieter as I walked away from the elevator, going to merely annoying instead of painful.

The fluorescent lights were the kind that made your skin look pasty and hurt your eyes. Despite the noise, most of the office doors were open, including 057, but the light coming out of Dr. Matoska's office was different, far closer to natural sunlight, and I wondered if the room had an outside window.

I stuck my head in. The room was a mess. The entrance was half blocked by a stack of broken-down cardboard boxes leaning against the doorjamb. Spools of wire or fiber spilled across the floor and stacks of books waited beside electronic devices and half-filled boxes. The desk was stacked with boxes, except for a corner with an open, half-filled bottle of scotch, two mismatched glasses, and a Marvin the Martian coffee mug.

The fluorescent bulbs had been pulled out of the fixture and a bank of different colored LED lights, approximating real sunlight, dangled from jury-rigged wiring.

But no sign of Cory Matoska, Ph.D.

The next office was open, too, and a young woman sat before a computer monitor. I said, "Excuse me," but she didn't even twitch. I looked closer and saw she was wearing earbuds, the wires hidden in her long brown hair. I stuck my hand into her field of vision and waved.

She turned to the door and pulled out one of the earbuds. "Yes?"

I jerked my thumb back down the hall. "Seen Professor Matoska?"

She nodded. "He was going to pack up his lab."

I raised my eyebrows expectantly.

She said, "Oh. You don't know where his lab is?"

I nodded.

"Keep going, turn the corner, and it's on the left. Still had his name on it at lunch."

"Thanks."

She went back to her music and I moved on around the basement. As I turned the first corner, the sound of raised voices emerged from the general background roar of the HVAC plant's ventilation fans.

I reached a short cul-de-sac off the main hall in time to hear:

"—prototype isn't university property! Its funding was not tied to the school at all!"

The man speaking had his back to me. He wore jeans, a polo shirt, and had a small bald spot in blond hair shot with gray. Beyond him, a man in an expensive suit and a female and male police officers stood in front of a closed door labeled "Lab 16" and "Dr. Cory Matoska" below a small rectangular window with wire-reinforced glass.

The man in the suit said, "That is yet to be determined. Our standard engineering-faculty agreement is pretty clear about intellectual property on work done here."

"And if I'd signed that awful piece of verbiage, you would be right, Hannum, but your predecessor agreed that it would not be appropriate, given my funding, and we deleted that entire section."

The female campus police officer frowned and shifted, turning so she could see Hannum—the man in the suit—as he responded to this.

"I'll be happy to review your contract with university legal, but if you think I'm going to let you cart off university property before I do that, you're insane!"

The man with the bald spot turned toward the police and pulled out his cell phone. He held it up and a flash went off.

The male police office said, "What are you doing?"

Dr. Matoska—it had to be Matoska—said "Dr. Hannum has been trying to get his hands on my research as long as I've been here. If you two help him, you'll be named in the criminal charges." He looked back at Hannum. "I have a complete video inventory of the lab."

I saw Hannum glance at the cell phone still in Dr. Matoska's hand with a look of speculation.

"The video's in the cloud, Hannum."

Matoska stepped to the side and looked directly at the female officer. "Officer—he leaned forward and looked at the name badge pinned to her uniform. "Ah, *Deputy Chief* Mendez, are you going to let me into my lab or not?"

Hannum said loudly, "It's *not* his lab. Not anymore."

Matoska clenched his fists. "Are you going to give me access to *my property*, then?"

Mendez said, "I hate to say it, but this looks like a job for the lawyers, Dr. Matoska."

"And will you also guarantee that this asshole won't be looting my equipment?"

"Are you seriously concerned about that?"

"It's not the first time Dr. Hannum has tried. Why do you think I was fired? I refused to collaborate on my research or give him a byline on my last paper."

"That's *slander*! Your contract wasn't renewed for *performance* reasons, Matoska."

"Slander, that's the spoken one, right? Have you seen the standby lists for my six-thirty seminars? Have you seen my students' surveys? Who's slandering now? You were all glowing compliments when you were trying to worm your way onto my last paper. What was that about fast-tracking a tenured position?"

"You're delusional," Hannum said, blushing.

Deputy Chief Mendez intervened. "We'll padlock the door then and put an evidence seal on it. It's Tuesday. You have three business days to come to an agreement with the university or to get an injunction. If we don't hear anything by Monday, we'll unseal it."

Dr. Hannum's eyes narrowed and his face went still and I knew that Dr. Matoska was right. Dr. Hannum *was* after the prototype. I didn't know if Matoska was legally in the right or if Hannum was but I didn't really care.

Because I was after it, too.

Dr. Hannum noticed me peering around the corner. "What do you want?" It wasn't a question, really. More of a "Get out of my business!" sort of growl.

"I'm waiting for Dr. Matoska," I said.

"He's not with the university anymore!"

I raised my eyebrows.

"He's right, I'm afraid," said Matoska, turning around for the first time. He was pale, with a mustache and a soul patch, but he hadn't shaved the rest of his face recently. He had the weirdest eyes—one was light hazel and the other one was dark brown.

I stared, unable to help myself.

"What did you need?" he asked. He was frowning now, not recognizing me. Not surprising—we'd never seen each other before.

"I can wait," I said. "Sounds like you're in the middle of it."

Hannum said, "I *told* you, he's not with the university anymore!"

With my face still on Dr. Matoska's mismatched eyes, I said quietly, "He *keeps* saying that."

Dr. Matoska snorted.

I turned back to Dr. Hannum. "I'm not with the university *either.*"

"Then what do you want?" he snapped.

I put a puzzled expression on my face. "Nothing from *you.*"

Matoska's lips twitched up.

Hannum's mouth worked like a fish out of water, but before he came up with something to say I added, "I'll just wait in your office, then, Dr. Matoska," and retreated around the corner.

Back in Matoska's office I put the cap back on the scotch bottle and moved it out of sight, behind one of the boxes.

Matoska came back ten minutes later, a profoundly irritated look on his face. He glanced at the desktop and then at me.

"I drank it," I said.

At his look of alarm, I said. "Kidding. Put it out of sight. Didn't know if the university police would be coming back with you." I moved the box aside, to show him.

"Ah. Good thought. Who *are* you?"

"I'm Cent," I said. "I'm here about the MCP suit."

Matoska stared at me. "Since you're not with the university, you're not trying to get into one of my seminars. Are you from MIT? Did Dava Newman send you over?"

I shook my head. My research had led me to Dr. Newman as well, but I didn't think she'd be able to help me soon enough. They were painstakingly working through the problems, but Matoska was closest to a working prototype.

"So what's your interest?"

I wanted to pull back the sleeve of my sweatshirt and show him the scab from my frostbite. I wanted to say, *I got this at forty-five thousand feet.*

I didn't think he'd believe me.

"I represent an investor."

He rolled his eyes. "You know, kid, this is not at all a good day to waste my time."

*Kid.*

I shouldn't have been offended. I'm only seventeen. Still, when I took the legal-sized manila envelope out of my shoulder bag, I flipped it out, to land on the desk in front of him, a lot harder than necessary. It was over a half inch thick, after all, and it hit the desktop with a resounding *thwap.*

He stared at it.

"What's this?"

"Funding."

He tore open the flap and stared at the bundled cash. "Are those hundreds?"

I nodded. "Ten bundles. One hundred notes each. Ten K a bundle." I let him do the rest of the math.

"A hundred thousand dollars?"

"Ayup."

Matoska opened his mouth to say something, but it took him a while before he managed, "What do you expect for it?"

"Continued development. Later, we want a working suit." I tilted my hand toward the money. "For more money, of course. *This* is for research."

He blinked like an *owl*, I swear.

"Do you have a draft agreement for me to look at? Do you expect rights to the IP?"

"IP?"

"Intellectual property. Patents etcetera."

"Oh." I shook my head. "It's a grant, not a loan. Your work is *your* work. Just spend it wisely."

"On my rent?"

"You can't do research without a place to live, Doc. I realize you just lost your job. If you have to use some of it to cover living costs, that seems reasonable."

He blinked. "This isn't *drug* money, is it?"

"No laundering going on here, Doctor Matoska. Or should that be Professor Matoska?" I *hoped* there was no laundering going on. It was from Dad after all.

"Call me Cory." He was still staring at the cash. "I'll need a hell of a lot more money than *this* if I don't get my prototype out of the lab."

"So, Dr. Hannum really *is* after it?"

"You heard that?"

"Pretty much," I said.

"He was courting me pretty hard but I finally ran out of maybes on Monday. I got the termination notice Tuesday."

"Where in the lab is the suit?"

"It's in the corner, on a stand, with the life-model pressure sensor."

I must've looked confused because he said, "The life model is like a mannequin, inside the spacesuit. There are two USB plugs coming out of the neck, one that powers the sensor multiplexor, and one for data. There's also a power supply hooked to the suit. I need to get that back from the bastards, too."

"Okay," I said. "I'll take care of it."

"What?"

"Later. But before your friend Hannum does."

He looked alarmed at that. "You don't think—"

I shrugged. "If everything else you said about him is true—"

He turned back toward the door.

I said, quickly, "I know *you* did that video inventory, but does *he* know what's in your lab?"

He paused and shook his head. "No. Kept him out of there."

"Then let me take care of it," I said. "I have resources."

He gestured at my shoulder bag. "Unless you have a law firm in your bag, too, I don't see what you can do."

I said, "I think *that*—" I jerked my chin toward the money.

"—earns a *little* trust. Besides, you get jailed by the campus police, you won't even be able to finish clearing out your office. Where you moving this stuff, anyway?"

He frowned and took a step back, turning to look at the boxes and piles. "I was going to rent a storage locker. I'm pretty sure I can secure another teaching position PDQ, but I don't have room for this stuff at my place—it's an efficiency."

"Hmmm. I can help there, too. You finish packing the boxes and I'll get them moved to secure storage."

"I'm supposed to be out by six," he said, doubtfully.

I pulled my cell phone out of my pocket and converted to the local time zone in my head. "Ah. Half past one. Not a problem."

He looked relieved. "That would be great."

I killed an hour and a half helping him pack, though we ran out of boxes before we ran out of books. I sent him off for more and checked the lab.

A freshly mounted padlock hasp had been attached to the metal door frame and door with tamper-proof screws. In addition to the security padlock in the hasp, a holographic sticker labeled *evidence seal* had been affixed across the gap between door and frame.

I looked through the wire-reinforced glass of the door's rectangular window. It was dark inside and I was blocking most of the light from the hallway. I pressed my cell phone to the glass and turned on the flashlight app.

That gave me enough light. I heard footsteps from around the corner and jumped inside, the flashlight still on.

The prototype was at the end of a heavy steel workbench, looking spookily like a man. Well, a headless man. The suit was light gray, with a rough-woven texture, leading up to a stainless steel neck flange. The two USB wires Matoska, uh, *Cory* had mentioned emerged from the headless neck, but the free ends were coiled loosely on the workbench, unconnected to anything. There was a plug just below the neck flange with a thick cable running over to a power supply which, in turn, was plugged into the wall.

I unplugged the power supply from both ends and wrapped

the cables around it, then jumped it to the warehouse in Michigan. I came back for the suit, lifting it from the two curved brackets that supported it under each armpit. Whatever the mannequin—the life-model pressure sensor—was made of, it was nearly as heavy as a person. I jumped it to the warehouse and lowered it carefully to the concrete floor.

I went back for the stand and that was when I heard the scraping. I held the cell phone against my side, to block the light. There was a shadow over the door window but it wasn't someone looking in. I slid closer and saw, just outside the door, a stepladder and somebody's feet on a step at my eye level.

I looked up, through the glass. It was Dr. Hannum and he was pushing a suspended ceiling panel up. I looked at the ceiling above me. Enough light was coming in so that I could see this ceiling was suspended, too.

I stepped back to the stand and jumped it to Michigan, then returned to the lab. Hannum's feet were higher up the ladder but the noise from the ceiling didn't seem any louder. I would've thought that an engineering lab would have firewalls above for safety, to keep fire or fumes from spreading.

Then I heard a clanking noise and hinges squealing. Perhaps a firewall above, but with an inspection door through it?

I jumped outside, to the other side of the ladder, and activated the camera function on my cell.

Dr. Hannum was perched on the top two steps of the ladder, his upper body in the suspended ceiling and leaning to one side.

"Dr. Hannum," I called loudly.

He flinched and one of his feet came off the ladder. His arm punched down through the adjacent ceiling panel, showering chunks of fiberglass and cellulose to the floor. He flailed and barely avoided falling the rest of the way down, hanging suspended by his other arm as his foot groped for the ladder.

I watched, interested, as instead of falling, he managed to get his foot back to a step and his weight shifted back over the ladder. He twisted his head to look down at me and the flash, as I took the picture, froze him, wide-eyed, shocked.

I examined the image on the phone. "Ah, good. It's got your face *and* the university police seal. Have a nice day!"

I turned and walked around the corner.

"Wait!" he yelled, but then there was the sound of a crash as the ladder went over and something heavy fell. I kept going.

I locked Cory's office door from inside, turned off the light, and spent five minutes jumping all the packed boxes to the warehouse.

As I returned from one of these jumps, I saw Dr. Hannum pause in the hallway and glance through the darkened window. I knew from experience how hard it was to see anything if the room was dark, so I just froze. If he unlocked the door, I'd leave.

Hannum shook his head and kept going. I stepped to the door to watch, then grinned. He was definitely limping.

By the time Cory returned with the last few boxes, I had the lights back on and the door open. He froze in the doorway, looking at the empty floor space.

"I guess your guys came."

"I took care of the suit," I said. "Just in time, too." I showed him the picture I'd taken on the phone of Hannum up the ladder.

His fists bunched. "That son of a bitch. I'm going to—"

"He didn't get it. I already had it by then. And he fell off the ladder right after I took that picture. He was limping the last time I saw him."

Cory stared at his fists and then exhaled, letting his fingers unclench. "How did *you* get the suit? Did you go over the wall like him?"

I shook my head. "I'm not an amateur. Look, I'll bet if you send this picture to Hannum, he'll renounce any claim to the rest of your equipment. Or you could send it directly to Deputy Chief Mendez."

The corners of Cory's mouth twitched up. "Where is the suit?" He looked around the office.

"I thought it best if it got off campus as soon as possible." I didn't add that it was also out of state.

"Oh. You had the guys take it when they took the boxes?"

"The same people, yeah." Person. "What sort of facilities do you need, to continue your work?" I was wondering if I'd need to set him up with a workshop and if the Michigan warehouse would be suitable.

"Depends. At some point I'll need a walk-in vacuum chamber—I'm betting we can get access to the eleven-foot chamber at Johnson Space Center. Or if I end up on the West Coast, Lockheed Martin has a great chamber in Sunnyvale. Here, we rigged a cylindrical chamber for our earlier tests, with a mating flange for the helmet collar, but the department repurposed it later for some vacuum-deposition tests."

He grinned, suddenly. "But while I was out I got a callback from one of my previous coauthors. He offered me a lecture post for the spring semester with immediate access to research facilities since I have—" He pointed at me. "—current funding."

"Oh. Great! Where?"

"Stanford."

My stomach clenched and I nearly jumped away.

Joe was at Stanford.

Well, at least I wouldn't need a new jump site.


My cell phone *doesn't*.

What I mean is, we completely killed its cellular radio when we rooted it. It can't connect to any cell towers. This is deliberate.

It *will* connect to WiFi hotspots, though, but every time it does, it uses a different Media Access Control address for the wireless Ethernet adaptor. My phone stores a block of four thousand MAC addresses harvested from obsolete and decommissioned equipment, and ranging from phones to computers to tablets to routers. Last time I checked, I'd used about half the list. The program is set to cycle through them again when it reaches the end, but I suspect I will break or lose the phone by then.

I also did the regular security things, like using encrypted browsing and changing accounts regularly, but mostly I depended on looking like a different machine every time I connected to the net from wildly varying WiFi hotspots.

When Joe first left for college, we used e-mail, instant messaging, voice over IP, and computer videoconferencing to talk during the week, and we saw each other on the weekends, usually with me taking him someplace.

When I found him in bed, with *her*, I'd screamed and jumped away, ending up sobbing in the reading nook under my bed.

I hadn't done *that* in a while.

An hour later, I connected to my e-mail account and found three e-mails.

The short version is that one of Joe's study partners had been dumped by her boyfriend. Beers and a shoulder to cry on had turned comforting into something more. It was the only time and he was so sorry and could I ever forgive him?

I sent a one-word message, *No*, and deleted the e-mail, instant messaging, and telephony accounts that we'd used. If he sent any other e-mails, they bounced.

Okay, *when* he sent them. I *know* he sent others. I read some of them off of his computer, while he was in class.

*Stalker* much?

Stalker.

I watched Joe for the better part of a month, several times a day, usually through binoculars. I looked through his stuff when I knew he and his roommate had class. I even thought about putting a remote camera on his shelf, hidden in a book.

Yeah, I know. *Mega* creepy.

I didn't put a camera in his bookshelf. I stopped visiting his room, though at first it was only because his roommate skipped class one day and nearly caught me.

Then I just felt embarrassed.

If some guy was entering *my* bedroom when I wasn't there, how chill would *I* be with it? It took me another week to apply the same logic to my following him around campus.

*Either go to him and make up, or leave him alone.*

And I was too afraid to go to him.

I stopped jumping to campus.

Exactly two weeks later, Dr. Cory Matoska tells me he's got a post at Stanford.

*Perfect.*

I connected to a coffeehouse WiFi hotspot in the Mission District of San Francisco and used an Internet telephony program to call Cory's cell phone a few hours after his scheduled arrival on the Stanford campus.

"How was your trip?"

"Uh, Cent? The number shows up as blocked."

"Using Skype. Don't have a dedicated number. You still have my e-mail, right?" I'd set up an account just for him and he'd sent me his new office and lab info as soon as he received it from Stanford.

"Oh, yeah—it's on my laptop. The trip was okay. Did the drive in three days. But I took your advice and had the movers do the packing. Talk about stress relief."

"How's your lab?"

"Great! Thanks for having the stuff delivered. Though there was some weird mix-up there. They've lost all record of receiving the shipment. No one even knows who unlocked the lab for the movers. They're *really* embarrassed about it."

*Oops.* Maybe I should've waited to deliver it until after Cory had received the keys.

"It's all there, right? Nothing broken, nothing missing?"

"Seems to be. Flexed the suit. Worked fine."

"Flexed? You bent it?"

"Oh, no. I just charged the EAP fibers and relaxed it."

"EAP?"

"Electroactive polymers. I thought you'd read my papers. That you knew how the suit worked." He sounded annoyed.

"Ah. I know it contracts when the power is off. That's the reason it doesn't have to be customized, right? We chose you because you were the first to achieve thirty kilopascals over a nonuniform surface without having to customize it for different people."

His voice sounded calmer when he said, "That's right. It's really quite dramatic. I could show you when you're in the Bay area."

"I'm local now," I said. "Are you in your office?"

"No. Unpacking. I scored a temporary faculty apartment in Stanford West. A petroleum-engineering professor is off doing an extended sabbatical in Abu Dhabi, research and teaching. Perfect timing. But I could bicycle to the lab in ten minutes."

"Is that convenient?"

"Well, if you give me half an hour."

"Yeah, could do that."

"Do you need directions?"

I'd been there already but I said, "The Durand Building right? Material sciences. Aeronautics and astronautics?"

"Yes."

"See you there, then."

I jumped directly to Cory's lab because, other than Joe's dorm room over in Stern Hall, it was the jump site freshest in my memory for Stanford. The lights were off and the door was closed, but unlike his previous lab, it wasn't tucked away in the corner of the basement. High northern windows lit the room and the adjoining office, which made both rooms much less claustrophobic than his previous digs, though they were about the same size. He'd already organized things, and the boxes I'd stacked here four days before were gone.

I let myself out the locked door into the hall and waited, sitting on a bench. I could hear people walking through the halls in other parts of the building but this little stretch was quiet. I could see down the hall and through another window. In the far distance was Hoover Tower and I remembered time spent with Joe on the observation deck when it was open *and* when it was closed.

I had to look away to keep from crying.

Cory came up the hall, still wearing his bicycle helmet. Velcro straps bound his khaki slacks at the ankles. He nodded at me.

"You must've been close. When you said you're local, does that mean you live here in Palo Alto?"

"No, but I've been out here a lot." The absolute truth.

"Well, if you can afford to fund me, you can afford the travel, I guess."

As he unlocked the door I said, "Travel is the smallest budget line item we have."

He uncinched the straps from his pants cuffs and put them in his helmet, tucking it into an empty spot on an otherwise full bookshelf. He ran his fingers across the spines of several books as he moved to the connecting door to the lab. "It was weird. Didn't feel right with these in the boxes."

I followed him.

The stand and suit were at the end of the room, their cables leading to the bench. This time the USB connections rising out of the headless neck were connected to a laptop computer and the heavier cable below the suit's helmet flange was connected to the power supply, as it was when I first saw it.

"So, electroactive polymers," said Cory. He handed me a piece of what looked like dark gray insulated wire, about six inches long. "This one is an ionic EAP. Pull it tight."

I held it between my thumbs and forefingers and pulled it straight. It wasn't at all stretchy.

Cory took a pair of leads from a smaller power supply on the bench and clipped each one to the ends of the gray piece where they stuck out past my fingers. "Hold it tight," he said, and flipped a switch on the power supply.

The gray piece suddenly thickened and was three inches shorter, drawing my hands together despite my best efforts to pull it back to its original length.

"Huh!" I said. "Muscular!"

"Yeah. In fact, that's one of the biggest applications under development. Artificial muscles for prosthetic limbs and actuators for small robots and drones." He turned it off and it relaxed, allowing me to stretch it back out to its previous length. "The molecules fold under current, pulling in on themselves. Now try this one."

He handed me a different length of what looked like a fuzzy cord, also six inches and, while I held it, he shifted the alligator clips from the gray rubbery piece to this one. "Give that a tug."

When I pulled hard on this piece it stretched out. I managed to pull it out to about eight inches but it retracted to six inches as soon as I relaxed. "This one has some elasticity. Is that what the suit is made of? It's pulling pretty hard now. I hate to think what it would do when you put the pressure on."

He smiled. "Keep some tension on it."

I did and he threw the switch.

It didn't bunch up or pull together. It *relaxed*. I was now holding a piece of thinner smooth cord nearly fifteen inches long.

"The ECP core of this one relaxes its molecular structure under current and folds back up when we remove current. We could've gone the other way, but we decided pretty quick that you wanted a power failure to enable, not disable, the suit."

For a moment I pictured my arm, the place where I'd had the frostbite, suddenly and unexpectedly exposed to vacuum. "That would be . . . bad."

He nodded. "Mind you, we're not talking about exploding limbs etcetera. Our skin is tougher than that, but you would get swelling and tissue damage. You know why the target is thirty kilopascals don't you?"

"One third an atmosphere. Twenty-nine thousand feet above sea level. Mount Everest."

He looked pleased. "Right. Your skin can handle that easily enough."

"Yes," I said, rubbing my wrist through my shirt. "Up to forty-five thousand feet, though that's pushing it."

He nodded and flipped open the laptop on the bench. The screen lit up as it came out of sleep mode. A chart of numbers appeared, with labels like *Anterior Torso 4*, *Right Leg 23*, and *Left Foot 16*. Above it were three larger numbers labeled *Max*, *Min*, and *Avg*. They were 31,250, 30,700, and 30,986. "It's in pascals." He reached over to the suit and dug his thumb into the chest. Immediately the max went up to 31,540 and the average crept up slightly, too.

"These are measured by strain gauges in the surface of the life-model pressure sensor. When we change out the underlying gel packs for different-sized life models, we get comparable results."

He reached out and turned a knob on the heavy-duty power supply connected to the suit. The suit *shifted* on the stand, going from a sleek, smooth surface, tightly covering the structure beneath, to suddenly looking like ill-fitting and wrinkled coveralls three sizes too big. Only the neck flange seemed the same as before, though the fabric of the suit now seemed to bunch together where it met the stainless steel.

Cory let me look at the suit for a moment, my mouth open, before he directed my attention to the laptop screen. Across the top of the screen read *Max: 320 Min: 0* and *Avg. 11*. "Those maxes are from the armpit sensors, probably, where it's resting on the stand."

I took a fold of the suit between my hands. It felt like midweight canvas, flexible, nowhere near as taut and rough as it had felt before.

"I'm impressed, Doctor Matoska. How does the suit feel on an actual human?"

He cleared his throat. "We've only done partials, but it's okay. Full range of mobility with only a little effort and good vacuum protection."

"Oh? But not a full suit yet?"

He opened his mouth but then closed it without saying anything. He turned to the suit power supply and slowly turned the knob, reducing the power to the suit gradually. This was just as magical as watching the suit expand. The suit shrank down, like it was alive, until it seemed to merge with the life-model pressure sensor inside. The average pascals climbed to 30,827 with a max of 31,602 and a min of 29,985.

Dr. Matoska said, "I blew through most of my previous grant and wasted over fifty thousand dollars of EAP fibers trying to solve the issue of a reclosable entry." He looked a bit shamefaced. "I was lucky the first time. It's a topology issue. All the tensioning fibers have to go from the anode—" He touched the front half of the suit, right below the flange. "—to the cathode." He tapped the back.

I stepped around the suit. Except for the rigid flange at the neck, it was seamless. No zippers, no buttons, no clamps.

"I tried to incorporate a pressure closure with the fibers looping through anchor islets, we got wildly varying pressure distribution, areas completely out of balance. A human would have gotten dangerous hematomas in some parts, and overpressures in others that would constrict circulation dangerously.

"Next I tried to put the anode around the closure and the cathode at the helmet flange. It threw everything off. I tried a secondary waist flange, splitting the suit into two separate electrical systems. That was closer but we couldn't get good pressures in the waist region. I tried an oversized helmet flange, big enough for a flexible adult to worm through, but the pressure distribution around the neck and shoulders was way off *and* we couldn't maintain the neck seal necessary to pressurize the helmet."

I tried to hide my disappointment. "So what's the next step?"

"A great deal of computer modeling," he said. "I've met with a multidisciplinary team here. They've got some applied mathematicians and guys from material sciences. I'm thinking we go back to the original design but we make the anode and cathode ring disassemble—" He held his hands together, touching at finger tips and thumbs in a circle, then spread them apart. "—instead of being permanently locked into the neck flange as they are now. Then the wearer can put the suit on, then bring the anode and cathode together and latch them to the helmet flange once he pulls it over his head."

Automatically I said, "Or her."

"Huh?"

"Or over *her* head."

He looked at me oddly. "Why did you say that?"

I'd said it because *I* needed the suit, but I answered, "We have men *and* women in space, Cory."

"We do. That's one advantage of this suit type, after all. It handles wide hips and narrow waists without any trouble." He cleared his throat and added, "But I was wondering if you'd heard about the testicle issue."

I blushed. "Excuse me?" For a second I wondered if he was turning into my Central Park stalker.

"I told you about the suit prototype that had the waist flange, right?"

I nodded.

"While it wasn't giving us good pressures around the waist, we thought it was giving us consistent enough pressure everywhere else on the life model to do some human-comfort trials. First we tried the upper body by itself and then we tried the lower body by itself, on one of my grad students.

"Turns out the testicles don't like thirty kilopascals of pressure, no matter how uniform." He winced. "I tried it, too. We semisolved the pinching with variations on an athletic cup and some gel padding, but it wasn't perfect. But when we had some undergrad females try the lower half, they didn't need any padding or structural support. They reported no discomfort."

I raised my eyebrows. It wasn't something I'd considered before. "The advantage of internal reproductive organs, I guess. What about breasts?"

He shook his head. "Not a problem, even with the one woman who wore a D cup. She wore an athletic bra and we went slow on the tensioning, making sure the pressure was uniform with no pinched flesh. She said it was the best support she'd ever had. Of course we didn't have it on that long."

"Why?"

"Breathing. We didn't have the suit in a vacuum and they weren't breathing pressurized air, so the suit squeezes in on the lungs. It's possible, but it's tiring. Once we solve the closure issues, we can do extended-period comfort tests by pressurizing the helmet above ambient."

I looked down the neck. "How do you resize the mannequin in this guy? You tried the suit with a large range of body sizes, right?" I was pretty sure that was in his paper.

He nodded. "The life-model sensor is modular." He tapped the protruding neck. "The neck is part of the central torso which goes all the way down to the crotch, then there's a right and left torso. The arms and legs are all one piece each. Each piece fits through the neck flange. We simulated several different body types, achieving thirty kilopascals from six foot four, two hundred and twenty pounds, all the way down to five foot even, ninety-five pounds."

I nodded. I was five three, myself.

I looked around the lab, "Where are your other life-model parts?"

"That was some of the equipment in my old lab."

"Oh. How did that work out?"

"I took *all* your advice. I sent the picture to the campus police, to university legal, *and* to Hannum." Cory grinned. "I don't think the legal department is happy with Dr. Hannum. The faculty senate is rather upset, too, about my termination midsemester. I've agreed not to sue and they are paying my next two months' salary. *And*, not only did they unseal the lab, they paid for shipping my equipment out here."

"Poor Dr. Hannum."

"Well, the bastard has tenure, so it's not like he'll get fired, but I suspect they might stick him with the department chairmanship an extra year or two."

"An *extra* year? That's a punishment?"

"You'll understand later, when you start teaching in grad school."

It was my turn to stare. That was not exactly a direction I'd ever seen my life going. Flattering, though. I don't think he realized how young I was.

I turned back to the suit. "If you could get a human into *this* suit would it protect him in a vacuum? Do you have a working helmet?"

"I have a helmet. Weren't you listening, though? I'd have to chop a person up to get him inside. No grown human I've ever seen will fit through this flange. Maybe some three-year-olds."

I nodded. "I understand, but let's just say *if*? Could it go into space?"

He shrugged. "Well, at least to vacuum testing. That's why this is so frustrating." He brought his index finger to his thumb until they were almost touching. "We're *that* close."

I nodded slowly.

I knew a human who could get into that suit.

I knew three of them.

# FOUR

## Davy: You don't drop your weapon

Davy thought of himself as a timid person.

He was a person who could jump away at the slightest confrontation and often did. He still thought of himself as the young teenager cringing in his bedroom when his alcoholic father came home.

He was not feeling timid, now, though. He suspected it had to do with losing his mother to violence. He wasn't willing to lose anyone else. The "doctor" from the nursing facility had pointed a gun at his mother-in-law and a Taser at his wife.

Davy didn't drop him fifty feet into the water of the pit—something he had been doing for thirty years. He wanted access to the man's cell-phone history and, if he had any documents, Davy didn't want to risk them becoming illegible.

But he did drop him into the pit—from fifteen feet above the island, into a stand of thorny mesquite scrub. The man pitched forward, flailing his arms to try and get his feet under him before he hit, but he only partially succeeded, slamming down through the brush. His breath left him with a heavy grunt and the Taser flew fifteen feet. He still clutched the automatic, though.

Davy snatched the Taser and jumped to the rim above.

The man wasn't dead. Davy could see his arms were twitching but suspected he hadn't managed to inhale yet. He was considering going back down to jump-start the man's breathing when he heard a wheezing intake echo off the walls of the pit. After several more wheezing breaths, the man managed to sit upright, pulling away from the thorns that snagged his jacket. He started to stand, but his left leg gave way when he tried to put weight on it.

His next attempt went better, using his arms and good leg, he staggered upright. After a few more labored breaths he limped out of the brush to a stretch of bare sand near the water's edge. He carried the gun pointed at the sky, one hand bracing the other, his elbows pulled tight into his sides. His head swiveled back and forth, looking over the island, then the walls of the pit, and then finally up toward the rim and the blue sky.

Davy aimed the Taser before jumping, appearing six feet behind him, his hand already squeezing the trigger. Two red laser-aiming dots appeared on the man's back and then the Taser bucked. Two wires shot out, sticking into the man's jacket four inches apart. His back arched and his arms spasmed. His legs didn't collapse as much as kick out, and he landed heavily on his back. Again, his breath left him.

Davy took the gun and two spare ammo clips, the wallet, the phone, and three spare Taser cartridges from the man's rear pocket. He found a pair of handcuffs tucked in the man's belt and there was a capped hypodermic in the breast pocket of his jacket.

Davy jumped away to the Yukon, to the cabin, and set his looted material on the kitchen table. He popped the battery out of the phone. He'd never been able to get a GPS receiver to work in the cabin—metal roof—but there was no point in taking chances.

The gun felt odd, unbalanced. He hit the clip release, but nothing came out. He turned it over and looked up the frame. There was no magazine in the weapon. He worked the slide in case there was a round in the chamber, but no round ejected. He pointed at the exterior log wall and pulled the trigger. Click.

He wanted to go through everything, but first things first. He left it all on the kitchen table.

When Davy returned to the pit he carried a broad-spectrum

radio-frequency detector with an antenna probe at the end of a cable. He also had a handheld metal detector hanging from a belt loop.

The man was breathing again, but even more labored than after his drop. His eyes were half open, but Davy didn't think he had control of his muscles yet. Still, he stood well back while he swept with the radio-frequency wand.

No transmitting bugs. No transmitting trackers.

Davy was almost disappointed.

He used the metal detector, paying special attention to the man's upper chest. Nothing.

He was *not* disappointed about that. The last thing he wanted to see was another exploding upper chest.

Sweeping lower, he got a strong beep from the man's buckle and nothing else. Davy snaked the belt out of the man's pants, slapping away the man's hand as he weakly tried to block Davy.

Davy stepped away. The belt buckle was heavy stainless steel and when he fingered it, it slid out of a pocket in the belt revealing a short, double-edged knife blade.

There was something odd about the snap on the man's slacks. Davy twisted it and it came away. He turned it over and saw a concealed push-out, plastic handcuff key.

He jumped away, leaving the man on the sand.

The wallet had eighty dollars in cash, a driver's license and credit cards for Mortimer S. Hunter from Maclean, Virginia. There was also a gym membership, a frequent-diner card from a sushi restaurant, and a worn picture of a girl, perhaps twelve. The town sounded familiar to him, but he couldn't place it. He took pictures of the ID and other cards, then put them back in the wallet.

He jumped back to Wichita, to a small, airless self-storage unit next door to Samantha's retirement village. A massive knee-high deep-cycle battery sat on the concrete floor. Welding-gauge wire ran from screw terminals to a DC-to-AC inverter. The power adaptor of a cheap netbook computer was plugged into the inverter. The netbook sat on a TV tray in front of a green plastic patio chair.

The camera Davy had installed in Samantha's room looked like the wall-plug transformer end of a phone charger and, in fact, was doing a good job of charging Samantha's cell phone, but it had a tiny wide-angle lens that looked like a screw hole. It also connected to the nursing facility's WiFi network, as did Davy's netbook in the storage locker.

Davy hit the shift key and the blank screen came alive, showing Samantha's room from the vicinity of the room's built-in vanity. Samantha was reading from her tablet, which was held above her by a gooseneck floor stand. Her arm was propped with pillows so she could change pages with just the flick of a finger. He turned up the volume on the netbook and heard the muted sound of a television from a neighboring room.

He nodded. He didn't think they would take her. Besides the logistics of moving a post-surgical bedridden patient, if Millie or Davy didn't know where she was, then Samantha couldn't be used for bait.

The netbook was recording the camera feed in space-saving fifteen-frames-per-second video. Davy checked the remaining room on the flash drive. He could store months at this rate. The battery would last weeks.

He switched to the web browser and searched for Maclean, Virginia, then sat back, surprised at the results. Sure, they *called* it Langley, but the actual address was 1000 Colonial Farm Road, Maclean, Virginia: Central Intelligence Agency.

Davy cleared the search from the browser history, reselected the monitor window, and jumped back to the Yukon.

When he replaced the battery and powered it on, Mr. Mortimer Hunter's phone asked for a key code. Davy shrugged, pulled the battery again, and put both the battery and phone in his pocket.

It had rained recently in Singapore's Sim Lim Square. The pavement was wet, but the sun was barely above the horizon and it hadn't turned steamy yet. The man Davy was looking for had already opened his kiosk, the International Phone Emporium.

"*Ni hao a*, Lucas?"

Lucas was taller than Davy, unlike most of the Singapore Chinese, but he tended to hunch over, to bring his eyes level with most of his customers. "Ah, me very well, one."

Davy smiled. "I have this phone. I need to get the logs, the pictures, the contacts, and the texts off of it." He handed the phone and battery to Lucas.

"Huh. *Wah lau!* So crap one! Five minutes. You want on a different phone or just thumb drive?"

"Thumb drive, please. Uh, I don't have the security code."

Lucas grinned. "This one can do *lah*."

Davy nodded. "Thought so."

"Wait *lah*."

"Sure."

While Lucas did his thing at the back of the kiosk with cables and a laptop, Davy stared at the phone displays that ranged from simple cordless phones for landlines, to cell phones of every make and model, up to satellite communications systems used at sea or other places without cell service.

Lucas came back and said, "What else you want or not?"

"Nothing else. Hundred dollar okay?"

"Singapore or U.S.?"

"U.S. dollar."

Lucas smiled. "Very okay."

Davy traded the cash for the phone, battery, and thumb drive, and shook Lucas's hand.

Back in the pit the "doctor" was up again, limping gingerly around the edge of the island. Davy thought his limp was less pronounced and, considering that the man hadn't *really* pointed a loaded weapon at his mother-in-law, Davy was glad he hadn't dropped him from any higher.

He jumped down to the island, thirty feet behind the man.

"Is it your ankle or your knee?"

The man jerked around at Davy's voice and dropped to one knee as his leg gave way again.

Davy winced. He felt a little guilty but he was pretty sure the man *had* intended to use the Taser on Millie. Then there was the knife. He wasn't sure what *that* was about.

"Ankle," said the man.

"I wouldn't have used the Taser if I'd known the gun was empty."

The man shrugged. "You didn't know that until after you got it, right? So maybe I could have threatened you with it."

"You were thinking that far ahead?" Davy asked.

"Well, no. Training—you don't drop your weapon."

"Why'd you unload it?"

The man shut his mouth.

"Did they tell you to? I mean, the scenario was obvious. Threaten the mother to keep her still, then Tase my wife, hoping that would give you enough time to use the hypo. But I don't see how having an unloaded gun fits that scenario." Davy kicked at a small rock. "So why empty, Mortimer? Is that what they call you? Mort? Morty?"

The man grimaced. "Hunt. They call me Hunt."

"So that's your real name? Not an agency-issued alias?"

"That's my name."

Davy noticed Hunt hadn't said *that's my* real *name*. It reminded him of what he'd told Cent when they were living in New Prospect. *Don't think of it as a* false *name. Think of it as who you are* now. "They must give you a lot of grief at the agency for that. Or is it something you try to live up to? And where's your agency ID? The folded one in the blue case, name up top, photo below?"

The man didn't say anything.

"You ever hear of the Daarkon Group?"

The man's eyebrows went up. "I . . . have."

Davy jumped within two feet of the man. *"Do you work for them?"*

The man's hands were up in a guard position instantly and

he lashed forward toward Davy's shin with his good leg, but Davy wasn't there.

Davy was impressed. The man's face hadn't flinched at all, just dropped slightly below the upraised hands. *Lots of training. Years, probably.* Davy resolved to keep his distance.

From four feet behind Hunt, Davy said, "Well, do you?"

Hunt dropped his hands back down and pivoted slowly on his buttocks until he could see Davy. "Can you believe anything I say? For what it's worth, I don't work for the Daarkon Group."

"Where did you hear about them?"

Hunt tilted his head to one side and eyed Davy. After a moment, he said, "I read it in your file."

*My file*? "Oh, really? Is this from eighteen months ago?" That was when Davy had discovered Daarkon, following links from twenty years before. Millie had passed the group to FBI agent Bekka Martindale after Hyacinth Pope escaped prison.

"I shouldn't say."

*Shouldn't*? "You already told me there was a file. Kinda late, isn't it?"

"Perhaps." Hunt sighed. "The first entry was eleven years ago. That's when they first filed incorporation papers in California. They got put in the file because many of their directors were affiliated with Lawrence Simons." Hunt watched Davy carefully as he said the name.

Despite his best efforts, Davy felt his mouth go tight. "Did I react enough?" With an effort he relaxed his face. "Are you agency or not? We're talking my old NSA file or its descendants, right? I'm actually thinking you aren't with the Daarkon Group or, if you are, you aren't aware of it.

"Just tell me why you emptied the gun. Did they tell you to or was it your own idea?"

Hunt blinked and looked *embarrassed.* "I didn't like the idea of pointing my weapon at a bedridden old lady who probably couldn't lift a weapon even if she *was* armed. And I needed my finger on the trigger, so your wife would believe me."

"Ah. And since it was a Glock, the safety projects from the trigger. You didn't want to risk a discharge."

"Yes. They specifically told me not to point my gun at you or your wife."

"But they were okay with you pointing it at a helpless old lady?"

Hunt looked away.

"So it was *your* idea to empty the weapon."

"I had spare clips!"

Davy shook his head. "What else is in my file?" *Maybe I should be spending my time trying to get CIA records instead of watching that building in LA.*

Hunt pursed his lips. "There's a lot from when you worked for the NSA and later, when you went missing. The stuff after that is peripheral, investigating known associates. That led to the Daarkon Group stuff, some surveillance of your wife's family, of your father until his death." Hunt licked his lips.

Davy wondered what was in the file that Hunt *wasn't* talking about.

"Then there was a new section dating from the recapture of Hyacinth Pope in New Prospect. *That* was eighteen months ago."

"Why this attempt on Millie?"

"Standing order, I'm told, but *I* wasn't assigned until your mother-in-law's health deteriorated and the likelihood of a contact increased."

Davy took a step back. "Why are you being so forthcoming?"

"*My* assignment is to get you working for U.S. interests again. I didn't come up with the snatch attempt on your wife and, in fact, deleted it from the early mission planning since it was more likely to turn you against us. But my supervisors put it back in and gave it priority one.

"I think I have a better chance of achieving my mission goals by being open with you."

*Forget the unarmed combat training—this guy is dangerous in* lots *of ways.*

Davy jumped back to the Yukon and uncapped the hypodermic. Returning to the rim above the pit, he marked Hunt's exact posture and position, and jumped.

"Shit, that stings!"

Davy was already twenty feet away but he'd left the hypodermic standing upright in Hunt's thigh, the plunger fully depressed. Hunt carefully pulled it out and stared at it, frowning.

"What was it?" Davy asked, hoping he hadn't poisoned the man.

Hunt didn't say anything.

"You should tell me in case I have to get you to an ER. You know: allergic reactions; overdose."

Hunt's head nodded or maybe it was wobbling. Reluctantly he said, "Haloperidol." His next words were slurred. "They were gonna use loraze . . . ze . . . ze . . . pam but it can depress resp–ration and they—" Hunt fell back onto the sand with a thud.

Davy didn't think he was faking but he tapped Hunt's injured ankle with the toe of his shoe just to be sure. There was no reaction. Hunt's pulse and respiration were slow but regular.

Davy carefully capped the hypodermic, then took a full-face picture of Hunt with his cell before returning to the cabin. When he came back to the pit he put Hunt's cell phone, battery, and wallet in the man's jacket pockets.

He left Hunt lying on the grass in front of a six-foot-high concrete bust of Einstein in Plaza Einstein, a tiny park on the Via Agentina in Panama City, Republic of Panama.

When Davy returned to the cabin, Millie was leaning over the kitchen table looking at the gun, Taser, hypodermic, and handcuffs. He breathed out, his shoulders dropping.

"S'okay?"

Millie nodded, then gestured at the weapons. "We can't leave her there. As soon as her physicians pull the surgical staples, we're bringing her home."

They'd already discussed it. They'd fought about it.

Davy wanted to move Samantha to a different nursing facility, under an assumed name, probably in another country. But Millie wanted her in *their* home.

She'd said, "I don't know how long I've got. If you knew *your* mother was going to die soon, wouldn't you want to spend as much time with her as possible?"

That was the clincher. He certainly hadn't known how soon his mother would die when she'd been killed thirty years before. He'd have given anything for more time with her.

"Have you talked to Cent?"

"Not yet. Mother only just agreed. I don't think she's ever had a gun pointed at her before." Millie's mouth drew down into a tight line. "I was worried she'd have heart failure or go into respiratory distress. Instead she just suggested that *you* stay longer next time."

Despite the grim look on Millie's face, Davy laughed, tried to stop it, then laughed some more.

Millie's mouth softened and one corner turned up.

Davy said, "Well, the gun was empty, at least. He had no intention of hurting her."

Millie raised her eyebrows.

Davy told her about his conversation with Mr. Hunter.

"God. That's got to be his real name. No one would assign that to an agent, would they? So, not *them*?"

Davy shrugged. "I don't think so. Doesn't mean someone above him isn't."

She sighed.

Cent appeared on the living room side of the island counter. "Hey."

"Hey, yourself," said Davy.

Cent spotted the gun and hypodermic on the table. "Anything wrong?" Her gaze moved back and forth from Millie to Davy.

Millie summoned a smile. "I told you about my mother's new injury?"

Cent nodded, her eyes wide. "She's not—"

"Oh, no. She's okay. But I don't know how long we've got. I'm bringing her home next week, to live with us."

"Oh. That's good, right?" She gestured at the gun. "What's with that?"

"CIA tried to snatch me."

Cent turned to Davy. "Are *they* okay? Do I need to avoid the pit?"

"They'll . . . be all right." He took out his cell phone and showed her a picture of Hunt's face. "In case you see him."

Cent studied it. "Right. About Grandmother, do you want to use my room? I could move downstairs."

Millie smiled. "I was going to talk to you about that. Would you be comfortable sleeping in the Eyrie? We're going to bring in some help and I was hoping to put *them* in the sewing room and the library."

Cent looked at Davy. "Uh, there's not exactly any privacy at the Eyrie. It's all one big room and all."

Davy said, "I don't have to go there."

"What about all those books, Daddy? You have as many *there* as you have *here*. What if I have . . . company?"

Davy grimaced. "I can move my books," he said. "I'm going to have to clear out the library here, anyway, so I thought I'd take over part of the warehouse. We're going to cut back on the relief work while we're taking care of Samantha, and the supplies we haven't used can all go into one corner."

Cent looked shocked. "Uh, Move the library? It's *always* been there."

"Not always," Millie said, smiling at Davy. "It's been moved before."

Davy rubbed at his forehead. "It was *smaller* back then, but yeah." He pointed at Cent. "I'm just moving the books. You can use the shelves in the Eyrie."

Millie nodded. "When do you plan on starting that? I want the room completely ready by next Tuesday."

Davy sighed. "I'll get right on it."

# FIVE

## Cent: Fainted? I don't faint

Friday afternoon I met Tara at her apartment while her mom was still at work. "What's the story?"

"I told her I'm visiting Jade."

I raised my eyebrows.

"I told her that the two of us went in on the price of a plane ticket," she said. "That I'm taking the bus to Salt Lake City International. The tricky part is that Mom's going to drive over there on Sunday to pick me up."

I winced. "I don't have a jump site in Salt Lake City."

"Shit! What airports do you have?"

"I avoid airports. They have lots of cameras." The last airport I'd been to was in San Antonio, Texas. But the main problem was that here in New Prospect I was as close as I'd ever been to Salt Lake City, and that was still a couple of hundred miles away. "I've got *nothing* near there."

"Should we cancel?" The expression on her face told me everything I needed to know about what *she* wanted.

"No. Don't worry, I'll figure it out." If worse came to worst, I could do my ballistic thing.

Tara phoned Jade and confirmed she was alone in her dorm room, so I jumped Tara directly there. It was already 5:30, dark, and near freezing in Northampton, but we bundled up and ate wood-fired gorgonzola pizza at Pizzeria Paradiso. The two made a show of including me in the conversation, but they really only had eyes for each other.

I gave up before dessert.

"See you Sunday afternoon."

I walked out into chilly Northampton alone, leaving the booth to them. Not their fault, of course, but too much a reminder of Joe.

The Eyrie is about twelve miles from the pit, deep in El Solitario, a cliff house two hundred feet from the bottom of a steep canyon.

Long before I was born, Dad took a ledge with an overhanging shelf and enclosed it with a wall of natural rock. He used dye in the mortar to match the rock, but you can't really see it from anyplace but the opposite wall of the canyon. From the floor, the ledge blocks it. From above, even on the opposite ridge, the shelf blocks it. Dad says he's seen hikers in the canyon, but it's been secure since before they got married.

I was surprised when Dad said I could have it, but Mom filled me in.

"He's not comfortable with the idea of live-in help. I insisted we have medical resources on-site, but he's worried we'll end up with a mole—with one of *them*. He was the one who suggested you *not* sleep here. He figures you'll be fine while awake, but he didn't want anyone sneaking up on you."

That I could understand. Dad is paranoid, but he has reasons for his paranoia.

I'd already helped Dad set up new shelves in the warehouse. He started loading them with his books out of the Eyrie immediately after that.

I jumped the contents from my bedroom shelves to the knotty pine shelves in the cliff house. It was clear why Dad hadn't moved them. The ledge that formed the Eyrie's floor sloped from one end to the other, a gradual descent. All the shelves had been built in place to be level on that uneven surface.

I spread out my collection of books and manga and videos,

leaving room for expansion, but there were still four empty units down at the far end when I was done.

Mom had me take my desk and chest of drawers, and we rigged some rods for my hanging clothes. We moved my bed, with the reading nook beneath, to the warehouse.

It was weird standing there, in the empty bedroom. The carpet was still there, but Mom said she was going to pull it for sanitary reasons. "Your grandmother has enough trouble breathing without dealing with old mold and dust."

I felt guilty. I was certainly responsible for any mold. My first jump put a couple of cubic yards of snow in this room. I offered to help strip the carpet, but Mom knew I had other plans.

"Go on. I've got this."

I jumped to the Stanford campus. Not only was it still light, it was forty degrees warmer. It was after hours for the observation deck on Hoover tower, so I jumped there and sat in the sun.

Of course I thought about Joe. I looked south toward Stern Hall. I could walk it in five minutes, but of course *I* didn't have to walk.

I tried to look away but it took a conscious physical jerk to turn my gaze west instead, toward Cory's lab in the Durand Building.

Cory wasn't in, which was good, 'cause I wasn't going to talk to him before I'd proven it could be done. Apparently he'd taken his laptop home, so I didn't have worry about disconnecting the USB cables. I slowly turned up the power running to the suit's EAP fibers and watched in fascination as it expanded and relaxed, sagging on the life-model form, hanging suspended from the arm supports and the helmet flange.

I couldn't see how the pieces of the life model were connected to each other and was about to give up when I saw the edge of a strip of Velcro sticking up between the neck and one of the shoulder sections. I gritted my teeth and, using a screwdriver, pried it apart. The Velcro let go with a tearing sound and I winced, sure I'd ruined something, but I hadn't. When I repeated the process on the other side, the entire central section of the torso, from neck to crotch, came up through the helmet flange. It was trailing six fine wires, but there was enough slack I could lie it on the floor by the suit.

Inside, the wires wound off toward the remaining modules, terminating, on the two I could see, in connectors glued to the surface of the left and right parts of the torso. Both sides of the connectors were clearly labeled so I unplugged them.

The two remaining torso modules were Velcroed in turn to the arms and the hips. I eased them out. At this point, I was able to unplug the remaining four wires, so I lay the torso pieces on the bench, face up, keeping their orientation to each other. The ease with which the arms and legs came out was comical after my initial frustrations. In all, it took a half hour, but half that time was just finding that first piece of Velcro.

I laid out the life-model legs and arms with the torso and the result was a bit disturbing—a headless man lying on the workbench. The sun was down and the light coming through the windows had diminished. I looked at the bench and shuddered, and turned on the lab lights.

Without the life model, the suit was much lighter when I put it back up on the stand. Sure, heavier than normal clothing, but less than seven kilos, including the helmet flange.

Though Cory hadn't been using it while the life model supported the upper part of the suit, the stand had a two-pronged fork on a hinge that, when flipped down, was the right width and height to support the helmet flange where it had been before.

The suit looked huge.

*Stop stalling.*

I peered carefully at the thing and thought about how I should hold my arms. I took a deep breath . . . then let it out again and stepped back.

Something wasn't right.

I looked down at the floor and swore. The feet were pointing away. The cable connector should've clued me in, since it was on the opposite side. I took the suit back off the stand and turned it around again, carefully arranging the feet and arms.

And then I did it.

I was standing in the suit.

The top of my head was sticking out of the helmet flange but my eyes were below it. I laughed. I flapped my arms—my hands came near the sausage-sized fingers at the end of the sleeve. It felt like putting on Daddy's clothes when I was a little girl, practically vanishing into the oversized shirts and pants.

I jumped back out.

*Well, that advances the timetable a bit.*

I turned my phone on, hooked into the Stanford guest WiFi, and loaded the Skype app.

"Cory, could you meet me at your lab tonight?"

I'd considered going to the next step by myself—the bit where I turned the power off and let the suit shrink, squeezing in, until the thing was pressing against my skin, hopefully uniformly, at the predicted thirty kilopascals. But for all I knew, it would bind or even trap me, not letting me move enough to reach the switch.

Awkward, at the very least.

I'd changed clothes by the time Cory, got there, though I wore my long dark-wool coat over all.

He'd seen the light was on and opened the door, the key still in his hand. "How'd you get in?"

I smiled. "The same way I got in when I delivered your equipment. Sorry. No one let me in, just as no one let me into your old lab when I recovered the suit."

He looked down at the doorknob. "Uh, these aren't cheap locks. You didn't 'bump' them open. And that security padlock at my old lab was a level up from even this."

I nodded. "Don't forget the evidence seal."

He frowned. "Right. Uh, this is a little creepy."

"I've been in the suit, Cory."

His head swiveled and he looked at the suit, hanging empty, still powered, at full extension, baggy and hanging. "Impossible—unless you ruined it." He walked past me, his steps quickening. He ran his fingers over the cloth, around the flange. He twitched the rheostat on the power supply, reducing voltage, and let it shrink in until it hung there like a thin-limbed child's onesie instead of a shroud for a giant.

He turned back to me and said, "I'm going with 'impossible.'"

I opened the coat. I was wearing my high-tech snowboarding skintight long underwear over briefs, bra, and ankle socks. "Expand it again."

He stared at me, then said, "Unless you don't have a human bone structure, you're *not* fitting through the flange."

I jerked my chin at the suit. "Expand it."

He turned and flipped the rheostat. When he turned back toward me, I wasn't there.

What he saw was my black coat dropping to the floor.

I had to stand on tiptoe and raise my chin to look through the flange. Cory took two steps toward the coat, tilting his head to look at the connecting door to his office, before he thought to look back at the suit.

"See," I said. "I didn't break it."


Well, *that* didn't go like I expected.

I was kneeling on the floor holding a plastic bag full of snow against the bump on the back of his head.

"Sorry, I should've had you sit down first."

He was still blinking. "What happened?"

"You fainted and hit your head on the floor."

"Fainted? I *don't* faint," he said, offended. He sat up and groaned, then reached up and touched his head. "Ouch." He glared at me. "Did someone hit me?"

"You fell. Your head bounced off the floor. Here." I handed him the Baggie of snow.

He touched it, squeezed it. "What's this? Shaved ice?"

"Snow," I said.

"Snow. In the Bay Area?"

"Let me see your pupils. Do you have a concussion?"

He glared at me again and told me the date, the day of the week, and the current president.

I said, "Tell me what happened right before you fell down."

"Uh, I turned the power back up on the suit and then looked

back at you, but you'd dropped your coat and moved while I was looking away. I checked the office then looked back at the suit and you were standing behind it, looking over the flange."

"I wasn't behind the suit," I said gently.

He blinked like an owl again, several times, and pressed the snow against his head, then said plaintively, "Why *snow*?"

"It's softer than ice. Against the bump on your head."

"*Where* did you get snow?"

"Canada."

He rolled his eyes.

There were two tall backless bench stools in the room, but I thought they would be more dangerous than standing. I went back into his office and rolled his desk chair back into the lab.

"Here. Sit down in this. You're a rational man, aren't you? Ph.D. engineer and all?"

He nodded reluctantly and let me help him up into the chair. I thought about going back into his office and getting his bicycle helmet, but he looked pretty secure in the chair. It had a cloth seat, not leather, so I thought he wouldn't slide out of it even if he fainted again.

I walked back to the suit, still in its expanded form. "Let's try this once more. Call it a reproducible result."

He was watching me, outwardly calm, but it was clear some part of him was not calm, for his fingers were clutching the arms of the chair hard enough to dimple the padding.

I jumped back into the suit, and looked over the rim of the flange as soon as I could. The seat was moving back a bit, but his eyes were still open and, in fact, he was sitting bolt upright, his hands still clenched to the arm rests. I lifted my right arm, twisting it back and forth until my hand found the sausage-sized fingers. I flapped them at him.

He stood up slowly and I watched him carefully. If he started to pass out again, I'd catch him this time, but though he clenched his eyes shut and leaned against the workbench top for a minute, he eventually walked forward, breathing slowly and deliberately.

"You okay?"

He licked his lips. "I'm not sure. I don't think I'm going to faint again, though."

"That's good."

He reached out and lifted the helmet flange off its supporting fork. "Step forward."

I shuffled forward, feeling the underarm supports scrape along my armpits, and then I was in front of the stand. When he lowered the flange so it rested on my shoulders, it was much less claustrophobic.

"How did you *do* that?"

He didn't scream it, but the intensity in his voice and face made me want to jump away. "We'll talk about that," I said. "But right now, let's just see if the suit fits."

He blinked again.

"Cory?"

He shook his head, as if to clear it. "I haven't cleared any human trials with the institutional review board. Uh, you *are* human, right?"

"We mean no harm to your planet," I said.

He didn't think that was funny at *all*.

"I'm human, honest. Very human. Ultrahuman."

"What does *that* mean? *Ultra*?"

I backpedaled. "Just human, Cory. I have this one thing I can do, and we'll talk about it, but I'd rather not go through the institutional review board. I promise not to sue you if you promise not to pinch me in two."

He blinked. "No, that won't happen."

"Well, how should we do it?"

"Slowly," he said.

First thing he had me do was shift my feet all the way into the legs, toes all the way into the ends of the feet, then get my fingers and thumbs into the corresponding sausage casings at the ends of the arms.

"Ready?" he asked.

I nodded, nervous, excited.

He slowly lowered the voltage, pausing several times to check how the suit was conforming to my body, but paying special attention to my hands. He got to the point where it fit, all over, like comfortable clothes, not tight, but the fingers felt like they were in oversized work gloves and the feet felt like they were in slippers.

"Walk around a bit, flex your joints."

I did.

"Okay, hyperventilate."

"Excuse me?"

He pointed at my chest. "Remember what I said about it being hard to breathe?"

"Oh, yeah. Squeezing in on the lungs."

"Right. Just want to make sure you're stocked up on $O_2$."

"And low on $CO_2$," I added.

"Yeah, that, too."

I took some deep, quick breaths and held up my thumb.

He took the rheostat all the way down.

It felt *good*, like the most complete hug in the world, like crawling under the couch cushions and letting them push down on you. Inhaling, though an effort, wasn't that bad.

I flexed my fingers. There was tension and if I relaxed my hand, the fingers and hand would straighten out into a slightly curved extension. When I relaxed my arms, the default position was with the elbows slightly bent and the armpits slightly open, with gravity pulling my hands down toward my thighs. I reached up and fingered the power-cable connector, finding it easy, the fingers, wrist, elbow not having to work harder than they would in a middleweight jacket and heavy work gloves. I unclipped it.

"Uh, don't do that!"

"Why not?"

"What if we can't reconnect it?"

"Don't you reconnect it all the time?"

His mouth opened and shut. Then, "Yes, but someone isn't usually wearing it! If we can't reconnect it, how do we get the suit *off* you?"

I shrugged. "Even if we can't get the connector to work, I'm sure you could jury-rig a way to energize the EAPs. Alligator clips or something. Worst-case scenario, we'd cut the suit off."

He looked like he might faint again.

"As a last resort." I walked down the length of the lab and back, then tried some jumping jacks. My feet slipped a bit on the linoleum.

When I'd jumped to the office, after changing into the long underwear, I'd worn the sheepskin boots that were my Yukon winter kick-about shoes. They were loose enough that when I slipped my suited feet into them, they fit snugly.

"The suit needs some grip on the soles."

Cory shook his head. "The suit is the underlayer. You put on utility overgear as needed. Boots, gloves, knee pads, insulated or electrically heated coveralls."

"For Mars, right?"

He nodded. "Eventually."

"But it would work in orbit, yes?"

"Yes. You might need high-albedo coveralls to keep the sun off. Cooling is more of a problem than heating. Vacuum is an insulator, after all, and the body produces lots of heat."

"But you wouldn't need active cooling? That's the idea of the open weave—evaporative cooling from sweating, just like on Earth?"

"That's the idea. How's your breathing?"

"Inhaling takes some effort but I'd forgotten about it until you asked."

"I wish we had sensors under the suit. Need to confirm the counterpressure."

"Don't trust your previous data?"

"I'd be very surprised if it wasn't thirty kilopascals, but we need to know before we expose you to low pressure. I'll have to rig up a bodysuit with strain gauges on it. What are you wearing—long underwear? What else?"

"Sports bra and panties and a pair of thin ankle socks." I told him the brand of the wicking base layers. "What did your other candidates use?"

"We used a dancer unitard with integrated feet, gloves, and hood." He gestured at me. "What you chose looked relatively slick on the surface," he said. "And like it conformed pretty well to your body." He looked away and I think his ears went bright red.

I felt my own ears warm up a little. "Very slick, yeah. Good movement when I'm snowboarding."

"So, no abrasion from the suit so far? No folds of cloth bunching up anywhere?"

I nodded. "Feels really good, actually."

He lifted my arms and pulled them right and left, working the shoulders. "Looks like you chose well. You'll have temporary marks from the seams."

"Duh." Well, he'd never worn a bra, probably.

I kept the suit on for a full hour, doing various range-of-motion tests, then spending some time at the bench, manipulating progressively smaller objects. Last, he handed me a device with an LCD readout and a label which read *Electronic Hand Dynamometer.*

"Squeeze." It was for measuring the strength of the grip. He took several measurements from each hand. "We'll need to measure your grip without the suit, when you've rested. Still okay on the breathing?"

"It's a little harder now."

"Does anything feel numb, like it's gone to sleep? How about your toes?"

I wiggled them. "Feel good."

"Ready to stop?"

"Sure." I pulled the sheepskin boots off. "Let's see if the connector still works."

Despite Cory's worries, the power cable snapped back on and he cranked up the voltage.

The suit let go of me in a way that was more unsettling than when it had tightened. It was like a bra strap breaking or a wet suit ripping or snaps coming open. It made my skin crawl.

As soon as the suit stopped expanding I said, "Hold onto the helmet flange, please."

"Huh? Oh!" He'd slowly relaxed over the course of the hour, excited to finally see the full suit working on a human, but now that he realized what I was about to do, his posture was wary again and his eyes wide. He took hold of the flange on both sides of my neck and then he was holding the empty suit.

I pulled up my left shirt sleeve and examined the lines imprinted into my skin by the cuff seam and the end of the sleeve. "Wow. You weren't kidding." It didn't hurt, and when I rubbed it vigorously with my thumb, it began to fade.

Cory hung the suit on the rack. He was breathing a little fast and I didn't think it was the weight of the suit. He turned back to the bench and turned the power down.

Again, I was surprised at how small the suit became.

He crossed his arms and said, "Are you going to tell me what's happening yet?"

"You mean that thing I do? Sit back down," I said.

"You're afraid I'll faint again?" He felt the back of his head and winced. "Maybe you have a point." He moved to the chair.

I put my boots back on. "We call it jumping."

"We?"

Mentally I groaned. "Well, I do."

"How many of you are there?"

I shook my head. "Need-to-know, Cory. Need-to-know. Anyway, I can jump to anyplace I've been that I can remember well enough, or to anyplace I can easily see." I walked slowly toward him while I was talking. "For instance—" I looked back, to the end of the lab beyond the suit stand, and then jumped there.

He flinched and I was glad I hadn't followed my first impulse, which was to jump from farther away to right in front of him.

"How do you do that?"

I shook my head again. "Need-to-know, Cory. I can tell you a few things, though. There currently doesn't seem to be a limit on how far I can go."

I jumped away to the Yukon and in the walkway behind our cabin, scooped up a double handful of snow, then jumped back to the office and slapped it into his hand.

Yeah, he flinched big time, dropping the snow on the linoleum between his feet.

I kept talking. "That was from the Arctic Circle. I routinely jump all over the planet and, here's the important thing, I jump from *higher to lower latitudes and vice versa with no problem*."

He was still staring down at the small pile of snow on the floor. "I'm not getting you."

Well, it *was* new to him. I was sure he'd get the implications in a minute.

"Watch." I used the lab stool to climb up and stand on the workbench. Yes, I could've jumped up there, but I wanted the point to be crystal clear.

I stepped off and dropped to the floor, but before I touched, I jumped back to the far end of the room, standing perfectly still.

Cory flinched again, but then his eyes widened. "You didn't carry the momentum of the drop!"

He blinked again, multiple times, and I couldn't help thinking of the owl again.

"And when you change latitude, you're not carrying any velocity with you?"

"Bingo, Cory. What's your conclusion?"

"You're matching velocities."

"And this means? . . ."

"You're *changing* velocities."

"Now we're getting somewhere," I said. "Watch this." I jumped in place but ended up facing the opposite direction. I slowly turned around and raised my eyebrows.

He was doing the owl thing again. "That looked so weird. You changed orientation, right?"

"Right, but mostly I wanted to show you I could jump to the same location but still change things. Watch carefully."

I jumped in place adding just under twenty feet a second straight up. I held my body still, making sure he saw that I hadn't leapt up using my legs. The ceiling was a good twelve feet up and I slapped it with my palm at the apex of the jump, then dropped back down again. Before I hit, I killed all my downward velocity, landing whisper quiet on the floor.

"What did I change, Cory?"

He wasn't blinking this time, but his mouth hung open. "Velocity," he said.

"I *knew* you were the bright one." I walked up to him and peeled back the cuff of my right sleeve, showing him the half-inch circle of scab where the blackened blister had been. "See this? It's a bit of frostbite. I got it at forty-five thousand feet."

If I thought I'd had his full attention before, I was mistaken. The intensity of his gaze as he lifted his eyes from my wrist to my face was scary.

"I want to go higher." I pointed my finger at the ceiling.

"I want to go a *lot* higher."

# SIX

## Millie: I should pay *you*

"Oh. My. God." Davy left his mouth open after the last syllable, slowly shaking his head.

Millie frowned. "Does she check out? Seeana's not one of *them* is she?"

"Oh, no. Like your mother said, she earns the median salary but she's paying off a lot of debt—two different boyfriends maxed out her credit cards. Unfortunately, it wasn't behind her back, they just didn't pay her back as promised. That's the main reason she lives with her mom.

"The last 'check' I did was to listen at the window. Her mother *never* stops talking even when Seeana *isn't* in the room. If she is with her, then it's 'pity you aren't more pretty' and 'too bad you have such rotten luck with men' and 'I don't know why you take after your father instead of my side of the family.' "

He covered his ears.

"We need to get her out of there."

"Most of the time I'm wearing earbuds and listening to audio-books on my phone." Seeana leaned closer, cupping her hand around her coffee. "I *tell* Mom that it's because I'm on call for my job and have to be ready to take calls. It's not like I turn it up so loud I *can't* hear her—more to give myself something else to focus on."

She hadn't seemed surprised that Davy overheard her mother. "These autumn days, people leave their windows open until late. Mrs. Lee in the next unit complained to Mother that she couldn't hear her television over Mother's constant chatter. Mother's still talking, but *they* aren't." She gestured toward Millie. "So, you had questions about home care?"

That's what Millie had told her when she'd arranged the meeting.

"Yes. If you were going to take care of Samantha in a home environment, what sort of resources—staff and equipment— would you need?"

"You thinking of putting her back in her apartment? Cause that would be much more expensive than where she is, since the staff is shared."

"No. Our home."

"Even more expensive. You'd need a health-aid worker full time, during the day, regular nurse visits, and *you* would have to respond at night."

"We were thinking three health aids, with you as supervisor. Unless you want four. Three shifts and some juggling for days off. I'd be around, usually, as well."

Seeana blinked. "You don't need a full-time nurse for one patient."

"We're remote. Staff need to live on-site. We'd be offering you ten thousand a month."

"Ma'am, the average staff nurse rate here in Wichita is sixty-five thousand dollars a year. I mean, really well-paying positions might get up into the eighties, but nobody pays one hundred twenty thousand dollars."

"My mother wants *you*."

"Ma'am, you're offering me a place to live away from my mother? I should pay *you*! How far away?"

Millie licked her lips. "How do you feel about . . . snow?"

So the first jump is always a shock. Millie left Seeana lying on the couch before the great fireplace and went back to the kitchen for a damp cloth and a glass of water.

Seeana hadn't fainted, but her knees had given way and she needed a moment.

Millie was returning when she heard Seeana give a gasping half scream. She rounded the pillar and saw Cent standing by the fireplace, looking like she wanted to scream, too, one hand up to her throat.

"This is Seeana, Cent. She helps take care of Grandmother in Wichita. We're hoping she'll continue to do so here."

Cent dropped her hand and breathed out. "Sorry. Didn't mean to startle you. Glad to meet you."

Seeana was sitting up, perched on the edge of the couch. She slowly settled back, leaning into the cushions. "Nice to meet you." She said, but it was tentative. "How many of you *are* there?"

Millie stepped forward and set the glass on the coffee table. "This is my daughter. The only other person living here is my husband, Davy." She offered the warm, damp cloth to Seeana. "Feeling any better?"

Less tentatively, Seeana said, "Yes." She sipped from the water. "Oh, nice water. That from your fridge?"

Cent said, "From the tap, from our spring."

From the couch, Seeana could see the view across the valley to the firs framed in white on the far side. She took another swallow of water. "Cold as melted snow," she said.

She stood up carefully. "Let's see this place of yours."

# SEVEN

## Cent:—while I'm making my own

I found Dad at the cabin, pulling up the carpet in my old room. He'd piled most of it in the middle of the room and was prying up the carpet anchors at the edges of the room.

"I thought Mom was going to do that."

Dad twisted around to look me. "Did she say that?"

"Uh, she said, 'I've got this.' "

He laughed. "See?"

"Yeah. I see. Do you have a jump site in Salt Lake City?"

He jammed the pry bar under another section of the anchor strip and pried up. Half of it levered up and then snapped further down, where the nails still stubbornly gripped the floor. "Shit! Uh, I've got a site in Washington Square Park."

"That's New York City, Daddy."

"*And* Salt Lake City. The old city-county building is there. The jump site is across the street from The Leonardo. Remember?"

I shook my head. "Doesn't ring any bells. What's The Leonardo?"

"That downtown museum—art, science, technology? We went there for the "Mummies of the World" exhibit?"

"Oh. Yeah, I remember that. When I was fourteen. I didn't realize that was in Salt Lake City."

"Why do you need to go to Salt Lake?"

I deployed my first-level response, a true but uninformative answer. "Doing a favor for a friend of Joe's." *Technically* true. Tara and Jade knew Joe. "Could you pop me over there so I can acquire it?"

Dad closed his eyes and pursed his lips. "Yeah—I think so." He threw the broken section of wood into the middle of the room with the piled carpet and stood up, gesturing to me to come closer.

He put his arms around me and then we were standing on brown grass, an icy wind swirling dead leaves past our ankles. The trees immediately around us were mostly bare, and I could see the blocky modern museum across the street, as well as a much older castlelike building in the middle of the park. Dad pointed to a huge building on the opposite side of the park from the museum—modern, yet with Greek columns. "I think that's the state supreme court. This good enough?"

I kissed him on the cheek. "Thanks, Daddy."

He smiled, then said, "What's the favor?"

I hated lying but I hated arguing with him about "security" issues even more. Out came the prepared lie. "A local specialty. Kid's homesick. Joe won't tell him how he got it."

He made a "go on" gesture with his hand.

"Fry sauce."

"Oh, *that*. Why doesn't he just mix mayo and ketchup?"

I shrugged. "Says it's not the same. Has to be from this one chain—Arctic Circle."

"Weird." He looked at his watch. "You good? I need to finish pulling the carpet so your Mom and Seeana can refinish the floor."

"Yeah, thanks."

He vanished.

I considered going back for a jacket but decided the hoodie I was wearing would be enough. Before long, though, I regretted the choice. There weren't any cabs cruising the streets so I asked a woman walking a dog. "Yeah. Your best bet would be to walk up to the Marriott City Center." She pointed north. "Like three blocks that way. There'll be cabs there."

I was chilled by the time I got there and, before taking a cab, I went inside, found a restroom, and jumped home for my wool coat.

Seventeen minutes and twenty-five dollars later, the cab dropped me curbside at Terminal Two, Salt Lake City International Airport. I kept my hood up and my face down and picked an alcove behind the Starbucks at baggage claim five. There was a camera, but it was blocked by a sign directing people to ground transport.

Good enough.

The helmet was a polycarbonate fishbowl, a true sphere, sitting on a metal collar with through fittings which in turn terminated in a flange and seal.

"It was tested to hard vacuum," Cory said.

"With a person in it?"

Cory tapped the fishbowl, "It did some time in the eleven-foot chamber at Johnson, on an experimental suit. It was an attempt to make a disposable suit—cheap enough to use once and discard. The suit design didn't work out, but the helmet never failed."

"How do you test it without a suit? And what do you mean by hard vacuum?"

"Hard vacuum is all over the place in the literature, but when I use it, I mean fractions of a pascal—the thermosphere and above.

"We test solitary helmets two different ways. One is to put them on a test stand and pressurize them to ten atmospheres. That's effectively the difference between one atmosphere inside and a vacuum outside. The other method *is* in a vacuum—in a chamber on a sealed test flange—one atmosphere inside, vacuum outside. We did both on this."

"And it passed?"

"To one atmosphere." He jabbed his thumb toward the suit stand at the end of the bench. "*We* only need a third of that four-point-nine psi, for the MCP suit."

"Where's your life support?"

He tilted his head. "Pardon?"

"What are your test subjects going to *breathe*?"

"Oh. You run an $O_2$ line, on a pressure regulator set to four point nine psi, and absorb the $CO_2$ with soda lime or lithium hydroxide in the helmet. We could just purge the $CO_2$ but that would contaminate the vacuum."

"Contaminate? A bit of oxygen and $CO_2$ is going to contaminate your pristine vacuum?"

"Contaminate as in 'pressurize.' The vacuum pumps are good, but you purge the helmet and you probably raise the pressure several pascals, and it will take a bit of time to pump it back down. You want consistent vacuum for the tests."

"Could you run the $O_2$ from a tank, instead?"

"It *was* run from a tank."

"I mean a tank on the suit."

"Oh, sure, no difference."

"And could you run *that* in space?"

"Just a tank and some absorbent?" He frowned. "You'd want something more robust than that, with backups. That's not my area of research, really. Just needed them able to breathe for my tests. But spaceworthy life support? Well, NASA has already done thousands of hours of EVA—they've got it wired."

He wasn't getting my point. "When will NASA test your suit in orbit, Cory?"

*And when will NASA give* me *a spacesuit?*

He frowned. "The design needs to be proven. It has to be tested in chambers and refined. I've got to solve the closure problem."

"I see," I said. "You want to contribute to the space program. You've got the long view. You're thinking about a push to Mars within the next twenty years."

"Well, yeah."

I leaned in and locked eyes with him, causing him to lean back, a bit alarmed.

"Cory, you give me a working helmet and an hour of breathable air and I'll test your suit in orbit *this week*."

His eyes widened and he licked his lips.

I said, "I'm fine with advancing the state of technology for NASA *and* every other space program, but I'm not waiting to buy a ticket. The difference between you and me is that you're depending on *their* space program—" I pointed at him and then jerked my thumb back at myself. "—while I'm making my *own*.

"You want to come along?"

The weekend had gone well for Tara and Jade, though Jade didn't want Tara to go back. They were more clingy than they'd been on Friday, if that was possible.

"Decide," I said. "Tara's mom is probably passing through Provo, now. When she gets to the airport and Tara doesn't show, I'm not the one who's going to call her. Pretty sure you'll get some interesting calls from *both* sets of parents."

Jade rolled her eyes and reluctantly let go of Tara.

I made Tara buy me a hot chocolate at the baggage-claim Starbucks at Salt Lake City International and hung around while she checked in with her mom by phone.

"Hey, Mom. I'm here . . . yeah, not for another hour, but the flight got in early to Chicago and they had an earlier flight just leaving and overbooking issues on my scheduled flight so they asked if I'd switch. No problem. I have a book. Just let me know when you're about to get here and I'll be curbside."

She stuck her tongue out at me and disconnected.

"I could've stayed with Jade another forty-five minutes!"

"Your mom could've been early, too. You guys decide about Europe?"

"She's going to try and sell it to her parents. You can really get me to Paris?"

"*Mais oui, enfant.* A lot easier than it was to get you *here*."

"Okay. She's selling it to her parents—her dad's onboard with it already. If her mom stops with the objections, I'll join them the second week of their trip. A week and a half in Europe wouldn't suck."

"Okay. You good? I'd keep you company, but I have to go get some calcium hydroxide."

"You need calcium? Remember to take vitamin D with. It improves absorption."

I laughed. "I'll keep that in mind." I doubted that vitamin D would help calcium hydroxide absorb more carbon dioxide, and I sure as hell wasn't going to try and swallow any.

I left from a bathroom stall around the corner.

This was the deal:

I would provide the required parts and materials and wait until Cory rigged up a pressure-sensor onesie so we could test whether we were getting thirty kilopascals evenly over my body. In return, he would create a life-support pack I could use in orbit.

Not that we didn't argue about some of the details.

"Do you know how much lithium hydroxide costs?" I'd said after five minutes online. "Why can't we just use diving-grade soda lime? Isn't that what you were going to use in the chamber tests?"

Cory was working on the sensor onesie, sewing the ends of flexible strain gauges onto a dancer unitard. "Too heavy," he said without looking up. "The price difference is negligible compared to how much it costs to get it out of the gravity well."

I shook my head. His habits of thought were still locked into the old system. I said, mildly, "How much does it cost NASA to get something into orbit?"

"With the Falcon Heavy, the rate has dropped to a thousand bucks per pound and that's the cheapest rate to date. So you see, it's worth it to go with lithium hydroxide for the scrubber. It's forty percent lighter."

"Cory, how much does it cost *me* to get something into orbit?"

He looked up from the work. "*Oh*. I don't know. I don't know if you *can* get into orbit."

I felt like punching him. I held up my arm, exposing the scab. "I can get a lot farther toward orbit than *you* can."

All right, maybe *I* wasn't so sure either, but the suit was the roadblock to finding out.

He nodded. "I guess."

"But the important thing, is, no matter how far up I get, it won't cost us any more than we've already spent. We have the suit, we have the helmet, and it's pretty trivial to rig air. Even if

I'm limited to fifty pounds of cargo, my cost to orbit is effectively zero dollars per pound."

"What? Even just going by the material costs of the prototype, that's not true. I've got over forty K in the EAP fibers alone. Call it twice that for the whole rig. That's still sixteen hundred bucks per pound."

"But if this works, I can go to orbit *more than once*, Cory, with no further expenses. I'll be able to go to orbit over and over again, as long as the suit lasts. These are capital costs, not operating expenses. If you're going to count them against the size of the payload, you need to multiply the size by the number of payloads."

Cory shook his violently as if to clear it.

"Whoa. That's so weird." He exhaled sharply then took two slow breaths. "Weight has always been a priority in this field, a major consideration in all design choices. Even the MCP suit was partly an answer to the problem of heavy, bulky EV suits."

"So, are you okay with soda lime? According to that chart you gave me, even with moderate exertion, two kilograms will give us over five hours. And the at-rest metabolic rate would give us over twenty hours."

He came over and said, "Show me your numbers."

I pointed at the online data sheet. "One hundred fifty liters of $CO_2$ per kilogram of absorbent. The chart says a person would discharge fifty-eight point six liters per hour at a walk, fourteen point four liters per hour at rest. So, two kilos is three hundred liters divided by all that."

"Where are your calculations?"

"Pardon? Nearly sixty goes into three hundred five times—five hours. And fourteen point four is less than a quarter of that, so four times five—twenty hours. Basic math."

His lips moved and I realized he was doing the numbers in his head like I had. "Okay. We can use soda lime, but I want a spreadsheet, not approximations in your head."

"Don't trust my math?"

He held his lower lip between his teeth. "It doesn't matter," he finally said. "It's not the probability of you being wrong—it's the *consequences* of you being wrong."

"Cory, I can be back on the ground *instantly*. I'm probably the safest test subject you could have."

He shook his head sharply. "If you *noticed*. The first symptom of $CO_2$ toxicity is drowsiness. Understand?"

I could tell he was serious, even a bit upset.

"Sure, Cory. A spreadsheet. And checked separately on paper and with a calculator."

"By more than one person."

"Okay." I smiled. "Nice to know you care."

He blushed. "Well, uh, wouldn't want to lose the suit."

"Sure, Cory. Sure."

Two days later, Cory finished wiring the pressure-sensor onesie. He calibrated each sensor using weights to exert known pressures, adjusting them in his monitoring program, then he went back and checked them all again, using weights of different sizes.

"Satisfied?" I asked when he finally stopped.

He shrugged. "I guess. This is how I calibrated the life-model pressure sensor and that worked out." He glanced at me. "I hope."

I jumped back to the Yukon to put it on. I had to be careful not to snag any of the wires or the multiplexor box where it clipped to the collar of the unitard. I returned, feeling like some kind of android, and jumped into the relaxed MCP suit.

Cory hooked up the multiplexor before tightening the suit, checking the readings. "Got the gravity thing happening on the soles of your feet, but pretty negligible right now everywhere else. Let's do it."

He reduced the voltage even slower than he had the first time, anxious not to snag any of the strain-gauge wires, but in less than a minute he'd reduced it all the way and the suit was squeezing down on my skin again.

"Feel all right?" He wasn't even looking at me when he asked, his gaze moving to the readouts on the laptop.

"Feels fine, Cory. How's it looking?"

"Average is good, but there's a low reading below twenty-seven thousand eight hundred." He was scrolling down through the individual readouts. "Huh, right armpit. Lift your arm, please."

I raised my right arm and rotated the shoulder.

"That's got it. Might have been twisted or there was a fold of cloth, but it's above thirty-one now. Lower it."

I did so and he nodded in satisfaction. "Good, excellent. Let's do some yoga."

It wasn't really yoga, but it involved me standing in various poses: crouching, bent over at the waist, reaching up, reaching down, sitting, crawling, kneeling. Then we cycled the suit, relaxing it completely, then back to tight again, and did it all over.

Cory was pleased. "It's good. Pretty much what we expected."

"Well, *I* expected it," I said. "You didn't seem so confident."

He shrugged. "I thought we had a pretty good chance, but I wasn't willing to proceed without checking."

"So, orbital, yes?"

"Whoa. So now we need to test the neck gasket."

The latex neck gasket sealed into the suit's helmet flange and clung to the neck like a turtleneck. Its job was to keep the helmet's air pressure from leaking out past the neck, and through the weave of the EAP fibers. You wanted the body's sweat to outgas past the fabric, but not your breathing air.

Even before you pressurize the helmet, it is squeezing on your neck. It doesn't quite interfere with breathing or blood flow, but for the first five minutes after you put it on, you get the feeling someone is gently choking you to death.

With the polycarbonate fishbowl helmet locked on me, Cory slowly pressurized it with a compressed air tank, first to 1 psi. As the air pressure in the helmet increased, it pressed the latex seal against my skin more uniformly, improving the seal. After 1 psi seemed to be holding, he increased the pressure in one psi intervals until we were at our operating pressure: 4.9 psi.

That was 4.9 psi *gauge*, meaning it was 4.9 psi greater than our sea-level room pressure, or a total of 19.6 psi. Operating in a vacuum, it would be 4.9 psi absolute.

Once at this operating pressure, Cory had me hold my breath, since the air going in and out of my lungs changed the pressure readings. After thirty seconds of steady readings—no leaks—he let me breathe normally.

For the first time, it was effortless to breathe in the suit. The air pressure in my lungs counteracted the suit's constriction of my chest. Initially there was a slight gag reflex, but that soon faded. We kept going for another five minutes and then stopped, as planned, because of $CO_2$ buildup.

"The seal looks good," he said. "We're obviously going to have to do something about the fogging."

"You said it." By the end of the five minutes I could barely see through the clear polycarbonate. "They pretreat with anti-fog solution in spacesuits, right?"

He nodded. "Yes, but they also pull excess moisture out of the mixture. If we're going with a closed circuit rebreather, we're going to have to deal with that."

For the next test, we tucked a mesh bag of commercial diving-grade soda lime pellets in the back of the helmet to absorb $CO_2$, and we extended the test to thirty minutes.

The neck seal performed well, but the interior of the helmet was coated with beads of water when we stopped.

"Right," I said. "We have to deal with the moisture."

The next day I shopped.

I'd already purchased oxygen tanks (Houston) and a forty-four-pound keg of commercial diving-grade soda lime pellets (Key West), as well as some very expensive laboratory-grade pressure valves (Seattle), but now I was after more fittings, armored hose, low-power computer cooling fans, activated charcoal, and a fifty-pound tub of silica gel desiccant.

While I acquired these, Cory spent his time in one of the engineering machine shops.

When we met back at his lab late in the afternoon, he suggested breaking for the day, but I could tell that he was as interested in proceeding as I was.

"Let's push on."

I'd splurged for the main tanks, choosing five composite M-15 medical tanks that held 425 liters of oxygen when fully charged to 3,000 psi. They were fifteen inches long and four inches in diameter.

Cory had insisted on a backup tank. "At least a half-hour's worth." I picked the smallest composite bottles I could find, five little one-hundred-seventy-liter tanks three and a half inches in diameter and less than ten inches long.

Cory made the rebreather chamber out of aluminum pipe, the same diameter and length as the main oxygen tank. One end was sealed with a welded plate and the other end was stoppered with a plug, with a double O-ring seal and exterior latch clamps. At both ends of the chamber, one-inch through ports connected to ninety-degree elbows.

By the time we quit, near midnight, both ends of the chamber interior had low-power computer fans mounted across the through ports with RadioShack three-AA cell battery mounts beside each of them. Three mesh cylinders, their outside diameters barely smaller than the inside of the pipe, filled the rest of the space. The first and longest mesh cylinder, taking up half the chamber's length, was filled with soda lime pellets. The other two, using the rest of the interior space, held silica gel and activated charcoal.

"How do you turn on the fans?" I was tilting the cylinder back and forth, looking for a switch on the exterior.

"Inside," Cory said. He lifted the lid off and pointed. The fan mounted on the lid had a tiny slide switch epoxied to the aluminum. He pointed at another switch glued to the side of the cylinder, just past the seal face. Tiny wires, also epoxied to the aluminum, ran down past the activated-charcoal carrier toward the other end.

"Why two, and why inside?"

"Redundancy. Either of them will give us enough air flow. Inside, because I didn't want to run more holes."

"Will the fans run long enough?"

"Yes. It's all predicated on at least five hours of midlevel exertion. Two kilos of absorbent, four hundred twenty-five of

$O_2$, at least seven hours of battery for the fans. If you want to push it longer, we'll need to add more double As, and you'll probably need to wear a diaper."

I knew the astronauts did when on their extended EVAs, but I didn't find the notion particularly attractive.

"Five hours sounds like plenty. I can always take bathroom breaks."

We broke for the night then, but we were both back early the next day.

We mounted the chamber on a commercial diving harness that I'd found when shopping for the $CO_2$ absorbent. It had a stainless steel back plate over form-fitting back padding, and fully adjustable shoulder, belt, and crotch straps that I could snug up directly over the MCP suit or over any number of extra protective layers. It also had several large stainless steel D-rings on the shoulder straps and belt for attaching additional equipment.

We clamped the main tank and the rebreathing chamber horizontally across the back plate. One-inch ID armored hoses ran from the elbows on the rebreather chamber to through ports on the base of the helmet at the rear, right: incoming, left: return. The incoming air was diverted up, toward the top of the helmet, before coming down to nose and mouth, and hopefully, keeping the face port fog free. The exhaled air was sucked back into the rebreather chamber from the return port, dragged through the soda lime to trap the $CO_2$, through the silica gel to trap moisture, and through the activated charcoal, to absorb bad breath, I guess, before returning.

A short quarter-inch armored hose ran from the main $O_2$ tank to the feed valve on the sealed end of the rebreather chamber. The feed valve released oxygen into the chamber (and therefore the suit) when the helmet pressure dropped below 4.85 psi. An overpressure valve mounted in the helmet released air to the exterior, if the relative helmet pressure exceeded 5 psi, but this was only expected to happen when I transitioned from the earth's surface to the upper atmosphere.

"Or if you have a catastrophic failure of the feed valves and it pumps $O_2$ in without stopping," said Cory.

The backup oxygen we mounted in front, on the side of the belt, running a quarter-inch armored hose up the shoulder strap to another underpressure valve mounted to the helmet's base. This underpressure valve would keep the helmet pressurized to 4.85 psi. If the rebreather failed, I could push a button on the overpressure purge and manually vent air from the helmet, also venting $CO_2$. Either of the feed valves, sensing the pressure drop, would add fresh oxygen into the system.

"At least that's the theory," said Cory. "We have to test it, but I skipped breakfast. You want to go get us some lunch? You know, *your* way?"

He meant jumping. He'd gotten used to being able to send me on errands, no matter how far.

"Okay. Stand up."

He did, asking, "Why?"

I did one of Dad's patented jump-grab-jump moves and Cory was staggering away from me in an alcove at Shinjuku Station. Though it had been early afternoon at Stanford, it was predawn here. Still, it was one of the busiest stations in the world and when I stepped around the corner, hundreds of people were walking toward this platform or that.

Cory recovered enough to step out beside me, his eyes wide. "Where are we?"

"Tokyo. Shinjuku Station."

"Why are we here?"

I raised my eyebrows. "Lunch!" I led him around the corner to a takeaway bento box vendor. They were always open, which is why I came here a lot. A clerk was putting out the boxes for morning rush hour, some breakfast boxes, but mostly lunches for passengers to carry away with them for later in the day.

The middle-aged woman clerk-in-charge recognized me and bowed.

Dad would call that bad security but I liked knowing people. I liked people knowing *me*. I smiled and bowed. "*Ohayo!*"

"*Ohayo gozaiamasu*! What today?"

"Cory." I pointed at the glass display cabinet. "What do you want? I've never had the squid, but everything else is good."

He picked the salmon, I took the *mochiko* chicken. I paid with two thousand-yen notes and took my change. Cory took the plastic bag and, after another round of mutual bowing, we went back to the alcove.

I jumped him to a beach and held onto his arm as he staggered. "Sit," I said.

He dropped to his knees and I sat cross-legged, snagging the bag away from him. The sun was rising out of the ocean before us and the air was warm and slightly humid, overlaid with salt and tropical flowers.

"Okay. Where are we *now*?"

"Queensland."

He looked at me blankly.

I added, "East coast of Australia."

He swiveled his head around, looking for kangaroos, maybe. "Australia?"

"That's right. You're now standing on your head. Also, you've time traveled. It's tomorrow, here. International dateline and all that."

I put his bento box in front of him and started eating from mine. After a minute, he opened his and began eating, too.

"Doesn't this mess you up?" he said around a mouthful of buckwheat noodles. "The sun coming up in early afternoon?"

I shrugged. "On the International Space Station, the sun comes up sixteen times a day. A little jumping around here on Earth doesn't even come close."

"Huh."

"I've done stupid things, though, where I've followed the sun around the globe for thirty-six hours without sleeping. I started seeing things. Now I try to get to sleep by two A.M. every morning."

"You mean two A.M. Pacific?"

I smiled. "Let's just say two in the morning in *my* home time zone."

He frowned. "Why are you so secretive?"

"I don't like being drugged, chained, and imprisoned."

"What? Has that happened?"

"It's been tried. It has happened to . . . others." I looked at him. "Uh, by the way, Cory, I know you agreed not to talk about this thing I do, but you should also know that if people find out that you're working with me, they might try to *use* you to get to me."

"What do you mean, 'use?'"

"My dad has a saying: When you squeeze a lemon, it's hard on the lemon. Interrogation. Hostage. That sort of 'use.' So, keeping quiet about me is good for both of us."

He was quiet for a moment. "I see that, I guess. What happens when I want to show NASA a fully working suit that's been tested in orbit?"

It was my turn to be quiet for a moment. Finally I said, "We'll cross that bridge when we get to it.

"We have to *get* to orbit, first."

# EIGHT

## Davy: I'd say we've outstayed our welcome

Once she realized that Millie was serious about the "no expense spared" thing, Seeana kept adding items to the facilities list. Then new items would remind Millie of other things and she would add items, then bring the new list to Davy.

"Get these, please."

Davy sighed and recruited Cent to help him shop.

"Oxygen? No problem. I've got just the place."

Millie said, "We'll need a small portable unit for when we transfer her. We're three thousand feet higher than Wichita, too. She may need to go with a nose/mouth mask instead of a cannula."

Cent said. "We'll get a few four-double-M tanks and get them recharged, two at a time."

"How big is a double-M?" Millie asked.

Cent held her hand flat next to her hip to how show tall they were. "Thirty-four hundred liters. About forty pounds. I'll also get extra regulators, cannula, and plenty of tubing. Do you want to consider a concentrator?"

Davy said, "What's that?"

Millie answered. "Plugs in. Produces oxygen from regular air. Well, produces ninety percent $O_2$, up to about five liters per minute. We should probably consider it for the long run."

Davy said, "But with tank backups, right? In case the unit fails, or we lose power?"

"Oh, yes."

While Cent dealt with oxygen, Davy hit general medical-supply stores for other equipment and expendables, ranging from bedpans to a suction pump with reservoirs, and monitors for blood oxygenation, pulse, blood glucose, and respiration.

Millie went over the equipment with Seeana. They kept adding things to the list, but, two days before Millie's mother was due to get her surgical staples removed, even Millie had to admit, "We're ready, I guess."

Davy said, "No. We need one more thing."

"What is it?" Cent asked.

Davy had put it on the top shelf of the master-bedroom closet and mounted the siren on the wall. It looked halfway between a laptop and a piece of lab equipment.

"Broad spectrum radio-frequency detector. Four kilohertz to eight gigahertz. That's why it has the three different antennas." He was standing on a stool to reach the screw-down terminals on the siren. He left one wire hanging, unconnected.

"Turn off your phone."

Cent fished her phone from her jeans pocket and powered it down. "You know we killed the cellular on this."

"Yeah, but you still have Bluetooth, WiFi, and GPS, right?"

"GPS doesn't transmit, does it?"

"Yeah, you're right. I'm more worried about GPS *trackers*: devices that actively transmit their location. However, any signal detectable can be tracked so I don't want anything going out from here."

"You worried about Seeana?"

"Not especially. Or the health aids. But someone *else* could plant a tracker on any of them, you know?" Davy hit the power switch and watch it go through its boot-up process, then went through a few menu choices. The device began beeping.

"Huh. Something at two thousand four hundred twenty-two megahertz. Oh. Two point four gigahertz. Go see if your mom is on her computer."

Cent walked out onto the landing. She stuck her head back in the room. "Yep. You want her to turn off WiFi?"

Davy shook his head. "Nope. If she has to remember to turn the WiFi back off every time she returns from downloading her e-mail we'll end up with a load of false alarms. The software lets me set allowed ranges." He thumbed through the manual. "If I block out twenty-four to twenty-five hundred megahertz, it won't alarm for WiFi or Bluetooth." He flipped a page. "I don't *think* we're using the five point six gigahertz stuff."

"Don't forget the walkie-talkies."

"Crap. Okay allowing four hundred sixty to four hundred seventy megahertz."

By the time all the medical equipment had been set up, Davy was pulling his hair out.

"How many things have transmitters built into them?"

Millie didn't even look up from her book. "Rhetorical question, right?"

Davy went back to Singapore and purchased a portable radio-frequency scanner he could walk around with to identify the offending monitors.

By the end of the day he had set the scanner in the closet to allow some specific frequencies in the fifty-two-hundred-megahertz range as well, but at least the thing stopped beeping.

He hooked up the siren. When he brought in a working cell phone and then a working shortwave radio, both borrowed for the test, the alarm went off in less than two seconds.

Millie asked, "Now are we ready?"

Davy said, "I have no idea."

"Does this mean you can't think of anything else, either?"

"Right."

Millie nodded sharply. "Tomorrow, then."

---

While the gravimeters that the Daarkon group used could detect the gravity of a small child from a few meters, Davy was confident that they really couldn't tell the difference between a jumper appearing and a passing truck from more than a few hundred yards, gravitational attraction being subject to the inverse square law.

Still, to be sure, they arrived at different times and used normal transport to approach the retirement village. Millie took a taxi, Cent took a bicycle, and Davy took the bus. They each wore a radio and earplug microphones.

Cent had never been to the intensive-care side of the facility. Once, dressed as a Girl Scout, she'd sold cookies on the assisted-living side, to cover a visit to her grandmother, but that was before she'd learned to jump, and she had no practical memory of the place.

All three of them had gone over the floor plan the night before, and Cent studied pictures from the facility's website.

None of them wore disguises but they came in at different times. Millie signed in to visit her old friend, Agnes Merriwether. While she distracted the receptionist, Cent cut quickly past and into the dining room. Davy went to his unit in the neighboring self-storage facility to access Samantha's room via the hidden camera.

By the time Davy had them on screen, Samantha was dressed in her own flannel nightgown—not the open-backed patient gowns the facility provided. Seeana had prepped for the move, under the guise of an extensive sponge bath. She'd removed the Foley catheter, the saline drip, and moved the oxygen tube for Samantha's cannula from the room's wall feed to the small portable composite tank that Cent had provided.

Davy spoke into his radio. "Status?"

Cent's voice came over the radio, "On station."

Millie's followed, "On station."

Davy thumbed the transmit button, "Copy both. Ditto."

Davy waited, watching the screen intently. Seeana would signal readiness by leaving the room, ostensibly for a bedpan.

The two paramedics pushing the gurney into the room were *not* part of the agenda.

Coincidence, or had Millie's entrance triggered something?

He turned up the sound in time to hear Seeana say, "—don't have any record of a move order." She turned to Samantha. "You didn't request this, right?" She looked hard at the paramedics. "She's her own guardian."

The first paramedic stepped closer to Seeana, ostensibly to show her something on a clipboard, but screening the second who reached under the gurney's disposable bedding.

Davy didn't wait for the man's hand to emerge.

He thumbed transmit—"Eyes open!"—and jumped.

He appeared in midair, three feet off the ground, his knee rising sharply into the man's jaw.

There was no time for the man to react. His mouth clicked shut and his head flew back, and a black submachine gun clattered across the floor.

Davy jumped eight feet to the side and watched the other paramedic's foot travel through the space he'd just vacated. Davy was going to take him when the man suddenly spasmed and dropped to the floor. Davy saw the wires then and jumped again, to another corner of the room.

For a second Davy thought that they'd been firing at him and hit the paramedic by mistake, but the man standing in the doorway was making no attempt to raise the Taser.

It was Hunt, the CIA agent, dressed as a doctor again. He wasn't even looking into the room, but swiveling his head to scan both directions of the hallway before he looked back at Davy.

Seeana had run to Samantha's side and was watching them both, eyes wide.

Davy pointed at the paramedics. "Not yours?"

Hunt shook his head. "And probably not *alone*, either. There's a lot more visitors here than—shit!" He stepped into the room as a bullet slammed into the metal door frame, chest high. He dropped the Taser to the floor and snaked an automatic out from under his white jacket. "You going to take her, do it! You should get the nurse out of here, too."

Davy pointed at Seeana and then at the bathroom.

Seeana shook her head, emphatically. "Not until Sam is safe."

Hunt dropped to a crouch and leaned his head out the door, and then jerked it back as another shot sounded in the hallway.

Then there was the sound of a heavy impact and an explosive exhalation of breath, and a loud crash segueing into a jarring cacophony of breaking plates and bouncing silverware. An automatic pistol bounced past the doorway and rattled on down the hall.

Hunt looked again. "Huh." He stood up and leaned cautiously out the door again before stepping out into the hall.

Davy followed.

A multidrawered meal-dispensing cart lay on its side, several drawers open and trays and food scattered. A man lay groaning against it.

Hunt said, "He was thirty feet up the hallway a second ago."

Davy's lips twitched. He touched the transmit button on his radio. "Status."

Cent's voice came back. "Sore shoulder."

Millie voice: "There's movement in the parking lot."

"Copy that. Cent, keep watch. Millie, come here."

Millie appeared by the bed, then jerked as she saw Hunt.

"Not a hostile!" Davy said quickly.

Hunt's eyes went wide. He slowly and carefully put his gun back in its clip-on holster, and leaned against the wall, his arms crossed, watching intently.

Millie raised her eyebrows at Davy.

"Later," he said. "You ready, Samantha?"

Samantha's voice was reedy, but she said, "I'd say we've outstayed our welcome."

Seeana moved the portable oxygen tank onto Samantha's lap and then helped her fold her arms over it. She locked eyes with Davy. "Gently. No jerks, right?"

Davy nodded and slid his arms carefully under Samantha's back legs, lifting carefully. Seeana supported Samantha's head until she could lean it against Davy's shoulder.

"Okay, Samantha?"

The reedy whisper was loud in his ear. "Yes."

Davy looked at Millie, who wasn't taking her eyes off of Hunt. "You got Seeana?"

Millie nodded.

There was another crashing sound from the hallway and Hunt looked out again. He reached back into his jacket, but then jerked back in the room as a body flashed past the door at head height. From the sound, the body hit something on the way down, too.

Cent's voice sounded in Davy's ear. "There's more coming."

Davy thumbed his transmit button. "It's okay. We're done here."

Millie tilted her head at Hunt and said to Davy, "Do we need to get him clear?"

Hunt was moving toward the downed paramedics, limping slightly. "No thanks," he said. "I'd like a chance at these guys." He pointed at the two paramedics. "And their friends."

"Daarkon Group, you think?" Davy said.

Millie jumped to the other side of the bed, behind Seeana. "Not *now*!"

"Right." Davy jumped directly to Cent's old room, beside the newly installed hospital bed, in the Yukon. He waited until Millie appeared with Seeana, and then, with Seeana supporting her head, he gently lay Samantha down.

Cent stuck her head in the door a minute later, rubbing vigorously at her right shoulder.

Samantha stared out the window, a view down a mountain valley, draped with snow and framed by evergreens. She looked from Millie, to Davy, to Seeana, and her eyes finally came to rest on Cent. Her eyes moistened.

Millie had to hand Samantha a tissue, and then kept one for herself.

"Well," Samantha blew her nose, then flipped her hand over, pointing at the window. "This is nice."

# NINE

## Cent: Testing

"Where were you?" Cory asked.

I rubbed my shoulder and said, "Had to help my grandmother move."

"Pull something?"

"Or pushed it. I'm okay. Let's get to it."

I spent next two hours in the suit.

We tested the feed valve first, simply by breathing. Just by breathing, I bound up oxygen into $CO_2$ which was then absorbed by the soda lime, causing the pressure in the helmet to slowly drop. When it hit the trip point, 4.85 psi, the valve let in $O_2$ from the high-pressure tank, closing again at 4.9 psi. Rinse, repeat.

We also tested it by bumping the purge valve, dropping the pressure far more abruptly. Again, it quickly adjusted and I made sure to hold my mouth open during these tests, letting my ears and lungs equalize as needed.

We shut the valve on the main oxygen tank and switched on the backup emergency oxygen. The backup feed valve worked identically to the main feed valve.

"I wish I had a chamber! We need to see how the purge valve works when exterior pressure drops!" Cory raised his voice to be heard through the helmet.

I pitched my voice up, too. "Be right back."

I jumped to the springhouse in back of the cabin in the Yukon, at an altitude of forty-five hundred feet above sea level, wiggling my jaw to make sure my ears would equalize. The purge valve worked as expected, venting out the excess pressure (a little over 2 psi) from the helmet, but unlike the hiss I got when opening the purge valve manually, the noise was more of a buzzing, burping sound.

Usually when I jumped home from sea level, the pop in my ears is immediate, sometimes painful, but this time it happened slowly, buffered by the venting.

I took a few deep breaths and then jumped back to the lab.

Cory was clenching the edge of the lab bench, his knuckles white. He let go abruptly and said something, but I couldn't hear because the feed valve kicked in and was boosting the helmet pressure back up.

He repeated himself. "Don't do that!" Then, slightly less emphatically, he said, "Where'd you go?"

"My house."

"Why?"

"It's at forty-five hundred feet. The purge valve kicked in and stopped. Just like it's supposed to."

His mouth made an "o" shape.

"Sorry. I'll discuss it first next time."

Now that he knew what I'd done, and the size of the pressure change, he had me do it ten more times with the main $O_2$ tank, and then ten more times with the backup.

The purge valve and both feed valves continued to operate as intended. When we quit it was not because I was running out of air, or there was too much $CO_2$, or I was too hot.

I was too *dry*.

Cotton mouth only *hinted* at it. I had trouble summoning saliva and my tongue felt like it was swelling.

But the polycarbonate helmet was crystal clear—not a trace of fog.

As soon as Cory lifted the helmet and I shrugged the harness off, I jumped to the Michigan warehouse and grabbed a case of bottled water from the emergency relief supplies and jumped back, thumping the case onto the lab bench. I didn't say anything until I'd finished the first bottle.

"Dry."

"Too much desiccant?" Cory said.

I shrugged. "Didn't have breakfast. Came straight to the lab. I'll need to drink water before heading out."

Cory shook his head. "It's going to be worse in orbit. For long duration EVAs, you'll need some way to drink. Especially if we're counting on perspiration for cooling. Dehydration could be serious. We'll need to rig some sort of hydration bladder with a bite valve in the helmet."

I started another bottle of water. "Suits me. But that can wait for the more extended trips. We're still going tomorrow."

Mom was washing dishes after supper and Dad was sitting at the kitchen table, talking to her.

I came quietly in and leaned against the wall by the fridge.

"—the health aides in Manila."

Mom rinsed a plate and stacked it in the drainer. "What did you think? Were they good?"

Dad looked at me and said, "Seeana liked them. They're all working in geriatric and they all have excellent English." He shifted in his chair so he was facing me more directly. "How's my investment coming?"

"We're testing in the morning."

A plate broke in the sink and Mom said, "*Shit*. Excuse me." She carried three triangular sections of broken plate over to the trash can and dumped them. "Testing, eh? What does that mean?"

"At altitude."

Dad stood up abruptly. "Already? I thought you just funded the project!"

"We have a prototype, but they weren't able to do human testing before." I told them about the MCP suit and how I could get into it.

"So you're the only person who can wear this suit?" Dad said.

I looked back and forth between the two of them. "There are three people who could wear it. They're all standing in this room."

Dad got that stubborn look in his eye and I added, "But on men, it squeezes the testicles something *fierce*."

Mom covered her mouth and Dad looked thoughtful.

"What do you mean by *altitude*?" Mom asked. Her voice wasn't as tense as Dad's, but her posture was.

"Forty-five thousand feet, for the first trial." I touched my wrist. "After all, I've already been that high. If *that* works okay, I'm going for the Kármán line."

Dad exhaled. "A hundred kilometers."

"Yes." I could hear the exhilaration in my voice.

Dad stared at the wall. Absently he said, "Space, by anyone's definition."

"Is that where the air stops?" Mom said.

Dad held his hand out and wiggled it. "Very, very thin air. It's the height where you have to go so fast to get lift that you exceed *orbital* velocity. What's that phrase, Cent? Where aeronautics ends . . ."

"Where aeronautics ends and astronautics begins," I said. "But there's still air drag. You really couldn't maintain an orbit there unless you used propulsion to keep your speed up. Better to get higher, above two hundred kilometers."

Dad nodded. "Like Sputnik. Or better yet, up around three hundred forty kilometers, like the International Space Station."

I could tell from Mom's expression that she wasn't sharing my enthusiasm.

"I'm not going to try for orbital velocities yet. I doubt my GPS is going to survive all the way to a hundred K anyway. Too many of the components aren't vacuum hardened. But I'm hoping it will last long enough to register my peak altitude."

"No way," Dad said.

"Because of the vacuum?"

"It will stop reading at sixty thousand feet."

"Why? The GPS satellites are all the way out at twenty thousand kilometers."

"The U.S. limits civilian GPS receivers to reporting altitude under sixty thousand feet and speeds under a thousand knots."

I wrinkled my forehead. "Why?"

"So bad guys can't jury-rig them to control missiles."

*Oh.* Crap. "That's only eighteen kilometers—barely into the stratosphere." How would I know when I'd passed the Kármán line? A really good vacuum gauge? Could you even measure thirty-two hundredths pascals?

"Wait a minute," I said. "That's the *U.S.* government. What about units sold outside the U.S.?"

"Maybe," Dad said. Reluctantly he added, "I know someone I could ask. Where are you going to do this?"

"I thought I'd do it above the pit. Nice empty space and all that. That's kind of why I'm telling you guys—wanted to know if you'd like to come watch."

"Yes." Mom said firmly. "Seeana can stay with Mother."

Dad was still frowning. "Perhaps you should wait until we can get you a GPS that will work in LEO? I mean, you wouldn't want to go too far by accident."

I shook my head vehemently. "We'll figure something out. If nothing else I can just head for the moon. It's big and bright and when it looks as big as the earth does, I'll know I'm in space."

Mom looked alarmed.

Dad said, "Don't worry—she's kidding. Cent won't go out that far until she's dealt with radiation shielding."

He was right. For the time being I was sticking to the protection of the near-Earth magnetosphere.

Mom said, "What does Joe think?"

As if I knew. The best defense is a good offense. "You think I need to get my boyfriend's permission? Really?"

Mom looked away.

I said, "I just thought you guys might like to be there. We're going to set up near the pit in that sandy wash, starting about nine A.M. mountain time."

"We?" said Dad.

"Dr. Matoska. The suit guy."

"You're jumping him there?"

"Yeah."

"What about Joe?" Mom said.

"I *told* you. This isn't Joe's decision."

Mom's eyes widened but she said mildly, "I *meant*, is Joe attending your test, too?"

I felt my ears heat up. "Oh. No. Classes."

*You'll have to tell them* some*time.*

"We'll be there," Mom said.

"I haven't told Cory—Dr. Matoska—about you two," I said. "I've implied that there are others who can jump, but . . ."

"Do you trust him?" Mom asked.

I tilted my head to one side. "I trust his self-interest. I don't think I'd tell him where we live or anything like that. He wants his suit to be tested in space. He's been very cautious about safety protocols. I would've tested last week, with just a tank of oxygen, but he balked."

Dad shifted uncomfortably. "He checks out."

I frowned. "What do you mean, he 'checks out'?"

"I had him screened, with an agency."

"Screened." My voice was flat and I could feel my eyes narrowing.

Dad waved his hand, "Like a prospective employer. He's gone from post to post, but usually he's the one who leaves. He did get involved with a graduating senior at one school and there was a complaint, but it was just after he got his Ph.D. He doesn't look like one of *them*."

I was wondering if I should be angry or not. It was Dad's money, after all, that was funding Cory. I guess he had the right to check.

"So, nine A.M., mountain," Mom said.

"Yes."

"I'll tell Seeana."

# TEN

## Davy: GPS

Luckily Davy had been there before and even had a video record he could refer to. He sure didn't want to get there the way he had the first time: three hours of highway travel from Las Vegas followed by four hours of back-wrenching off-road driving.

The makeshift gantry, two football fields away, was empty, and the only person around was a red-headed man in shorts, a hoodie, and combat boots sitting near the tents at a portable table, with a laptop in front of him.

The redhead heard Davy's footsteps and turned, saying, "Did you find—" He froze, blinking. "Where did *you* come from?" He stood up and looked over at a Jeep Cherokee parked by a set of tents. "Where's your car?"

Davy smiled and said, "I'm Davy. Is Wanda Chappell around?"

"Lou," the redhead said, tapping his chest. "Wanda and the guys are out looking for the bird."

"I see I missed the launch. How'd it go?"

Lou was still scanning for Davy's vehicle. "Pretty good at first. Made twenty-eight thousand feet. We got good data the whole flight. The drogue deployed right after apogee. But then the main chute didn't. Telemetry had it hitting at twenty-one meters per second."

Davy translated that in his head. "Uh, forty-six miles per hour? How fast was it going on the way up?"

"It passed Mach three in the first fifteen seconds. At least the drogue *deployed*. If the rocket had come in ballistic we would've needed shovels and tweezers."

There was a flash of light in the distance as a windshield caught the sun. They both turned their heads. Vehicle dust resolved into two trucks cresting the rise about a mile out.

"Ah. Guess they got it," said Lou. "*How* did you get here?"

"I'm parked around the corner," Davy said.

"*What* corner?"

"Exactly."

The trucks got down onto the flat and picked up speed. They could hear them now.

"Damn," said Lou. "They'd be coming a lot slower if the bird was intact."

The trucks circled around the tents to park by the Jeep, kicking up a cloud of dust that drifted back over the campsite. Lou squawked and ran to shut his laptop. "Idiots!"

Davy held his breath and squinted, trying to keep the fine grit out of his eyes and lungs. But the breeze blew it past quickly. When he opened his eyes again, men were getting out of the truck cabs and clustering around the bed of the longest pickup.

A thin black woman with close-cropped hair got out of the passenger side of the first truck. She was cradling a three-foot-long aluminum tube capped with a stainless steel cone. She said, "Lou, sweetie, the electronics bay is okay but the main body is buggered to hell."

"Did the main deployment charge go off?" said Lou.

"No. I don't know if the TeleMetrum didn't close the circuit or the e-match failed."

"Damn," said Lou. "Well, don't take it apart before I check the settings with the wireless link."

Davy said, "Did the electronics survive the crash?"

Wanda's eyes went wide at the sound of Davy's voice. "Davy? I didn't recognize you. It's been, what, seven years? I'm used to seeing both of you. I think that's what really threw me. How is your daughter?"

Lou said, "Wanda, I have no idea how he got here. It's like he came out of thin air."

Wanda laughed. "Exactly. And when he leaves, he'll go back into it." She turned back to Davy, "You working on another rocket? Your daughter still likes things that go high?"

"Something like that."

Wanda handed the aluminum section to Lou. "Here, baby. See what you can figure out."

Lou glared at Davy, then turned around and walked back to the table, grumbling.

Wanda shrugged. "I could tell him the truth but it would make him even more grumpy. Do you need something? Cause I could sure use the income. I'm going to have to do a complete rebuild of the main body and it *wasn't* in the budget."

"I do. Need a GPS that's not restricted by ITAR."

Wanda's brows went up. "What's getting you, the speed limit or the altitude?"

"Both."

"Ambitious. What sort of range do you need on the telemetry? You get too far above sixty thousand feet and we may have to go with a separate transmitter."

"I don't need any telemetry. I do need a display." He touched his forearm. "And some kind of strap."

Wanda looked around. The men had unloaded the body of the rocket, a mostly intact tube that bent sharply above the fins. She said, "Let's walk." She headed out toward the gantry. When she was well away from the others she said, "You're talking about a *person* being above sixty thousand feet, aren't you?"

Davy grimaced. "Not my idea, but yeah."

"Knowing you, it's not a government deal, right? Do you need some crew for this shot?"

"Not exactly, though we may need some operations help eventually."

"This isn't something that a normal person can do, is it." It wasn't a question.

"*Lots* of people go into space. The count's over five hundred now, isn't it?"

"Over six hundred. But something tells me *you* aren't doing it the usual way. You never gave me a clue this was possible back when you were doing those hobby rockets with your daughter."

Davy smiled weakly. "I didn't know it was. Still don't know, really. Would kinda prefer to *not* know."

Wanda tilted her head and squinted at him. "Not you, then. Your daughter?"

Davy looked away. After a moment he said, "She's done forty-five thousand feet. And that was before she had a suit."

"*Damn!*" said Wanda.

"Damn it all to hell," said Davy. "Can you help me?"

"Oh, yeah. What should the display handle? I mean, in altitude and speed."

Davy pinched the bridge of his nose. He didn't even want to *think* about the speeds much less say them. "I think we're safe topping out the range at fifty."

"Fifty miles?"

He pinched harder. "Fifty kilometers per second. Altitude better read all the way out to the Navstar satellites. Might as well make the readouts kilometers all around except for longitude and latitude."

Wanda's eyes got bigger. "I like a girl with ambitions. To be honest, I don't know how GPS functions when you get out past the satellites. It'll definitely work in low Earth orbit, though. When do you need it?"

"Tomorrow. Nine A.M."

She blinked. "Left it a bit late, didn't you?"

"The suit wasn't supposed to be *ready* this soon. It's happening with or without the GPS and I'd really rather it was with."

"Vacuum?"

He nodded.

She winced. "I can't do a vacuum-hardened display by tomorrow. To be honest, I'm not sure I can do a vacuum-hardened display from off-the-shelf components in *any* time frame." She licked her lips. "We could put it in pressure housing, though. How much are you willing to pay?"

He looked back toward the tents and jerked his chin at the mangled rocket body. "How much to retool?"

Wanda grinned. "*Now* you're talking. Pricey part is the phenolic/graphite nozzle, but I'm going to start over on the casing and fins, too. I'll need to get back to Vegas, though. I *know* you can arrange that, right?"

Davy nodded.

"Let me tell Lou you're giving me a ride home. He's gonna be jealous as hell, so make sure your wedding ring shows."

"Wanda, are you taking advantage of that young man?"

She licked her lips lasciviously. "You have *no* idea."

# ELEVEN

## Cent: 624

I was on oxygen and had been for fifty minutes when I arrived at the lab. I was an hour early, wanting to make sure we had everything ready, but Cory had beaten me there. He was printing out lists and proofing them.

"What's that?" I asked, speaking loudly to be heard through my mask.

"What?"

The demand-regulator mask I was using not only covered my mouth and nose, it was made of moderately dense plastic.

I pointed at his stack of papers and raised my eyebrows.

"Procedures," he said.

"Oh. Checklists?"

This time he understood me.

"Yeah—to make sure we don't skip steps, even if we're nervous or bored or tired." He put the stack in a clipboard.

I nodded approvingly. "Did you prep the backpack?"

He shook his head. "Nope." He held up a list. "We're going to do it by the numbers."

Theoretically we had more than three hours endurance left in the pack and oxygen bottles after yesterday's tests, but we weren't going to use it at altitude with anything less than maximum capacity—not this first time. Cory started to hand me the list but I said, "No," and handed it back. I pointed at my chest. "I'll do it."

Yes, he had a checklist for emptying the backpack, too.

"Release latches."

I unsnapped all three. "Check."

"Remove hatch."

I pulled and twisted on the end plug until the two O-rings slid past the seal surface and it released with a slight popping sound. "Check."

"Remove filter packs."

I turned the frame ninety degrees so the open end of the tube faced down and the mesh packages with soda lime, silica gel, and activated charcoal slid out, forming a stack on the bench. "Check."

"Dump contents."

We had a disposal can set up for these, but the mesh cylinders were tricky to open without destroying them so it was the longest part of the operation. "Check, check, and finally check."

I filled them in reverse order: activated charcoal, silica gel, then soda lime, using an electronic postal scale to standardize each load. As soon as I filled each one, they were sealed in ziplock bags. "Check."

"Dump batteries."

I pulled the alkaline batteries from their holders at both ends of the cylinder, bagged, and dumped them. "Check."

"Install fresh batteries." We'd bought retail packs of six AAs so that the new ones always came from sealed packages. I popped them one by one into their holders, paying careful attention to polarity. "Check."

"Test outflow fan."

I clicked on the switch for the bottom fan and it whirred to life. I put my fingers in the helmet to feel the airflow up the back of the helmet. "Check."

"Turn outflow fan off."

"Check."

"Test return fan."

I turned on the fan in the cylinder's lid. It whirred to life and the breeze moved across my fingers. "Check."

"Turn return fan off."

"Check."

"Load activated-charcoal filter."

I took it from its bag and slid it all the way down into the chamber. "Check."

"Load moisture absorbent."

I loaded the silica gel pack and slid it in until it touched the charcoal mesh. "Check."

"Load $CO_2$ absorbent."

I slid the last mesh cylinder in. "Check."

"Apply lubricant to the seal surface."

I took the tube of silicone grease and put a thin film all the way around the O-ring seal surface of the rebreather cylinder. "Check."

"Insert hatch."

I eased the plug back into the end. "Check."

"Secure latches."

I snapped all three shut. "Check."

"Document maintenance."

I wrote on the cylinder itself with an indelible marker: *Batt & filters repl* followed by the date and time.

"Check."

The procedure for replacing oxygen was similar, though both used tanks would go back to the medical-supply house for refilling. When I'd made sure the new ones were secure in their clamps, I screwed on their regulators. I opened the valves briefly to read the gauges, confirming their fully charged state, then shut them back down again. I wrote their psi reading, and the time and date right on the tanks themselves.

"Next, Cory?"

He handed me a sealed packet with an optical wipe, the kind used for cleaning glasses. "Antifog treatment."

I nodded and carefully wiped down the entire interior of the polycarbonate fishbowl. "Check."

He took a deep breath. "We're going to do the donning checklist there, right?"

"Right, but I should put the suit on here. Don't want to get sand in the mesh."

He nodded his head. "Right, we don't want that."

I was wearing my wool coat over my underwear, base layers, socks, and a pair of Merrill Moab Mid Ventilator ankle-high lightweight hiking boots one size too big for my feet. I kicked these off and hung the coat while Cory relaxed the suit.

I took off the oxygen briefly and held my breath, for the transition.

I was in the suit immediately, and even though I had to put the oxygen back on and Cory took his time tightening the suit back over my body, I was disconnected from the power supply in under two minutes. I put the hiking boots back on over the suit feet, and laced them up, stepping forward and back, then bouncing in place. Good fit over the thickened suit.

"Ready, Cory?" I said, strapping the aviation GPS onto my left wrist.

He sighed. "I guess."

I checked the clock. Local time was five minutes until seven. Five minutes until nine at my destination.


First I took a tarp.

Mom and Dad were there, sitting on folding lawn chairs, a cooler between them.

I pointed at the cooler and raised my eyebrows.

There were staring and I realized I must look pretty odd between the oxygen face mask and the suit. Absently Dad said, "Water. What's with the mask?"

"I know," said Mom. "She's prebreathing oxygen to outgas nitrogen from her bloodstream."

Dad nodded. "Right. Bends. Got it." He shook his head. "Knew that. Forgot about it. Glad you guys are on top of it."

Mom said, "Cent was doing that from the beginning." She touched the suit fabric. "That doesn't seem like very much protection."

I rolled my eyes.

Dad helped me spread the tarp on the ground and anchor it with rocks against the slight breeze.

"Back in a sec," I said through the mask.

I ferried extra oxygen, the helmet, and attached backpack to the tarp, and then finally, Cory and his clipboard of checklists.

Cory staggered, but recovered quicker than he had his last jump. He looked from Mom and Dad to me and then back again, focusing finally on Mom.

"These are your parents."

Ah, well, the resemblance is there, of course.

They stood and shook Cory's hand. "I'm David. This is Millie. Pleased to meet you, Dr. Matoska."

"Call me Cory," he said, automatically. "You understand what Cent is trying to do?"

"Return to the mother ship?" said Dad.

If he weren't out of reach I would have kicked him.

Mom said, "Behave!"

Dad smiled. "She wants to conduct activities in low Earth orbit. More importantly, she wants to *survive* activities in low Earth orbit. Is that pretty much what she's told you?"

Cory nodded. "Amounts to the same thing. She said she was building her own space program."

Mom looked at me over her sunglasses. "Indeed."

I blushed and turned to Cory, pointing at the checklist.

He lifted the clipboard and looked at it, almost as if he was surprised it was there. "Ah. Checklist. Yes." He looked back at me. "Hydration."

I took a bottle of water out of the ice chest and, temporarily lifting the mask, chugged it. Before breathing in again, I purged the mask. "Right. Next?"

He looked at his watch. "When did you start prebreathing?"

"Six fifteen, Pacific."

He scribbled on his clipboard. "We'll do another twenty minutes and do the last bit of flushing in the suit."

Dad took a bag from beneath his chair.

"Here," he said. "I talked to someone."

He took out a clear-plastic box about two inches by three, and an inch thick. Inside I could see a nine-volt battery and a double stack of circuit boards. The top board had a surface mount, multiline LED display. The bottom of the box had four thumbscrews clamping it shut on a black rubber gasket and the same lockdown posts passed through brass grommets on a Velcroed wrist strap.

It was already turned on and I compared its readings to the aviation GPS on my wrist.

The longitude and latitude differed by less than a tenth of a second, but the altitude was completely different. "Ah, metric?" I compared them. "And in *kilometers*. Great!"

Dad had been listening carefully, his head tilted, and he understood me. "And it won't stop working above eighteen kilometers or at speeds faster than half a kilometers per second."

"How'd they get around the ITAR regulations?"

"The manufacturers limit it in the firmware. This one uses open-source hardware and software so, even though they also have the limits, you can overwrite them. The GPS module has an integrated antennae. It handles data logging and display using an Arduino processor."

It didn't do map displays but it had the information I needed: altitude, bearing, horizontal and vertical speed, longitude and latitude, and time.

"Thanks, Dad."

He smiled. "How do you guys communicate while you're up there?"

"We don't."

"What if you need help?"

"Well, I'll come back and get some. It's not as if anyone can come to my aid."

Mom's eyes narrowed and Dad's jaw did that thing where it juts forward, and he tapped himself on the chest.

"Only one suit," I said. "Maybe later. Don't worry. Something happens, I'm back on the ground like *that*." I tried to snap my finger but it didn't work with the suit fabric on my hands.

Dad looked unhappy but he didn't say anything. Good thing, because I was doing this, with or without his permission.

Cory had been watching the back and forth intently, wondering, I think, if my parents were going to halt the proceedings. But when neither Mom or Dad said anything, he checked his watch again.

"Fans." He read out the procedures while I did them—unlatching, removing the hatch from the rebreather chamber, switching on both ventilation fans, and sealing it back up.

"Check," I said.

"Don life-support harness."

He handed Dad the clipboard for this next part. While I slung the backpack on and fastened buckles and snugged up straps, Cory held the helmet up, keeping the armored hoses out of the way. I moved my shoulders around and twisted my waist back and forth. Secure *and* comfortable. "Check."

"Remove prebreathe mask."

I held my breath again. While it took two hours to get rid of the nitrogen, a few full breaths of regular air would put dangerous amounts back into my bloodstream.

"Don helmet and latch."

He lowered the helmet over my head, and I took it, guiding it into the flange fifteen degrees off center to engage the threads. I then rotated it to the locked position, and latched the safety clamp. I held up my fingers and thumb in the okay sign and he checked off the next line.

"Turn on main oxygen."

I reached back with my right arm and felt for the main oxygen valve. I eased it on and the feed valve hissed, pressurizing the helmet, and my ears popped. The hissing stopped as pressure reached the valve's set point. "Check" I said, and my voice bounced oddly in the helmet.

"Test purge valve," he said. His voice sounded distant through the helmet, but still easy to understand.

I bumped the purge button and it hissed, oxygen jetting into the weave of the suit over my fingers. Immediately the hissing switched to the feed valve, then stopped again when the pressure was back up. I took deep breaths and held up my forefinger and thumb.

"Turn off main oxygen."

I reached back and twisted the valve in the other direction. "Check."

"Turn on backup oxygen."

"Check."

"Test backup feed valve by purging helmet."

I bumped the purge valve and the backup oxygen-feed valve repressurized the helmet immediately. "Check."

"Turn off backup $O_2$."

"Check."

"Turn on main $O_2$."

"Check."

He nodded. "Right. Let's say you end up someplace else, where I'm not there to read the checklist. What's the shutdown procedure?"

"I turn off all oxygen, then I slowly vent the helmet with the purge valve, and then I can breach the helmet seal." I saw him start to open his mouth and said, "Yes, I know. *Exactly* in that order so I don't pull off the pressurized helmet and blow an eardrum."

"*If* I'm here, though, *wait* for the checklist."

I held my thumb up.

He turned a page on his clipboard and then said, "Okay. You want to swap the GPS out?"

I looked at the two units. "Let's do the first test with both." I strapped the one Dad gave me onto my left forearm, next to the off-the-shelf unit.

"Altitude above sea level?"

"At three thousand seven hundred fifty-three feet and—" I tapped the new unit. "—approximately one point forty-four kilometers."

"Okay. Starting life support log at nine-thirteen." More formally Cory said, "You are cleared to forty-five thousand feet."

I could've jumped directly there, but I guess I wanted to

wow them. I left the ground at about two hundred miles an hour, more speed than I'd normally add in the atmosphere, but I wanted to make some noise that they could hear. When the altimeter passed two kilometers above sea level, I jumped another five kilometers up, exhaling sharply. My ears popped and the purge valve dropped the helmet pressure, but my breathing was still effortless. The old GPS read twenty-three thousand feet. And it still worked when I jumped to thirty-five thousand feet, then forty-five thousand.

The sky above was black but it was blue at the horizon.

It was cold.

I checked the new GPS: 13.7 kilometers up.

The problem was that there was still enough mass in the air at this altitude for thermal transfer, so the thin but very cold air was leaching away my body's heat. I didn't want any *more* frostbite.

I turned face down and fell, feeling the air shrieking past, then jumped all the way back to the tarp on the ground, my jaw working and my mouth open.

My ears adjusted without a problem.

"Why are you sitting like that?"

Cory was off the edge of the tarp, sprawled in the sand.

Mom said, "He was surprised, when you took off like that. I think we all were. He fell down. I just expected you to jump straight to altitude."

I couldn't help grinning. "First time and all that."

Dad rolled his eyes. "You wanted an audience."

"I wanted a *launch*," I said, still grinning.

I held my hand out to Cory and helped him stand.

"You weren't up there very long," Cory said. "Was there a problem?"

"Cold," I said. "Breathing was fine. I just didn't want any more frostbite."

Mom said, "And you want to go higher? Won't it be colder?"

Cory explained to her about thermal transfer in a vacuum. "Just like a thermos," he said. "Once we get out of the atmosphere, it will cease to be a problem."

*That's right*, I thought. *We'll have a whole* different *set of problems.*

But no need to tell Mom that. Not yet.

Cory turned back to me. "Are you ready?"

I nodded inside the helmet. He checked the time and recorded it.

I waved at my parents. "Five minutes."

Dad asked, "What about five minutes?"

"Back in five," I said.

He stood up. "Where are you going?"

"The Kármán line."

He held out his hand, palm out. "One hundred kilometers? Space? Don't you thin—"

I was gone.

I cleared my ears at twenty-five thousand feet, then forty-five thousand, then added velocity, hitting the two hundred miles per hour the first time—eighty-nine meters per second—and increasing the velocity each time I coasted to a stop.

As Dad had warned, the civilian aviation GPS went from fifty-nine thousand feet to an "Invalid Data" message as I passed eighteen kilometers.

By the time I passed twenty-five kilometers my upward velocity was over 244 meters per second. Though my ears popped slightly, the air around me was so thin that significant pressure changes took longer and longer.

The display on the civilian GPS flickered and then died completely at fifty kilometers. At seventy-five kilometers I stopped feeling cold. I didn't know if I was going so fast (six hundred meters per second) that I was getting friction warming, or if the air had finally thinned enough that it wasn't carrying away my body heat. I wasn't hearing the rush of air past the suit, like I had in lower altitudes.

My eyes were glued to the display and when I passed one hundred kilometers I was coasting upward at seven hundred meters per second. The only thing I could hear was the whir of the circulation fans, my own breathing, and the thudding of my heart.

I looked away from the GPS and down.

*My god.*

When you cry in free fall, the water does not run down your cheeks. It doesn't even leave your eyes. I had to blink hard and shake my head to clear my vision. Forty-five thousand feet had been impressive but it was *nothing* compared to this.

I floated.

I'd plummeted before, but it was always in the atmosphere, quickly pushing against an almost solid wall of air, a dragging, noisy beast that plucks at your clothing and screams in your ears.

A glance at the GPS showed I was still coasting up, but it was utterly silent and I felt nothing pulling at me. The GPS showed me when I passed 102 kilometers, but I couldn't really feel the motion.

I wiggled my fingers and moved my arms and legs. The suit was still comfortable. My breathing was still easy.

Per the GPS, my upward trajectory was slowing, slowing, and shortly, it would reverse. If I jumped again, but added velocity sideways, building up to 7,840 meters per second parallel to the surface of the earth, I would be in a circular orbit, but it wouldn't last long.

Though I couldn't hear it rushing past, there was still enough atmosphere at this altitude to generate drag, to decay the most circular of orbits.

Earth still made up most of my field of vision but at the edges it was curving away, clearly a globe, a sphere, a "big blue marble." The weather below, in West Texas, was clear, but up in the panhandle a front was coming through, knife sharp, crystal clear to the south and brilliant white clouds to the north. I twisted my head to the right and flinched. It was just the briefest glimpse of the sun but I was seeing violet spots.

For a second I was seriously worried about my eyesight. Could I jump if I couldn't see? Is that all it would take, a glimpse of the unfiltered sun, to maroon me up here?

Well, not maroon. I was at the upper end of a ballistic trajectory that was about to change direction. One way or another, I would return to the world below me.

I held my eyes shut until the spots faded. When I opened them back up, I had trouble focusing and then I realized it was the tears again, water balling up on the surface of my eyes. Blink, shake, blink, shake.

Below, the snaking progress of the Rio Grande cut through rough terrain thrown into sharp relief by the shadows cast by the midmorning sun. I looked at the GPS. My upward velocity was slowing, slowing, and I'd just passed 104 kilometers.

As of yesterday, when I'd looked it up online, the total number of humans who'd traveled into space was 623.

Not anymore.

My upward velocity finally slowed to zero and the GPS seemed to hang there for a second before it registered movement back toward the planet. Careful not to look at the sun again, I changed my orientation, jumping in place with no change in velocity, so that I was looking away from the bright globe, out into the black.

I could see stars, though not as many as I thought I'd see. Sunlight was entering the helmet from the side and bouncing around. I held up one hand, trying to block it, which helped a bit. Then I saw movement to the south, a bright pinprick movement, moving away—really moving—and then it seemed to swell as it became much brighter, and then faded back to its original pinprick.

*Ha.* I'd seen one of these before, though from the ground. It was an Iridium flare, a reflection from the main mission antennae of an Iridium Communications satellite. They were in polar orbits 780 kilometers above the earth, nearly 700 kilometers higher than I was. I watched it until it passed the terminator of Earth's shadow and blinked out.

I wanted to chase it.

*Five minutes.*

Right. Maybe next trip.

I returned in three jumps, brief pauses to let my ears equalize at twenty kilometers above sea level and then ten and then—

All three of them were standing. Mom and Dad were looking at the tarp and Cory had his head tilted up.

I staggered sideways, but regained my balance before they reached me. I held up my hand, forefinger to thumb, okay. I guess even four minutes of microgravity could make normal gravity seem odd.

Cory raised his eyebrows. "Well?"

I spoke up, to be heard outside the helmet, "One hundred and four kilometers."

Mom's lips were moving, then she said aloud, "Sixty-four miles?"

Dad said, "Close enough."

"Were you cold?" she asked.

"No. Not a bit. Maybe I should try for orbit, Cory."

He glared at me. "We had a *deal*."

I sighed. "All right." I started to reach for the main oxygen valve and stopped myself. "Checklist."

It took only a minute to depressurize the helmet and get it off by the numbers.

"Your right cheekbone is sunburned," Mom said, as she handed me a fresh bottle of water.

I touched the cheek with my suited hand. "Yep. Sure is. Sun was on that side."

Cory leaned in and peered at it. "Damn. Polycarbonate is supposed to cut out most of the UV. Could be near-UV, I guess. We'll need a protective visor."

"Not sunglasses?" I said.

"How are you going to adjust between sunlight and shadow? Sunlight and eclipse?"

I nodded. "Got it. When are we going to be ready for the next test?"

He ran his finger down my arm, across the fabric of the suit. "Let me get this back into the lab. We tested the suit in a vacuum before and we even hit it with high-energy UV, but we want to make sure it's not degrading now that it's met the real thing. Also, there are other things we need to examine, remember?" He raised his eyebrows at me.

I blushed. "Right." I turned to Mom. "Could you meet me back home after we get the suit off? I need some help."

Dad swiveled his head. "What kind of help?"

I bit my lip, but not telling him would just cause him to imagine terrible things. "My skin. The suit seems to work fine, reinforcing it, but we need to check it."

Dad looked puzzled.

"*Everywhere*, Daddy."

"Oh. Got it. I'll, uh, just work on that other thing, then."

Cory and Mom nodded.

*My* turn to imagine the worst. "*What* other thing?"

"A way to handle the communications issue. We were discussing it while you were 'out.'"

Mom muttered, "Longest five minutes *I've* spent lately."

Cory said. "Satellite phone. If they work down here on Earth, with atmosphere and buildings and mountains, they should work even better in orbit. Your mom suggested it. She says she sees them used in remote sites in relief work."

Dad gestured sharply at the sky. "The wait would have gone a lot easier if you were talking. When you have longer-duration tests, it's just going to get worse. At least for us." He made a little circle movement that took in Mom and Cory.

They still couldn't come after me if I got into trouble, but I could see their point.

If I was out there, I could be fine, I could be dying, I could be in need of advice, I could just need to hear *their* voices.

Sort of like Joe.

I ground my teeth together.

It was the not knowing.

# TWELVE

## Davy: Satphone

Davy jumped to Sim Lim Square and flinched immediately back to the Yukon, his hair, shoes, and shirt soaked. Rain had been falling so heavily that he could barely see across the square. He changed his shirt and toweled his head dry, then put on foul-weather gear.

When he returned to Singapore, the standing water was up to the ankles of his rubber boots. He kicked his feet like a child splashing in a puddle as he walked across to the International Phone Emporium.

Lucas was standing inside the glass door staring out at the rain. He pushed it open for Davy, smiling as he recognized him.

Davy nodded. He waited under the overhang for a few seconds, to let the worst of the water drain off his gear, then ducked inside.

"Come in, come in! I never see such rain, *ar*? Every *Ah Tong Ah Seng* stay away today like they melt. What you want or not?"

"Satellite phone, Lucas. I need a satellite phone."

Lucas's face lit up. "Good *lau*! For where? You want for Europe, Africa, and Asia, make you very good deal on Thuraya phone. GSM *and* satellite handset."

"I need it for everywhere."

"What you mean, everywhere *ar*? Even way up north?"

"*Ya.*"

"You need Iridium, then. I give you very good deal for pre-paid SIM card. Okay deal for contract."

In the end, Davy handed over several thousand dollars in cash and Lucas, smiling, gave him a bundle double wrapped in plastic against the rain.

Davy paused at the door and then turned back. He really couldn't leave without warning Lucas.

"Uh, Lucas? When we start using this phone, people might come looking, right? I mean, the SIM will trace back to you, *ya*?"

Lucas frowned. "Why they looking? You kill someone?"

Davy smiled. "Of course not. But maybe you should not know who bought these."

Lucas shook his head. "No, man. Next time when they ask I act blur."

"Next time? They asked already?"

"Oh, no. Singlish. Next time." He waved his hand forward. "Future time. Like 'Next time when you married' or 'Next time get out of way' *ar*?"

"Oh. Okay. You act blur. More better."

Lucas grinned. "I blur like *sotang*." At Davy's expression, he translated, "Like squid."

Laughing, Davy went out into the rain.

# THIRTEEN

## Millie: Not Fair

"Looks like a hickey," Millie said. She smiled. "Sure it was the suit?"

Cent winced. "You're kidding, I hope. That would be an odd place for a 'hickey.' If it's not an odd place, then I don't want to know the details."

Millie said, "Different strokes."

Cent said, "Well I'm sure it's not a hickey. Not *that* kind."

Millie thought Cent sounded a little defensive.

Cent continued, "When we were testing, we sometimes got a marginal reading there, but not consistently." She poked at it. "Doesn't hurt."

It was in Cent's right armpit, a reddish bruise no bigger than the ball of Cent's thumb. She'd told Millie that her skin had been a bit dry, too, but after showering and putting on some lotion the dryness went away.

There was only the one hickey.

"How much water do you lose out there?" Millie asked.

"I don't know," Cent said. "How would we find out?"

"Weigh yourself, before and after. If you pee, weigh that, too."

"Cory probably already has it in his test protocols but I'll mention it." She handed Millie her phone. "Take a picture of the bruise for the records, okay?" She held a towel across her front while Millie did it.

"Let's do the other armpit," Millie said. "For comparison."

Cent switched sides. "Sexy," she said in a flat voice.

"Oh, go get dressed!"

Millie was standing at the kitchen sink staring out the window into a light snowfall when Davy returned.

Without looking at him, she said, "What were you *thinking*?"

She heard him lean back against the opposite counter before saying, "I was *thinking* that it would take a lot longer to develop a practical suit."

She turned around. The minute he saw her face, he crossed his arms and his mouth got tight. She shook her head and then rubbed at her face with both hands, forcing the muscles to relax. "Didn't exactly work like that."

"He lost his funding. The people I asked said it would take him *years*. How was I to know that his one insurmountable problem could be solved by a teleport?"

"What are we going to do?" Millie's voice contained a strain of hopelessness that made her want to slap herself.

"You'd have to *ask* her to stop."

"For what reason?"

"Only the truth would work."

"What? That I want her to stop because *I'm* terrified she's going to get herself killed?"

Davy sighed. "You're allowed to say we're *both* scared she'll kill herself."

"Why don't *you*, then?"

Davy looked down at the floor. "She's not my mother."

Millie frowned. "That doesn't make any sense. Of course Cent's not your mother. Or do you mean me, being Cent's mother?"

Davy shook his head. "I mean Sam. *I'm* not the one who's in danger of losing their daughter *and* their mother." He jerked his thumb up and back, toward the bedrooms on the second floor.

It was unexpected and it rocked her back, taking her breath away. She shut her eyes, squeezing tears down her cheeks. "Dammit. I'm the one with the training. I didn't see that." She wiped at her face with her hands. "That is, obviously I was doing everything I could to *avoid* seeing that."

Davy handed her the tissue box. "It's grounds for *asking* Cent to stop. She could be brought to understand why this is such a bad time. *Telling* her to stop wouldn't work—we both know that. She's as stubborn as you are."

Tears and all, Millie couldn't help laughing.

Davy stared at her, perplexed, then got it. His face relaxed. "Okay, maybe I'm a little stubborn, too."

Millie blew her nose. "But *you* don't want to ask, her, do you? Why?"

Davy looked away.

Millie nodded. "Right. Because it wouldn't be fair."

Davy exhaled heavily.

Millie went on. "*We're* afraid, but it isn't as if she doesn't know what she's doing. *I* didn't know about the bends thing until *she* told me. Dr. Matoska seems to be moving cautiously, too. She'll be eighteen soon. She can be a thousand miles away in an instant."

Davy nodded. "Yes. It's probably less dangerous than her little adventure in New Prospect."

Millie shuddered. "Less? At least those people would want her *alive*."

Davy held his hand out and rocked it. "At least the hazards are known. Vacuum, heat, cold, collisions, radiation. Humans have been operating up there for over half a century.

"But when it comes to *those* bastards, it's hard for her to know what smiling asshole is holding a hypodermic needle or a Taser behind their back. Or, my biggest fear, when a sniper is waiting completely out of sight for her to show up." He stabbed his finger at the ceiling. "At least *they* can't get at her up *there*."

He dropped his hand and his shoulders slumped. "And, no," he said. "It wouldn't be fair."

# FOURTEEN

## Cent: More Prep

Cory had reloaded all the parts of the life-model pressure sensor into the suit and was taking readings. I Bluetoothed the pictures from my phone to his laptop. He frowned. "The *right* armpit?"

I nodded.

"To be honest, I half expected mild pressure hematomas at *every* joint." He blew the picture up on the screen until square corners of the pixels started to show. "Skin was intact, right? No sign of bleeding?"

"Definitely not." I stabbed at my T-shirt over the armpit with my finger. "Can't even tell where it is."

He checked the pressure sensor readouts for the corresponding region on the life model. "The pressure is nice and uniform under these conditions, but I must admit, the model doesn't exactly have armpits—no hollows there. You may need some padding under there, to compensate, to keep the pressure up."

"How does the suit look?" I said, gesturing at the magnifying loupe he'd set upon the bench.

"Good so far, but you were only in vacuum for five minutes, right?"

I nodded.

"We need to test for longer durations, but I want to solve the sun visor and the water issues first," he said. "Plus communications, right?"

I groaned. "How long?"

"What's your hurry?"

I glared at him. I had my own agenda, but I wasn't sharing it with *him*.

He spread his hands. "Look, we wouldn't even be testing without your ability to get inside. We'd be months or years away even with your funding. Have a *little* patience. Your dad said I should remind you about the 'surviving activities in low Earth orbit' part if you got pushy." He took a step back suddenly and his eyes got wide. "Cent?"

I rubbed at my face with both hands and exhaled. When I took my hands down some of the tightness had left my cheeks. Anyway, Cory wasn't leaning back anymore.

"How long?" I asked again, only milder.

Cory said carefully, "Your dad says he can have the satellite handset by tomorrow, but I need to work out how we're going to integrate it into the helmet and harden it for vacuum. I was thinking we'd make another aluminum chamber to hold the phone and the water bladder. We'll position the oxygen tank lower, the rebreather chamber a little higher, and put the new section in the middle. And we'll need to pressure test it and the connections. If things go well, I'm thinking four, five days. No, dammit, then there's the visor."

I held up my hand.

"*I'll* take care of the visor."

"*Tinkerbell* piggybacked on a Delta II launch delivering three multisensor oceanography platforms into low Earth orbit. We had a liquid gas propulsion system to get us to our target altitude of eight hundred fifty kilometers. Unfortunately the thruster solenoid failed open and we ended up blowing the entire store of hydrazine on one continuous thrust. *Tinkerbell* ended up in a highly elliptical orbit with an apogee of eleven hundred kilometers and a perigee of two hundred.

"For a while, we were in deep doo-doo with NASA and the

U.S. Strategic Command because they predicted a potential collision with the *NOAA 9* meteorological satellite."

We were on the fifth floor of Rudder Tower and the room was half full, perhaps twenty-five student and faculty members of the campus Makers Club.

Roberta Matapang, the guest speaker, was a graduate student working on her Ph.D. in astronautical engineering. She was describing her work on a nanosatellite designed and built by a consortium of Texas A&M and University of Texas students and faculty. I liked her but so far, every question asked, no matter how stupid, was a "Good question."

"Was a collision really likely?" asked one of the two guys on the front row.

I rolled my eyes, then took a deep breath and let it out. Probably wasn't being fair. After all, I'd been researching the low Earth orbital environment for *months.*

Ms. Matapang said (you guessed it), "Good question. The chances of any one object running into another are *very* low. However, there are over nineteen thousand pieces of debris bigger than ten centimeters. So while the chance of any particular *one* of them hitting another are pretty low, the chances that one of the many *does* have a collision approaches certainty.

"Over two thousand of those pieces were the result of just *one* collision in 2009, when a defunct Cosmos satellite collided with *Iridium 33* at over forty-two thousand kilometers per hour."

"Jesus," said the other front row student. "Were they orbiting in opposite directions?"

Ms. Matapang shook her head. "Roughly right angles. *Iridium 33* was in a polar orbit and the Cosmos was highly inclined, too."

"But your satellite, uh, *Tinkerbell,* didn't collide?"

"No. As its orbital track was refined by CelesTrak, the risk was downgraded. They passed more than three kilometers apart."

"What about your mission—could you do any science in that orbit?" the same boy asked.

"Good question. The main mission of *Tinkerbell* was to rendezvous with a discarded Delta II second stage, but now we don't have the fuel to do it. We've used the onboard camera for some Earth imaging, but that's about it."

"Is there a danger that it will run into something else?" asked the first student to speak.

"Another good question. Probably not. She's experiencing considerable atmospheric drag at perigee and we don't think she'll survive another two hundred orbits."

"Why did you want to rendezvous with the Delta upper stage?" *Did I say that out loud?* I'd been wondering for two days, since I'd found out about the talk, and researched what I could online.

She smiled at me and most of the students turned their heads to see who'd spoken. I was not the only woman in the room, but you could count the rest on one hand.

"Good question. The first part of the mission was to image the booster's exterior. It's been in orbit for over seventeen years, much of it in regions thick with orbital debris. Since we have exact prelaunch specifications, the idea was to examine the degree of micro- and macro-collisions."

"Or one of those fast collisions?" the first boy in the front row suggested.

I shook my head and Ms. Matapang noticed. "Do you want to tell him why?"

"Is the booster still its original orbit?" I asked.

She nodded.

"Right," she said. She looked back at the front row. "A major collision would've changed the orbit as well as torn it apart. The second part of our mission, though, *was* to change the orbit."

"Oh. But you ran out of fuel," said the second boy on the front row.

She smiled at him. "Yes we did, but that fuel was only to rendezvous. To deorbit the upper stage, *Tinkerbell* was going to hook onto one of the Delta's support-truss struts, then kick out a five hundred meter spool of woven aluminum tether. This stretches out along the local vertical and degrades the orbit."

The guys were puzzled.

"Why does that degrade the orbit?"

"Why do you think?"

One of the faculty in the middle of the room suggested, "Atmospheric drag?"

Ms. Matapang held her forefinger and thumb close to each other, "A tiny, tiny bit. What else?"

One of female faculty members said, "Solar wind?"

Ms Matapang shook her head. "Let me give you a clue. The tape is electrically conductive." She looked around the room but nobody reacted. She added, "And it would be moving through Earth's magnetic field."

"Like a wire in a generator," said the woman who'd spoken.

"Yes," said Ms. Matapang. "The wire generates current and the empty spool, dangling down, acts as an electron emitter. The current creates a magnetic field along the wire which generates electrodynamic drag as it moves through the magnetosphere."

A kid on the front row held up a piece of wire, pulled out of his pocket and waved it around. "I'm moving this wire through the earth's magnetic field and I'm not really getting much in the way of current."

Okay, *he* didn't get a "good question" response.

"How fast are you moving the wire?" Ms. Matapang asked.

"Oh, a meter a second? Roughly."

Ms. Matapang said, "Besides being considerably longer, the tether moves through the magnetosphere at orbital speeds. That's over seven *thousand* meters per second. You can understand how that might be a little more significant? It does take a while to degrade the orbit, but it's a matter of weeks or months, not the years atmospheric drag would take."

"So it's a remediation test?" I asked.

Matapang lit up like a light bulb. "*Exactly*. None of us want an ablative cascade."

I nodded. *I* certainly didn't.

Some of the audience knew what an ablative cascade was, but the rest had to have it explained.

"The amount of orbital debris has reached a point where a

hypervelocity collision has the possibility of creating more debris which in turn causes more collisions, which in turn—" She spread her hands apart, flexing her fingers sharply over and over. "It would put so much debris in LEO that it could render the polar orbitals unusable."

When she finished taking questions, I sprang out of my chair and walked briskly up to her, arriving while others were still getting out of their chairs. "Do you have the NORAD Catalog Number for *Tinkerbell*?"

She blinked. "Uh, yes, in my phone." She pulled it out and went through her contacts. "It's five three four two zero. You want to track it? It's small but if conditions were right, you might be able to acquire it with binoculars."

"Sure," I said. "Thought I might try and 'acquire' it at perigee. Two hundred orbits? How many days will that be?"

"Two hundred orbits is a wild-ass guess. Small as the cross section is, we're not getting as much drag at perigee as we expected. Thirteen, fourteen days. Maybe. Plus or minus a week."

"Do you have a card?"

"I think so. Looking for an internship? What's your major?"

I shook my head. "Oh, I'm already working on a project, thanks. I don't have a major yet."

"Undeclared, eh?" She dug into the bottom of her satchel. "Ha." She pulled out a dog-eared business card with the university seal. "Here it is." She peered at it. "Still current, too, for another three months."

I thanked her and made room for the others. Two guys started walking toward me, smiling, one of whom was tall and gangly like Joe. I turned and slipped out the door. As soon as the frame blocked their view of me, I jumped away.

"Gunner" Lee was a guy on eBay selling reproductions of the Apollo moon mission gear, including a reproduction helmet with the Lunar Excursion Visor Assembly for six hundred dollars. He was grumpy in e-mail about my wanting to inspect it before purchase. He was even grumpier when I showed up at his door in a suburb of Fort Worth and turned out to be this teenage girl. He wouldn't let me in to see the thing until I held up a wad of cash. Even then, he made me put on disposable gloves before handling it.

I don't swear much, but I wanted to. "The visor is completely opaque!"

"It's a replica," he said, as if I were an idiot.

"It's not *replicating* the original very well!"

Gunner held up his hands, thumbs extended like a frame, and peered at the helmet through them. "It looks just like the original!"

"You said on your entry it was *wearable*."

"It is. You can see through the main helmet. Just don't close the visor. If you're *not* going to buy it, you should pay for wasting my time."

For one brief second I considered jumping away *with* his stupid helmet. *Who wasted whose time?* It had taken me half a day to get a jump site in Fort Worth and then taxi to Gunner's house.

"That would be *no*." I handed the useless assembly back to him.

"If you weren't *serious*, you shouldn't have come out here!"

I wanted to punch him. I pointed behind him. "How much is *that*?"

When he turned his head, I jumped away.

It was mean of me. He was probably thinking I ducked away and hid in his house. With any luck, Gunner would waste the rest of the day looking for me.

I was okay with that.

But I still needed to solve the visor problem.

Motorcycle helmets have visors. Some of those have metallic coatings. But, none of them have the needed geometry.

Even though it wasn't the solution, it led to one.

A plastics factory in Lancaster, Pennsylvania made visors for a leading Japanese motorcycle-helmet company, which they shipped all the way to Japan before they came back attached to high-end, full-face, brain-pan impact protectors.

*I* went there because of the wide variety of coatings they could produce, including my preferred one, vacuum-deposited gold.

The technical sales rep took one look at me and said, "I have a call from the Pentagon in two minutes, but perhaps I can get someone less busy to help you." He waved a hand out the door and said, "Patel, come here!"

Patel wore a button-down shirt with a loud tie, jeans, and combat boots. "Yes, Dr. Brunson?"

"Help her," he said. He shooed both of us out of the office, barely acknowledging my thanks before he shut the door.

"What you need to know?" asked Patel. He had a Philly accent, where window ends up sounding like "wind-ah" and eagle rhymes with "iggle."

I smiled. "I need an optical-quality hemispherical polycarbonate visor externally coated with five hundred angstroms of gold."

He shook his head, not in denial but as if to clear it. "Polycarbonate. Hemispherical. Optical. An infrared-filtering gold coating."

I nodded.

He looked back toward the sales rep's office. "Did you tell Dr. Brunson that?"

"I didn't get a chance. He has to talk to the Pentagon."

Patel grinned. "Yeah. Security of the nation and all that. He really does talk to the air force. The company is making some visors for helmet-mounted displays, but he doesn't talk to them as often as he'd like people to think."

I was surprised he was speaking so frankly. "Work here long?"

"Just the semester. I'm on work-study from Drexel. So, what kind of helmet? Flip-up, full-face, off-road?"

I opened the padded bag I was carrying.

"Uh, that looks like a—"

"A fishbowl?"

"That's not what I was going to say."

I shrugged. "Want to show me the visors?"

He shook his head. "None of our motorcycle visors are going

to fit that. What's the diameter on that? It looks like a true sphere. Is it symmetrical?"

I nodded. "Yes, It's a true sphere with a planar intersection five centimeters from the bottom." I tapped the mounting flange. "Outside diameter is thirty-three centimeters. We need three-to four-millimeters clearance."

"How many visors do you need? We can custom make anything, but if we only make a few, the unit price gets really expensive."

"One. Well, maybe three. Spares."

He moved to small cubicle against the far wall. "Let me check something." He sat down at a computer and typed. After a moment he looked over at me and said "How would you feel about *five* millimeters clearance?"

I leaned over his shoulder, looked at the picture, and then read the specs. "Wow. That'll work. That'll work just fine."

"Wow," said Cory. "That'll work. What is it?"

"It's a protective dome for a roof-mounted closed-circuit television camera."

I'd put the helmet on the bench and perched the dome atop it like Don Quixote's Golden Helmet of Mambrino. The camera dome was a perfect half sphere, coming halfway down the helmet, a one-inch flange sticking out all around like a hat brim. When I titled the dome forward, it covered the entire forward face of the helmet.

"It will need a housing at the back and some sort of pivot, and we'll need to cut the flange off," said Cory.

"We'll cut the flange *mostly* off," I said. "If we leave it intact here—" I held out my forefinger and thumb, spread about eight centimeters apart, at the very front of the helmet. "—I can use that part as a handle to raise and lower it."

The finished visor assembly was like a hood for the helmet, coming all the way around at the neck where it buckled together near the chin, but only rising to the top of the helmet at the back and sides. We made it out of two sets of quilted sheets, each a double layer of fire-resistant Nomex/Kevlar cloth stiffened by an interior sheet of heavy aluminum foil. The gold-plated visor slid back between the quilts when stowed, pivoting on two thick aluminum clevis pins which went through grommeted holes in the inner layer of quilting, through drilled holes in the plastic visor, and through more grommets in the outer quilt, where they were secured with locking rings in their cross holes.

When I pulled the visor forward and down, it pivoted smoothly on the pins, sliding out from between the quilted pieces and down over the face. However, when I tried to raise it, it had a distressing tendency to stick, catching and bunching up the cloth.

I took the assembly apart and lined the visor pocket, top and bottom, with an additional layer of Teflon-coated cloth. That fixed the sticking issue, both reducing the friction and increasing the hood's stiffness so it stopped the bunching.

The Nomex/Kevlar cloth was off-white and it bothered me that it didn't match the light gray of the MCP suit.

"Maybe we should we paint the hood gray?"

"No," said Cory. "Let's keep the reflectivity up."

"You worried about heat? I thought we didn't have to worry about that. Perspiration and all that."

"Sweating *inside* the helmet isn't going to get rid of the heat in there. Purging is the only thing that will and that wastes $O_2$. So let's do what we can to keep the heat out in the first place."

"Got it. What about solar radiation *on* the suit? Is that going to be a problem?"

"Possible. We always thought the MCP suit would be used under outer layers, for scuff resistance and micrometeorite protection." He fingered a scrap of the Nomex/Kevlar cloth. "Do you want to sew an oversuit as well?"

"Cory, they *make* Nomex coveralls for industry. We can buy them off the shelf."

"Oh. Right."

I did end up sewing a Nomex/Kevlar/aluminum quilted cover for the life-support backpack, with openings for the new and old hoses, the main oxygen valve, and the satphone antenna.

One of the new armored hoses carried water from a plastic bladder in the left side of the new chamber, but setting up the communications side took the most time. We needed multiple insulated conductors through the aluminum walls, a four-conductor port for the headset, and a coaxial port for the exterior antennae. Both of the fittings failed pressure tests, proving, on investigation, *not* to have been rated for vacuum despite the sales rep's claims. Cory made some phone calls and then had the appropriate, quite-expensive ceramic-and-metal parts overnighted from South Carolina.

"Order twice as many as you need," I said.

Cory winced. "That's over a thousand dollars just for the headset connector!"

"You might need a spare later."

"Thank god we only need *one* antennae through port."

While Cory waited on his parts and then repaired the phone housing, I bought some Nomex industrial coveralls in the same off-white as the visor assembly and backpack cover. I removed their collars, and adjusted the neckline to fit closely around the suit neck, just below the helmet flange.

We did ground tests the next day.

Okay, the helmet was no smaller than it had been the last time I'd used it, but it sure seemed like it was.

First of all, there was a lot more stuff inside.

We went with a full-sized comm headset with over-the-ear earphones because they had the best chance of staying in place without resorting to a Snoopy cap. I could still turn my head side to side, but if I tilted left or right, the earpieces knocked into the polycarbonate dome. Then there was the water-tube bite valve. It came in the back of the helmet and was mounted off to my left side. When I turned my head and dropped my chin it was right there, relatively easy to get into my mouth, but when I was facing forward, it occasionally brushed against the edge of my jaw and if I'd just taken a drink, a drop of water would linger there, like a cold, wet kiss.

Then there was the visor assembly. It wasn't inside the helmet but it hung there in my peripheral vision to the left and right, and if I turned my head all the way to one side, half of my field of vision was blocked, like my head was in a hole. Combine that with the constriction from the neck gasket and claustrophobia kicked in big time.

Fortunately, after ten minutes, I adjusted completely.

I only saw the satphone when we pulled it out of its pressure chamber to swap out the batteries. It was thick, like the cell phones from when I was a kid. Dad delivered it with an auxiliary external antennae and two high capacity 3.7 amp-hour packs, each capable of 6.5 hours of talk time and forty-two hours of standby.

We could call any phone on Earth, really, so we purchased an anonymous prepaid cell phone to be our base station. With the satellite handset entombed in its aluminum chamber, I couldn't dial *numbers*, but the answer/terminate call button which Cory mounted on the front of the helmet flange would redial the last number called by the phone.

The satellite phone couldn't get a signal inside the lab (there were two more stories above us) so I jumped out to the desert, beneath the open sky. After ten seconds I heard the ring tone in my ears and hit the button.

"Cory?"

"Check. Oh, that's nice and clear. Imagine what it will be like when you're two hundred kilometers closer to the satellites and there's no atmosphere in the way."

*Imagine how clear it will be when I'm among them.*

I didn't say that out loud.

Speech on the satphone was clear, but a bit odd. The compression codec they used clipped the voice and about every fifty seconds, when it handed off to another satellite, there was the briefest quarter-second pause.

I looked up.

I wanted to go straight to one hundred kilometers again, but not only had I not flushed the nitrogen out of my system, I'd promised Cory we'd test for six hours total. I walked around the wash for a while, flipping the visor up and down, staring at the morning sun through it. It was working quite well down here at the bottom of the atmosphere.

The water made a huge difference. I didn't guzzle it, but taking a sip every five minutes made all the difference in the world from the cotton mouth I'd experience before. When we stopped after the first two-hour block, I had to get completely out of the suit and head for the restroom.

We did that two more times.

During the third session, I kept my water consumptions light, just moistening the mouth and, at the beginning, purged the helmet completely, exhaled, and did it again. At the end of this two-hour period not only *had* I purged the nitrogen out of my system, I'd also completed the promised six hours of testing.

"The call might drop for second, Cory. I'll call you back."

I jumped to ten kilometers, let the helmet purge and my ears pop, then twenty kilometers, and then a hundred.

*Oh, glorious.*

I didn't try to go sideways, to achieve orbital velocity—that was for tomorrow. Instead, I just let myself fall, looking at the feast below.

I hit the phone switch. It took a few seconds before I heard ringing and an answer.

"Cent?"

"Right."

"Where'd you go?" Cory's voice was clear as a bell.

"I shifted a hundred klicks. Good signal on my end. You?"

"Nice and clear. Look, we're at six hours and ten minutes. I know you haven't been exerting yourself, so we probably have another six hours of capacity, but let's call it a day."

I pulled the visor forward and down and twisted to look at the sun, a tiny disk, bright but bearable, through the gold coating.

"Sure, Cory. Be there in a minute."

At one hundred kilometers you don't accelerate at 9.8 meters per second per second. Nearly, but you *are* one hundred kilometers farther away from Earth's center of mass than you are at sea level. Gravity's grip does slack off inversely proportional to the square of the distance. So, call it 97 percent.

Still, there was no air to slow me and I was headed for the ground at over three hundred kilometers per hour in less than seven seconds.

It would only get faster.

I jumped away.

# FIFTEEN

## Davy: Hunt at the Gym

Davy was leaning against the wall when Hunt came out of the health club. He nearly missed him. The CIA agent had gone in wearing a suit and polished oxfords. Now he was wearing jeans, a T, and running shoes, and carried a largish gym bag.

He started counting but the man made him before he got to ten. Davy stayed where he was and let Hunt walk to him.

"I thought it would be here or the sushi place," Hunt said.

"Is that why you had them in your wallet? So I'd have a point of contact?"

"No. I realized you probably saw them when I was writing up my post-mission report."

"I'm not seeing the limp."

"No. The ankle is maybe ninety-five percent back."

"Ah. Not going to apologize. You were going to Tase my wife."

Hunt nodded. "And I pointed a gun at your mother-in-law."

"An unloaded gun."

"You didn't know that. I'm lucky you didn't kill me. But you don't do that, do you?"

"Tell that to Lawrence Simons."

Hunt shook his head. "I've read the autopsy. I saw the report on the device they took out of you, too. Did you know they got the one out of Hyacinth Pope intact?"

Davy blinked. "No. No, I didn't." He thought about Agent Martingale of the FBI. "I don't think the FBI knew that, either."

"Right. The NSA classified that. Anyway, I don't think you were trying for Simons's death."

"Forget about that," said Davy. "I've made my peace. What did the NSA find out from the implant? Did that lead anyplace interesting?"

"Sort of." Hunt looked down and scuffed the toe of his shoe on the sidewalk. "The implant started out as a Cyberonics vagal nerve stimulator for the treatment of refractory partial epilepsy, but someone retrofitted a larger case, a larger battery, and added physiological sensors. The programming was changed to allow higher voltage levels based on feedback from the sensors. Debilitating."

Davy couldn't help shuddering. "If by debilitating you mean convulsions, vomiting, shitting yourself and, what was that last one? Oh, yeah, *not* breathing." He paused to take a couple of deep breaths. "You're not telling me anything new. Could you trace the purchases from Cyberonics or the vendors on any of the sensors?"

Hunt shook his head. "Dead ends. Companies that never existed or, in the case of the sensors, cash purchases. The only thing that led someplace was the code."

"Code?"

"The overwritten firmware. When the NSA decompiled the machine language, they found a set of unique assembly language-library subroutines. They could only find one other piece of hardware that used that library."

Davy raised his eyebrows.

"It was a DoD contractor. I'm sorry, but I'm not allowed to say which one."

"So they're *still* a DoD contractor."

Hunt didn't say anything.

Davy let it go for the moment. That was twenty years in the past. "How about our friends at the nursing home?"

"We got four of them. All of them are U.S. citizens. Two of them have residences in LA county, but two of them came in from out of the country."

Davy raised his eyebrows. "Costa Rica?"

"How'd you know?"

"Some of the employees of Bochstettler and Associates ended up there. Same kind of business, different name—Stroller and Associates. There's a link between them and the Daarkon Group."

Hunt took out his phone and began typing on the keyboard. "Stroller like baby stroller?"

"Yeah. CEO is William Stroller. I first found Daarkon Group by following him there. There's a Facebook photo with James B. Gilead and William Stroller at a Daarkon Christmas party."

Hunt nodded at the mention of Gilead's name. "Gilead surfaced two months ago for his daughter's wedding but then vanished again. Except for that, he hasn't been seen in almost two years."

Davy nodded. "Yeah. Not since I visited their offices in LA and they went to ground."

Hunt said, "What did you do to them?"

Davy wasn't going to tell the CIA about gravimeters and jumping. "Just looking but they made me. It spooked them."

"What were your intentions?"

*To never be a target again. To make sure Millie and Cent aren't targets.* "Know thy enemy. I certainly did no more than show up, but the wicked flee where no man pursueth."

Hunt blinked. "Well, it's hard to pursue when you didn't see them go."

Davy said, "So, where's the Retreat?"

"Ah, you've heard of it? We have no idea. There was a mention of the Retreat in an e-mail between Gilead and his wife in the weeks before the wedding. The only other mention was in a phone conversation between a lower-level Daarkon exec, Todd Hostetler, and Kirsten McAdams, one of Gilead's known personal assistants. Ms. McAdams shut him down as soon as he said the name. Like ice. Hostetler apologized profusely."

"Anything else?"

Hunt shook his head. "*Nothing.* No *where*, no *what*, no *who*. Communications going in or out from there have to be blinded, possibly double blinded. All previous cell phones associated with the top-tier executives have either been canceled or are moribund. Not only no calls, but none of them have connected into any cell network in the last fifteen months."

"Well, it makes me feel better knowing *you* can't find them either, but why are you trying?"

"Well, initially we were wondering if you got them."

Davy didn't bother responding to that.

Hunt looked off to the side. "There has always been some concern when people are so highly connected and you don't know who's pulling *their* strings."

"It should damn well be a matter of national security. Far more justifiably than your pursuit of *me*."

Hunt turned to watch the street traffic. Without turning back to Davy, he said, "Well, *I* agree with you. But the job has a certain amount of, well, following orders, you know?"

Davy showed his teeth but it wasn't a smile. "Yes, but *whose* orders? If you knew *all* the hands tugging that string, that would be one thing, but there's still the chance one of those hands belongs to a person like Lawrence Simons. Like James B. Gilead."

Hunt turned away from the traffic. "Then why are you *here*?"

"I'll work with you but I won't work for you. I gave you Stroller and Associates. You told me about the guys who came for Samantha. This stuff I can do. But if one of your bosses gets anxious again and tries for some kind of snatch . . . well, afterward he won't think it was a poor decision—he'll think it was a disastrous decision. A career-ending decision."

Davy pointed at Hunt. "But the way things work they'll make sure you take the blame."

"As you say," Hunt said. "That's the way things work."

Davy nodded, stepped around the corner of the building into deep shadow, and jumped.

# SIXTEEN

## Cent: Good enough for Yuri

"I just think you should stick to under two hundred kilometers."

I hate it when they argue with me while I'm wearing the pre-breathe mask. This time it was Cory *and* Dad.

"Why?"

"Radiation," said Cory.

I took a deep breath, lifted the mask away from my mouth and said, "Are you kidding?" I put the mask back on and purged it before inhaling again. Took it off. "I'm staying equatorial and below the inner Van Allen belt. No real difference!" I put the mask back on.

Dad said, "If you stick to under two hundred klicks, the orbit will take less time—therefore less radiation."

I lifted the mask again. "Two hundred three miles, three hundred twenty-seven kilometers. If it was good enough for Yuri, it's good enough for me." Mask on, deep breaths. "And the difference in orbital period is less than five minutes!"

Dad wasn't giving up. "He didn't have a circular orbit. His perigee was only one hundred five miles—one hundred sixty-nine kilometers!"

I just shook my head.

Dad glared. "I hate arguing with you when you're wearing that mask!"

He couldn't see my mouth but he could tell I was smiling.

We "launched" from the lab. There was no real point in having the "ground crew" in Texas, especially since the prepaid cell phone wouldn't get a signal there. When I jumped to ten kilometers, it *was* over the pit because that was the site I had. Ditto for twenty kilometers and then 104.

The phone rang in my headset and I hit the answer button.

"Status?" asked Cory.

"At one hundred four klicks altitude. Adding velocity now." I flipped the visor down to protect my eyes.

It was a weird thing.

When I was learning to add velocity while jumping, my first clue, my first feedback, was the sound of air rushing by. Not much air rushing by at *these* altitudes. See the problem?

Now all of my feedback was visual, the motion of the earth below or the stars above or the readings of the space-enabled GPS. I faced southeast and tried to imagine the earth spinning below me.

It stayed still.

I was station keeping, jumping back to that spot 104 kilometers above the pit, to zero my vertical velocity, but with each jump, trying to add horizontal speed to the east.

It wasn't working. I'd drop again, but I wasn't moving sideways that I could tell.

Well, maybe if . . .

I watched the readout on the GPS instead, looking at the heading and imagining it reading 120 degrees, one kilometer per second.

Suddenly the earth was sliding slowly under me, moving west and a bit north. I was still dropping, though, since one kilometer per second wasn't anywhere near orbital velocity for this altitude.

"Status?" This time it was Dad's voice and I could tell that Cory had put the cell phone on speaker.

"One kilometer per second, altitude ninety-nine kilometers. Heading one hundred twenty-eight degrees. Central Texas."

I jumped again, back to altitude, trying to double the horizontal velocity. I peered at the GPS. Had it changed? It still said 1.0 kilometers per second, but the earth seemed to be really spinning below. I looked at the display again. Not 1.0, but 10.0—*ten* kilometers per second.

*Whoa, Bessie.*

I barely kept myself from flinching back to my bedroom. Wouldn't *that* have surprised Grandmother.

This wouldn't take me in a circular orbit. This was fast enough to take me all the way out past the geosynchronous satellites, 35,800 kilometers away, before swinging back in a highly elliptical orbit. If the vector was in the right direction, it might even be enough velocity to get me gravitationally captured by the moon.

"Ten kps, One hundred five degrees bearing, one hundred forty-eight kilometers altitude."

Cory said, "What was your speed? I don't think I heard that right."

"Ten kps."

"Do you think that reading is right?"

"Pretty sure. Longitude is changing far more rapidly than it was before and my altitude is jumping. And the earth's spin, well, let's just say it's zippin' along."

"Cent, from LEO, it only takes ten point nine kps to escape Earth's gravity!"

"Don't worry. Just using it to reach my target altitude. I'll trim it *way* back."

When the altitude read three hundred kilometers, I started trimming the horizontal speed back, paying more attention to my vertical speed.

"Status?" Dad's voice was a bit strident.

"Crossing Cuba. Eight kps. Altitude three hundred seven kilometers. Heading one hundred twenty degrees."

I kept increasing or decreasing the horizontal component until my vertical speed was barely changing, a very slight rise, less than a tenth of a kilometer every few minutes.

"What's happening there, Cent?"

"Altitude three hundred forty kilometers. Bearing one hundred twelve degrees. Velocity seven point seven two kps."

I bit down on the bite valve to take a sip of water and it squirted hard, jetting into the back of my throat and airway. I began coughing furiously and beads of water splashed off the inside of my faceplate and began floating around my face.

"Cent what's wrong?" Cory said, his voice rising slightly.

Dad said, "Return, Cent, abort! Christ, her life support must be failing!"

I got my throat clear and took a wheezing breath, then another, finally saying, "S'okay. Got some water down the wrong pipe."

Dad said, "Jesus!"

I heard Cory exhale before saying, "Microgravity can be tricky. Liquids don't always behave like you expect."

*Tell me about it.* Though I didn't think it was microgravity that was the problem.

When we'd tested the suit the day before, the water feed had behaved like any earthbound hydration pack—bite down to open the valve and suck to get the water into the mouth.

I cautiously bit down on the bite valve again, barely squeezing, and water sprayed hard into my mouth. I released the valve and swallowed the water.

"We've got a bit of an overpressure problem in the water compartment, Cory."

"What? Oh!" I heard him smack his forehead with the palm of his hand. "The compartment is at a full atmosphere and the helmet is now a third of that! It must be squirting like a fire hose. It's not leaking through the bite valve, is it? It wasn't designed to hold a pressure differential—just open so you can suck water through the tube. *Last* thing you want is a helmet full of water."

I glanced at the drops that were floating in front of my eyes. They were drifting past my cheeks, heading for the air return to the rebreather. The first filter cartridge the water would hit in the rebreather chamber was the activated charcoal, but next one after that was silica gel and it would probably soak up the drops.

*Unless—*

I realized that, really, the first thing the water would encounter on entering the chamber was one of the circulation fans.

I hoped it wouldn't short out.

"The bite valve seems to be holding," I said. "Maybe we can put an overpressure valve on the water compartment, to vent the excess when I'm, uh, exoatmospheric?"

"Sure. I've even got a spare that's set to five psi. It'll take less than a half hour to drill, tap, and install it. You want to come back and take care of that now?" From the tone of his voice, I knew which one *he* preferred.

"No. I'll keep an eye on it. Besides, as I drink, there will be more room in the chamber and the pressure will drop."

"Understood. Give me your stats again. I'd like to get the elements of your orbit."

"I just crossed the equator and I'm well out into the Atlantic. Altitude is three hundred forty one kilometers, speed is seven point seven two kps." I gave him the longitude and latitude.

"How's your temperature?"

"I feel comfortable. It's local afternoon, but I'm not feeling anything heating up." I was feeling a little thirsty so I took another cautious gulp from the water "jet."

Over the next ten minutes I gave him updates as the sun sunk lower behind me.

"Okay," he said, a few minutes after the last update, "Pretty circular. I've got an apogee of three hundred sixty-two kilometers and a perigee of three hundred twenty-two. Inclination of orbit is twenty-four point three degrees and period is just under ninety-two minutes. Were you going to adjust it anymore?"

I thought about it. Our biggest concern was radiation and, as long as we were below the inner Van Allen belt, it was moderate. The earth's magnetic field funneled the sun's charged particles around the planet or trapped them in the radiation belts. Because the inclination of my orbit was low, I also wasn't going anywhere near the South Atlantic Anomaly, where the inner Van Allen Radiation belt drops within two hundred kilometers of the surface. Lots of high-energy particles *there*.

"Ninety-two minutes. Copy that. Let's leave things as they are."

When I first started looking at orbital speeds and periods, I thought there should be more of a difference between 200 and 340 kilometers of altitude. I thought of it as a 60 percent increase. What I didn't realize was that it was the *radius* of the orbits that mattered. Not the distance to sea level but how far it was to the center of the earth. So it was really the difference between 6,600 and 6,740 kilometers, a change of just two percent.

The entire earth was darkening below me as I reached the west coast of Africa. For me, the sun was still brilliantly bright through the visor and a full hand span above the horizon, but the curvature of the earth put everything below me into night. A few minutes later, when the sun dropped over the horizon, the entire western edge of the planet lit up, a bright thin band of atmosphere, and then it faded.

*Wow.*

And then it was *too* dark.

For a second, I waited, thinking my eyes would adjust, but finally I remembered the visor and pushed it up. There were stars above and man-made stars below when I crossed the African coast over Benguela, Angola.

For me it was a line of lights defining the coast and a splotch of light where the city and airport were. But Cory identified the location for me. Now that he had the orbit, he was running an active plot on computer. When I passed a brightly lit city, he was able to name it for me.

It took less than seven minutes to cross the continent, three thousand miles through Angola, Zambia, the Democratic Republic of the Congo, Zambia (again), Malawi, and Mozambique. Two minutes later I zipped past the northern tip of Madagascar and my ground track bent north again over the dark Indian Ocean and brighter swaths of moonlit clouds stretching east toward Australia.

"Hey, Cent," Cory said.

"Yeah?"

"You might want to look up."

I tried to turn, like I would on Earth, twisting my hips, but my legs went one way and my torso went the other, then returned, and I was still facing the earth. So I ran in place, pumping my legs in circular motion, as if I was running forward. My entire body began rotating backwards. I stopped running and my body stopped rotating.

*Ha! Just like on the videos.*

I did it again until the earth was to my back and I was looking out into the black. The three-quarter moon was quite a ways north of me and the amazing Milky Way was off to my left, but I don't think that's what Cory meant.

"What am I looking—*OH MY GOD!*"

I'm not religious, really, but some things.

"That's sixty kilometers above you," Cory said. "It's crossing your path at about thirty degrees. You're going faster, of course."

At sixty kilometers it was only a jagged dot, but I could make out the panels sticking off the main truss and crossing it, a thicker white line of modules running from the standby Dragon personnel capsule off the Harmony node all the way to the standby Soyuz off the Zvezda service module at the other end. To my eye it was drifting backward in orbit, and from north to south, though we must have been going the same direction (south to north) or it would've crossed my path like a bullet, at several kilometers a second.

They were only sixty kilometers away—the eight humans currently in space.

*Nine total.*

I could *see* it. I could *jump* to it.

And I would, but not today.

Sunrise, like sunset, was *spectacular*, happening sometime after I crossed Papua New Guinea into the Pacific proper. I had to grab the sun visor to flip it into place quickly, and in my haste, I hit the headset button, disconnecting Cory and Dad.

*Oops.*

I floated on, secure in the knowledge that they would call back, so, when the phone rang after thirty seconds, I tapped the button and said, "Sorry, about that. Accidentally hit the disconnect."

"Oh, really?"

My teeth clicked together. It wasn't Dad's voice and it wasn't Cory's. "Hello?"

"This is Mark Mendez. Who am I talking to?"

"You have the wrong number," I said.

"I'm pretty sure this is the handset I'm interested in. I'm calling from the Iridium Communications Satellite Network Operating Center in Leesburg, Virginia."

*Uh-oh.* I tried bluffing. "Then you *know* how expensive my satphone minutes are."

Dad had prepaid four thousand dollars for five thousand units when he purchased the phone, which did take the price down to eighty cents per minute. Still, some people bought smaller chunks that weren't as discounted, costing over a $1.25 a minute. Our minutes were "global," supposed to be good *almost* anywhere, but Dad had added, "We might not be able to use them above North Korea."

"Your account minutes are not being deducted for this *diagnostic* call," the voice said. "We're seeing some aberrant behavior from your handset. The call you were just on, was it working all right?"

My breathing slowed a little. I hadn't realized it had increased. "Sure, awesome. Though I hung up on my peeps by accident. They're probably trying to call me *right now.*"

I heard him say something to the side, not into the mouthpiece. "What? No, that's not possible. Check it by footprint." His voice strengthened. "Oh. Your party, yes, they were. An associate at the Tempe gateway station is talking to them now."

"You intercepted their call? That's kind of creepy."

"They wouldn't have been able to reach you while I was on the line. We just wanted them to know that your handset was still operational."

"And why wouldn't it be?"

He chuckled. "This will sound a little crazy, but according to our Doppler shift data, the handset is traveling nearly twenty-eight thousand kilometers per hour. We're trying to find the glitch in our system."

Someone spoke to him in the background and I heard, "—not sure it's a glitch."

"Hold please," he said. The sound went away. I think he muted his mike.

He was gone long enough that I thought the call had dropped. I was about to hit the disconnect when he came back.

His voice was accusatory. "Your *handset* is switching between satellites in completely different orbital planes as often as it switches between units in the same orbit."

*Well, damn.* I stalled for time. "The same orbit?"

"Our satellites are in polar orbits, in six different orbital planes, thirty degrees apart. If your handset was sitting in one location, the handoff would be between one of the eleven satellites in the same plane, with occasional sideways transfers as the rotation of the earth took the handset under a different plane. During your previous call, your phone was handed off to satellites in a different orbital plane *seven* times."

"Seven? I thought you said there were just six."

"Your handset encountered the first plane again on the *opposite side of the planet*."

"Why do you keep saying 'handset?' "

"You've mounted the handset in some sort of microsat. Those are *orbital* speeds. You're linking to it by a separate transceiver, then using our system to check your radio link, yes?"

*Oh. He doesn't think* I'm *in space. He thinks the* handset *is*. "I suppose that's one possibility," I said.

I could hear the other person speaking in the background again and Mendez said off to side, "Not possible." Pause. "Well *which* is it?"

I didn't hear the response.

He spoke back into the headset. "What is your satellite's NORAD ID?"

"We didn't apply for one."

"You don't *apply* for an ID. NORAD assigns them on launch! We've got a rough plot of your satellite's orbit and there's nothing in the Joint Space Operations tracking database that matches."

"Perhaps we recently changed orbits?"

"No, there would've been a collision evaluation if a change had been detected. And it *would* have been. Unless you've managed to get your satellite smaller than five centimeters. The nine-five-five-five handset you're using is fifteen times longer than that."

"I *knew* we should've told somebody we were launching."

He exhaled sharply. "Right. As if you could launch without detection."

Obviously, *I* could, but I understood his conviction. Peaceful rocket launches look a lot like nonpeaceful ballistic missile launches and there was a lot of technology out there to detect *those.*

I could hang up, or I could tell him the truth. "All right, Mr. Mendez, I *am* using your system for orbit-to-ground communications. My associate—" Dad "—looked through your TOS and didn't find any restrictions on altitude. Is orbital use a violation of your terms of service?"

He didn't say anything for five seconds. Finally, speaking slower than before, he managed, "That's . . . incredible. Uh, no it's not covered in the TOS. I guess they didn't consider it a possibility. Our Iridium NEXT constellation includes a system to communicate with space-borne assets, but it won't be completely deployed for four more years. Anyone putting packages in orbit for the U.S. works with the TDRS System in geosynchronous or uses transceivers and ground stations. Why are *you* using ours?"

"I would think that would be obvious: So we can communicate from any part of our orbit—no waiting to come around to a ground station. Are we messing up your network by calling from altitude?"

"Uh, no. Since you're not transmitting through the atmosphere you have excellent signal strength. But we *should* probably have a different sort of user agreement. If nothing else, people capable of putting a satellite in orbit can afford premium rates."

"Greedy, much?"

"Just good business. Let me to speak to your boss."

"My *what*?"

"Your boss—put him on."

*Him?*

I looked down at the deep blue of a Pacific striped with low cumulous clouds and calmed myself by thinking, *He can't see what I'm seeing.* I loved how the cloud's shadows trailed across the water to the west as the sun rose. I took two deep breaths before saying, "I can't do that."

"Can't or won't? I *will* shut your handset out of the system."

"On what grounds? Who's violating the terms of service now? You've already interrupted today's mission."

"This is not our usual usage," he said. "It needs to be discussed!"

Emphatically I said, "I *knew* we should have gone with Inmarsat or Globalstar. Your network probably won't work for us anyway when we're working the high orbitals."

"Working the high—? Never mind—let me speak to the person in charge!"

"You already *are.*"

Someone said something to him and he covered the mouthpiece of his handset, but I still heard a muffled, "No additional delay? That's not possible." Then, to me, "We're not seeing a delay on your radio-to-orbit transmission. How are you doing that?"

"Because I'm *with* the handset, Mr. Mendez. I'm not sending a separate radio signal to a satellite and using Iridium to check it. I'm using the satphone to communicate with my *ground crew.*"

I heard his sharp intake of breath. "This is a *manned* mission?"

I gritted my teeth. "This is a *womaned* mission. Now are you going to get off the line and let me talk to my peeps or not?"

"That's *not* possible," he said, but the certainty wasn't there.

"You keep saying that. I'm not sure it means what you think it means."

"You're in orbit."

"Pretty damn sure. At seven point seven two kilometers per second, three hundred fifty-one kilometers above sea level. I'm coming up on the International Date Line. There's some islands below. Don't know which ones but they have a lot of ring-shaped barrier reefs. Uh, atolls? Where is the Iridium bird I'm connected to?"

"Uh," I heard his head move against his handset. "It's just south of the Marshall Islands."

"That would be it. You wouldn't believe how the water color changes as it gets shallower. Makes me want to go snorkeling." I took a sip of water and in a flat voice I said, "Besides talking to my nonexistent boss, what do you want, Mr. Mendez?"

"Uh, how long are you going to be doing this?"

"Oh, we're going to be operating for several years. Or did you mean today? Just this one orbit. We'll be off the air in another thirty minutes, but depending on our post-mission analysis, I'm deorbiting a satellite tomorrow."

I heard a sharp intake of breath.

"Oh, don't worry. It's not one of *yours*."

I disconnected the call.

My heart was pounding and my stomach felt a little sick. For a second I thought something was wrong with my life support, but I realized it was just reaction. It's not that I *like* confrontation. But it doesn't really scare me since I can always jump away from it if I have to and, I must admit, I tend to be a little impulsive.

Before Mr. Mendez called back, I hit the headset button to redial our base-station phone.

"Are you all right, Cent?" Dad's voice.

I sighed with relief. "I'm fine, but let's go with call signs from here on out. I just talked to the most annoying man." I told them about Mr. Mendez of Iridium Communication's Satellite Network Operating Center and their very all too accurate conclusions.

"Yeah. We talked to one of his people. You think they're listening in?"

"Maybe."

"Call signs, then. Roger that, Baby Bear."

I rolled my eyes. "Okay, Papa Bear. I can see the Hawaiian Islands. Coming up on Oahu."

Cory's voice spoke. "I am *not* going to be Mama Bear."

"Roger that, Porridge."

Dad laughed.

Cory said, "I prefer, 'Capcom.' What's your environmental status, Baby Bear?"

"Can we come up with something besides Baby Bear? But I'm not too hot, not too cold. I guess that makes it 'just right.' I've drunk enough water that the pressure has dropped—just a trickle when I bite the valve. Doesn't Capcom stand for 'Capsule Communicator?'"

"Used to. Now they translate it as 'Spacecraft Communicator' and they use it for everything, including talking to the ISS. 'Capcom' is a nice clear word, easy to understand on noisy transmissions."

"Roger that, Capcom."

I passed over the West Coast halfway down the Baja peninsula. It took me fourteen seconds to cross the Sea of Cortez. On this pass, I was going to be well south of the pit, but I wanted an entire orbit, just like Yuri. I waited until I reached my starting longitude, 104 degrees west, before jumping down to ten kilometers for an intermediate pressure adjust, then straight to Cory's lab.

"Forget the checklist," I said loudly, to be heard through the helmet. "Get the satphone turned off. I don't *think* it will acquire a signal, but I don't want them figuring out where we're based."

Cory unclamped that side of the compartment and, rather than power it down, he popped the battery out.

Then, we did the rest of the checklist by the numbers.

"Think Iridium will shut you down?" Dad asked when my helmet came off.

"They can't shut *me* down. I don't know if they'll turn off the phone. They won't if they know what's good for them."

Dad frowned? "Threat?"

"No, though I guess I could start deorbiting their satellites. Or threaten to. Take some close-ups of their birds and send them e-mail: 'Nice little satellite you have there. *Shame* if anything happened to it.'"

Dad smiled briefly but said, "No."

"Make that 'hell, no.'"

He nodded. "You catch more flies with honey—"

"I've always thought that was disgusting. Dead flies in honey. Yuck. If they cooperate, perhaps I'll offer advertising."

"Advertising?"

"Well, product endorsement. Put an Iridium patch on my coveralls. Take a few pictures floating in space next to one of their birds. 'Apex Orbital uses Iridium. You should, too!' "

"Apex Orbital? Is that what we are?" asked Cory.

I shook my head. "Apex Orbital is what *I* am. You'll need to come up with a company, too. Cause—" I deepened my voice. "—'Apex Orbital uses Matoska MCP Suits for superior mobility in exoatmospheric environments.' "

"Suits? There's just the *one*." But he was grinning at the thought.

"We'll have to fix that, right?"

When I was completely out of the suit I weighed myself, and Cory measured the remaining water.

"So, you're down six hundred six grams. If we assume it was all water loss . . . heat transfer in a vacuum is six hundred twenty-five heat calories per gram of evaporated water—" He stabbed at a calculator. "—call it three hundred seventy-nine kilocalories of cooling over ninety-four minutes. The at-rest heat production for an average human is fifty-eight watts per square meter" He looked at me, head to toe. "Average human has a surface area of one point eight square meters but you're on the small side—let's call it one point five." More calculator clicks. "That's eighty-seven watts—seventy-two kilocalories an hour, one hundred eight kilocalories for the whole orbit. Looks like you picked up an extra two hundred seventy-one kilocalories from solar radiation."

Dad looked concerned. "Is that dangerous? Would that burn her up?"

Cory grinned. "No, it's fine. About the same amount of heat she'd produce from moderate exercise—say walking briskly. I'd say the white overalls are doing their job, so don't plan on too many endorsements—or at least make sure their patches are highly reflective."

I'd carried four film dosimeters into orbit, flat, credit-card-sized pieces of plastic that self-developed when exposed to gamma and X-ray radiation. One was clipped to the outside of the Nomex coveralls, one inside the coveralls, and one we slipped between my base-layer shirt and the MCP suit, just below my right collarbone before we snugged the suit up. (That one left a rectangular outline.) The last one we taped to the inside of the helmet, at the back.

As expected, the outside, unprotected badge picked up the most, somewhere between twenty and fifty millisieverts, an amount that if accumulated yearly, every year, would increase your chances of getting cancer by 10 percent. Fortunately, the Nomex coveralls alone cut it to under ten millisieverts, and inside the MCP suit it was below five. The dosimeter at the back of the helmet, shielded by the polycarbonate dome and the visor assembly with its four layers of Nomex/Kevlar, two of heavy aluminum foil, and two layers of Teflon-coated cloth, had no reading.

"I'm sure there was radiation," said Cory. "Just not an amount within this unit's sensitivity. This gives us an idea, but these badges were designed for first responders in some kind of radionuclide exposure. Reactor accidents. Spills. What you were exposed to was mostly high-energy particles from solar and cosmic radiation.

"If you're going to hang out in orbit for long periods of time I'll want more shielding. No, forget the 'if.' In the radiation belts and the high orbitals you'll need shielding even for brief exposures."

"What do they use for the Constellation suits?"

"For EVA's they use a hard torso, but they have all sorts of oversleeve and overleg coverings, depending on the environment. Mostly it's multilayers of aluminized Mylar with an outer micrometeor protection layer."

"I could put on *two* coveralls."

"We'll see. Sounds like a really good test for the material-science lab here at Stanford. Fortunately, we're a long way from working outside of LEO."

I just smiled.

When Mom helped me check, we found another pressure hickey, this time on my left ankle. Again, no pain, no external bleeding, just a bluish-red patch between the heel and the ankle bone.

"I wonder if this will happen every time."

Mom said, "You sure it doesn't hurt?"

"Painless, I promise." I thought back to my three months in high school. "If hickeys were life threatening, then there'd be a lot more deaths among teenagers."

"True. Come tell Grandmother about your day."

I grinned. "Absolutely."

# SEVENTEEN

## Samantha: Poker Face

The first three days after Samantha moved to the cabin were rough.

Samantha's routine oxygen supplementation in Wichita (elevation 1,299 feet) was three liters per minute through a nasal cannula. After an hour in the Yukon, at forty-five hundred feet, she was in respiratory distress, with oxygenation levels around 85 percent. Seeana put her on a nose-and-mouth mask and upped the flow to nine liters per minute. Her oxygenation levels crept up above ninety, again. When they added IV liquids, she got up to 95 percent.

"Why is that?" asked Millie.

Seeana said, "Dry lungs, probably. Too much fluid in the lungs is bad, but not enough also interferes with oxygen uptake. You get this thick, dry mucous which doesn't clear. We need to keep her hydrated *and* keep her oxygenated. Her lungs are in pretty good shape, but her diaphragm isn't working near as hard as it should."

Millie sighed. "None of her muscles are."

Seeana nodded. "But they *could*. Her neurologist blames the inactivity from the fractures. He says her type of muscular degenerative disease *can* be countered with physio, but she's so brittle it has really interfered with exercise." Seeana sighed.

By the end of three days, they had Samantha back on a nasal cannula at four liters per minute oxygen flow, with oxygenation in the low nineties.

Seeana was cautiously optimistic. "But if we end up with a respiratory infection it could go bad. We need to be prepared to mechanically assist her breathing."

"A ventilator?"

"Not an invasive ventilator. If she's intubated *or* tracheal, she'll need to be in an ICU. *I'm* not willing to do that in this environment. But there's noninvasive ventilation with a nose mask or full-face mask."

"Like a CPAP machine?"

"Yes. Or BPAP. Far less chance of ventilator pneumonia. But if we can keep her oxygen levels up, her neurologist and her pulmonologist both felt the harder she works her muscles, the better."

Samantha improved, but with Seeana's guidance, Millie purchased a high-end ResMed Stellar 150 noninvasive ventilator.

"At this rate, we're going to need a cash infusion," Davy said. "I wonder where Daarkon keeps its cash."

Millie shook her head sharply. "No."

"If not them, who?"

Millie tapped him on the chest. "We don't have to steal. We have skills. Unique skills. We can earn it."

"You want me to work for the NSA again? That didn't exactly work out for the best."

"No, it didn't. But let's see what we can come up with, okay? We've had offers from the non-governmental relief organizations." She licked her lower lip and added, "And Cent seems to have some notions, too."


All three of the health aides were from Metro Manila; Bea and Jeline were from Quezon City, and Tessa from Muntinlupa, in the south.

"Don't jump where they can see if you can help it," Millie told Cent when they were both in Samantha's room. "We blindfolded them and had them sit in a chair. Your dad jumped the chair without touching them."

"What do *they* think happened?" Cent asked.

Samantha laughed softly. "Well, once it was clear that I didn't care what they said or thought, they've been speculating up a storm. I've heard a dozen suggestions including drugs and airplanes."

Millie said, "We paid substantial recruiting fees, which went to their families, and I think they're okay with things so far. The real test will be when their shifts are up and we take them back for their five days off."

"Five days?"

"Yeah. Ten days on, five days off. All three are here to begin with, for training, but in five days Tessa goes home. She comes back five days after that and Bea goes."

"Doesn't that put, uh, Jeline on for fifteen?"

"Yes. That's what they decided. Jeline's family is trying to buy an additional car for her brothers and she wanted the extra pay."

Bea was the tall one, nearly six feet. Jeline and Tessa were the same height as Cent, but Jeline's face was more angular and Tessa tended to bob her head every time someone spoke to her. Their English was excellent and all three had several years' experience in geriatric care.

Their previous employers had required them each to take care of several clients. They considered their current working conditions luxurious, especially after Davy installed a satellite dish to pick up Filipino TV channels.

Samantha had them set up a card table against the bed and taught them, and Seeana, to play bridge, patiently working through basic contract bidding.

They, in turn, taught Samantha and Seeana to play *Pusoy*, a card game where each of four players has to make three ranked five-, five-, and three-card poker hands out of their hand. Players got points based on whose individual front, middle, and back hands they beat, and whose they didn't.

Sometimes Samantha was too tired to play, unable to hold up the cards, even with her arms propped on pillows, but she enjoyed watching and she enjoyed the company. They would move the table slightly off to one side and some combination of the health aides, Seeana, Millie, and Cent would play, not just *Pusoy*, but Texas hold 'em, which Seeana had gotten hooked on from watching televised tournaments.

The health aides jumped at that and wanted to play for outrageous amounts. Millie provided a massive set of colorful poker chips, but limited the actual money to ten or twenty dollar buy-ins. Big piles of chips changed hands and vehement Tagalog oaths were sworn.

Cent did a little reading on the subject and, using a decent understanding of statistics and probability, usually finished in the money.

One evening, after the card table had been packed away and Cent ended up alone with her grandmother, she said, "Why do they do that? They bluff or they try to make their hand on the last card no matter what the odds."

Samantha chuckled. "Playing it safe is boring. *You* fold eight times out of ten, right? They're in it for the narrative, the struggle, the drama. For them, losing big is almost as good as winning big. They *do* enjoy themselves."

"I *enjoy* myself!" Cent protested.

"I noticed," Samantha said, drily. "After you fold, what are you doing?"

"I'm watching *them*. I'm watching how they bet, what their faces are doing each time a card flops. Then I'm comparing it to their final hands, if I get to see them. I try and predict which of them really has something and which of them is bluffing, what hands they have, based on the board and how they bet, even when it's the *wrong* bet." She shook her head. "Seeana's the real challenger. She plays the odds *and* she knows just how to bet, or how reluctant to act to get *them* to bet bigger. After that, it's Tessa. She doesn't make good choices, but I can never tell when she's got a great hand or nothing. It's always that little head nod, good or bad."

Samantha nodded. "I noticed. But she's not the only good bluffer."

"What? Seeana? She doesn't have to bluff. She's got the goods most of the time."

"I was thinking about you, dear."

Cent frowned. "Huh. Really? I thought of myself as just playing the odds. Don't need to bluff."

"Not talking about the *cards*. What's really going on with your young man, Joe?"

Cent blinked. "What do you mean?"

Samantha smiled. "Nice. Just the right amount of confusion. But I've been here over a week and all I've heard is excuses why he can't visit at this time. Your mother suspects something, but she's been more occupied with my stuff—" She waved her fingers, taking in the oxygen tanks, saline stand, and monitors. "—so hasn't been pushing it. Your father is distracted by *your* other endeavor." This time Samantha's finger pointed straight up, toward space. "I was wondering if that was what they were to you: a distraction." She frowned. "No, that's not exactly what I mean. I'm not suggesting you're doing what you're doing because of *boyfriend* problems. But you wouldn't be the first person to put more energy into a project because you were avoiding pain in another part of your life."

Cent's jaw dropped open and she turned bright red.

Samantha raised her eyebrows. *Have I offended her*? "Are you all right?"

Cent moved her mouth but it took her a minute to get the words out. "It . . . it just . . . took me by surprise."

*Oh*. "So, I was . . . close?"

Cent turned to take a tissue from one of the bedside tables and blew her nose. "Yes. For values of 'close' equaling 'dead on.'" She shook her head. "No, there's other stuff, too. A bit of 'I'll show *him*!'"

Samantha sighed. "So you *did* break up."

Cent threw her hands in the air.

Samantha hazarded, "Is it complicated?"

"I found him in bed with someone. I haven't talked to him since."

"Oh. *That's* not good."

"You think?" Cent said bitterly.

"Your mother didn't mention that."

"I haven't told her."

"So it's over? Have you ended it?"

"As I said, I haven't talked to Joe, either way."

Samantha tilted her head. "Do you *want* to end it?"

Cent clenched her fists and said in anguished tones, "*I don't know!*"

Samantha didn't have the strength to pull Cent closer, but her body language and the motions of her fingers did the trick.

Cent buried her head in her grandmother's lap and Samantha's fingers stroked through the girl's short hair as she sobbed her heart out.

# EIGHTEEN

## Cent: K4K Plan

As part of our new preflight checklist, I jumped out into the West Texas desert and powered up the satphone. There was a voice-mail indicator on the display.

I was afraid I knew who left *that* message.

The phone rang and I hit the answer button, but I didn't speak.

"Apex One, Comm check," said Cory's voice.

I was wearing the oxygen prebreathe mask, which Cory knew. I hit the keypad number five twice, the arranged reply.

"Comm check complete. Capcom out."

I disconnected. At this point, I was supposed to power the handset down and we wouldn't turn it on again until I was completely suited up and ready to go. Instead I dialed up the voice mail and listened.

"Mark Mendez, Iridium Satellite Network Operations Center. Please call me or, if you prefer, e-mail." He gave a number and an e-mail address.

I created a contact for him and his number in the satphone directory, adding the e-mail in the notes field. Then I powered the phone down and jumped back to the lab.

Anyone can go online and get the current speed, position, and orbital parameters of most active satellites and spacecraft.

Once I was fully suited, Cory did this for USSPACECOM catalog number 53420, Ms. Matapang's errant satellite, *Tinkerbell*. He tapped the screen. "Perigee over the Pacific in ten minutes."

I held up my thumb and jumped.

After a ten-K equalization jump, I hit my circular orbit of the previous day, thinking about the turquoise dots of the Pacific atolls bordered by water shading into deep blue ocean.

Cory connected within thirty seconds.

"Apex One, your position?"

"Capcom, ten degrees, fifty-nine minutes thirty-eight point three four seconds north. One hundred sixty-nine degrees, forty-nine minutes fourteen point six four seconds east. Altitude three hundred forty-five point six two klicks. Velocity seven point seven two kps. Heading fifty-three point six degrees."

"Roger that, Apex One. We need you at seventeen degrees north and one hundred seventy-nine degrees west. That's twelve degrees farther to the east, copy?"

"Roger that." I concentrated on the GPS readout, visualizing the numbers that should change and the ones that shouldn't.

The call dropped, but I was farther east, and farther north, still at the same speed, heading, and altitude. The phone rang in my ears and I connected.

"Capcom?"

"No."

Mendez again.

"This is *not* a good time."

"You skipped a satellite or two there. What are you *doing?*"

I gritted my teeth. *None of your business.* "I can talk to you this afternoon but you have to keep my line clear. We're *working* here!"

"What time?"

"Four."

"My time zone?"

"Eastern, right?" Leesburg, Virginia he'd said the day before. "Yes. Do you need my number?"

"No!"

I hung up.

Cory rang in. "Apex One, it went to voice mail!"

"Sorry, Capcom. What's my next adjustment?"

"Drop one hundred klicks altitude. Increase speed to eight kps. Come right to forty-five point five degrees."

And so we went on.

We homed in. Going from adjusting degrees, to minutes, and then finally seconds, with further adjustments to velocity and heading.

Cory said, "It should be pretty much *right* there."

I scanned the sky behind me, in front of me, above me. "I'm not finding it." The sun was coming up in front of me with lots of glare, but it should have lit up the target, too.

Then I saw a wink, a tiny, brilliant flash of bluish white, but it was down, hiding against the ocean.

"Ah. There's something down . . . down and forward."

I jumped, keeping the velocity and heading. As I closed the distance, it went from being dot of reflected sunlight to a bluish speck, and, finally, to a slowly spinning rectangular box coated with solar panels on four sides, two antennae on the fifth, and a smaller cylinder and a grappling mechanism on the sixth side. Not counting the antennae, it was about the size of a small carry-on bag.

*Hello,* Tinkerbell.

I jumped within touching distance, but didn't—touch, that is.

It had been in orbit for twenty-five days and, unlike sweaty little me, it didn't have an active cooling system. On the plus side, it had just come out of the earth's shadow. Still, possible temperatures ranged from well below freezing to hotter than boiling water.

I took the infrared thermometer out of the Velcroed breast pocket of my Nomex coveralls. It was a cheap unit that I'd picked up at an auto parts store, designed to check engine block, exhaust, and radiator temperatures. We had no idea if it would survive vacuum, but it was cheap and its sensor range was between twice-boiling and forty below. I'd replaced the alkaline batteries with stainless steel-cased lithium ion cells, which were less likely to bulge or leak at low pressure. We didn't know, though, if there were any electrolytic capacitors in the circuit. Cory said that those had a tendency to pop in a vacuum.

I pointed it carefully at the satellite and pushed the button. The LCD display came on, but though I twisted it this way and that, I couldn't read it through the sun visor. I jumped to the far side of the unit, so the sun was at my back, lifted my visor a few inches, and did it again.

Four degrees below zero Celsius. Good. I put the thermometer away.

I was wearing Nomex insulated firefighter gloves over the suit. I took hold of the top and bottom edges, trying not to put pressure on the solar cells. I was half expecting this to be a struggle; that it would pull against my grip, suddenly lifting me into a higher orbit.

Silly.

Of course it didn't—I'd matched heading and velocity. If I just hung there, I was *already* headed out toward an apogee of eleven hundred kilometers, but we didn't want that.

"CapCom, Target acquired. Returning to base."

The instant I appeared in the lab, the solar panels went white with frost.

"Hope *that* doesn't hurt anything," Cory said.

I went through the checklist to depressurize the suit on my own while Cory used a Torx screwdriver to open the antennae end of the satellite. By the time I was out of the suit, he was reaching into the interior with a pair of insulated needle-nose pliers.

"There," he said. "Batteries disconnected. Hand me that tape." I looked over his shoulder as he used electrical tape to cover a multipin plug-in terminal on a bank of flat batteries mounted on a circuit board. "Powered down. Not transmitting. Not receiving."

Using a soft cloth, Cory carefully wiped beads of water off the solar panels.

"Maybe we should have waited until it was above freezing?" I said.

Cory shook his head. "The radiation exposure of this mission was less than fifteen minutes. That's a *good* thing."

Ms. Matapang's cubical was in the Munnerlyn Astronomical Laboratory and Space Engineering Building, an older two-story yellow-brick structure on the north side of campus dwarfed by a huge four-story parking garage on its east side.

I had changed out of the undersuit base layers into jeans, button-down, and a Stanford sweat shirt Joe had given me. I'd located this building before, but not her cubicle. Before I started looking, though, I heard her voice through an open door on the first floor.

"It had to be a collision! It wasn't low enough to be atmospheric drag. It was dead on track when it last passed over the multistatic array."

"But there's nothing in the database that even comes *close*," said a man's voice. "Nothing passed closer than eighty-five kilometers in that time frame."

The sign by the door said *AggieSat Lab*. I peered around the edge of the door frame. The room had three rows of tables in the middle, with computers and chairs. More tables lined the walls, some empty, some stacked with other equipment. To one side, two men and three women stood talking.

The younger of the two men—a student?—said, "Doesn't have to be in the catalog. A meteorite coming in at interplanetary speeds wouldn't be. It could be tiny, too."

The other man was older with a salt-and-pepper beard, and wore khaki slacks and a white dress shirt. "There's no debris. Something that fast would have smashed it to pieces. Sure, some of the debris would've reentered but we would have seen *some*."

I stepped into the room, pulling the rolling suitcase behind me. It clipped the door frame with a thump and all five of them turned toward me.

*Damn.*

I'd been hoping to talk to just her.

"Hi," I said.

The older man said, "Can we help you?"

"Looking for Ms. Matapang," I said, gesturing toward her.

Ms. Matapang narrowed her eyes as she looked at me. "I know you, I think. Where from?"

"I was at your talk last week, about *Tinkerbell*. At the Makers Club."

She nodded. "*That's* right. You were the one asking questions about orbital remediation. Funny you should come in right now. The satellite, uh, left orbit two hours ago."

"Yes." I took a deep breath and added, "I know."

I spun the suitcase so it was rolling in front of me and pushed it closer.

The older man said, "You know? How do you know?" He gestured toward my torso. "Were you tracking our beacon at Stanford?"

I looked down at my sweatshirt, then shook my head. Easier to show them. I bent down to unzip the suitcase. It was one of Mom's old bags and the zipper was sticky.

"This is Dr. Perez," said Matapang, tilting her head toward the older man.

The student who'd offered the meteor hypothesis said, "We didn't get its beacon on the last two orbits and it wasn't responding to our downlink commands. Dr. Perez had to ask Joint Space Operations to *look*."

I flipped the lid of the suitcase to the side and lifted out the top piece of foam padding.

They stared.

"We disconnected the battery," I said. "Didn't want to risk a short. And we retracted the antennas because," I gestured at the bag. "Suitcase."

I paused in case one of them wanted to say something but

they were still staring. The satellite may have started in this very room, but their minds still had it in orbit or burned to ions in the upper atmosphere. They hadn't caught up yet.

"We snagged it just out of eclipse; the exterior was four degrees below freezing. Some frost formed when we got it down, but we wiped off most of the moisture and put a fan on it to dry it. I hope there wasn't any water damage."

Instead of speaking, Ms. Matapang took three quick steps forward and dropped to her knees, all her attention on *Tinkerbell*.

"It must be the engineering prototype," said the Dr. Perez, but one of the women lifted her hand and pointed at one of the tables against the wall. I looked—there was another *Tinkerbell* on a stand, antennae deployed.

"A replica?" suggested the male student. "The plans *were* open sourced."

Ms. Matapang lifted it, handling it like I had, by the frame at the top and bottom. She hefted it. "It *feels* right. Put that foam there," she said, jerking her chin at a clear space on the closest table.

I stepped over and set the slab of foam down, then backed away, making room. She laid the satellite carefully down on one of its solar cell-covered sides, then leaned to the right and examined the bottom.

She pointed, and the others came forward, leaning in to look.

At my expression, she said, "We all signed it, preflight, permanent marker. It's faded, but the signatures are there."

"It could still be a copy," one of the girls said. "Jamie put a photo of that on his Facebook page."

The other girl said, "Not the whole thing. Only the corner with *his* name."

The male student said, "Maybe someone else posted the whole thing. A lot of people took pictures."

I went back to the suitcase and knelt to zip it closed.

Matapang swiveled to watch. "How did you get it?"

"Well, maybe I made a copy," I said, with a little smile.

She wasn't amused. "That *would* be impressive, but there's a micrometeorite impact *in the middle of my signature*. Besides, I assembled and took that thing apart about twenty times. I recognize tool scratches. *How* did you get it?"

I handed her a newly printed card.

---

**APEX ORBITAL**

Green Satellite Insertion and Retrieval
Packages to 50 kg
LEO to GEO, Polar to Equatorial
***We deliver!***

Info@ApexOrbital.com

---

She stared, then said, "What does that mean? 'Green?'"

"Well, our carbon footprint is pretty low, but besides that, we commit to removing three kilograms of orbital debris for every kilogram we put up."

She worked her jaw to say something, but nothing came out.

"We're just getting started. No charge for this retrieval. If you're interested in us putting it *back* in orbit, say, about eight hundred fifty kilometers up, and attached to a certain Delta second stage, we would be willing to do that, too."

"I don't believe—how much do you charge?"

"For LEO? That would be our KforK plan. One thousand dollars per kilo."

Dr. Perez snorted. "One thousand dollars per kilo? Impossible. That's less than half the Falcon Heavy price. *We* were piggybacking and it still cost us eighty K to get this into an orbit lower than we needed!"

"Expensive," I said. "I weighed *Tinkerbell*. Thirteen kilos, right? So, thirteen kilo-bucks. Or, if you'd be interested in barter, it happens we're in the market for three microsats destined for LEO, MEO, and geosynchronous. Nothing fancy. Solar, battery, repeating audio-message radio beacon somewhere in the five hundred milliwatt range. Don't need downlink or uplink. One year endurance."

Dr. Perez's eyes kept straying back to *Tinkerbell*. "I can't believe one thousand dollars a kilo."

I shrugged. "Well, as the card says, we do have a fifty-kilo upper limit. But all *our* insertions are low-gee. You don't need to vibrate test, just vacuum and temperature."

"Impossible!" Dr. Perez said.

I nodded, then glanced aside to Ms. Matapang and stage whispered, "We get that a *lot*."

I pointed at *Tinkerbell*. "Maybe you should download your GPS log. E-mail us if you want to talk."

Pulling the suitcase, I turned and walked through the door.

Dr. Perez walked after me, saying, "Wait a minute, young lady! You still need to explain how you got hold of our—"

I stepped out of sight, past the door frame, and jumped.

"Mendez."

I was sitting in the grass, out among Central Park's Great Lawn softball fields, far enough away from the surrounding Manhattan buildings so they wouldn't block the satellite signal.

"Good afternoon, Mr. Mendez. How's your day going?"

"I've had better," he said, somewhat bleakly. He paused. "You're actually on the ground, aren't you?"

"Yes. Sorry to hear your day is sucky. Anything I can do to help?"

"Give me five hours back."

"Five hours?"

That's how long I've had the air force in my hair. They want to talk with *you*."

*Ack.* In as light a voice as I could manage, I said, "You guys are really going to run through my phone minutes."

A different voice came on. Not deep, but firm. "This is General Lionel Sterling, Air Force Space Command. With whom am I speaking?" I could believe he was a general. He sounded like someone who gave orders all day long.

For a second I considered disconnecting, but we knew this would happen sooner or later.

"This is Apex One."

"Your call sign? I was hoping for your name."

I lay back on the grass and covered my eyes with my forearm. "Have you been bugging my calls, General? I didn't tell Mr. Mendez that."

"I have a recording of your communications from this morning."

*But not yesterday's?*

"Did you get a warrant?"

"The Defense Intelligence Agency did. The FISA court issued it immediately. National security and all that."

"National security? How do you figure?"

"You just took a satellite out of orbit."

"I returned it to its *owners*." I winced. I hadn't meant to give him that much. "It seemed better than letting it burn up in another dozen orbits or so."

I heard a hand cover the mouthpiece and indistinct words spoken briskly. Orders, I thought. Someone was probably calling Texas A&M right now.

"Did they arrange this with you?"

"We did it on spec," I said. "We're just starting to grow the business."

"*What* business?"

I hesitated. It wasn't like he wasn't going to hear about it once we started advertising.

"Apex Orbital. Packages up to fifty kilograms between LEO and GEO, polar to equatorial. Delivery *and* recovery." I was going to need a jingle if this kept up.

"Never heard of you."

"Didn't I say we've only just started? And you've heard of us *now*, haven't you?"

"I . . . suppose. Where are you launching from?"

I licked my lips. Eventually they'd figure out that I wasn't doing things *their* way. "We have an equatorial volcano island in the Pacific guarded by genetically engineered crab soldiers."

I think he might have actually laughed there but he turned it into a cough. "Really, where?"

I remained silent.

He continued. "I should let you know we tracked your orbit the day before yesterday. You flew directly over our multistatic radar fence in Texas and we got a very good read on your orbit, but you deorbited before coming around again." He paused to let me respond. When I didn't he said, "We know you're using some sort of stealth technology because the radar return was tiny, nowhere big enough for a capsule. You must've launched in West Texas or New Mexico, but your stealth worked even better on air-traffic radar."

I nearly burst out laughing, but managed to control myself. "So you can't detect our launch—that's, uh, good. The technology is working much better than we expected."

He cleared his throat. "Perhaps. Last week the Tethered Aerostat Radar System at Marfa picked up something odd."

I winced. I'd seen that blimp on a cord. They used it to do low-level radar surveillance of the Mexican border. Marfa was sixty miles north-northeast of the pit. I guess they'd seen me when I did my "launch" for Mom, Dad, and Cory.

Looked like they weren't getting my equalization jumps, though, several kilometers above that. Or, if they were, they were discounting the short, isolated blips as noise.

"What do you want, General?"

"We need to inspect your facilities and do security clearances on your staff."

"Why?"

"National security concerns. Safety concerns. Last thing we need is more orbital debris up there."

"Well, *that's* the truest thing you've said. We see debris remediation as a growth industry."

"*Where* are your facilities?"

"We really don't want any government contracts, General, so no thanks on the offer of an inspection."

"How old are you, young lady?"

Huh. Hadn't expected *that* question.

"Is that pertinent, General?" I paused, torn between discretion and pride. Pride won. "I'm the first teenager to orbit the earth. It's been *nice* talking to you."

"You need to cooperate with us!" It was not a request. I imagined his junior officers snapping to attention when he used that tone of voice. I nearly sat up, myself.

"Huh. And here I was thinking that I *don't*."

The tone of his voice changed, less barking, more conversational. "You *really* sent up two missions in two days?"

"What does your data tell you?"

"Oh, we think you were up there. We just don't know if you *stayed* up there both days."

"No. Two separate missions. Me, both times. We've also been up before, but those missions were suborbital."

*Now you're just bragging.*

"We can have Iridium terminate your satphone account." It was spoken like a suggestion—not *quite* a threat.

"I suppose you could. But do you really want to eliminate your best chance of tracking our orbital activity?" I heard him breathe in sharply, but when he didn't say anything, I added, "The satphone is really convenient, but it's not essential. It was more of a concession to my ground crew. Bunch of worry-warts."

"You clearly don't know what you're doing!"

I got mad, probably because he wasn't completely wrong.

"No, *you* don't know what I'm doing. That's what *really* bothers you." I took a breath to calm down. "Look, if you really plotted yesterday's orbit, you'll know I passed sixty kilometers under the ISS. I seriously considered dropping by, but it *was* my first orbit and all."

"Is that a threat?"

"God, no. Just wanted to say hi. New to the neighborhood and all that. Believe me, interfering with our space program is the last thing I want."

"Our? You're an American?"

Mom and Dad were both U.S. citizens, but I was born in Canada. Should be dual citizenship but my birth wasn't registered anywhere. I didn't want to get into the details, so I said, "It's the *International* Space Station, General. *Poneemaetsee*?"

"I *do* understand, barely. Your accent is awful."

"Better than my Chinese. May I please speak with Mr. Mendez?"

"What? Why?"

"I want to arrange for some more satphone minutes."

"Uh, I doubt that's his department."

"It's not a normal purchase. I suspect he'll consider it."

He put me on speaker.

"Hello."

"Hi, Mr. Mendez. I was wondering if you would talk to your management for me."

"What about?"

"I'd like to trade services for ongoing minutes."

"What kind of services?"

"To start, I can give you video inspections of your active satellites."

"Uh, we get good inspections through the air force. They give us images taken by their—" I heard General Sterling clear his throat meaningfully. "—facilities."

"Ah," I said. "Spy satellites, eh? Taken at orbital speeds from tens or hundreds of kilometers away? I can give you high-definition video taken from two meters—*all* surfaces. Just one such video should be worth a lifetime of phone minutes."

"Uh, if you can do that, can you put more units in orbit?" asked Mendez.

"Fifty kilos is my upper limit—you want to go modular on your units, we'll talk. But I *can* attach deorbiting devices to your nonfunctioning birds. Electrodynamic tethers or solid fuel rocket motors."

"You're kidding, right? I mean, how could you possibly do that?"

"Look, I tried to get a paper route instead, but the newspapers keep burning up on reentry. Talk to your guys, okay? I'll send you an inspection sample within the week."

General Sterling said, "Wai—" but I hung up.

Joe told me that the palm trees on Stanford's campus are Canary Island date palms, which he learned at freshman orientation.

They can be over thirty meters tall or they can be short, squat things that look like giant pineapples. It was one of these short ones that he was sitting under when I saw him outside of his dorm, Stern Hall. He had a book open and a pad of paper, but he was staring off into the distance, eyes unfocused. Three tall, stereotypically Californian blondes dressed for *warmer* weather walked past, swaying like something out of a music video.

I wished I were that tall.

Joe glanced at them and looked away, back into the distance, and I decided that maybe I was tall enough.

I checked in with Cory and filled him in about General Sterling of the Air Force Space Command. "I'm thinking we might want to move the working equipment out of here."

He frowned. "You think they might come here?"

"They might track the cell we're using for the ground station. They'll already have figured out which cell tower it went through. Fortunately there's probably half a million people in Palo Alto who could've connected to that tower. Still, if they start paring targets down by their technical expertise, you might show up in the list. Eventually they're going to get an image of the suit and, what, maybe two dozen people have published in the last decade on mechanical counterpressure suits? Combine the two and they might come knocking." I tapped the power supply we used to relax the suit. "I'm gonna need a portable one of these. Doable?"

Absently, Cory nodded. "Sure. We always planned for it to be part of the suit, anyway. Something with a vacuum safety, of course." But he wasn't letting go of the main thread of our conversation. "Are they going to arrest me?"

God, I hoped not. "What for? You just sold me a suit, that's all. You're not responsible for what I do with it, right?"

"What about my voice on the recorded call?"

I shrugged. "We'll see, but I've been thinking about that. My dad should probably take that part over. He's not exactly someone you *can* arrest. He can also move the base station all over the place, making it harder for them to zero in."

Cory looked a little hurt. "But I *liked* participating."

I wanted to hug him, but instead I said, "Oh, you will, Cory. You will." I pointed at the suit. "First things, first. You need to solve the closure problem. I know two more people who could get into your suit as it is, but it needs to work for *everyone*, right?"

He nodded seriously at that. "Yeah. Even if just to get one for myself." He hesitated. "If I had a suit, am I wrong in thinking you could get me up there?"

I looked away.

"What? You couldn't?"

"I could. But keep in mind, Cory, *you* can't jump away in a second, should something go wrong. If the suit fails and I'm not there to pull you away—"

He nodded. "Of course. That's how *most* of us have to deal with space. Believe me, I know. Why do you think I'm so pushy about redundancy? But you could get me up there? And back?"

I nodded.

He exhaled. "We need to get on this then. The applied-mathematics group I've been working with has created a computer model of the existing suit that's working really well. I mean accurate in the behavior we've seen and measured. This week we're running simulations on several anode/cathode flange designs and I ordered enough electro-active polymer for two suits." He held up crossed fingers. "That's taken over half your upfront funding. Did you mean it about paying for a suit? Cause, really, you ended up getting that a lot sooner than we both planned."

He was right. I promised him funding and that later, I'd also purchase a suit. "That's fair. Apex Orbital will be an income producer pretty quick."

"Okay, then. I need to hire some assistants."

I was a little surprised. "Grad students? You ready for them to start writing up your research?"

He winced. "Just hands, really, when I start wrapping the next suit. Some bright undergrad would be fine." He frowned. "We'd have to keep them out of the loop on your, uh, operations, I guess."

It was like microgravity; my stomach lurched, and my heart felt like it was pounding. There was some nausea, too.

Cory reached out and grabbed my arm, his face concerned. "You just went white as a sheet! Are you okay?" He steered me over to his office chair and I sank into it. "Do you want me to get you a drink?"

I waved my hand. "No. It's okay." I took several deep breaths.

Cory reached out with his foot and slid the trashcan closer, trying to be surreptitious about it.

"I'm not going to puke," I said. *Could I? Should I?* "Remember when I said I was out here in Palo Alto a lot?"

He nodded. "First time we met here? Though of course, *you'd* actually been in here before me."

"Well before you got this position I already had a friend on campus. He's an engineering freshman—thinking about aerospace or ocean engineering." I tapped my sternum. "He knows about me." I took another deep breath.

"You might give him a try."

"O . . . kay. I'll need more than just one, though, especially if he's a freshman. They hit them hard and he won't be able to work that many hours."

I nodded. "Okay. I've got one or two others. They're not local, but since they *also* know about me, transportation is not an issue. But they'll have to work weekends. Let me see if they're interested." I wrote Joe's e-mail on the lab's white board. "The Stanford freshman is Joe Trujeque. You can say I recommended him . . . but don't tell him I'm actively involved, okay?"

Cory frowned. "You want me to lie to him?"

"Ohhhh, just describe the job first and see if he's interested. If he is, then you can . . . tell him . . . I guess."

# NINETEEN

## Cent: How do you DO that?

At 1:30 P.M. I watched Ms. Matapang leave the Astronomy and Space Sciences Engineering building from the top deck of the huge parking garage next door. She walked east along University Drive, crossed with the light at College Main, and continued along Northgate until she reached the Dixie Chicken.

I didn't see anyone enter after her. No one had drifted along and loitered outside. It was the end of the lunch rush and most people were heading away, moving back onto campus.

I found her inside, seated alone at a table for two. I pulled out the chair across from her and sat down. She froze, a burger in her hands, her mouth open to take a bite.

"Don't let a fly land in there," I said.

She took the bite and began chewing. After a moment she said, "The air force took *Tinkerbell* away."

I tilted my head back and looked at the ceiling. "How am I supposed to put it back in orbit?"

She shrugged. "They *say* they'll bring it back." She dipped a French fry in ketchup and popped it in her mouth. "After they've finished their tests."

"What on Earth are they looking for?"

"Not on Earth. Radiation. Chemical traces."

"From being in orbit?"

"Oh, no. They believe *that* part. The logs, etcetera. Plus the amount of activated metal radiation jibes for that much time in orbit. They're looking for physical evidence of *your* spacecraft—especially the drive."

"Huh. What do they expect to find? Fibers from my seat covers?"

"Well, traces of fuel or oxidizer? Or combustion byproducts of same? One of them mentioned a NERVA drive. They figured that was the only way you could pop into orbit with such short turnaround."

"NERVA?" It sounded familiar, but I couldn't remember where I'd read or seen it.

"Nuclear Engine for Rocket Vehicle Application."

"Oh! The old fission-reactor-heats-up-reaction-mass idea! I guess *Tinkerbell* might see more radiation if that was what I was using. But that would be *crazy*! It's bad enough dealing with orbital radiation as it is. And wouldn't that be a *huge* amount of hot exhaust? I'd think that would light up every SBIRS launch-detection satellite on that side of the planet."

Matapang, having taken another bite of her burger, could only nod.

I felt odd asking this, like I was asking another girl what some guy had said about me, but I was curious how they were handling it. "What did the air force say about me?"

"I don't know what they're saying to Dr. Garcia. They certainly weren't volunteering anything to *me* about you. For the most part, they just ignored my questions." She grimaced. "They are treating me as a security risk, despite the fact that I'm a naturalized citizen. Guess they think I'm spying for the good ol' Republic of the Philippines." She lifted her beer as she said this. "Dr. Garcia isn't talking to me, either. I'm thinking my Ph.D. dissertation is about to go down the toilet."

"Really?"

"It's about deorbiting debris with electrostatic tethers. My paper is all math, but the proof was going to be in the pudding, and now the air force took away my pudding and my faculty advisor isn't answering my calls *or* e-mails." She took a healthy slug of her beer. "I don't normally drink, but today is an exception."

"I can still hook a tether to that Delta booster. You have a spare tether or do you want to wait for the air force to return *Tinkerbell*?"

She froze in the act of putting her beer down, saying carefully, "I'm not holding my breath, but . . . we can use the *Lost Boy*—the engineering prototype. It's identical to *Tinkerbell*. We ran all the same tests. It doesn't have any propellant in it, but if you can get it latched onto the Delta, we should be able to deploy the tether *and* track the beacon."

I nodded. "While I'm at it, I can get you some high-def video of the micrometeorite wear."

"Hi-def video? We were going for stills. You need too much bandwidth for video."

"Ah, yeah, but I don't have to worry about bandwidth."

She stared at me. "You do this and I'll move heaven and Earth to make your microsats."

I held out my hand.

She stared at it, then said, "Oh! Certainly." She shook it twice, firmly, formally. "It's a deal."

I took out my phone and looked at the calendar. "How does tomorrow work for you? About nine A.M.?"

She blinked. "For what? To pick up *Lost Boy*?"

I smiled. "Yes. Make sure it's booted and charged up. Leave the antenna deployed. Don't tell anyone, okay? Not until after I've picked it up."

I could see doubt creeping back into her face. "That's nine A.M. In the AggieSat Lab?"

I punched the appointment in, then stood up and nodded firmly. "Nine."

I went out the back door, threaded my way between the mostly empty outside tables, and then jumped away from between two SUVs in the tiny parking lot.

There were a lot of suitable cameras, but very few suitable camera cases. We chose a camera designed for sports, capturing up to 120 frames per second at 720 pixels or up to 48 frames per second at 1440 pixel. We bought it with a sixty-four giga-byte storage card and a plastic case good to sixty-nine meters underwater.

And that was the problem.

Underwater cases are good for keeping pressure *out*, not so much for keeping it *in*. They usually *depend* on external pressure to push the sealing surfaces together.

Cory solved it, though, by designing, making, and then installing a set of clamps for the door's perimeter, providing the external pressure for the seals.

The next morning, after I went through my nitrogen-purge prebreathe and suited up, I took the case all the way to orbit, a pressure gauge where the camera would normally go. Fifteen minutes later it was still holding at 14.7 psi. I came back down and Dad powered up the camera and switched it to "record," then sealed it in the case. He handed it to Cory, who positioned it on the bracket attached to my chest harness and snapped it home.

I twisted my torso left and right, watching the camera track with it. I held up my thumb and forefinger in an okay sign.

Cory nodded and said loudly, "Looks good!"

For today's mission, Dad had a workstation set up in an un-tenanted office suite in Cincinnati, using the adjoining firm's WiFi. He stood to the side with our "base station" cell phone in his hand, poised on the balls of his feet.

When I held up my thumb, he nodded, then vanished.

I appeared in the AggieSat Lab in College Station. Matapang was standing at the door, looking down the hallway. She didn't see me appear. The computers on the central table had been shifted to one end, clearing a space for the satellite, where it rested across two strips of foam. It looked like *Tinkerbell*, but when I glanced at the bottom, it only had one signature—Matapang's.

I banged my gloved and suited hands together and she jumped, jerking her head around.

*Please don't faint. Please don't faint.*

She didn't, but she did end up sitting on the floor, her mouth open. I walked to the white board and uncapped the marker there. The felt tip was dried out, but it still made faint letters when I wrote, "good 2 go?"

Her jaw worked, but I didn't hear anything. To be honest, I don't think she managed any words.

I tapped the board, by my question. She managed a jerky nod. Below, I wrote, "Cell phone call 5-10 min."

She wasn't looking at the board. She was studying my suit, the harness, the connections.

*Typical engineer.*

Again I tapped the board and wrote, "OK?"

She managed a jerky nod, reached in her pocket, and held up her cell phone.

I gave her a thumbs up, walked to *Lost Boy*, and picked it up by the ends.

She started to climb to her feet, saying something, but I didn't hear it and I was gone, before she stood all the way up.

*Please don't faint.*

My first stop was the "Yuri" orbit, 350 kilometers over the Marshall Islands, local dawn, headed for Hawaii. The phone rang immediately. I carefully released *Lost Boy*, letting it float in front of me while I hit the button.

"Apex One here. Do you read, Capcom?"

Dad's voice said, "I read. Do you have the package?"

"Roger that, Capcom. Let's do this thing."

When I'd rendezvoused with *Tinkerbell*, we'd done it in stages, adjusting location, velocities, and headings until I'd gotten a visual. This time, Dad gave me the whole set of numbers: longitude, latitude, heading, speed, altitude, *and* a time. From what I could tell, the Delta second stage was coming over northeastern Russia and headed toward Peru. It was in an orbit several hundred kilometers higher and at a right angle to mine.

I took hold of *Lost Boy* and held my wrist so I could see the GPS screen. Dad's voice counted down to zero and—

I was much higher, 623 kilometers above sea level. The view

of Earth was different, still huge, still gorgeous, but more of a sphere. There was a coast below me and I was headed out to sea, but it took me a moment to realize it was the Sea of Okhotsk and Japan would be south.

The phone rang. I connected.

"Apex One."

"Capcom. Do you see it?"

Oh, crap. I'd been looking at the scenery again. I jumped in place, but turned 180 degrees, face out to the black. "Read me the present track, Capcom?"

He read out the numbers. My altitude and speed and heading were good, but the longitude was off by three seconds. I looked west.

"Got it, Capcom."

It was a lot easier to spot than *Tinkerbell* had been, but then it was over nineteen feet long and eight feet in diameter. The bell of the AJ-10 rocket motor was dark, a quarter of the overall length sticking down from a clump of pumps and tanks. Everything else—the support trusses, the mating collar for the first stage, and the payload collar—was white, catching the rising sun. I closed on it in a series of short jumps, towing *Lost Boy*.

"Capcom, connect to the client, please."

Dad used the cell phone's conference feature to call Ms. Matapang. By arrangement, he didn't talk. It rang three times before she answered.

"Hello?"

"Hello, Ms. Matapang. This is Apex One. I have your package ready for delivery."

"Uh, what does that mean? Are you about to launch?"

"I'm about to connect *Lost Boy* to the Delta-K booster. Is there anything special I should know?"

"Uh. Is this for real? I know you got hold of *Tinkerbell*, but *how* can you possibly be at the Delta II second stage?"

"I've got another satellite rendezvous after this. Do you want us to latch it, or not?"

"Uh, *yes*! Just shove the jaws onto any of the trusses. Stay away from the pumps though."

"Certainly."

The booster hung in front of me, scary big, and I felt like a swimmer floating next to a humpback whale. The "jaws" were two projecting rails with a wire across the bottom. When I pushed it onto the truss and the pipe hit the trip wire, two spring hooks sprang across from each rail, capturing the truss redundantly.

I unsnapped the camera from its mount and while I floated close to *Lost Boy* and the truss assembly of the Delta-K booster, I held the case out at arm's length and pointed the lens back toward my sun-visored helmet, then, for good measure, I imaged the GPS readout on my wrist.

"It's engaged, Ms. Matapang. Do you want me to release the tether?"

"Uh, no. It's not just a test of the tether, but our deploying mechanism, too. If *you* do it, it won't be a good test. Uh, I called up the booster's track—where are you now?"

"If you called it up, you *know* where I am."

"Humor me?"

"I just passed over that string of islands that goes north from Hokkaido up to Kamchatka. My altitude is six hundred twenty-three kilometers, heading one hundred sixty-nine degrees, forty-eight to thirty-six north, one hundred fifty-four to thirty-three east. My velocity is seven point six six kps. My camera is on. I was hoping to record the deployment of your tether for you."

"Oh." Dead air for a moment. "The Kuril Islands, right. It's still hard to take in. When you vanished in the lab . . . well, I thought I was hallucinating. But I see why Dr. Garcia never caught up with you when you returned *Tinkerbell*. And that suit, are you—"

"Stop." I didn't want her speculating about the suit and my lack of a spacecraft on a line bugged by the Defense Intelligence Agency. "When can you deploy the tether?"

"Ten minutes. We'll be line of sight then."

"It will take a *lot* longer than that before Texas clears horizon!"

"We've got Internet access to a transceiver at the University of Hawaii."

"Ah." That made more sense. "I can chill for ten."

"It won't mess up your next rendezvous?"

"Not an issue. I'm going to take some video of the booster while I'm waiting. Uh, why didn't you want me to hook onto any of the pumps?"

"The leftover fuel is hypergolic."

"Pardon?"

"If the Aerozine 50 fuel touches any of the dinitrogen tetroxide oxidizer, it will ignite. Makes for simple motors that can be stopped and started, but that's why they want to deorbit these guys. If the tanks deteriorate, the fuel can explode on its own, creating more debris *without* having to collide with anything else."

"Oh, really?" I eyed the booster, nervously.

"Really, really," she said. "So *don't* bump it."

"Roger that. Apex One out."

I disconnected and, as I waited for Dad to call me back, I took video of the booster, giving myself very slight relative velocity down its various sides. On the shadowed side, it was barely visible, lit by reflected earthlight, but I was not at all tempted to wrestle the booster's dark side around for better-lit shots. As soon as I'd imaged each side and both ends, I backed a hundred meters away, down orbit.

The phone rang.

"Apex One."

"This is General Sterling."

I just groaned.

"You did it again, didn't you? How many launches is that?"

"A bit *busy*! What do you want?"

"What are you doing?" I guess he realized how inane that sounded because he immediately modified it to, "What operations are you conducting?"

"You're the one with the phone tap. You *know* what I'm doing."

"It's not a live feed. They give me recordings later. The Iridium Network Center texted me you were back in orbit."

"Huh." It sounded like the truth. I giggled.

"What's so amusing?" He sounded annoyed.

"Laughing at myself, General. Not at you."

"Oh?"

"You have kids, General?"

He paused, then slowly said, "I do. Grown, now."

"How self-centered were they when they were my age?"

That surprised a laugh out of him.

"My mom says it's normal, but when I realized you weren't spending all your time listening in on my phone calls, I had to laugh at myself. It's not always about *me*, is it?"

"Hmmm. Well, monitoring your, uh, activities is actually interfering with my regular duties. So, what are you doing over the Pacific?"

"I just attached a nanosatellite to NORAD two six six two three, the Delta-K booster from the 2000 launch. The Aggies will take it from here, deploying a tether to bring it down over the next few months."

I checked the time on the GPS. Eight or nine minutes had passed since talking to Matapang. I was about fifty meters above the booster, maintaining a good camera angle on the attached satellite.

"We brought their unit in for analysis."

"Yes. You did. I put their engineering prototype up."

"Oh, really? Dr. Garcia mentioned you offered a launch."

"We don't offer launches. We offer *deliveries*."

He cleared his throat. "Well, Dr. Garcia certainly didn't report commissioning a *delivery*."

"*He* didn't, but if he would answer his grad student's e-mails, he might be aware of these things." Enough about Dr. Garcia. "I'm very interested in seeing how this tether works. It's quite simple for me to add tethers to the multi-ton debris. It's too big for me to deorbit otherwise. Any of *your* old birds need retrieving?"

The general cleared his throat. "Is that a serious offer?"

"We're in the biz, remember?"

"I thought you said you weren't interested in government contracts?"

That was right, I had. "Ah. Well, you're right. But we *are* committed to remediating three kilos for every kilo we put in orbit. We just put a seventeen-kilo satellite up, so we need to get fifty-one kilos down."

"You don't count the Delta-K booster? What is that, seven tons?"

"It's not down yet so, no. I'll deorbit at least fifty-one kilos today."

"Don't you *plan* this stuff ahead of time?"

"Oh, I have a target, just wondered if you had anything you wanted to offer instead."

"Surely it matters what orbit it's in?"

"Only altitude, really. Promised my ground crew I would stay inside the Van Allen belts, and I'm avoiding the South Atlantic Anomaly. Oops. Excuse me."

A hundred meters away, a piece of stainless steel about the size and shape of a two-quart flowerpot kicked off the end of *Lost Boy* and was moving briskly away, trailing a barely visible silver ribbon. I jumped closer, holding my hands clear of the camera. From only a few meters, the ribbon was more substantial than it had first seemed, composed of multiple strands of aluminum wire, loosely cross woven with Teflon.

I gave myself some velocity down the length of the tether, catching up with the "flowerpot." It was spinning on its axis, unwinding the tether and gyro-stabilizing the spool/terminator. When I looked down the length of the tether I could see it was developing a gentle curve as the spool responded to the local gravity gradient, bending slowly toward Earth.

"AggieSat Lab deployed the tether and I needed to get some video. It's looking good. So, any thoughts on an air force remediation target before I go to my next rendezvous?"

I heard him lick his lips. "If you're serious, there's a chunk of debris from the 2007 Chinese antisatellite test that has caused ISS evasion maneuvers several times in the past few years and will again in a few months."

I looked at the Delta-K booster. "Doesn't have a bunch of hypergolic fuel on it, does it?"

"Onboard fuel was nitrogen gas but even that probably didn't survive the impact. It hit head on at over eight kps. More debris than even the Iridium-Kosmos collision."

"I know. How big is the piece you want me to get?"

"It's a compact mass about fifty centimeters across."

"Half a meter? What kind of closing velocities—for the ISS that is?"

"Well, depending on the crossing angle—nine to eleven kps."

"Whoa." That was booking. I'd read that the impact of a ten centimeter object at ten kilometers per second was the equivalent of twenty-two sticks of dynamite. This would be more like a bunker buster. "What is it?"

"Could be any of a number of things. NiCad batteries. The reaction wheels. The nitrogen tank. One of the two onboard radiometers."

Half a meter was about the size of *Tinkerbell* and that had been a pain to locate. "How bright is it—high albedo?"

I heard him ask somebody off to the side. The answer didn't come back very quickly and he said, "One second. Looking it up."

I took some more video of the tether deploying. The curve was even more pronounced, now.

General Sterling came back. "Not as bright as some, but we've tracked it optically. Shows up fine on radar."

*I don't* have *radar*. I'd really have to look into that.

I wondered if doing this would buy more cooperation from them. "I might need some active tracking input to locate that. Are you still in Leesburg?"

"No. I'm back in my office in Colorado."

"Ah. So, e-mail a phone number where we can call you, okay? Info at apexorbital dot com. I've got this thing to do, but I should be able to call you back in ten or twenty minutes."

"What kind of thing?"

"Inspection video, remember? You were there when I made the offer."

"The Iridium bird? Which one?"

I disconnected.

Dad was a bit upset. "I've been calling forever!"

"Sorry. It's that air force general. You told me to be polite, remember?"

"Politely hang up, next time! Thought you were *dead*."

"Sorry. I need the setup for Iridium four."

Iridium birds four through eight all launched aboard the same rocket, a Delta II from Vandenberg in May of 1997. These were the first Iridium satellites in orbit. One through three were prototype test units that never launched.

Dad read off the coordinates, bearing, altitude, and the speed, then added, "Northern Russia, headed for Mongolia, China, and Thailand. Mark in twenty seconds."

The Iridium sats are triangular prisms a meter on a side and over four meters long. They orbit perpendicular to the earth's surface, a double set of solar panel wings on the end away, and four microwave horn-gateway antennae for ground stations pointing down from the other end. Just above the gateway antennae, another set of flat-plate slotted array antennae point sideways, cross linking with the other satellites. Then, above that, three flat-panel antennae, each about the size and shape of a standard door, lean out from the sides of the prism and communicate with subscriber handsets over seven hundred kilometers below.

Well, not *all* of the handsets were that far away.

After my jump, I was still thirty kilometers distant, but my target was easy to see. Those big, flat, door-shaped antennae catch sunlight like nobody's business.

My seventy-eight-hundred-kilometer jump from the Delta booster had dropped the call, of course. I waited a few minutes, seeing if Dad could connect. When the phone didn't ring, I closed in on the satellite in a series of jumps. The phone rang while I was still a kilometer away.

"Apex One."

"Capcom. You okay?"

"Just fine. Did it go to voice mail?"

"Yeah," he said. "You take another call?"

"No. Being this high, and away from the bird, I think I was

outside the broadcast cone. I'm *still* probably outside the cone, but I'm only a klick away, so we're probably getting side lobe leakage."

"Right. Get your vids. I'll be happier when you're down."

"About that. There should be an e-mail in the Apex Orbital account. Can you pull it up while I get the inspection video?"

I was done with the overall survey in two minutes. "Capcom, there's some wear and tear, here. Please connect me to Mark Mendez at Iridium."

"Connecting."

Mark Mendez answered. "Mendez"

"Hey, Apex One calling."

Sharp intake of breath. "What's with this number? That's not the handset."

"Calling through my ground crew, Mr. Mendez. I *am* using the handset."

"Boy howdy, are you ever. You're on number four but *there's no Doppler shift! HOW CLOSE ARE YOU?*"

"Wow. You totes need to chill. Why do you think I'm calling you?"

"Can you see it?"

"Dude, I'm three meters away. Listen, you have a few micrometeorite impacts on your solar panels and several on those big flat antennae—what do you call them?"

"The L-band phased arrays? We call them MMAs. Main Mission Antennas. You know, most people say antennas, not 'antennae.' Not that it's wrong."

"Sue me. Reason I called is you have this tear in one of those flat cross-link antennae—antennas. Something punched through it pretty good."

"I'll bet. Happened back in 2004. Rotated the unit and perturbed the orbit. It was offline for six hours while we moved it back and reoriented it. Amazingly, that antenna still works, but its signal strength is a third the others. That bird is scheduled for replacement with an Iridium NEXT unit in two years."

"Okay. I'm going to spend some extra footage on the impact. Anything particular you want me to look at?"

"Um, the analysis team always wondered why there wasn't more damage further inboard. Any sign of impacts behind the antenna?"

"No, because it's ripped *outward*. From the angle I'd say that whatever hit it travelled diagonally across the face of the MMA above and just caught the edge of the aluminum plate. It didn't hit anything else."

"Ah. One second." I heard him talking with somebody else, quick sentences back and forth, but couldn't make out the words. When he came back, he said, "One of the downlink horns is mounted right below the torn antenna. Any sign of damage there?"

"I'll look."

"Wait! What do you mean, you'll look? You aren't using propellant near the antennas are you? Are you in danger of colliding with it?"

"I'm—" How to say this without giving away too much? "—EVA. Our spacecraft—" my *nonexistent* spacecraft "—is nowhere near the satellite. I can assure you there is no propellant hitting your bird."

I unclipped the camera and jumped closer, but I avoided floating directly in front of the microwave antenna. "Did you hear from your management about my request?"

"They're still waiting for the air force to get back on that."

"What does the air force have to do with it?"

"DoD is still our biggest customer, you know? And you weren't very cooperative that last call."

"Oh."

"At least they haven't told us to shut down your account."

"Hmph. See you." I disconnected.

I spent another thirty seconds filming the impact site from different angles, making sure I got the underside of the downlink horn Mendez had asked about. Last, I held out the camera to take another selfie, then moved well away from the microwave horns, but perpendicular to one of the MMAs.

Dad reconnected. "So, I've got an e-mail from Sterling. It says, 'My direct number.' What's that about?"

"A favor. I asked if there was anything the air force needed to have pulled from orbit. There's a piece of debris that periodically passes close to the ISS."

"You want to do a favor for the air force? What are they going to do for *us*?"

"Da—Capcom, it's the International Space Station!"

Shit. Needed to be careful. Nearly said "Dad."

"Please connect us."

"What? From *this* phone?"

"He already has that number, remember? Phone tap?"

I heard Dad exhale. I bet his jaw was jutting forward the way it does when he's feeling stressed, but he kept it together. Guess he didn't want to argue in front of an audience. "Connecting."

General Sterling answered.

"Sterling." His voice sounded intent, so I think he recognized the number.

"Apex One, General. Can you give me the rough coordinates for your problem debris?"

"I can. Do you want the two-line element set?"

"The NORAD ID will do just fine."

"Three zero six nine two."

"Capcom?"

After a second, Dad said, "Coming up from Antarctica to Australia. Altitude is four hundred seventy-two kilometers. Bearing three hundred thirty-three degrees at seven point eight two kps. Coordinates sixty seconds out are—" He read them off.

"General, call me direct, after the break."

Dad began counting down and I concentrated on the numbers.

I was in eclipse, dark, barely able to make out anything. When I flipped up my visor, I could see the lights of Tasmania off to the east. The stars were amazing, but I hoped the target wasn't above me. I doubted I'd be able to see it against *that* canvas.

The phone rang.

"Apex One."

It was Sterling. "How do you *do* that?"

"How are you tracking me?"

"I'm not. I get texts from Iridium. Every time you connect to a new bird, they tell me, and where that bird is. That is, when it's a bird that's not contiguous with others."

Well, at least I knew how to operate in space without letting him know—turn that damn phone off.

General Sterling continued. "In two minutes, though, I can get active laser tracking from Mount Stromlo near Canberra—accurate within one meter."

"Uh, is that safe? I mean, for me?"

"Eye safe, you mean? Yes. Picosecond pulses."

I flipped in place to put my back toward the earth, anyway. Lasers? *Could they target me with a weapons-grade laser?*

Someone was talking in the background, feeding General Sterling information. To me, he said, "We've got two objects. We're pretty sure we know which one is the debris. You've got laser stealth, too? Your signature is *tiny*, nearly as small as the target."

He was getting size info—that *was* accurate tracking. "Our cloaking department will be pleased. *Assuming* I'm the second object, where is the debris?"

Sterling said, "Thirty-one klicks northwest, and one klick higher. Speed is close. Heading is diverging slightly. You're heading point three degrees more north than it is."

I jumped, first higher, then northwest.

Someone in the same room as the general swore loud enough that I heard it.

I heard General Sterling say, "If she can move halfway across the globe in seconds, you shouldn't be surprised at twenty-eight klicks." He kept feeding me info. "Two klicks away, still diverging west. Altitude close."

I jumped again.

"Five hundred meters north. Less divergence."

I jumped again.

"Ten meters west of you. It's reading higher by a few meters."

I couldn't see light reflecting off of it, but I was finally close enough that I could see stars winking off and back on as it passed in front of them.

I jumped again.

"We're not seeing any separation," Sterling said.

It was a hunk of junk—like something torn out of the middle of a commercial copier, or any other large electronic appliance, except with more gold plating. It was tumbling slowly.

I didn't have the IR thermometer with me. I held my gloved hand to it but it didn't feel cold or hot through the suit or the Nomex glove as the surface slid across my fingertips. It had been in shadow for a bit, and, at this altitude, it spent a decent amount of time shadowed.

I grabbed it carefully, trying to avoid the jagged bits, and, as its rotation slowed, I began rotating.

"I've got it, General."

"What are you—"

I jumped.

# TWENTY

## Davy: Guilty Thoughts

"What is it?" Davy asked.

He'd just returned to Cory's lab from Cincinnati, his computer under his arm.

Cent had removed her helmet and life-support backpack but still wore the MCP suit and her off-white Nomex coveralls. She was looking over Cory's shoulder as he crouched on the floor examining a hunk of metal that had been ripped forcibly from other pieces of metal. Most of it was shiny silver, but there were sheets of gold-colored foil, wires, tubes, and screw heads.

It was sitting on a bathroom scale.

Davy stepped forward to get a better look. He made out printing in Chinese.

"We think it's a scanning radiometer, but it's pretty smashed up," said Cent.

"What's a radiometer?"

Cory answered. "Like a camera for detecting specific frequencies of light. There were two on Fengyun 1C used to gather atmospheric data for weather forecasting."

"It's one hundred thirty pounds, eh?" Cent said, reading the scale. "What is that, fifty-five kilos?"

Cory stared off into the distance for a second. "About sixty-one point three-ish. How fast a collision?"

"He said somewhere between nine and eleven kps."

Cory stood up and scribbled on the board, muttering, "One half the mass times the square of the velocity. Split the difference, call it ten kps." He wrote down *3,065* and then began adding zeros. He stopped at six. "Whoa. *3,065* megajoules."

Davy said, "Give me a clue. What are we talking? A car wreck? A train collision?"

Cory bit his lower lip. "Kilos of TNT?"

Davy nodded. "That'll help.

"About four point six megajoules per kilo. So—"

Cent had grabbed the calculator off of the bench. "Six hundred and sixty-six point six kilos of TNT. Two thirds a kiloton."

Cory nodded. "To be avoided at all costs."

Davy gestured at the object. "What are you going to do with it?"

Cent said, "I think we should deliver it to General Sterling."

Cory turned his head and stared at her. "You gave *Tinkerbell* back to the people who made it. Shouldn't this go back to the Chinese?"

Cent shook her head. "I could maybe see doing that if they hadn't deliberately destroyed it for their antisat test. I think it might be a good thing if the air force saw we were *useful*, you know? If they chill, Iridium might chill. Would help if they weren't actively against us."

"I tried that with the NSA. It didn't exactly work out."

Cent looked at him, frowning. "Well . . . I don't really need the ground communication. If they tell Iridium to cut the account I can do my stuff without ground-to-orbit chatter."

Davy winced. "Okay. You win. Where is the general?"

"He's attached to USAF Space Command headquarters, Peterson Air Force Base, Colorado Springs. With NORAD and the 21st Space Wing," said Cent. "I looked it up."

Davy nodded. "I'll do it."

Cent squinted at him. "You sure? I don't have a site, myself, but I was considering dropping in from above."

Davy rolled his eyes. "Oh, great. You want to show up on the radar on a ballistic heading into *NORAD's* headquarters? You don't see the problem with that?"

Cent giggled. "Well, I guess you're right. And I do have a bunch of video to edit."

Cory provided a shipping tag and some tape. Cent, whose handwriting was light-years more legible than Davy's, wrote "Brig. Gen. Lionel Sterling, USAF Space Command, Peterson AFB. Compliments of Apex Orbital Services."

"Where will you leave it?" said Cent.

Davy shook his head. "I would put it in his office, but that would just make them nervous. Better I leave it outside their security perimeter."

Cent blinked. "Riiiiiiight. Don't make them nervous. We're an asset, not the enemy."

Davy felt his lower jaw projecting and his eyes narrowing.

Cent saw it. "What? What did I say?"

"Asset."

Cent's forehead furrowed. "Yeah?"

"I was an NSA asset." He tapped his left collarbone.

Cent made an "o" shape with her mouth. "Right. Keep them at arm's length? And by arm's length we mean miles away, right?"

Davy nodded, but he wasn't particularly happy about it. He was seeing all sorts of scenarios. Millie would call it engaging his "hyper-paranoid" mode. But she would also say, *Just because you're paranoid doesn't mean they aren't out to get you.* "Miles. Going forward, we're going to need a way to screen your, uh, packages. The packages you're going to deliver to orbit, yes?"

Cent asked, "For? . . ."

"Well, bombs for one thing."

Cory, using a cable tie to connect the tag to an intact electrical lead running between the radiometer and a bus connector, jerked his head up. "Bombs?"

"Or gas dispensers. Or Tasers. Contact drugs. Poisons."

Cory said, "You're kidding." He looked from Cent to Davy. "You're *not* kidding."

Cent shrugged. "I told you we have enemies. We need to move operations away from your lab, for sure. Besides, you have the suits to work on, yeah?"

Cory stared at her for a moment before he nodded.

Cent glanced sideways at Davy and then said lightly, "You hear anything about the suit-tech position?"

Cory answered, "He's coming in for an interview this afternoon."

Cent licked her lips. "Ah. Good." She glanced at her father and went bright red.

Davy abruptly stopped thinking about bombs and other satellite-shaped booby traps. "Are you blushing?"

She raised her eyebrows and pointedly said nothing.

Cory was looking at her, too. "Is there something I should know, for the interview?"

Cent shook her head. When Davy kept staring at her she said, "It's Joe, okay? I asked him to try Joe."

Davy nodded slowly. "Oh. Okay. You embarrassed about getting your boyfriend a job? Dreadful partisanship and all that."

She shrugged.

Davy said to Cory, "He's really smart. *I'd* give him a reference."

Cent pointed at the radiometer. "If you've got this, I've got some video to edit."

Davy nodded and she vanished.


Davy had a jump site for the Broadmoor hotel, a five-star hotel in Colorado Springs where Millie had attended a high-end donor conference on NGO relief work. He liked the restaurants, eighteen of 'em, and had been back often enough that he didn't have to review the video reminders.

He took a taxi from The Broadmoor to the Airport Value Inn and Suites and walked six hundred feet over to the Dairy Queen on Peterson Boulevard. He ate a dip cone and scoped out the main gate of the air force base.

After dark, he returned, appearing in the stand of bristlecone pines to the northwest of the gate and easing the chunk of debris to the pine-needle-covered ground.

There were two air police on duty at the gatehouse, both inside during lulls in the traffic.

A car turned, came down the off-ramp of US-24, and merged onto the boulevard. It slowed below the speed limit, and then nearly stopped before pulling up tentatively to the gatehouse. The car window rolled down as the first guard stepped up to the car, then turned her head to say something over her shoulder. The second guard stepped out and began gesturing, pointing back north and then west.

Davy jumped the piece of debris to the interior of the guard house and eased it down to the floor. He was back in the trees before the guards finished their directions and the car made a U-turn around the gatehouse and headed back up US-24.

As soon as the guards returned to the gatehouse, they popped back out. One of them did a quick search around the perimeter of the building, and the other walked farther out. He pulled out his flashlight and shone it around, but the mercury lights around the gate area were so bright, it made little difference. The guards met back by the door and conferred, then one stood outside while the other went in and picked up a phone.

Davy waited until the two air police units pulled up before jumping away.

*Well, at least they didn't call the bomb squad.*

There were four extra people in Samantha's room and two of them were swearing.

Davy stuck his head in, alarmed.

"Can I help?"

He couldn't see Samantha's head and shoulders past Bea, the tall health aid, and Seeana. Jeline was on the other side of the bed and Millie stood next to her, holding Samantha's hand.

Millie turned to Davy, her eyes wide, and she shook her head sharply.

Davy retreated.

He was staring blankly into the refrigerator when Millie joined him twenty minutes later.

"Either get something out or shut it," she said. "You're as bad as Cent."

He blinked, then pushed the door shut and raised his eyebrows.

"Her oxygenation was down into the eighties. We had to put her on the positive-pressure ventilator, but there was also some dry-mucous issues—some choking. Selena suctioned it out."

"Oh." He pulled her into a hug. "Scary?"

He felt the catch in her voice, but she continued calmly. "It was scary for *me*. Seeana took it in stride. Even Mom took it in stride. I'm the one who isn't used to it." She buried her face in his neck, then stepped away. "Dammit! We were supposed to be doing physical therapy by now! We can't improve her muscle tone because of the breathing and we can't improve her breathing because of the muscle tone."

She crossed her arms and her shoulders rolled forward, curling in on herself.

Davy filled the kettle.

"Second thoughts?"

She breathed in sharply through her nose. "*Guilty* thoughts. Not sure this would be happening if we hadn't moved her."

"You can't know that," Davy said.

Millie just shook her head.

Davy continued, "What you *do* know is that she chose to try this. To have some time with you and Cent."

Millie blinked back tears. "*And* you. You always leave out you."

Davy shrugged, uncomfortable, as always, with the notion of his extended family. It wasn't that he didn't appreciate them, but he was afraid they might suffer, that his enemies might use Millie's family to get at him. *Ah. I guess more than one of us has* guilty *thoughts.*

He got down the mugs.

# TWENTY-ONE

## Cent: What the HELL do I call you?

Tara designed a logo for Apex Orbital Services and, once she roughed it out, Jade took over, refining it into a sleek and polished graphic. The *A* in Apex was like mountain peak and an orbital ellipse encircled the entire word, broken only by a satellite icon floating above the *E*.

I created an animated version for the videos. Each opened with a thin slice of Earth arcing down across the top of the screen against the black of space. The word Apex part of the logo appeared, white; then the satellite icon popped into existence and orbited the letters, drawing the ellipse all the way around to its final position. To finish, the words "Orbital Services" faded in below, with our e-mail address below that.

Ms. Matapang's video showed my approach to the Delta-K booster, the latching of the unit to the truss, and my selfie shot with the GPS readout. I jump-cut to the inspection passes of the Delta-K booster, then to the moment when the tether deployed and unspooled. I particularly liked the last shot, a view from beyond the "flower pot," with the completely deployed tether curving off to the booster a half kilometer away.

For good measure, I repeated the logo animation at the end.

For Mendez at Iridium Communications I put in my approach to Iridium 4, the inspection passes, the close up of the cross-link antenna damage, and finally my selfie. Like the other video, the logo animation started and finished the file.

I put them both on our Singapore-based web server in their full, high-definition glory, then sent e-mails off to Matapang and Mendez with secure links to the video so they could download them.

I showed Mom and Dad the unedited video on my laptop, seated between them on the big couch downstairs.

This video started in Cory's lab and included my visit to the AggieSat Lab to pick up *Lost Boy*. When I clapped my hands to get Matapang's attention, her pratfall—dropping to the floor and ending up seated with her back to the door frame—was dead center on the screen.

"Did she get hurt?" Mom asked.

"Oh, no," I said. "Talked to her on the phone five minutes later. She was fine." *I hope.* For all I knew she took the call from the floor. No—she mentioned calling up the track of the Delta-K. Doubt she did *that* from the floor.

Once the video moved into space they both leaned closer, watching intently while I narrated. They watched all the way to the end, including the last bit where I strained to lower the suddenly heavy Fengyung debris to the lab floor before opening the camera case and powering down.

At the end, Mom's eyes were wide. "That . . . that is a good camera. Does it really look like that? The earth, the sky?"

"This is a good camera but in person it's better . . . it's *much* better."

"I'd like to see that someday."

"Mom, you could see it *tomorrow*."

Mom smiled. "Not just yet. Grandmother needs—well, *I* need to be with your grandmother."

I pointed at the screen. "Do you think she'd like to see this?" I said.

Mom and Dad exchanged glances and their faces set.

"Is she all right?" I said.

Mom held her hand out, rocked it side to side. "We had to put her on a ventilator. I'm hoping we can take her off of it soon. At the very least, we're hoping she can go off of it when she's awake. I'm sure she'd love to see that—" Mom gestured at my computer. "—but you might have to break it down into shorter sections. She gets . . . tired easily."

"Oh," I said.

I was feeling odd. I'd just gotten comfortable with Grandmother. I mean, she should've been a major part of my life, but she hadn't been. And I was kind of pissed about that. *Was she going to die?*

My stomach felt funny and my heart seemed to be racing. I didn't *want* her to die.

Dad was looking at both of us. "Hey, we all have ups and downs. It will be all right." He was trying to sound assured, and I was glad he was making the effort, but it wasn't really working for me.

Mom said, "Yes."

I don't think it was working for her, either.

I took my laptop up the stairs. Seeana was just leaving Grandmother's room. I waited at the first landing and said, "How is she?"

Seeana searched my eyes, looking, I think for my need. Did I want to be reassured or did I want the truth? I don't know what she found in my eyes but she said, "A little better. We've got her off the ventilator for now, and she's . . . maintaining. Oxygenation is right on the borderline, but we've got her fluids up and she's eating some soup." She watched my face then added, "I don't know what the long term prognosis is. Uh, prognosis means—"

I held up my hand. "Got it. Thanks."

Jeline was on duty, sitting off to the side, at the card table, playing solitaire. I smiled at her as I came in. "What is this, your fourteenth day?"

Jeline nodded. "Yes. Going home tomorrow. And *so* ready." She grinned.

Grandmother was propped up slightly, which, with her

bowed back, brought her head nearly upright. An insulated mug sat on an over-bed tray and she was using an accordion straw to sip. She was wearing the oxygen cannula and the oximeter sensor was clipped to her ear. I glanced at the readout and had to step to one side to read 90.2. The instrument had been twisted so that it was facing Samantha.

She smiled as she saw me stretch my neck to the side. "I insisted," she said in her whisper-like voice. "They like to put things back behind the patient, so *they* can read them, and the patient can't. I guess they're afraid I'll work myself into a tizzy."

I took one of the chairs from the card table and carried it around to the other side. "A tizzy sounds like an old automobile."

She snorted. "Like a Tin Lizzy? That's what they called the Model-T. What do you have there?" She gestured at my computer.

"Home movies," I said, and moved my eyes sideways toward Jeline.

Grandmother twitched her forefinger up and held it pointed toward the ceiling. She raised her eyebrows.

I nodded.

She looked over at Jeline. "Why don't you go have dinner? Cent needs to consult with me about her love life."

Jeline frowned. "You have a *love life*? How come *you* get a love life?" She stood up and came over to the bed, running her eyes over the instruments, the saline drip, and the oxygen feed. She looked at Samantha's face, then nodded. "Okay." She turned to me. "If any of the alarms go off, we'll hear it on the repeaters, but you can hit the call button, too." She pointed at it, where it was clipped the blanket, close to Grandmother's hand, then left.

I was blushing. "Love life?"

She winked at me.

I showed her the shortest video, the Iridium inspection, and she wanted more. So I queued the unedited video to just after hitting orbit, and, contrary to Mom's expectations, Grandmother stayed awake for the entire film. I was getting better at narration, too, but at the end, she said, "How come there's no sound from the video?"

This wasn't entirely true. There were points where I brushed against the case with my arms or when I was holding it out at arm's length to take the self-portraits that there was noise from the contact.

"Vacuum, Grandmother. Sound does—"

"Don't be silly—I was complaining about *Star Wars* and sound in space since before you were born. But Millie said you talk to your Dad on the phone, and some other people, right? Why aren't we hearing those?"

"Microphone is in the camera case. I'm in my helmet." I held my hands out. "Vacuum between."

"Hmmph. There should be a way. Thing I always liked best about the NASA channel was listening in on control room-to-mission chatter."

That was a really good idea. If I was taking inspection videos I could talk about the stuff I was seeing. I bet there was some sort of wireless microphone that would work with the camera. "I'll see what I can do."

"You need to take more footage of *you*. And maybe with your visor up, so we can see your face."

"Seems a little, uh, egotistical."

"Aren't you trying to make some money at this?"

"Uh, yes."

"It's all about the branding. I liked your logo but it's missing something."

Oh, yeah. Back when she was working, Grandmother had been in advertising. I sat up. "What's that?"

"You. Now I know you've got a lot going for you. You can put stuff up there cheaper, but that's not quite enough. You want *everybody* talking about you. I mean, you're not replacing SpaceX with their capacity . . . what can they lift?"

"Sixty tons to LEO in the Falcon Heavy."

"Right. What is your limit?"

"Well, we picked fifty kilos. I might be able to do more, but I'm pretty sure we can do that."

"Right. But you have other advantages. The big boys plan their launches months or years in advance, right? You can be up in minutes."

I shook my head. "Not minutes. I need a couple of hours to flush the nitrogen out of my system. But, yeah. I can move stuff on pretty short notice."

"You need to sell that. If a customer wants to put something up he needs to schedule it with you. He wants to put something up *now* you should charge a premium."

"Or to get something down on short notice?"

"Right. But that's operations and pricing—not so much my thing. My thing is branding and for that, we've got you: teenage girl in a spacesuit. Space Girl."

I mimed sticking my finger down my throat.

Grandmother chuckled.

"You need to take a bunch of footage of yourself. You're not just selling stuff to orbit, you're selling bragging rights. 'Yeah, *our* satellite was put up by Space Girl.'"

"Not Space Girl! Apex Orbital Services! Besides, I can't exactly take a camera operator up with me. Not *yet*. We only have the one suit."

Grandmother's eyes widened when I said that. "Maybe you can't, but you can do something with the camera. I have faith in you.

"Burn me a copy of your movie, okay? And bring me your logo designer. I want to talk to them."


To: info@apexorbital.com
From: rtmatapang@tamu.edu
Subject: cubesat specs

Greetings,

We are working on your cubesat design, but have questions about launch configuration. Are you limited to actual cubesat dimensions? If high acceleration and high vibration are not a factor we can quickly create units using off-the-shelf components, especially if you are good with larger than $10 \times 10 \times 10\,cm$ and greater than 1.33 kilo.

You didn't mention station keeping or attitude control capabilities—need them?

Please contact me.

> Roberta Matapang
> AggieSatLab
> Texas A&M University

ps. What the HELL do I call you?

pps. The Delta-K Booster is already 11 kilometers lower in orbit than pre-tether. Cool beans, right? I defended my dissertation yesterday.

---

To: info@apexoribital.com
From: lionel.sterling@peterson.af.mil
Subject: Fengyun 1C

Greetings,

Your 'package' was delayed. Perhaps you could call first next time. I would've been more than happy to take delivery personally. The Air Police commander is not happy with me as I cannot give him the background.

I am impressed, though, that you brought it back rather than let it burn up in the atmosphere.

We've told NASA that this particular piece will not be bothering them again. They think WE disposed of it which is embarrassing since I could neither confirm nor deny. I will pass on their sincere thanks to =you=, instead.

Please reconsider my offer to inspect your facilities. We could definitely send some business your way.

> Brig. Lionel Sterling
> HQAFSPC

ps. What the HELL do I call you?

———

To: rtmatapang@tamu.edu
From: info@apexorbital.com
Subject: re: cubesat specs

Dear DOCTOR Matapang,

Congratulations on the Ph.D.!

Correct. Vibration and acceleration not a factor. It can be as big as you like, dimensionally, as long as you keep it under 50 kilos. I would prefer under 25 kilos.

Don't need station keeping. Would antenna effectiveness be affected by tumble? How about the solar charging?

> —Space Girl

———

To: lionel.sterling@peterson.af.mil
From: info@apexorbital.com
Subject: re: Fengyun 1C

Thanks for the offer of business, but we'll pass. If you have any ISS emergencies, though, drop us a note.

> —Space Girl

———

To: info@apexorbital.com
From: rmatapang@tamu.edu
Subject: re: cubesat specs

Space Girl (Really? Space Girl?)

It's cheaper and more reliable to put solar cells on all surfaces instead of doing active attitude control (since we only need to power the transmitter) but there's an advantage to earthward orientation for antenna effectiveness. If you're really okay with unlimited dimensions, we could passively orient the bird with a telescoping, 10-meter mast, putting the solar cells, batteries, and transmitter at one end, and a counterweight at the other.

Like the tether from *Lost Boy*, this would align with the local gravity gradient, putting one end slightly above the orbit and the other slightly below.

While this isn't very critical in LEO, it would greatly improve signal strength in MEO and GEO. I'm sure we could do each bird well below twenty-five kilos.

—Roberta

———

To: jchilton@smith.edu
joseph.trujeque@sanford.edu
TaraBochinclonny@hotmail.com
bcc: info@apexorbital.com
From: cory.matoska@stanford.edu
Subject: Fabrication Team Meeting

As we are coming up on the winter break and some of you are traveling during that time, I'd like to get together and discuss our schedule and timetable for fab sessions in late January or early February. I propose this coming Saturday at the lab, 9:00 A.M. Pacific. It shouldn't take longer than an hour.

Please let me know as soon as possible if this works for you.

———

To: rmatapang@tamu.edu
From: info@apexorbital.com
Subject: re: cubesat specs

I think the mast idea is AWESOME. Please proceed.

To: info@apexorbital.com
From: cory.matoska@stanford.edu
Subject: Transport for Fab. Team Mtg.

You got my bcc on the meeting, right? They all rsvp'ed, so can you get Jade and Tara here?

To: cory.matoska@stanford.edu
From: info@apexorbital.com
Subject: re: Transport for Fab. Team Mtg.

Right. I'll bring 'em.

I jumped Tara from New Prospect directly to a large handicapped stall in the women's restroom on the top floor of the Durand Building. I'd jumped from there, and locked it first, so there were no surprises when we returned. I wasn't expecting any—it was Saturday and the top floor was mostly admin, deserted on the weekend.

I gave her Cory's office number and said, "Elevator's to the right as you come out."

"You're not coming with me?"

"Well, no. I'm not going to the meeting. Joe's gonna be there."

She blinked, her eyes large. "Well, then I'll wait here for Jade, so we can go down together."

"Oh." She was nervous. I'd been working with Cory for six weeks; she'd never met him. "Sure. Go wash your hands or something." I pushed her out of the stall and relocked it.

Jade wasn't in her room, but came in right after saying, "Sorry. Wanted to brush my teeth." She grabbed a jacket and nodded. She was also nervous.

"You okay? I thought you Smithies did all sorts of interviews and things."

"It's not *that*," she said. "You've always transported Tara from home. You never . . . *I've* never done it—travelled your way."

I looked at the ceiling and laughed.

"What?"

"Tara's nervous about the *interview.* Come on. Let's go before she has a panic attack."

I didn't even let Jade put on her jacket.

I was getting pretty good at it. Not as good as Dad, perhaps, but I knew to keep supporting Jade's weight after we appeared since it was probable her knees would buckle.

They did.

At her gasp, Tara's voice came over the partition, "Jade?"

I opened the door and let Tara take over steadying Jade.

Tara said, "So, come back *here* after the meeting?" She gestured at the tile and sinks.

I wrinkled my nose. "Out there. By the elevators. There's a couch and chairs." I bit my lip. "Uh, don't let Joe follow you."

Jade looked at Tara and raised her eyebrows, but Tara just nodded. "Okay." She looked at her watch. "Seventy minutes from now?"

I nodded. That was five minutes' buffer on both ends of the meeting.

As they left the bathroom, Jade asked, "We're really in California?"

"Guess so," said Tara. "Look—palm trees!"


I had seriously considered setting the camera on the shelf in Cory's lab and letting it record the meeting, but in the end, I behaved.

Okay—Cory was using one of the conference rooms and he would've noticed if it showed up there.

I jumped to the cabin, thinking I'd do better if I had someone to talk to while I waited. But when I stuck my head into my old room, Mom was holding Grandmother's hand and Grandmother was back on the respirator and either sleeping or unconscious. Seeana was taking her blood pressure and Tessa was doing something with the respirator settings. None of them were smiling and they were so concentrated on Grandmother that they didn't notice me.

It didn't look like a good time.

I went looking for Dad.

For a time, after we had to leave New Prospect, Mom, Dad, and I had recorded our destinations and expected time back in the kitchen. Lately, with Seeana and the other caretakers in our space, we'd stopped it rather than answer awkward questions.

Dad wasn't anywhere in the cabin and the white board in the kitchen was blank. I checked the warehouse, but he wasn't there, either.

I jumped to the cliff house. I was still having trouble thinking of it as "my" place, but I'd been sleeping there for three weeks. I stared at the books and vids on the shelves, but I wasn't really seeing them. I remembered looking at other books on other bookshelves, but not alone.

I jerked away from the books.

The propane-powered refrigerator was mostly empty. There were two sodas, one leathery apple, and a piece of cheese that had gone fungal in a ziplock bag.

Without thinking I popped the bag open.

I don't know why. Distracted, I guess. I nearly vomited and jumped, but I didn't do either. Instead I held my breath and sealed it shut.

Just like Joe.

No, Joe wasn't a piece of decomposing cheese. But, what had happened, it was like that, somehow. A good thing spoiled and made worse because I'd left it sealed away, unexamined.

For one brief second, I considered dumping the plastic bag onto Joe's dorm bed, but my stomach heaved at the thought. I jumped to Stanford and threw it into the Dumpster behind the Durand building, where Cory's lab and office were.

When I looked at my phone, it was still forty minutes away from the scheduled end of their meeting.

Right.

––––––––

Joe nearly fell out of his chair when I walked into the conference room. Jade and Tara looked at each other, eyes wide.

Cory just said, "Thought you had a conflict." His eyes shifted slightly toward Joe and back again.

"I was able to move some stuff around." I pulled out a chair at the far end of the table and sat, carefully looking at Cory. "How's the scheduling going?"

"We think we're good. Joe's return flight isn't until four days after we were going to start, though. Can you transport him as well as Tara for those work days? That would give us a four-day stretch to get started—that would really give us a chance to ramp up."

I glanced at Joe. His hands were clenched on the table top and his eyes kept flicking from me to his hands and back to me.

I thought about saying, *we could reschedule his flight*, or *we could reschedule the start of the program* or *he isn't necessary at the beginning*. I looked back at Cory.

"Sure. Is that coming back early or working from home, like Tara?"

Joe said, "I . . . I can't get into the dorm until after."

My stomach twisted. I wasn't sure how I felt about transporting him eight, nine times. "What will your folks say when you disappear for the last four days of vacation?"

He looked away. "I can probably find someplace to stay in Palo Alto."

Only one trip, then. I wondered if he was thinking of staying with his study partner.

Cory said, "I've got a couch you could use." He eyed Joe. "You might have to scrunch up a bit."

Joe looked relieved. "That would be good. It would be better if I told my family I had to return early for my new job, which *is* the truth. I was going to hit up a classmate who lives here for crash space, but I don't know him *that* well." He looked at me. "It would be really expensive to change the flight, now, so a lift would be very helpful. That way I could use the flight later, for spring break, or end of semester."

Stanford was providing a lot of aid for Joe, but they weren't

covering transportation and I knew his family was still stretching to cover the rest.

It wasn't exactly fair to say that he'd gotten spoiled when
we were together, but I *had* taken him surfing in Australia,
snowboarding in New Zealand, and to the theater in London.

Now he was scraping for airfare. I thought I'd be happy
about it, but I wasn't.

I looked off to the side and said, "Right."

Cory spent the next twenty-five minutes talking about the
work. The next suit was going to have the split-neck flange.
The process would be identical to the way my suit was made, but
there would be additional steps along the way to test certain
automation methods.

The process was both complicated and simplified because
the suit weave was assembled while the electroactive-polymer
fibers were under current—in their relaxed state. The form they'd
wrap corresponded to a seven-foot-tall, four hundred-pound
human. At that scale, the weave was wide and didn't require a
lot of precision. But it had to be kept electrified until the entire
suit was completed.

It was a good thing I knew most of this already. I was working very hard to appear attentive, but Cory's voice was mostly
going in one ear and out the other and it was all I could do not
to watch Joe out of the corner of my eye.

Cory finished his summary with, "What we do in four days,
this first time, we hope to cut down to two on the next suit, so
I'm hoping we can schedule those for weekends. Questions?"

Jade and Tara shook their heads, but Joe said, "How have
you been testing the suits—vacuum chamber?"

Cory looked at me and raised his eyebrows.

I blinked. "You didn't tell him?"

Cory shook his head. "Didn't know what *you'd* told him.
Them." His gesture took in all three of them.

"Uh, I told Tara and Jade—they designed that logo on the
video." I took a deep breath. "One second."

I just jumped from the chair.

This is a bit tricky since, arriving without the chair's support, you promptly fall on your butt. After discovering that one the hard way, I learned to add a slight bit of velocity upward and rotation forward when I appeared, so it would pop me up onto the balls of my feet, as if straightening from a crouch.

In the Eyrie, I grabbed my laptop and returned to the conference room. I queued up the raw video, put it in full screen, and set the computer on the table in front of Tara. Joe and Jade leaned in from both sides when I hit "play."

All three of them leaned forward when they saw my suited hands pick up the satellite, but when the footage switched into orbit they practically bumped heads. I let it run until we got to the first selfie I'd taken with the Delta-K booster and the *Lost Boy* AggieSat, then froze the video. You could see my extended arm and the camera reflected in the gold visor, with a background of half black sky and half brightly lit Earth.

Joe's mouth was half open and he stared at the screen wide-eyed.

Cory said, "So, yeah. We're on that testing thing."

Tara leaned back and said, "We've got to get some logos on your suit. Do we have to use paint? I thought the suit was supposed to be tight?"

I said, "That's just Nomex/Kevlar coveralls. The suit's underneath."

"Oh. So we could use patches and embroidery?"

I thought about it. "Uh, Probably. Something that can take high temps, though."

Joe blurted, "That was *you*?"

I looked at him. He was staring at me with wide eyes.

"Well, it wasn't Sailor Moon," I said.

"Are you *insane*?"

Jade and Tara flinched back from Joe's raised voice.

I felt my jaw muscles bulge and my teeth grind together. "We all heard that, right?" I said. I pointed at the door. "They probably heard that in the next *building*."

Joe held up his hands and looked at Cory. In a *somewhat* quieter voice he said, "That can't be safe!"

I reached over and picked up my laptop, closing it before

tucking it under my arm. "We're not hiring a health-and-safety officer. You want the job we *are* offering, great. But *you* don't get to tell *me* what I can and can't do."

He clamped his mouth and dropped his gaze to the table. I think his ears were turning red, but I turned my head to Tara and said, "You know where to meet me when you're done."

I jumped away.

I waited in the bathroom because I wouldn't put it past Joe to follow them and I was right. Jade, second through the door, shut the door behind her rather than letting it close on its own, and leaned against it.

I raised my eyebrows and she nodded. "Yep."

There was a knock on the door and Joe's voice said, "Is Cent in there?"

My mouth opened by itself but I shut it quickly before I actually said anything.

He tried to open the door. Jade said, "Hey!" and pushed hard against it with her back. I joined her, back to the door.

"Cent? I just want to talk!" He tried the door again. Tara added her weight. I put an arm around each of them and jumped.

We fell in a heap in Jade's dorm room, Tara falling across the bed and Jade banging her elbow on her desk.

"Shit, shit, shit!" Jade said, hopping in place and cradling her arm.

I'd never jumped two people at once, but it hadn't been any worse than jumping Joe and his backpack.

"Sorry," I said to Jade. "You okay?"

She held her elbow up so she could look at it in the room's tiny mirror. "Funny bone," she said. "S'okay."

"So he followed you guys?"

Tara said, "Yep. He did. We didn't let him in the elevator, but he ran up the stairs."

Jade nodded. "He saw us push the 'up' call button."

"What did he say?"

Jade laughed and Tara covered her own mouth before saying, "Joe said, 'What did she say?'" Tara looked over at Jade and shook her head.

I looked at Jade. "What did you tell him?"

She stopped laughing and shrugged. "I just went with, 'You mean, did she tell us you slept with your study partner?'"

I looked away.

Jade said, "I'm not going to lie—we have to work with him. Better we're all up front, you know?"

"I . . . guess." I raised my chin to nod but instead of dropping it I hesitated, then shook my head.

Tara nodded as if I'd just confirmed something.

Jade said, "Why'd you have Cory hire him? Revenge?"

I sighed.

"Leave her alone," said Tara. "She doesn't know."

Jade said, "Doesn't know what?"

"She doesn't know why she had Cory hire him. She's still working it out."

I met Tara's eyes.

*That* I could nod to.

# TWENTY-TWO

## Cent: You should include some Chuck Berry

I found Dad in the living room scooping ash out of the fireplace. I told him, "I need to know how to do that thing you do."

He looked at me frowning. "Really?" He dumped a load of ashes in the bucket and hung the shovel with the poker, then stood up. "I would've thought that you and Joe were working that out for yourselves, but okay. When a guy and a gal love each other very much—"

I struck out but my fist passed through empty space and he was standing behind me saying, "Missed him. *Darn* that guy."

My elbow caught him in the stomach. I'm sure he *let* me, damn him. He gave an exaggerated "Oof" and staggered back.

"You done?" I said.

He straightened. "What thing that I do?"

"Twinning."

"Hmmm. Really? What for?"

"Airflow. You know: *lots* of air."

"Oh?" He raised his eyebrows and pointed at the ceiling.

"Let's go try it."

"Where?"

"We could do it right here." He glanced back up at Grandmother's bedroom. "But then we might scare the horses. Let's go to your launch site. The sandy wash, okay?"

I jumped.

Dad appeared thirty feet away. He turned in place, carefully scanning all around.

I glanced around, too. It was in the upper sixties and the air was still. It was overcast but you could just barely make out the sun through the clouds. It was a bit past midday. No one was in sight. I jumped up a hundred feet and spun around as I fell, then jumped back to the ground before I'd dropped thirty feet.

Dad said, "Well?"

"There's a vehicle moving off that way, heading north. I could see the dust, but nothing we have to worry about. Had to be over six miles away."

Dad nodded.

"What's the drill?"

He turned to the side, facing east. "The first thing you want to do is to look at yourself. Not with a mirror, mind you." He jumped to a spot five feet in front of him but appeared facing west, looking to where he'd just been standing. Then he jumped back to his first spot, facing east. "Back and forth, like that, but faster." He jumped again and again, very little pause between the jumps—and then, just like that, he was in both places at once. His voice, distorted oddly, said, "I am looking at myself."

I could see through him. Through both of him. The backgrounds were distorted, too. The Dad on my left had a boulder behind him at the edge of the wash. The Dad on my right had a creosote bush in the background, but when I looked through them, the backgrounds had merged, a mixture of bush and rock, no matter which "Dad" I look at.

"You can move the ends," he said, and suddenly the right hand figure was ten feet further away. And then it vanished.

At first I thought he'd just stopped doing it, but I realized I could still see through his other image and that the background had changed, darkened. His voice was quieter but I still understood him when he said, "I'm in the warehouse." Then one side of his figure brightened so much, I blinked and looked away for a second. I heard surf and he raised his voice to say, "The beach, in Queensland." A warm wind pushed through my hair.

And then he really stopped twinning and was back, solid, present, blinking. "It was bright there—full sun."

His voice was normal again. I could no longer hear the surf and the breeze had died.

"Any questions?"

I'd seen it before, a long time ago, before I could jump, but I found it weirder, for some reason, than I had as a child. "When you do the water thing, is there anything different you do?"

He shook his head. "No. It's just like the air. You felt the air, right?"

I nodded.

"There was wind on the beach but what you felt was from the air pressure difference. Sea level versus? . . ."

"At three thousand seven hundred fifty," I said, remembering launch day. "About 2 psi difference."

He nodded. "If you're venting to orbit, you could be pushing it out at fourteen point seven, eh?"

I nodded. "I wouldn't vent air to orbit, though. Into a container, maybe."

"You could fill up a balloon pretty darn quick. That could be interesting." He rubbed his chin. "The first time I did this, I was exhausted, but after I got the hang of it, it didn't seem any more difficult than any other jumping. How about you? When you started adding velocity?"

I shook my head. "In atmo, if I do it long enough I get exhausted just being buffeted by the wind." I pointed up. "The orbital stuff, though—not so much." I had an odd thought. "Did you want *me* to teach you how to do the velocity thing?"

Dad smiled. "I'll give you credit, Centipede. You beat me there. But no, you don't need to show me. For instance—"

He left the ground too fast for me to track. I had to jerk my head back to see him, a rapidly shrinking dot against the gray clouds above. Then the dot blinked out and he was back at my side.

He fingered his shirt. "Oops." Two buttons still held his shirt closed but the others were gone. "Your mom will be annoyed. Let that be a lesson to me."

"Somebody's been practicing," I said.

"I do have one more trick," he said. "Something I haven't even shown your mother. If you figure out the twinning thing, I'll show you."

"What?" I asked. "I might *never* figure out the twinning thing."

"Consider it an incentive." He vanished.

It took me over an hour before my first success, and it shocked me right back out of it. I saw myself, all right, but it was wrong. Besides the transparency and the merging backgrounds (I was seeing through myself twice), I didn't look properly like me. The Stanford sweatshirt I was wearing actually *said* Stanford, not brofnatS. My hair was parted on the wrong side and my face just didn't look right.

So, weird, that.

It took me another half hour to get it back and hold it. Other than my own image, the landscape was a mess as my visual cortex tried to make sense of two different slices of desert, combining it in ways that didn't make sense.

I had to stop, nauseated, and breathe heavily until my stomach settled.

I kicked at the ground, sending coarse sand flying. Except for some very early effects when I started "plummeting" I didn't get nauseated in orbit. Felt unfair to feel it now.

I jumped to the Eyrie.

Dad had installed blackout-quality drapes so he could sleep there when his clock was set to different parts of the planet. I liked light so I kept the curtains open. There aren't privacy issues—to see in, you'd have to climb two hundred feet up to the ledge or be clinging to the far wall of the canyon.

I went from window to window drawing the drapes, taking the interior to dark shadows. When I turned off the kitchen light the darkness was profound.

I waited, breathing slowly, until the nausea was completely gone, then jumped back to the bright wash, to the dark Eyrie, to the bright wash, faster and faster, and then it clicked.

I could look at myself, but the sunlit desert completely washed out the dark interior of the Eyrie and I only had one landscape to contend with. The only parts of the Eyrie I saw were where light from the wash shone through me, lighting the floor around my feet.

I shivered, suddenly cold, and my concentration dropped. I was back in the Eyrie, in the dark. When I turned to switch the light back on, I felt sand grate between my shoes and the stone floor. Examined in the light, you could see where I stood, my footprints defined by a border of coarse sand.

I guess water and air isn't the only thing that could flow through the me-shaped hole. I shivered again. The Eyrie was cold today. I'd been sleeping here, but that usually involved dropping my jeans and crawling under flannel sheets, a quilt, and a down comforter. In the morning, I'd grab my clean clothes and jump to the Yukon for a shower.

I eyed the woodstove, but didn't really want to go through the motions of starting a fire.

Back in the Yukon, the snows buried the first story of the house most years. When extra-heavy snowfall threatened to bury the second floor, too, Dad melted it away by twinning to a hot place at low altitude. I pulled back one of the curtains and opened the window six inches.

It wasn't much warmer outside, but I knew someplace that was. It was over ninety degrees Fahrenheit in Perth, Western Australia, and it was still morning. I found a sheltered spot in a back alley, hidden from traffic and pedestrians, and twinned to the Eyrie.

I'd like to say that it happened immediately but it took me several fits and starts before I held both spots continuously.

I was trying for ten minutes but dropped to my knees as my watch display passed six. I was in the Eyrie and though the floor under my knee was still cold, the chill of the air was gone. There was condensation on the walls. Right. It had been humid in Perth.

After one attempt to stand, I *climbed* up onto the bed and

flopped onto my back. I thought about taking off my shoes and fell asleep instead.

To: info@apexorbital.com
From: rtmatapang@tamu.edu
Subject: Discussion

Need to talk in person about your stuff. Could you meet me where we made our deal, tomorrow, at the same time of day?

                                                                    Roberta

She hadn't named the Dixie Chicken. Dr. Matapang clearly thought someone else was reading her e-mails and, probably, watching her movements.

Crap.

I shot off an affirmative. I was hoping she was imagining things, but if she was right, I hoped it was just the DIA and not Daddy's old friends.

I arrived ten minutes early, coming in through the veranda entrance in the back, and took a seat in dark corner. I ordered a Coke and waited, the Coke untouched. If she *was* being tracked, I had no intention of drinking anything here.

That's how they caught Dad.

At 1:30 a young woman in a denim jacket and khaki pants walked through the front door. She looked around and then took a manila envelope out of her shoulder bag and began walking through the room, holding it so anyone could read the letters APEX ORBITAL writ large upon it.

I raised my hand when she neared me, watching her warily.

She blinked and said, "I'm supposed to ask if you know who this came from."

"Roberta?" I said.

She nodded and handed it to me. "Right."

"Is Roberta okay?" I asked.

"Was when she gave me this. Roberta said, 'The note explains all.'" She jabbed her finger toward the envelope. "I'm not supposed to linger."

I nodded. "Well, thanks."

She turned around and left. I bent down behind the table, as if to tie my shoes, and jumped away.

The handwritten note said:

Hey Space Girl,

They're definitely watching me. This note is being delivered by my landlady's daughter.

I had one of the students put the first unit on the roof of the lab. It's in a cardboard box next to the elevator stack.

I'm eating lunch over in Bryan at the same time this is being delivered to you in hopes they will be following me. Instructions are in the box, but let me know (via e-mail) if you have any questions. I have the parts for the other two if this one satisfies.

Roberta

I could look down on the space-engineering building from the top level of the massive parking garage next door. The cardboard box sat in the shade, up against the north side of the elevator shack.

It could be a trap. There could be guys waiting inside the roof-access door. It could be booby-trapped. For one brief second I considered getting Dad, but that thought didn't last long.

With Dad involved it might take all day to get the thing off the roof. Or worse. I could practically hear him saying, "Not worth the risk."

Well, it wasn't *his* satellite.

I jumped to the roof and crouched by the box.

The top wasn't taped and one of the flaps fluttered in a breeze. I flipped it back gently. When nothing went boom or emitted scary hissing noises, I flipped the rest of the flaps open. All I could see was gray foam, but when I peeled back one corner, I could see a rectangular section of solar cells and aluminum framing.

Well, it *looked* like it was the real deal.

I replaced the foam, closed the box, and jumped it to the sandy wash in West Texas. I set it down gently and jumped a hundred feet away.

When it hadn't exploded after five minutes, I hit the cabin for Dad's portable radio-frequency sweeper. I started from a hundred feet away and walked slowly toward it, but there was no RF from the box, nothing *active*.

You might ask why I didn't sweep the box back on that rooftop? I could justify by saying there would be so much radio-frequency stuff happening on campus, it would've been meaningless. That it was isolated from local radio out here.

The truth was I didn't think about it.

I jumped it to the Eyrie and unpacked it carefully, still not convinced it wouldn't explode. The sheet of instructions said:

> The OBC, transmitter, EPS, and batteries are all COTS. The solar cells are space-qualified triple-junction cells. Aluminum frame and pop rivets from Home Depot. I was going to get all fancy with the extendible mast but then one of our undergrads saw these snap-together fiberglass tent poles at REI. The mast needed to be nonconductive or it will generate electrodynamic drag like the tether you attached for us.
>
> There is an elastic cord down the center of the pole and simply unbundling the section should cause it to self-assemble. Manually check that the sockets are fully engaged, though, as the elastic will degrade rapidly from temperature swings and outgassing of plasticizer into the vacuum.
>
> The counterweight is hollow and half filled with steel shot to dampen oscillations from deployment or thermal perturbation.

Lot of acronyms. I had to go look them up online. COTS had several meanings, including "Commercial Orbital Transfer Systems" but the one that clearly pertained here was "Commercial Off-the-Shelf," meaning that they were components not purpose-built for the satellite. OBC turned out to be "On Board Computer" and EPS was "Electrical Power System."

> To add your audio message, connect a computer to the USB port and the onboard nonvolatile flash will mount as an external drive. Put an .mp3 or .wav file in the root directory and the radio will transmit it on continuous loop. Make it 5 minutes long and it will loop every 5 minutes. Make it 90 minutes long and it will loop every 90. There's 4 gigabytes of storage so you have substantial message-length flexibility. If there is more than one .wav or .mp3 file in the root, the system will play them in turn, in name-sort order, before looping.
>
> Currently there is a 60-second test.wav file in the root directory comprised of 59 seconds of silence and a 1-second 400 hertz tone. You can delete it or leave it in place as part of your broadcast set.
>
> The batteries are currently charged and the OBC will boot on master power ON and begin broadcasting at 145.990 MHz as soon as the Power On Self-Test is complete.
>
> Let me know when it's up and we'll monitor.

"You should include some Chuck Berry," said Grandmother.

Tara stared at her, appalled and worried. Both Grandmother and I started laughing but that stopped pretty quickly when Grandmother started wheezing.

"Calm down there, girl!" said Seeana, a worried look her face. She cranked the oxygen regulator up, increasing the flow.

I'd brought Tara to Grandmother to discuss branding issues, but we'd segued into planning the audio message for *AOS-Sat One* pretty quickly.

Grandmother's wheezing stopped after a few more breaths

and she closed her eyes for a minute. "Sorry, Tara, your face was just so funny. You must've thought I'd gone all senile on you."

Tara shook her head and said, "Of course not."

This nearly set Grandmother off again, but she held it to a chuckle. She looked at me and said, "She's a very *polite* liar."

Tara grinned. "Okay, *who* is Chuck Berry?"

My computer was open before me and I flipped over to my music app. The opening guitar riff from "Johnny B. Goode" screamed out of my speakers.

Even before Chuck Berry began singing, Tara said, *"Oh.* I know that song." I stopped the music after the first verse and she added, "But why do you want *that* on the recording?"

"Tradition," said Grandmother.

I was the one whose father used the space program for history lessons. I filled Tara in. "It was sent out on a gold-plated record on Voyager 1 and 2 that included greetings in different languages and various kinds of music. 'Johnny B. Goode' was one of the samples."

Grandmother nodded. "What do we have so far?"

Tara read the draft. "Greetings from *AOS-Sat One*! *AOS-Sat One* was fabricated by Texas A&M University's AggieSat Lab and placed in orbit by Apex Orbital Services: providing orbital insertion and recovery for spacecraft up to fifty kilograms in mass, placed in Low, Medium, and High Earth Orbits. Apex Orbital services, the home of—"

I interrupted her. "I thought we agreed that we weren't going to include that part!"

She ignored me, continuing with, "—the home of Space Girl. For prices and endorsement opportunities, visit our website at apexorbital dot com. Apex Orbital—we deliver!"

Grandmother flipped over a piece of paper on her bedspread. It was Tara's new design, a five line squiggle of a space-helmeted figure, clearly female but not obnoxiously so. She was pulling the satellite in the Apex Orbital logo as if it were a suitcase. *"We* didn't agree," Grandmother said. *"You* disagreed. Everybody *else* likes it."

I rolled my eyes.

Tara said, "You may know loads about orbits, but you don't know nuthin' about advertising." She bounced her eyebrows up and down. "Space. Girl."

I looked at Grandmother and said, "There's never a snowball around when you need one."

Grandmother said, "How many different messages could we fit on there?"

"Hundreds, why?"

"It just might be nice to vary the message. The order, the emphasis. It could get very boring, the same message over and over, even if we do play 'Johnny B. Goode' between every spot."

"I don't mind boring. What's important is that it comes from orbit."

Tara said, "Put the new logos on the site tonight, Space Girl."

I told Grandmother, "I'm going to drop her into a snowbank on the way home."

"I wish you'd let *me* edit the web page directly," said Tara. "It's frustrating having to run the iterations through you."

I winced. "I can give you access, but not from your computer and definitely not from this country. Not unless you want all the three-letter guys camped on your doorstep."

Tara said, "Three letter guys?"

Grandmother said, "NSA, DIA, CIA, and the ETC."

"ETC?" I said.

"Etcetera," Grandmother said.

"Ha." We hadn't mentioned the DoD and General Sterling of the Air Force Space Command. I added, "ABC, CBS, NBC, and CNN."

Tara laughed but then sobered, looking sideways at me. "We should get Joe to do some of the recording. He has that great baritone. Remember when he narrated that piece for the snowboard club?"

I looked away.

Of course I remembered. It was a YouTube compilation of epic snowboard crashes, mostly starring my old slalom partner, Carl. Joe did the voice-over epic-movie-trailer style. "One man doesn't amount to a hill of beans in this world, but he can run into a hill. OF. SNOW." It was the juxtaposition of Carl's spectacular crashes with the voice-over that made it fall-over funny, but of course now it just made me want to cry.

When I looked back, Tara had a concerned expression on her face.

I said, "You work it out with him. He's back home, right? I want to put the bird up on Sunday."

Tara blinked. "Can we watch?"

I raised my eyebrows. "Watch? It's not like a rocket launch. There's no ground-shaking roar of flames and all."

"You have to suit up, right? If we're going to work with Cory on making more suits, I want to see how it works. We should *all* see it but Jade will have to wait until she's back from Europe." Tara looked down at her hands. "I understand if you don't want Joe there."

Grandmother was watching me very carefully.

Tara put her hand to her mouth. "Oh. Uh, about Joe—"

I waved my hand. "Grandmother knows. My parents don't, though." I was scheduled to transport Joe back to Stanford in January, when it was time for them to start winding the next prototype. I hadn't counted on having to transport him—to touch him—before that.

"If he wants," I said.


Saturday afternoon, I picked up the USB thumb drive with the edited audio from the apartment Tara shared with her mom in New Prospect.

"It's the file called beacon.wav," she said. "We did six messages, as discussed. And Joe *does* want to come tomorrow. What time are you doing it?"

I felt nauseated.

Tara took one look at my face and said, "You *said* he could."

"Nine Pacific. I'll pick you all up here, is that okay?"

Tara said, "Mom'll be here."

"Damn. Right. Behind the coffee shop, then. At ten A.M. Mountain. Make it straight up ten, so you don't freeze your butts off."

"Our cute butts," said Tara.

I smiled but it wasn't very convincing.

Back at the Eyrie, I listened to the recording with my computer. They'd switched up the wording on the message each time, but always conveying the same information.

Joe did three different voices, one extra deep, one natural, and one in a dead-on pommy BBC accent. Tara did one of hers natural, one with a deep southern accent, and, to my surprise, one in Diné. Each of them was separated by "Johnny B. Goode" and the Morse tones for AOS-Sat One and, damn them, a vocal sting in two-part harmony of the first five notes from *Also Sprach Zarathustra*. The root, major fifth, and octave were hummed, but that dramatic last two notes were—you probably guessed— "Space Giiiiiiiiiiiiiirl!"

I laughed until I cried.

Well, I laughed and then I cried.

I made a copy and edited out every bit of Joe's voice until there was just Tara and Chuck and the Morse tones and loaded that one onto the satellite.

When I powered up the satellite, it took five seconds before the broadcast started showing up on Dad's portable radio-frequency scanner. When I plugged in earphones, it came across, loud and clear.

*Dammit, dammit, dammit.*

I powered the bird down, reconnected it to my computer with the USB cable, and put Tara's original version back on the satellite, "Space Giiiiiiirrrl," and Joe and all.

# TWENTY-THREE

## Cent: 2100 Kilometers

I jumped to the rooftop of Krakatoa ten seconds before 9 A.M., breathing oxygen and dressed in my undersuit outfit, but with my long wool coat and sheepskin boots over that. When I peeked over the parapet at the back, Tara and Joe were below, cupping something hot in Krakatoa's distinctive paper cups. Their breath fogged the air around them.

I scanned up and down the alley, then checked out the side street as well. All seemed clear.

I appeared behind Joe, lifted the edge of the mask and said, louder than necessary, "Ready?"

"Shit!" he said, jerking around.

For a second it looked like he would drop his cup, or maybe squeeze it so hard it would pop the top off and spill his mocha, but to my disappointment, he managed to hold onto it.

Tara put one hand over her mouth. After a second she said, "Ready."

I jumped her to Cory's lab where she burst out laughing. "That was *mean*."

I said, through the mask, "Who's doing the laughing? Were you there long?" *Did you talk about me? What did he say?*

Tara tilted her head to one side and studied me. "We were inside for fifteen minutes but we'd walked out back about five minutes ago. You should go get him. It's friggin' cold there and your boy has gotten used to California."

I nearly snapped at her. *He's not* my *boy anymore*. Instead I jumped back to the rooftop of Krakatoa and peered over. Joe had put his back to the wall so I couldn't appear behind him again.

Still, when I popped in six feet in front of him, he inhaled sharply.

I beckoned with one hand and said through the oxygen mask, "Let's go."

He stepped forward warily.

I used to teleport him face-to-face, sometimes while kissing. Sometimes jumping him led to a different sort of jumping him.

This time I did it Dad's way, jumping behind him, grabbing his coat, and jumping away without pause.

When I released him in the lab he staggered forward and caught his balance on the workbench.

"Dammit, Cent. I dropped my coffee!"

I looked down at the clean floor, then realized he meant back where I'd grabbed him. I jumped back to the alley and there it was on the ground, a brown puddle.

I tried to feel vindicated, but it just made me feel petty. I picked up the lid and cup and threw it away in a nearby Dumpster.

Five minutes later I reappeared in the lab and put a fresh medium mocha down on the bench. Rather than say anything, I just turned my hand palm up.

He picked up the cup, avoiding my eyes. "Thanks."

Tara stared at me and raised her eyebrows. I turned to the end of the workbench and said, through the mask, "This is our satellite."

That distracted them.

Three thirty-centimeter-square solar panels were mounted to aluminum angle iron, forming a triangular prism with the circuitry mounted in the space within on insulated ceramic standoffs. The top was closed by an aluminum sheet so thin that it almost qualified as foil. The bottom was open, allowing access to the master power switch and the USB port. An antenna with three cross pieces was mounted at one of the corner edges, pointed the same direction as the open end. Directly opposite the antenna, the base socket for the mast was through bolted into the aluminum angle iron, and its bundled extension sections and the terminal fist-sized counterweight were strapped to it with Velcro.

"What's this?" Joe asked, pointing at the top of the satellite. On the thin aluminum sheet I'd written *2100 K, 6.859 KPS, 45 deg true, 0 lat.*

"We're going for a circular orbit at twenty-one hundred kilometers. Technically, that's just outside of LEO, but it's far less crowded than the lower orbits."

"More radiation, though," Joe said.

"A bit, yes, which is why this mission will be very short."

Cory and Dad wouldn't be there for another fifty minutes. I'd told Cory we'd be doing the checklists as a training exercise but that he could verify things after.

I made Tara read each item off and had Joe do the steps, except when the steps had to be done by me or when I had to show him how a latch worked, where a seal was, and where supplies were kept—the desiccant, soda lime, and batteries.

Cory showed up just after we'd finished recharging life support, filling the hydration bag, and turning on the circulation fans and satellite phone. Dad stuck his head in a bit after Cory positioned the radiation dosimeters and double-checked everything *we'd* done.

Tara complained, "Hey! We used the checklist and everything!"

Cory nodded. "Good. We double-check, though, because while the chances of you messing up are slight, the consequences of you messing up are death. And not your death, right?"

Tara blinked. "Oh. Right."

Joe didn't say anything, but his eyes got bigger.

"Trust but verify," I said. "Let's put it on."

Cory relaxed the suit and I kicked off my boots and took off my coat. I did a last-minute check of the undergarments to make sure all the seams were flat and none of the cloth was bunching.

I looked up to see Joe staring and I glared at him. He cleared his throat and looked away.

Dad held my oxygen mask while I jumped into the suit, and I resumed oxygen breathing before Cory tensioned the fabric. After he tightened it we did our bend and stretch.

Cory held up the okay hand sign. "Comfy?"

I held up my hand, thumb up, then pulled the Nomex/Kevlar coveralls on, complete with our newly created "Space Girl" patch on one shoulder and "Apex Orbital Services" patch on the other.

I let Tara lace up my boots, though the suit was flexible enough for me to do it myself. When she finished and settled back on her knees, I put on the comms headset, took off my oxygen mask, and held my breath while Cory lowered the helmet into place.

We went through the final checks: purge valves, backup oxygen, GPS, camera, and lastly, gloves.

Cory did a two finger salute. "Cleared for deployment to twenty-one hundred kilometers. Don't linger."

Dad nodded to me and held up our "base station" cell phone.

Tara grinned and held up two thumbs.

Joe looked stricken.

I picked up *AOS-Sat One* and jumped.

Dad called first, of course. "Space Girl, how do you read?"

"Loud and clear, Capcom."

"So, whatever happened to Apex One?"

I sighed. "Talk to our very annoying director of marketing and public relations."

"Hey!" I heard Tara's voice in the background. "I'm *right* here, you know!"

Dad came back. "Right. Space Girl. Status?"

I said, "Staging orbit." This is what we were calling my usual starting place: 345 kilometers above the Marshall Islands, booking along northeasterly at 7.72 kilometers per second.

"Right. ECLSS would like a status."

Cory, he meant. ECLSS stood for environmental control and life-support systems.

I wiggled my fingers and toes. "Optimal, Capcom. Breathing easy. Temperature good. I'm transitioning to target orbit now."

"See you on the flip side."

"Right." We weren't going to be talking during this next bit. The target orbit was fourteen hundred kilometers above the Iridium satellites and we weren't expecting to get a signal.

I got it pretty close on the first try, a forty-five degree inclined orbit at twenty-one hundred kilometers, booking along at seven kilometers per second but not circular, not yet. After a few tuning jumps I settled at 2,097 kilometers above the earth and 6.86 kilometers per second.

I watched the readouts for another two minutes. Vertical speed was at a mere three meters per second, putting perigee and apogee within sixty kilometers of each other, well under half of a percent of eccentricity.

Earth looked different this high. I could see all the way from Papua New Guinea to Hawaii. I was tempted to just float there and watch, but I'd agreed with Cory that my max exposure at this altitude would not exceed ten minutes. I'd already used three.

I ripped open the Velcro closure on the mast bundle and the sections started unfolding. I gave the counterweight a push toward the ocean below, and then backed off so the camera could record the self-assembly. The elastic contracted, pulling the sockets together in short, percussive jerks, leaving the entire assembly—satellite, mast, and counterweight—oscillating back and forth, the midpoint on the fiberglass rod moving a good meter side to side.

I could already see that it was damping, but I didn't want to take the time to linger and watch the entire thing calm down, so I moved to the counterweight and began working my way from joint to joint, making sure each socket was fully engaged, and using my mass to damp the last of the vibrations. By the time I was up to the solar panels, the oscillations were negligible.

I turned on the master power, double-checking that the switch was fully engaged, then I took thirty seconds to record some selfie footage in front of the satellite.

I held the camera at arm's length, twisted to the side so that the new Apex Orbital patch was visible, then did the same with the other arm to get the Space Girl patch.

The last thing I did was move back five meters and position the camera so it took in the entire satellite, counterweight, mast, and all. I carefully released it trying to get the camera to just hang there but it took me three tries before it was still enough. I jumped back into the frame, hanging in space beside the mast, the entire arc of Earth's horizon floating behind and slightly below. I waved. I did a two finger salute. And then I held my arms out to the side and jumped in place adding *spin*, revolving slowly, but then pulling arms in like a figure skater and speeding to a blur. I held that for a two count and then jumped back out of frame, to the camera, spin killed.

My mouth filled with saliva and I thought I was going to vomit.

*Don't you* dare, *Cent.*

I grabbed the camera and jumped back down to my staging orbit over the Marshall Islands and stared at the horizon, breathing deeply. It took several breaths before I felt good enough to snap the camera into its mount and then hit the redial button.

Dad answered. "I read you, Space Girl."

"Capcom, the package is deployed. I'm back in my staging orbit. You want to patch me through to Matapang?"

"Roger that."

When Roberta answered I said, "It's a beautiful morning in orbit. Our baby should pass two thousand ninety-seven kilometers over Hawaii in about five minutes. Do you still have access to that U of H radio?"

"What? Oh. It's up—did you say two *thousand*?"

"Yeah. Cleaner vacuum up there and all."

"Harder to deorbit, though. Oh, that's right. You'll just go get it, won't you?"

"That's the plan. The radio?"

"Yeah, we've got access, if they aren't using it. Uh, now's a good time—it's predawn there. Less competition. Give me a few minutes."

I heard her typing rapidly on a keyboard. "And frequency is . . ." More typing. Then I heard her say, *"What?* Chuck Berry! Oh, that's PERFECT." She pushed the cell phone against something and I heard, "—never learned to read or write so well." And then she was back. "Loud and clear. Are you going to be sued for copyright infringement?"

"I hope not. We licensed it for a year."

"Okay. What's the catalog number?"

"For 'Johnny B. Goode?' "

"No. The satellite catalog number."

"Oh. Who assigns that?"

"USSPACECOM. Usually at launch, though it took them a week to assign *Lost Boy* a number after you attached it to the Delta Stage."

"Ah," I said. "My very next call. Thanks!"

I disconnected, then used redial to call Dad back. "As discussed."

"Time to be good space citizens? Right. Putting you through."

One of the reasons I'd chosen Sunday was because I hoped *this* call would go to his voice mail, but he answered immediately.

"Sterling."

"Good morning. Don't you ever take a day off?"

"Ah, Space . . . Girl. This phone routes to my cell when I'm not in my office. And what are we up to today?"

I went with the literal. "I'm at three hundred forty-five kilometers right now," I said. "But earlier I was at twenty-one hundred. I think that might be a new nonlunar record." I *knew* it was. Gordon and Conrad reached 1,371 kilometers during Gemini 11.

And, yeah, I was bragging.

"Congratulations. How many astronauts went farther?"

"Twenty-four." *All men.*

"I see. And what were you doing so far out? Dropping off? Or picking up?"

"Dropping off. Our first satellite. Who do we talk to about getting a satellite catalog number?"

"Uh, I think that's someone in launch monitoring. I'd have to check. Why is *this* one your first? I thought your first was that AggieSat Lab bird? Why doesn't that count?"

"Oh, that counts as our first *delivery.* Today was *our* first satellite. *AOS-Sat One.* So we thought we should let SPACE-COM know. I mean, you're going to notice it soon enough when it crosses your fence. It's a lot bigger than five centimeters, after all."

"When did you do this?"

I looked at the time display on the GPS. "Nine minutes and forty-three seconds ago. It has an audio beacon at one hundred forty-five point nine nine megahertz. I deployed it over the International Date Line near the equator, but it will be over North America pretty soon."

"Did you do a collision assessment?"

"Within our limited means. But that's the reason we put it out so far, you know? Way outside most of the junk in LEO. Also why I called. You guys are all about the tracking."

"Christ on a crutch. Young lady, that's no way to run space operations!"

"Hey, how much space debris have *you* guys deorbited? And I *did* call. You *don't* want us to tell you guys when we put something up? Isn't that what the Chinese do? If there's a potential collision, let me know. I'll be *happy* to adjust it."

I heard a sharp intake of breath. It sounded like Dad when he's getting ready to yell. I put my hand over the headset button, ready to hang up if he exploded, but however tempted he was, he held it together.

He sounded almost resigned when he said, "Give me as many of the orbital elements as you have."

"I left it at two thousand ninety-seven kilometers so the semimajor axis would be—" I added Earth's radius to the altitude. "—eight thousand four hundred seventy-one kilometers. Inclination at forty-five degrees. Eccentricity is darn close to zero. The longitude of the ascending node is approximately one hundred eighty west. Velocity was six thousand eight hundred sixty meters per second. Changes in altitude were less than three meters per second but, frankly, that's within the error bars of my GPS."

I heard a pen scratching as he took the numbers down. "A two-line element set would be better," he muttered.

I knew about two-line elements but I didn't quite understand them. They didn't cover that in high school physics. I changed the subject.

"I'm going to remediate some more junk—you have any other problem debris?"

"Uh, I'm not at the office, but I don't recall any pressing issues this week. You have something in mind?"

"Yes. A chunk of *Cosmos 1375,* if it doesn't turn out to be too big."

I heard him typing on his computer. "Ah. *That* one. We will watch your operation with interest."

"Toodles."

I disconnected.

*Cosmos 1375* was put up just to be destroyed as part of a Soviet antisatellite test. According to my research there were fifty-six major pieces of it still in orbit. I caught up with mine as it passed 903 kilometers over the Aegean Sea.

It was like a dishwasher if a dishwasher were tumbling slowly and egg-shaped, with flattened tubing and twisted structural elements projecting at odd intervals. It was spinning slowly, perhaps once every three seconds. One hemisphere was blackened with carbon scoring while the other side was covered with torn sheets of gold foil. I think it was a fuel or oxidizer tank.

The first piece I grabbed, a section of tubing that extended out furthest, bent, twisted, and then snapped off in my hand. The tank tumbled on, only now with a slight wobble.

The next bracket I grabbed was firmly attached. The tank slowed down and I began rotating with it, or, more exactly, we started orbiting around a midpoint that corresponded with my elbow. This made me think the debris massed as much as I did, suit and all.

*A bit larger than your fifty-kilo limit.*

I *thought* I could jump it, but I didn't want to go all the way back to the lab with it. What if it fell on me?

I looked at the GPS readout and concentrated.

The earth was suddenly noticeably bigger, nearer, and darker. I flipped up the visor. I was back in eclipse over the Marshall Islands and headed for Hawaii. My altitude was one hundred kilometers but my speed hadn't changed: still 7.417 kilometers per second.

I let go and jumped to the southwest rim of Diamond Head crater, to the observation deck on top of the fire control station. The sky was brightening in the east but the state monument's parking lot in the crater floor was still in deep shadow. The lights of Waikiki were blazing, of course.

It was going by gut. I hadn't done any calculations, but I'd placed it five hundred meters per second too slow to maintain orbit. So I figured that between atmospheric drag and its trajectory, it would enter the atmosphere some—

The streak started low in the west and blazed halfway to the eastern horizon before it faded into the dawn.

Even if it wasn't burned completely to plasma, it would drop into the ocean long before it reached California.

Cory pulled the dosimeter from the coveralls' outer pocket while Tara and Joe were still going through the suit-depressurization checklist. As soon as the backpack and helmet came off he said, "Less exposure than your full orbit lower down. I still want to beef up the coveralls' shielding so the exposure at epidermis—" He checked the helmet dosimeter. "—is at least as good as it is in the helmet."

Joe's eyes got a bit wide, but he said, "Do you know Professor Seck?"

Cory shook his head. "I heard the name. Material sciences, yes?"

Joe nodded. "The TA I had in statics is one of her grad students. She was just funded for her work on hydrogen-rich polymeric nanocomposites for radiation shielding."

Cory said, "Nice catch." He scribbled the name and a note on the white board, circled it, and added the phrase, "lunch or something."

When Cory relaxed the suit, I said, "Back in five" and jumped directly to the Eyrie, where I changed into street clothes rather than hang around the lab in my long underwear . . . in front of Joe.

Dad and Tara were gone when I returned and Cory was doing something to the front of the shrunken suit as it hung in its stand. Joe leaned against the bench, watching.

Without turning his head Joe said, "Your dad gave Tara a lift back to Krakatoa. Could you make it part of the flange assembly going forward? Maybe an interlock with the helmet?"

I realized the questions were for Cory. I stepped forward to see better.

Cory held a piece of circuit protoboard with a large slide switch, a rheostat with an oversized knob, a cluster of resistors, capacitors, and IC chips, and a flat, rectangular lithium ion cell. A short cable ran from a connector on the edge of the board to the connector on the helmet flange.

"What's your thinking on the interlock?" Cory said.

Joe said, "Well, if the helmet is still on, you wouldn't want to relax it, right? You could still be in orbit. It would be another safety beyond the vacuum sensor."

Realization hit. I said, "Oh, is that the portable unit?"

Cory grinned, flipped the switch and twisted the rheostat. The suit expanded to full floppy mode. "Conservatively, we've got ten minutes of extension per charge cycle. If you expand it right before donning, and contract it immediately, I'd say you could go through ten don-and-doff cycles before you had to charge it." He patted the old shoebox-sized unit on the bench, "Though we'll always have this for backup."

"How do you charge it?" I asked.

He twisted the board to show the other connector.

"Ah, USB, nice."

"At least a two-amp charger, though."

"Vacuum hardened?"

"Designed and specced for. Hasn't been tested but all of those components are good for vacuum and derated below fifty percent."

I frowned. "Derated? What does that mean?"

Joe blinked. "You don't know that?"

I snapped, "We aren't all able to go to Stanford University, Joe!"

Cory's eyebrows went up but he said, "When a component is going to operate in an environment that will stress it—high temperature swings, extreme vibration and acceleration—you *derate* its capacity." He tapped one of the black rectangles on the board mounted on a multifinned heat sink. "This voyage regulator can handle up to ten amps, but for this application, we'll never pull more than five. The heat sink is oversized, too, since it can't count on air convection for cooling, only radiation. It's like building a bridge to handle fifty tons but never allowing a truck bigger than twenty-five tons to use it."

Joe held up his hands. "I was just surprised. You know so much more than me about this—" He gestured at the suit and at the life-support pack, ending with a gesture that took in the ceiling, and, I guess, the sky. "I wasn't trying to insult you. I only learned it myself last month in my intro-to-aerospace class."

My ears turned red and I had to look away. "You have this opportunity that I'll *never* have," I said. "I barely got six months of high school before they took that away."

Cory looked at me, puzzled. "Then where did you do your undergrad?"

I turned my back to him but it wasn't enough, I had to jump away.

I fell to my knees in the Eyrie. It was worse than crying, it was those wracking sobs, three of them in succession, and then I was yelling at myself. "Shut *UP*. Stop feeling sorry for yourself!" I wanted to smash something.

I jumped to ten thousand feet and let myself drop, twisting

deliberately, turning it into a tumbling flailing plummet, cold air stabbing through my clothes and yanking at my hair.

The ground rushed toward me and then I was crouched in the sandy wash panting, but at least the tears had stopped.

Back in the Eyrie I washed my face. The water from the kitchen cistern was cold and that helped too, but when I looked in the mirror my eyes were puffy. I didn't like that person.

I felt guilty for misleading Cory. I felt guilty for feeling sorry for myself. Sure, Joe got to go to Stanford but he wasn't able to go as far afield as I had. Forget Australia, Asia, Europe—I'd been to *space*.

I was wearing sunglasses when I jumped back. Joe was standing at the bench with the helmet over his head, one hand bracing the flange, the other sliding the reflective visor up and down.

"Doesn't feel right unless you've got it locked into the suit," I said.

He jerked and I heard his head bang against the polycarbonate. He was biting his lip when he lifted it off his head. "Just wanted to see—"

"Of *course* you wanted to. Who wouldn't?"

He set the helmet back on the bench, resettling the armored hoses and the backpack. "Cory had to go to a thing. I told him we'd make sure the lab was locked."

I nodded.

He gestured at the helmet. "Bigger than I expected—not as claustrophobic."

He hadn't tried it with the headset and the neck gasket. The sensation of being slowly strangled might have changed his mind, but I just nodded again.

The camera was sitting on the workbench, case open, the memory card beside it. I gestured at it.

Joe said, "Tara grabbed the video from today. She wants to cut some clips for the website." He kept looking at the camera, then said, "She wants me to do some more voice-over work on that, if it's okay with you."

I shrugged. "Certainly. Uh, you guys did a great job on the audio loop."

"Well, that was Tara. Hard taskmaster."

"Uh, the spots were, what, thirty seconds? How long did it take you?"

He grimaced. "She kept me in front of the mic until two in the morning. We must've done twenty-five takes on the 'Space Girl' jingle alone. I gave up and went home after about the tenth take on the Diné spot and she still wasn't satisfied. I don't know how much sleep *she* got."

I didn't know what to say, so I just nodded.

He changed the subject. "Cory was surprised to learn you hadn't any formal university-undergrad time."

I winced. "I should've told him."

"I don't know. He said you never *told* him you had. He just assumed you were at least a third-year undergrad from your level of comprehension and maturity."

I blushed. "I didn't mean to mislead him."

Joe shook his head. "If anything, he was more impressed knowing you've done what you've done with homeschooling and self-study. Then insulted you and we had words before he had to leave."

"He insulted me?"

"He said you were the most impressive autodidact he'd ever met. Not fair. I told him sure, you could be a bit didactic—well a lot didactic—but there was nothing automatic about it. When you're doing that you're being *deliberately* annoying."

My mouth twitched and, dammit, he *saw* that.

He said, "I should be careful before you go all autodidact on my ass." Then he sobered. "I know you wanted to go to college, Cent. But I thought it was because you wanted to be with me." His mouth turned down. "Self-centered?" He made a checkmark in the air. "Achievement *unlocked*."

I said, "I *did* want to be with you, too." *Still do.*

His face twisted and it was his turn to look away. "You were just so good at everything. Like you didn't need to study or work. I was able to keep up this semester because I busted my ass. I had to do that in high school, too."

I'd seen his graduation ceremony from the back of the mezzanine. "You were a straight-A student!"

"Because I *worked* at it. I was a D student in middle school. I skateboarded. I smoked pot. I tried to get laid. That was *it*. When I went into high school I didn't have the habits and I didn't have the material and that was obvious to me the first week of school."

"I *know* how smart you are," I said. "Getting Ds had to take some work."

Joe raised his eyebrows. "Well, yeah. You have to *not* do the work *and* skip the tests *and* alienate your teachers. It was *exhausting*."

"You could've coasted through high school without much work. Why not do that?"

"My last year of eighth grade, a second cousin of mine dropped out of his high school, got mixed up with a gang, and went to *prison*.

"His mother fell apart. I mean, she couldn't hold it together, lost her job. My parents ended up taking her in. I got to listen to her talk about it for an entire summer. I had to go with her to *visit* her son."

"You thought *you* would go to prison if you didn't get good grades?"

"Well, I didn't think *that* would happen—Matt was pretty much a jerk all his life—but I wasn't ruling out some other spectacular failure. It wasn't what happened to Matt that scared me—it was what it did to his mother. I didn't . . . I couldn't do something like that to my mom."

I'd never heard this before. We'd talked a lot about our childhoods, but not this.

"I never had that choice," I said.

"Huh?"

"I wasn't in elementary or middle school. My parents both knew *exactly* how I was doing on my school work. I had a formal study schedule when I was *four.* Distracted by friends? Smoke pot? Get in trouble with boys? Ha! You and I both have good study habits, but it wasn't like I *decided. You* got to make that choice."

Then I smacked myself on the forehead and started laughing.

"What's so funny?"

"Our first-world tragedies. 'Oh, no, I must work hard because I am attending a world-class university. Oh, no, I'm able to travel all over the world and I have multiple homes.'" I squeezed my eyes shut. "There are kids who will die today because they don't have clean water. Try and convince *them* of my troubles."

"Stupid comparison. Maybe we're luckier than ninety percent of the people on the planet, but no matter how expensive the shoe, it still pinches when it doesn't fit."

Okay, every time Dad tried that *Eat your dinner, there are kids starving in Bangladesh,* I'd shoved the plate toward him and said *Then give it to them.* Joe was right. Misery isn't a bloody competition.

Joe was chewing on his lower lip.

"Go ahead," I said. "Say it."

He shook his head. "No."

"Why not?"

"I'm supposed to be home for dinner tonight. What the hell am I going to do if you hear what I want to say and then bug out, leaving me twelve hundred miles from home?"

Now that set my heart to pounding. What hurtful thing did he have to say that would make me do that to him? "Oh, I don't know. That might be the *least* of your troubles." I wondered how he'd like to try a flailing plummet from ten thousand feet.

"Bring it," he said.

I sighed. "Get your coat."

"Where the hell are we?" Joe said.

It was bitter cold and we scrambled through crusted snow to get across the parking lot and into the closest door. The one that said, *Employees Entrance.*

We were in a hallway, a time clock and a rack full of cards mounted to the right by a series of workplace safety posters. There was a sign that said, *Reception at the East Entrance.*

"We're in Franklin, Wisconsin. We're going to talk to a guy about a blimp. Well, sort of. BlimpWerks makes remote-control scale-model blimps that can be flown around stadiums with advertiser signs on them. They create special shapes, too." I pointed at a framed photo on the wall. It showed an SUV-shaped blimp floating above a crowd at a basketball game. The next photo showed a burger-shaped blimp for one of the national fast-food chains dropping leaflets on a crowd at a hockey game. Several more photos showed classic zeppelin-shaped blimps with logos painted or hung on the sides. "But they also have some prototypes I'm interested in."

Joe looked at his watch and I said, "I'll have you home for dinner. I promise."

We found receptionist at the other end of the hallway and I asked her for Mr. Papadopolis, the sales engineer.

Mr. Papadopolis was not as tall as Joe, but muscular—not just a weight lifter but a body builder. He took one look at the way I was hunched over my crossed arms and offered us something hot to drink in the employee break room. Joe had coffee, I had tea.

Mr. Papadopolis had a distressing tendency to want to talk to Joe, but Joe, bless his heart, just pointed at me. "I'm just along to look pretty. She's the buyer."

Mr. Papadopolis adjusted quickly enough. "Right. What kind of blimp do you need? Is this a school branding for stadium games?"

I shook my head. "I was talking to your Ms. Wilde in R and D about your new fabric and she mentioned the test spheres."

"Oh! I don't know what you'd do with them. They were really just an assembly-and-performance test. We needed to make sure the new fabric heat welded properly and held pressure at least as well as our standard envelope. They'd make awful blimps."

I nodded. "Yes, wrong shape, not a problem for *our* application. Could you give me and my, um, *colleague* the details on your new fabric?"

Joe glared at me.

"Well, it's a tougher version of our standard three point two-ounce helium-tight envelope. *Our* proprietary material is a treated three-ply ripstop nylon that will hold its helium long term. Our competition uses polyurethane and has to have helium added midperformance to keep buoyancy. But not our stuff. We can save you thousands on your annual helium costs."

He looked in danger of going all-in on his sales spiel so I said quickly, "So what's different about this fabric? Ms. Wilde said something about incorporating Kevlar now?"

"Yes. The middle layer is now Kevlar for decreased pressure deformation, and we added an aluminized Mylar layer on the outside for UV protection. Some of our clients have experimental designs that need higher pressures. They're working toward lifting body rigidity, for slightly-heavier-than-air vehicles, you know. They want to achieve lift below three knots of air-speed, so they needed something scuff-resistance for takeoffs and landings."

Joe asked, "How much heavier is this fabric than your standard envelope?"

"A slight increase, just a half an ounce for twice the strength and hardly any deformation."

Joe frowned and Papadopolis added, "That's per square yard."

I said, "Ah. So this is three point seven ounces per square yard? Could we see the prototypes?"

"Right."

He led us through their assembly bay and into the attached warehouse.

The first thing Joe and I saw was a half-inflated, sixty-foot-long puffer fish hanging from the rafters. I froze, looking up at it. "Wow."

He glanced at me and then up. "Yeah. Cool, huh? We made it for the triple-F, but they went bankrupt before we got more than the deposit."

I stared at it. It had obviously been designed to depict a puffer in its fully inflated defensive mode. Fully inflated, it would be nearly spherical with a white bottom and a mottled brown top. It had the distinctive spines projecting out everywhere but the face. "Triple-F?"

"Fukushima Fugu Festival. You know, where they eat the fish?"

I nodded. "Oh, yeah. Fugu sashimi. Expensive yet poison."

He chuckled. "That's right. A few people die every year. I understand the trick is to get a tiny bit of the poison. Just enough so your lips go numb."

I shook my head. "Not for me, thanks. But *that*—" I pointed up. "—is beautiful."

"We're trying to interest the Macy's parade people but they prefer to commission their own sponsored balloons." He started walking again. "Ah, over there." He threaded his way through rows of stacked boxes and rolls of fabric to a pallet rack against the wall. He pointed to the fourth row up.

"*That* pallet. I'll go get the steps."

I was tempted to jump up to the shelf, but that would have freaked him out. He went down to the corner of the room and started pushing a large rolling set of steep stairs, about fifteen feet tall, with a railing on one side only. Joe helped him guide it into place, and Mr. Papadopolis threw a lever, causing the wheels to lift up, dropping it onto sturdy, nonskid feet.

When we got to the small platform at the top, the pallet was chest high on me but came up to his stomach. He slapped a bundle of silver fabric about the size of a rolled-up sleeping bag. "Here's the first test sphere. Four yards in diameter." He pointed up at the ceiling. "For the helium test it bobbed around the rafters for four weeks. We were going to wait until it lost buoyancy but gave up finally and had to haul it down for the scuff tests."

I fingered the cloth. I could make out the texture of the weave but it was through a coating or coatings. "How were the scuff tests done?"

"We pumped it up to twenty psi with an air compressor and played soccer with it."

"Soccer? It was, what, over twice as high as you?"

"Well, maybe it was more like uh, polo. We used golf carts

to push it. It was fun until a northwester came up. It bounced over the fence and took off for Racine. Fortunately it caught in some woods before it crossed I-94." He shook his head smiling. "Hell of a scuff test, though."

"It didn't get punctured or ripped?"

"Nope, it was still holding at twenty-one psi."

"I thought you pumped it to twenty."

"It was spring. Sun came out from behind the clouds." He held his hands out, fingers spread, suggesting a ball shape. "You see when the air heats—"

"Boyle's law, we know," I said quickly before he could mansplain it to me. I tapped a bundle on the same pallet, the same color but nearly twice as big around. "Are these all the same material?"

He nodded, tapping and speaking in turn. "Four yards, ten yards, twelve yards. After hockey season we're starting on a lifting body."

"Would you sell these?"

"What, *all* of them?"

"The small one to start. If it works out, then the others."

"Have to talk to my sales manager to cost it out." He eyed me doubtfully. "If you've got the resources."

"Right. I don't expect to pay a *huge* amount, though. They're used, right?"

"They're unique."

"Well, give me your card and I'll call you midweek to see what your manager said."

Rather than go out into the icy wind again, I jumped Joe to the alley behind Krakatoa from the stairwell.

He checked his watch. He was gnawing on his lip again.

Against my better judgment I said, "You aren't twelve hundred miles from home, you know." I was still poised to jump away.

Joe looked at me and his eyes teared up. That, alone, made me want to run screaming.

"I'm sorry." He was staring down at my feet. "I . . . I betrayed you. I violated your trust. I know an apology is nothing against the hurt I caused you, but I need to say this because the words just keep circling through my head over and over and over, all day and all night. I wish it had never happened. I wish I hadn't been so *stupid*, so *weak*, so . . . *afraid*."

He looked at me and, dammit, a tear spilled down his cheek.

I opened my mouth but I couldn't say anything.

He nodded slightly. "There. That was it. I've been trying to get that out—just that. The early versions were all begging and asking and totally wrong. I've deleted them and burned them and flushed them. I don't need a response. I don't expect one." He turned on heel and as he walked away, I heard his last words echo off the wall of the alley.

"I don't deserve one."

# TWENTY-FOUR

## Cent: Going Viral

I knew the commercial-satellite community would take notice as soon as *AOS-Sat One* made it into the space command tracking catalog, but I wasn't expecting the rabid subset of amateur radio hobbyists who tracked satellites. And I didn't count on them directing *everybody* on the Internet to our website, specifically to Tara's new video spot: thirty seconds of me and the universe and every satellite and piece of debris I'd recorded, finishing with my nausea-inducing spin cross-fading into the Space Girl logo.

The video went viral over twelve hours and our hosting service crashed hard at hour fifteen. At first they thought it was a denial-of-service attack, but when they saw it was legitimate traffic, they offered me five years of high-bandwidth service if they could manage ads on our sidebar. Tara said, "Hell, no," and took over the e-mail negotiations.

In the end, *they* got an ad for their hosting service on our home page and the site got its own dedicated server on the main backbone.

"*I'll* manage the advertising," said Tara. "Last thing we want to do is to cheapen our brand with a bunch of erectile dysfunction ads. I'm thinking Iridium Communications and Merrell apparel."

The info@apexorbital.com inbox choked on incoming fan mail, interview requests, and business inquiries, and our hosting service had to upgrade *that*.

Twenty-four hours later the video started showing up on network news. Grandmother recorded as much of the coverage as possible.

Dad was *not* pleased.

I told him, "You *knew* we had to go public to grow the business. What did you want me to do? Start a lemonade stand?"

He scowled at me. "At least your visor is down in all those clips."

Our site crashed again and our service replaced the dedicated server with a server cluster.

I gave up on keeping Tara off the site. Someone had to deal with the e-mail, but I didn't give her access until we'd set up two offshore virtual private network accounts with advanced encryption.

She VPN-ed into the Norway account and, from there, VPN-ed into the Singapore account. Only then did she touch the hosting service to download e-mail and update the site.

Journalists were not just sending *us* e-mails.

USSPACECOM's press office said, "We have no comment on that."

Iridium Communications did confirm that the image on the video *was* their Iridium 4 commsat and that they had received the full inspection video referred to therein. They did *not* mention that my orbit-to-ground communications were via their network.

A junior member of the House Armed Services Committee announced his intention to call for an investigative hearing on this threat to national security. The chairman said drily, "I wish the representative from Florida good luck with that."

Roberta appeared on CNN, introduced by the interviewer as Dr. Matapang of Texas A&M University. The titles beneath her face said, *Dr. Roberta Matapang, Satellite Designer, Ph.D. in Aerospace Engineering.*

"Who *is* Space Girl?"

Roberta raised her eyebrows. "I believe that is the call sign of Apex Orbital Services' CEA."

"CEA?"

"Chief executive astronaut."

The interviewer did a double take. "Oh. But what's her name? Her nationality?"

"American? Don't know for sure."

"But you *have* met her?"

"Yes. Three times. Once when she delivered our failed *Tinkerbell* research satellite after recovering it from orbit. A lunch meeting to arrange the delivery of our *Lost Boy* unit *into* orbit. And when she picked up *Lost Boy* prior to that mission."

"What does she look like?"

"A young woman. American? Canadian? Very intelligent. Direct. I like her very much."

"Are you in communication with her now?"

Matapang looked from the interviewer to the camera and winked. "Depends on whether or not she is watching, doesn't it?" She looked back at the interviewer. "I've talked to her by phone twice, during missions. Other than that, we exchange e-mails."

"During missions? What does that mean?"

"She was in orbit, both times."

"How do you *know* that?"

"Well, she was delivering satellites to orbit both times."

They split the screen and put up a still taken from our video, a full frame of *AOS-Sat One,* but before I moved into the frame. "Was one of them this satellite? Made by your lab at Texas A&M University?"

Roberta held up her hands. "Assembled, rather." She talked about the various parts and functions of the satellite, spending most of the time discussing the fiberglass mast while a clip of it self-assembling ran in the foreground. "I was the primary designer and fabricator but I was ably assisted by Ritchie Winodgrodzki and Amber Cosby."

"Are they other faculty at the Texas A&M?"

"Undergraduate students, but I have high expectations."

"So . . . tent poles?"

Matapang grinned. "Yes, tent poles."

The interviewer leaned forward, face serious. "You've heard the arguments about this being a hoax, the product of computer special effects. The fact that there were no detected launches that corresponded to these orbits."

Robert grinned. "Of course."

"What to do you have to say to that?"

"Nothing."

"What? You're not going to argue it's *not* a hoax?"

"Your producers don't think it's a hoax. I'm on your show because dozens of amateur satellite trackers reported the bird's existence. CNN flew me to Atlanta because millions of people have watched the video and found it compelling. But for me, the best reason you're taking this seriously is that the U.S. Space Command issued *AOS-Sat One* a catalog number and is issuing tracking statuses on it, just as it does every other spacecraft around the planet.

"Talk to *them* if you think it's a hoax."

"But how did it *get* there?"

"No idea. If you find out, I would *love* to know."

The newly famous (notorious) firm of Apex Orbital Services offered every university in North America the chance to orbit their microsats (anything up to twenty-five kilos) at the low, low price of one thousand dollars per kilo, with a thousand dollar minimum.

We did not require vibration or temperature testing, but for this low, low price we would be releasing them in low, low orbits where atmospheric drag would deorbit them within three months.

We weren't expecting the number of takers.

"Three hundred and fifty-five satellites?" I said.

"That's just the ones who've paid so far," said Tara.

"Three hundred and fifty-five thousand dollars?" I was having trouble wrapping my head around it.

"Oh, no, girlfriend. It's over half a million so far, though our

Singapore credit-card handler is taking three percent. Over half of them are one-cube units under a kilo, but we've got a lot of three-cube units and a surprising number of units over ten kilos."

Cory said, "I think you can blame Matapang."

"What does Roberta have to do with anything?"

Cory grinned. "She open sourced the plans for *AOS-Sat One*. You said it yourself back when we were arguing about soda lime versus lithium hydroxide: So many decisions are made because of weight constraints. When you put things up *your* way, you don't have to account for acceleration and the high cost of extra weight.

"I'd say a lot of these units were heavily modified in the last two weeks when they realized they didn't have to fit all their stuff in a standard cubesat deployer or follow all the red tape in '91-710.'"

"What's that?"

"'USSPACECOM Manual 91-710: Range Safety User Requirements.' It has seven volumes. Not to say that most of these didn't jump through all the hoops. Most of these are standard cubesats that were on launch waiting lists for years or were rejected for not doing *important* enough research. Some are probably practice units, the functional engineering prototypes created to test a design before making the *approved* one.

"At our launch rates, it's okay if they don't survive first contact with space. It's a reasonable risk."

Tara said, "At least thirty of these had their launch fees paid for by Kickstarter campaigns."

"Great," I said. "Now we're taking *lunch* money."

The other caveat for our customers was that they had to deliver their units to our designated agents at Denver International Airport *inside* security. In other words, they all had to go through TSA X-ray and explosives sniffing before we saw them.

It was Joe's idea. Cory told him about Dad's worry that *they* could use a satellite as a way to attack us. Cory thought it was very clever. Tara did to. So did Dad.

Okay. It was clever.

It eliminated a few units that were using propellants like hydrazine or used explosive bolts for deployment. If they used cold nitrogen-gas propellants they had to arrive empty with instructions for charging. Electric propulsion units that used arcs to generate plasmas that were in turn accelerated by electromagnetic fields made it through. Most of the satellites, though, didn't use propulsion, just attitude control using gyroscopes or a passive gravity gradient like *AOS-Sat*'s mast, or magnetorquer rods to interact with the ambient magnetosphere. The TSA had no problem with these.

We hooked up the clients with college students flying home for the holidays through Denver. Dad took delivery and put them in a storage vault rented for the purpose, 650 feet under the prairie near Hutchinson, Kansas.

Dad said, "It was a salt mine. Now it's a document-storage facility. After all, these satellites are designed to be tracked, and rather than worry if we got all the power off—well, unless they're sending messages with neutrinos, nothing is going to get through."

I said, "That works for me."

I made a deal with General Sterling: We'd give him a list of the day's deliveries ahead of time and USSPACECOM would do a COLA evaluation (Collision Avoidance on Launch) to avoid creating more debris.

We put the first set up on New Year's Day.

I hadn't planned on asking Joe for help but when I showed up to pick up Tara, he was there, waiting with her. It was easier to jump him to the lab than to talk to him—to tell him I didn't want his help.

Especially when I wasn't at all sure what I wanted.

Dad jumped Cory into the vault with a folding table. Tara and Joe ran the checklist on the suit and I prebreathed oxygen.

Deep underground, Cory carefully connected batteries or threw switches. When I was fully suited up, Dad met me in a field in Oklahoma holding a plastic milk crate with eight activated cubesats nestled in duct tape and foam pockets.

A piece of duct tape stuck to the outside of the crate said,

*Polar Set: 1340 UT, 7.895 kps, 205 k Alt., 87° Inc., 190 west, 0 north.*

I managed this orbit immediately, still near the Marshall Islands but lower and headed almost due north. I only had to do one tweak to smooth out some eccentricity before I released them, one at a time, pushing them gently away in different directions.

Cory had said, "You can probably just dump the whole crate since *any* change in velocity will move them into slightly diverging orbits, but let's keep them from banging into each other."

I tried to report the deployment to General Sterling, but when I called, someone else answered his phone.

"General Sterling's office, Captain Soldt, speaking."

"Uh, is the general available?"

"He's on an urgent call. If this is Space . . . Apex Orbital, he asked me to receive your information and request that you hold for him."

"O . . . kay. The first eight are deployed, parameters as agreed."

Soldt said, "Ah. I see it on the list. The polar orbits?"

"Right. Still no problem? It's not too late to retrieve them."

"Uh. I believe the track is good. *Wow.* Sorry, I'm just a bit amazed you're calling from orbit."

"Is there any problem with doing the next ten, the set that's scheduled for fourteen-forty Zulu?"

"I don't think—ah, the general's available, now."

Sterling came on. "Are you in orbit?"

"Yes, General. How was your Christmas?"

"Lovely thanks, but never mind that. I have an urgent situation with the International Space Station."

I blinked. "Debris?"

"No. A medical emergency. Flight Engineer Mikhail Grebenchekov presented with acute lower-back pain last night. Ultrasound imaging revealed a ten centimeter-diameter abdominal aortic aneurism below his kidneys with evidence of bleeding into the abdomen. He needs emergency surgery right *now* and it is the consensus of the mission flight surgeons that reentry deceleration in either the Dragon capsule or the Soyuz will rupture the aneurism."

My heart was suddenly very loud in my ears. "Are you asking for my help?"

"Depends on what you can do. If you can get him down without five Gs of acceleration, I'd phrase that as 'We're begging for your help.' "

I stammered, "Cer-certainly, General. Where does he need to go?"

"Texas Medical Center in Houston? Brooke Army Medical Center? Russian Academy of Medical Sciences? *Someplace* with a competent vascular surgical team."

I didn't have sites for *any* of those places but I'd walked past the emergency entrance of Stanford Hospital several times with Joe, back before the . . . incident.

"I can put him outside the emergency room of Stanford Hospital. That's about the best hospital I can get to. The only other site I have is a second-class regional medical center in the southwest."

"Stanford—as in Palo Alto?"

"Yeah."

"Let me talk to NASA. Perhaps you should move closer to the ISS while I'm doing that?"

"Where is it right now?"

"Uh, just now passed the Queensland Coast, headed northeast. You want elements?"

"Longitude, latitude, bearing, altitude, horizontal and vertical velocity."

"That's *so* wrong." He read them off to me.

I said, "Transitioning. Call me back."

I appeared in eclipse and flipped up the visor. The station was ahead of me in the orbit, and above, lit by the half moon behind me. I could see the truss and the panels and the pressurized modules, but it stretched no farther across the sky than the moon did behind me.

The phone rang and I answered, "Space Girl."

"Sterling. I've got mission control at Johnson patched in. They, uh, want to interface with your control systems so you can *safely* approach the ISS."

"Oh, really?"

Another man's voice came on. "This is Flight Director Grimes. We have you at ten kilometers on the Warden system. We didn't see you enter our no-fly sphere. What is your propellant?"

I rolled my eyes and jumped.

The ISS went from thumbnail size held at an arm's length to bigger than my spread fingers.

In the background I heard a voice say, "—under a thousand meters!" and Flight Director Grimes said, "Abort your approach! Abort your approach!"

"General? Do they want assistance or not?"

Sterling sounded exasperated. "It's not just Grebenchekov. There's seven other people on the station and a hundred and fifty billion dollars in infrastructure investment."

I closed my eyes. *I* knew I could get there without breaking things. "What does the crew want?"

The flight director said, "They are, of course, very concerned for their crewmate, but it's *our* job to weigh all the factors when—"

I just disconnected.

My next jump took me to fifty meters under the Destiny module just as the station passed the terminator. Sunlight ran golden fire down the length of the solar panels and I flinched, flipping down the visor and blinking my eyes.

I'd seen photos, but really, just like everything else, the photos don't do it justice.

All the shutters were open on the observation cupola on the Tranquility node, making it look like an exotic six-petaled flower. I could see two faces in the central circular window, both looking down—out?—at me. I added a few meters per second velocity in that direction, adjusting sideways as the entire station tried to slide away from me.

Go fast to raise. Slow down to drop. Moving in orbit is not

intuitive. I killed all relative velocity one meter away from the cupola.

A woman whose wildly spreading hair was constrained by the headset she was wearing was waving at me, grinning widely. The man next to her was shaking his head, but not, I think, in disapproval.

The phone rang.

"Space Girl."

General Sterling sounded amused. "The flight director has given up on the official docking procedures. Commander Elliott reports that you're right outside the cupola?"

"Yes. Am I good to enter?"

"One second. They're going to patch—"

A woman's voice came over my headset. The words didn't quite sync with the woman's lips on the other side of the glass, but I could tell it was her, her words lagging as they were routed through multiple satellites and ground stations.

"—can hear her. Can she hear me?"

I held up my thumb. "Loud and clear."

"Hey! Ditto that. I'm Flight Engineer Alis Nagata. This is Commander Ken Elliott. Where is your spacecraft?" She craned her neck to look through the side ports, scanning.

Ah, well, I knew it would come out eventually.

"I'm wearing it," I said.

They looked at each other.

She said, "How is that—"

"Even possible?" I channeled Matapang. "That's a *very good* question. First things first—didn't you declare a medical emergency?"

"Uh, roger that. We're clearing the suits out of the Quest Joint Airlock so we can depressurize it for your entry. Shouldn't take more than—"

I jumped.

The call dropped as the metal skin of the ISS cut out my satphone signal. My ears popped and the automatic feed valve buzzed loudly, jetting oxygen into my helmet to raise it above the station's one atmosphere.

I'd jumped past Elliott and Nagata in the cupola into the middle of the Tranquility node. I put my hand on a bright blue handrail and twisted back toward them.

They were staring, wide-eyed, and a buzzing alarm was audible even through my helmet.

I flipped up the visor and held up my hand with a "Wait," motion. It only took me ten seconds to shut off my oxygen feed, purge the helmet, and disengage the flange. The alarm was louder now and I left the headset on to protect my ears. Despite knowing it was okay, it felt dangerous to let go of the helmet, but when I finally did, it just hung there, above my head.

Commander Elliott turned and spoke into an intercom box, "Override the depressurization alarm and double-check it with ETHOS." The alarm cut off and he said, "Un-fucking-believable!"

I removed the headset. "What was that?" I pointed at my ear.

"Rapid depressurization alarm, when you, uh, came aboard," he said. "For a second there, I thought we'd left the screen door open. The pressure drop stopped as soon as it started, though."

Flight Engineer Nagata said, "I . . . guess we don't need the air lock after all. Welcome to the International Space Station."

Even without the alarm buzzing, the space station is *noisy*. There's coolant pumps and control moment gyroscopes and humidity control and $CO_2$ scrubbers and water reclamation and motors for pointing the solar panels. But mostly it's fans, everywhere, circulating air, their whirr and whine echoing off of every metal and plastic surface.

I shucked my life-support pack, helmet, headset, and gloves in the Tranquility node, and left them secured, tucking one of the harness straps, doubled, under a handrail. Flight Engineer Nagata led the way and Commander Elliott brought up the rear.

I was trembling.

First of all, it was *the International Space Station*. Sections of it had been up longer than I'd been alive. I'd sat on dark mountainsides or in the middle of deserts, watching it burst through the terminator into sunlight and streak across the night sky.

Then there was the weightlessness. Yes, I'd been experiencing microgravity for a while now, but never without a helmet on. I wanted to shed the rest of the suit and bounce from bulkhead to bulkhead, unrestricted.

We floated into the Unity node and hooked a rail to turn, ninety degrees, into Destiny, the U.S. Lab. For a second I thought we were floating down, but then Alis changed her orientation, and when I twisted to match her, the far wall wasn't down anymore, but level, like entering any room back on Earth.

"That's Grebenchekov on the CMRS," Nagata said. The man was loosely strapped to what looked like a cot, fastened to the "floor." He was tucked into a thin sleeping bag with armholes, but the zipper was pulled down to expose his abdomen and upper legs. He was wearing boxer briefs and a T-shirt.

Commander Elliott said, "Crew Medical Restraint System."

Another woman "stood" beside him, one foot hooked into the frame of the "cot." She had a blood-pressure cuff on Grebenchekov's upper leg and a stethoscope pressed to his inner thigh, listening intently as she bled the pressure from the cuff. She wrote a number down on the clipboard Velcroed to her pants leg.

Her eyes went wide when she saw me, but then she patted Grebenchekov on the shoulder. "Hey, Misha! There's a pretty girl to see you, you lucky bastard."

Flight Engineer Grebenchekov did *not* look good. His color was pasty white and his eyes were unfocused, but he made an effort, twisting his head and then shaking it slightly as he took in the neck flange on my suit, the coveralls, and my face.

"*Chyort voz'mi!* I must be sicker than I thought."

I trotted out one of my few phrases of Russian, "*Ya ochen rad poznakomitsya.*" *I'm very glad to have met you.*

"*Kozmos devushka?*"

Wow. So "Space Girl" was getting Russian coverage, too? I turned my shoulder to show him the Space Girl patch. "*Da.*"

The other woman held out her hand. "I'm Kate Rasmussen." When I shook it, she held onto my hand, staring at me. "My *daughter* is older than you are."

"Probably. How old is she?"

"Twenty-two." She released my hand.

I held it up and extend all five digits.

"Five years older?" she said.

I nodded.

Commander Elliott was using a communications handset near the hatch into Unity node. "Hey, Space Girl. USSPACECOM says you can deliver Mikhail to Stanford Hospital—is that their med school?"

"Yep. Whenever you're ready."

"*Without* deceleration?"

"Well, there'll be a one-time change to one G." I shrugged. "Can't avoid it. It's what we *use* down there."

Commander Elliott's lips twitched and he said, "Right. He's been up *here* for one hundred and fifty-six days. There's going to be some stress, regardless."

Three more men floated into the room, one of them coming from the Harmony node at the far end of the lab and the other two from the Unity node, behind us. They'd probably come from the Russian end of the station. That's the language they were speaking, anyway.

Both of them did a double take when they saw me. The one in front held out his hand, but when I tried to shake it, he began examining the suit fabric, bending my fingers and wrist.

His English was excellent, with an accent more British than Russian. "That's all?" He tried to push up the sleeve of the coveralls. "Just the one layer?"

"That's the *important* layer. I've got a pair of overgloves back with my helmet for thermal and abrasion protection." I pulled my hand gently out of his. "They don't hold pressure."

"But it allows transpiration? Cooling by evaporation?"

I nodded. "Yes. A mechanical counterpressure suit. It keeps me quite comfortable." His companion was reaching out to touch the helmet flange, peering over it at the neck seal. I waved them off. "Guys!"

Nagata said, "Oleg! Pyotr! *Vesti sebya!*"

They backed off, abashed.

"*Izvinyayetsya,*" said Oleg.

"Sorry," said Pyotr.

I looked at Commander Elliott and motioned at Grebenchekov. "Are they ready for us at Stanford?"

"They don't believe it, but, yes—they're ready. They have a vascular surgical team scrubbing and mission control sent them the video of the ultrasound exam." He turned to the Russian who'd been palpating my hand. "Oleg, will you get Mikhail's Orlan suit?"

I shook my head. "He won't need it. We'll go directly."

Kate Rasmussen said, "Directly." Her voice was flat, her eyebrows raised.

Nagata said to her, "You felt the pressure drop?"

"Of course."

The other Russian—Pyotr?—said, "Everybody felt the drop. Everybody's ears popped."

I blushed. "Sorry. That was me."

"Did you cycle through the air lock before it was fully equalized?" asked Rasmussen. "I mean, you couldn't, really. The pressure would hold the door closed."

Commander Elliott said, "She didn't come through the air lock. One second she was outside the cupola, the next she was in the middle of Node 3."

Both the Russians looked extremely doubtful. So did Rasmussen

"Like *this*," I said, and jumped back to Node 3—Tranquility—where my life-support pack was.

I heard the combined shout—well, part gasp, part shriek, part yell—come around the bend, even over the ventilation fans.

I slung the pack and tightened it, put the headset around my neck, and returned to the U.S. Lab, pulling myself along one handed, holding the helmet and gloves under my arm.

Commander Elliott was floating through the hatch from the U.S. Lab, looking toward me. "Ah. Good." He turned back into the lab, clearing my way and calling out, "She went for her gear in Node 3."

As I floated back into Destiny, Rasmussen's mouth was open. Even Grebenchekov was staring.

"See?" I said. "Directly."

Flight Engineer Nagata asked, "Why wasn't there a pressure drop when you did that?"

"Why do you think?"

She narrowed her eyes and then said, "Because there's no pressure differential between here and Node 3?"

"Yes."

Nagata nodded. "Unlike when you came in from vacuum—seven hundred forty-eight millimeters of mercury difference."

"Sorry? Millimeters of mercury? Like fourteen point seven psi?"

She laughed. "Close. One atmosphere is seven hundred sixty millimeters of mercury. Call it a quarter-of-a-pound difference."

"Ah. Well, the transition isn't instantaneous, so I *leak* a bit between locations." *Or a lot.* I was definitely not going to describe twinning to them. "So, you'll get a *bump* in pressure when I take him to Stanford. That's sea level."

Before they could get started on the phenomenon—I could see the questions forming in their eyes—I lowered the helmet over my head.

Rasmussen held up one hand, stopping me. "I *thought* the suit was unnecessary since you're going *directly*." She was unwrapping the blood pressure cuff from around Grebenchekov's thigh.

I paused with the helmet flange just above my eyes. "If I don't put this back on, it will drop to the ground, or, worse, land on Mikhail here, when we're in gravity again." I made an 'X' over my heart. "I promise I won't expose him to vacuum."

Commander Elliott said, "I think we're going to have to trust her, Kate."

Rasmussen bit her lip. She zipped the sleeping bag three quarters of the way up, then took the sheet of paper off her clipboard and tucked it inside, over Grebenchekov's chest, before pulling the zipper up the last bit. "These are my notes on his initial symptoms, his vitals, and his history and medications."

She pulled herself down and kissed Grebenchekov on the lips. *"Ya lyublyu tebya*, Misha."

His lips twitched and he said, *"Ya tozhe moy dorogoy doktor."*

I latched my helmet but I didn't bother turning on the oxygen—the rebreather fans were still running. Pulling on my gloves, I tucked one of my hiking boots into the frame of the CMRS and crouched down, putting my other knee against the bulkhead.

Rasmussen unstrapped Grebenchekov and floated him into my arms. I put one arm under his shoulders and the other across his chest. She locked eyes with me, staring through my helmet, searching for something—reassurance, I guess.

I winked at her and jumped.

I arrived crouched, cradling Grebenchekov's head and shoulders, then fell backwards, onto my rump, still holding him, and he ended up across my lap. His legs bumped into the sidewalk and his eyes went wide as he felt gravity for the first time in 157 days.

I twisted off the helmet one handed and lifted it slightly. "Are you all right?"

He stared blankly ahead and seemed to be having trouble breathing.

"Misha! Okay?" I said, louder.

He blinked and focused on my face. *"Da."* He reached up and patted my arm weakly.

Then the ER's automatic doors opened and organized chaos wearing multicolored surgical scrubs descended upon us.

"Let me," said an orderly, sliding a backboard under Grebenchekov. Others stooped and I was edged back. "And LIFT," a women's voice said and they all stood in unison, raising him waist high. A gurney rolled under the backboard and he was lowered to it.

I lifted my helmet all the way off.

Grebenchekov turned his head toward me and reached out his hand. *"Kozmos devushka!"*

I grabbed his hand. "What?"

"Tell Kate!"

I leaned closer. "Yes?

"*Mne nuzhny ochki!*"

They started rolling him back into the building and I took quick steps to keep up with them. "*Chto? Vo angliyskiy!*"

I saw him grope for the words, then he pointed two fingers toward his eyes. "My glasses!"

"Oh! Okay." I grinned and he smiled back, then the glass doors swallowed him and his attendants.

I was thinking about following them in when a camera flash went off to my right. A man with a massive DSLR camera stood two yards away, clicking madly. Behind me I heard a screech of tires and I turned to see a television news truck bump over the curb from Pasteur Drive, parking illegally on the grass. A reporter jumped out of the passenger seat with some sort of audio recorder in his hand. Equally quick, the driver pulled out a pro video camera from the rear compartment and tossed it up onto his shoulder.

I heard the hospital door open again. Two men were approaching me—one in a suit and tie, the other in Military BDUs.

For a brief moment I considered snatching both cameras and jumping away, then saw a closed-circuit camera mounted above the door.

Dad was going to kill me.

I put the helmet on, took three steps sideways to clear the overhanging roof, saluted toward the news camera, and launched, adding two hundred miles per hour velocity straight up.

It was loud in the helmet.

I hope it looked good on TV.

# TWENTY-FIVE

## Cent: Avtoruchka

I made a satphone call from the roof of Stanford Hospital two hours later. I wasn't exactly revealing anything if they tracked the location. They knew I'd been here, after all.

"Sterling."

"Any news on Grebenchekov?"

"Yes—good news."

I took a deep breath. Relief, I guess. I was surprised; I wasn't aware of how tense I'd felt until then.

Sterling continued. "The aneurism was as big as a grapefruit with a dime-sized hole on one side. Fortunately the pressure from the ballooning vessel pressed that opening against the wall of the abdomen so it was seeping, rather than gushing.

"They clamped and did an aortic resection with a Dacron graft, restoring blood flow to the legs in under ten minutes. They took another twenty minutes to close him back up but the urgency was gone, at that point.

"The surgical team confirmed that a high-G reentry would've been fatal. Or, for that matter, even just waiting a few hours. You definitely saved his life."

I felt my ears get red. "Well, then, uh, good on *you*, General. You're the one who thought of asking."

"I could *ask* all day. It wouldn't make *me* capable of the mission. *Thanks*. That's unofficial, but I'm working on getting permission to formally thank you on behalf of U.S. Space Command. What can I do *unofficially* to show my appreciation?"

I thought about it. "Could you expedite the decision about Iridium Communications? They said they were waiting for DoD permission before they could negotiate a deal to compensate us for our video inspections."

General Sterling clucked his tongue against the roof of his mouth.

"I'll see what I can do."

Okay, I knew I'd get a lecture from Dad, but I guess I wasn't expecting one from Joe. That didn't mean I was going to put up with it.

"So what was I supposed to do, let him die?"

"Why did you take off your helmet? That flight engineer has already tweeted two pictures of you from the ISS!"

Dad had left the "ground station" cell with Tara because it couldn't reach out of the underground storage vault any more than the satellite transmitters could, so I hadn't been able to call him and I *still* hadn't connected.

"Which flight engineer? Except for Commander Elliott, they're *all* flight engineers."

Joe looked at his phone. "Uh, Nagata."

"Show me," I said.

I hadn't even seen her holding a camera, but the first picture she'd posted was of me floating outside the cupola (sun visor still down). Compared to the standard NASA EMU suit, I looked sylphlike, almost a dancer in a unitard.

"I don't see what you're complaining about."

He swiped to the next picture and stabbed his finger at it.

*That* picture was inside the U.S. Lab with me and Rassmussen shaking hands over Grebenchekov, Commander Elliott in the foreground. My short hair was standing up in a way I didn't remember at all and zero G changed the shape of my face, too. My skin color was definitely better than Grebenchekov's.

No helmet. Face in three-quarter profile.

"That is *so* cool," said Tara.

Joe scowled.

I bit my lip. "I understand, Joe. You're worried that they'll connect me to you and you'll get the heat."

"Fuck no! I was worried about *you*! But while you're on the subject, what about Tara? What about Jade? You're telling me this won't have repercussions?"

*Ouch.* Maybe he had a point, there. I locked eyes with Tara.

She shrugged. "They might connect you with *you*, I suppose. I mean, *you*, Space Girl, with *you*, Cent-that-lived-in-New-Prospect-for-a-while. But I doubt it will lead to Joe. I wasn't aware you guys were still dating until after you weren't anymore."

Joe looked away.

Dad jumped into the lab with Cory.

"Where were you? We've had the next set of satellites ready for the last forty-five minutes."

"Sorry. You never took me down into the vault so I couldn't jump there to tell you."

"Tell me? Tell me what?" He blinked, finally noticing I was wearing jeans and a sweatshirt. "You're *not* in the suit. Are you all right?"

"Fine, yes."

Tara said, "Everyone is fine, including Flight Engineer Grebenchekov."

Cory said, "Who is Grebenchekov?"

All three of us started talking at once, Tara excited, me matter-of-fact, and Joe angry. I shut up and let the two of them tag team it, but I got ready to defend myself.

When he'd got the whole story, Dad said, "You saved his life?"

I nodded.

He walked up to me and put his arms around me. "I'm very proud of you."

Tears are so much easier to deal with in gravity, especially if you have someone else's shirt to wipe them on.

Then Dad held me at arm's length and shook me halfheartedly

by my shoulders. "But the photos! Why'd you take off your helmet?" He shook me again, but the corner of his mouth kept twitching up. When he let go, he glanced sideways at the others and then back at me.

I sighed. "Lemons. Yes. I know."

He shut his mouth, but he mimed crushing something in his hand, the other hand cupped below to catch the squeezings.

I spread my hands and changed the subject. "We're behind schedule. We should double up on the remaining satellite insertions."

Tara said, "We've got e-mail reports from all of this morning's bird's owners. All are transmitting. One of them had trouble uploading commands, but that seems to be a software problem."

"Maybe I can go retrieve that one later and let them fix it?" I said.

Tara glared at me. "No more freebies! If they want to pay for retrieval, fine, and they'll need to pay for relaunching, too!"

I held up my hands. "Yes, ma'am!"

Cory said, "Tara's right. Even at *your* rates, they need to take responsibility for shoddy work."

I nodded. "Right. I have my own projects, after all."

Cory frowned. "The new suits?"

I shook my head. "No. *My* space station."

Okay, I thought the first wave of press response after *AOS-Sat One* went live and the first video went viral was crazy.

SPACE GIRL SAVES ISS COSMONAUT.

EMERGENCY MEDICAL EVACUATION ON INTERNATIONAL SPACE STATION.

FORGET 911: SPACE GIRL TO THE RESCUE

IS IT A BIRD, A PLANE, AN AMBULANCE?

And, inevitably, to prove it's never what a girl can do, it's how she looks:

SPACE GIRL IS HAWT!

During a scheduled in-flight video interview with the Associated Press, Commander Elliott and Flight Engineer Rasmussen were asked about my actions. Rasmussen said, "I've been asked not to discuss this pending the formulation of NASA's official response." She looked away from the camera and when she looked back water was accumulating in her eyes in that annoying zero-G way. She flicked the water away from her face with a finger and said, *"I'm* grateful as hell."

Commander Elliott added, "The entire crew is grateful. We are overjoyed that Misha is safe and out of danger."

NASA and the hospital kept press away from Grebenchekov, but when the first officials from Roscosmos (the Russian Federal Space Agency) arrived, they brought representatives from the Russian press with them.

"I love *kosmos devushka!*" Grebenchekov said. "She speaks very good Russian!"

Ha. Take *that*, General Sterling.

The vast majority of our new customers in the university microsat promotion did not need specific orbits. They did need enough inclination to reach the latitudes of their tracking facilities. The universities (and three *high schools*) were distributed from Miami to Fairbanks. Most of the exceptions had already been taken care of in the first set of polar-orbit launches.

Confident now in the precision of our deliveries, USSPACE-COM approved a faster insertion rate. "It would simplify things if you distributed the rest of these short-lived units in the *same* orbital plane," General Sterling said. "It would make the COLA evaluations for *our* launches simpler."

I was talking to him via the base-station cell phone, sitting on the roof of "Gunner" Lee's house in Ft. Worth. As much trouble as it took to get *that* jump site, I figured I might as well use it, and I didn't really care if they tracked the call there.

"Ooh. Our own orbit! Some of the tracking stations are moderately north. We'd need to match the fifty-degrees inclination of our previous nonpolar deployment. Would that work?"

"Yes. Can you handle two-line orbital sets yet?"

I grimaced. "We've got the CelesTrak software running ground side. It's just not as intuitive to me as lat-long ground track with altitude, or even uncoded Keplerian elements."

He groaned. "This is no—"

"—way to run a space program? We're working on improving our space-side hardware. My girls are seeing if we can work out a deal to test MiGHO."

"MiGHO? Why do I get all my space news from a seventeen-year-old girl?"

"Oh, surely *you* have heard of it? Multi-System GPS for High Orbits?"

Sterling growled. "The one *I* heard about was in a *classified* briefing. Perhaps you're talking about something different."

I raised my eyebrows. "I'm talking about the German project with the ESA? Uses side-lobe transmissions from *all* the GPS systems—U.S. Navstar, EU Galileo, Russian GLONASS, and Chinese Compass navsats—to get position and velocity fix as far out as lunar orbit?"

"Hmph. We're flying it on a DoD mission two years from now. How did *you* find out about it?"

"I don't know about your briefing, but it's not exactly a secret. The company generated several academic papers and they sounded very interested when we queried." My turn. "Who told *you* I was seventeen?"

He paused. "Well, *you* mentioned it to Flight Engineer Rasmussen . . . Ms. Rice. Or is it Ms. Harrison-Rice?"

*Oh, fuck.* "I didn't mention *that*."

"Once they saw the news stills and video from your delivery of Flight Engineer Grebenchekov, it was a matter of minutes before the NSA delivered a file to the DIA. I got a heavily redacted version, but it includes you and your parents."

I almost hung up. "And does that change anything?"

"Well, it sort of clears up why we haven't seen your launches. And it helps that you're not foreign nationals. There had been some fears expressed that you would start removing some of our orbital intelligence assets."

I remembered what I'd said to Dad back when space command first "discovered" me. I repeated it: "Nice little spy sat you have there, *shame* if anything were to happen to it?"

"Yes. Like that. I suggest you don't repeat that."

"You don't have to worry about *me*." *I'll play nice if you guys will.*

"From what I can see, you would be putting these birds into orbit regardless of our approval. Better for *us* to insure they go into safe orbits, so we're cooperating . . . for now. But my boss flew to Washington to discuss the matter with . . . well, with people. It's all way above *my* pay grade."

Sterling's boss was the head of U.S. Space Command. *He* reported to the air force chief of staff. I didn't want to think about who was in that meeting.

Sterling cleared his throat. "I will say that it is a *good* thing your identity became known in conjunction with your medevac of Grebenchekov. Saving his life, plus your remediation of the Fengyun 1C debris, has earned you substantial good will from *some* parties. We'll just have to see, Ms. Rice."

"It's Cent."

He *hummed.* "Yes. That was in the file, too, but I didn't want to presume.

"We'll just have to see, Cent."


Over the next three days we put 108 satellites into what we were calling the Apex Standard Low Earth Orbit. At 205 kilometers altitude, the circumference of the orbital track was over forty-one thousand kilometers. Evenly distributed, that was one of those tiny cubesats every 115 kilometers.

I also made one quick trip to the ISS, prearranged through General Sterling. He patched me through to Johnson who patched me to the station.

Commander Elliott said, "The package is on the RMS above the Terrace."

The "Terrace" was the Exposed Facility outside of Kibo, the Japanese Experiment Module. A small air lock with a sliding table allowed the crew to move experiments from inside the station to outside, where the RMS—the Remote Manipulator System, a Japanese-built arm not unlike the larger

Canadarm—moved the experiments in or out of one of the many slots on the Terrace.

The "package" in this case, was a small foil envelope.

Flight Engineer Rasmussen was looking out the right-side window on the end of the Kibo module.

When I had my hand on the foil envelope, she turned back to the RMS operator station and opened the jaws of the manipulator, releasing the envelope. I tucked it into one of the large coveralls pockets on my leg and made sure the Velcro was closed.

Then I held up *my* package and pointed at the manipulator. She turned her head and said something. Commander Elliott floated up to the left-hand window and I heard his voice. "What is *that*?"

"That" was an eight-quart aluminum pressure cooker that Cory had modified by replacing the automatic pressure release with a manual valve. It also had a simple pressure gauge, currently showing the internal pressure was 14.6 psi higher than the vacuum outside.

"I've got five pounds of seedless grapes, five pounds of Honeycrisp apples, and five pounds of navel oranges. You haven't had a supply flight in six weeks, right?"

I saw Rasmussen lick her lips and the jaws of the manipulator closed firmly on the pressure cooker's handle.

There's always enough food on the ISS, but fresh fruit only lasts a week or two after resupply flights.

Commander Elliott said, "Fruit? Really?"

"There's also two pounds of my mom's Christmas fudge."

Elliott turned his head. "Flight Engineer Rasmussen! We have an *urgent* experiment to recover. The Kibo air lock is still unpressurized, yes?"

I heard Rasmussen's voice come distantly through Elliott's mike. "Affirmative."

"Open that outer door and extend the sliding table. We need to get that puppy on board!"

"I'll come get my container later," I said. "Any messages for Misha?"

Through the window I saw Rasmussen reach her hand out for the headset that Elliott wore. He gave it to her.

Her voice came over the link. "Choose a date."

I repeated it back to her. "That's the message?"

"Yes. By the way, the crew *already* liked you because you helped Misha. When they see the fruit, there may be a few marriage proposals."

"Aren't they *all* married?"

"And your point would be?"

I laughed. "Tis the season," I said.

And jumped.

I ended up jumping past the Roscosmos people and hospital security. Nobody recognized me. I was wearing my Stanford sweatshirt over jeans and a T-shirt.

Grebenchekov was in a hospital bed but, I was relieved to see, he wasn't even on an IV. He wore regular pajamas, not a hospital gown.

The other man in the room was talking at—not to— Grebenchekov in rapid-fire Russian, while Grebenchekov stared impassively at the ceiling. When he saw me, the man switched to English and said abruptly, "You are in wrong room."

I ignored him. "*Privet*, Misha. I brought your *ochki*."

It took Grenbenchekov a moment—I wasn't wearing a space suit, after all. "*Kosmos devushka?*"

I handed him the foil envelope.

He dumped the contents onto the bedspread. The eyeglasses were round lensed, with a slider on the nose bridge that allowed the wearer to adjust the focus of a secondary lens as needed. NASA had been flying them for several years because zero G altered eyesight significantly in some astronauts over the course of a single mission. Misha was one of these. "Ah. *Slava bogu!* Come here and let me kiss you."

The other man said, "*This* is Space Girl? Surely you're joking?"

"No kissing," I said to Grebenchekov. "What would Kate say? She sent a message, by the way."

The other man started out irritated but now he sounded angry. "Is she talking about your American mistress? They spoke of this at the training center. What would your wife say?"

Grebenchekov looked *furious* and I became acutely aware that he'd had major surgery just three days before. "Sergei, time for you to walk out of room before someone throws you out window."

I don't think I've ever seen someone actually *sneer* before but I'd have to say that's what Sergei did. "You don't get rid of me so *easy*, Misha. Even without the surgery, you have been five months in space! You can't push me around like you did in—"

Sergei's chair toppled over onto the grass of the Campus Oval, a good mile away from the hospital. He did an awkward back roll and ended with his legs flopped over his head. I didn't help him up, or wait for him to struggle upright, or even pause to talk.

Back in the hospital room, I returned the chair to its place in the corner and lowered it to the floor.

Grebenchekov was sitting up and had twisted around, one leg out of bed. I held my hand out in a "wait" gesture and he sank back onto his pillows.

"I don't like Sergei," I said. "He isn't very nice."

Grenenchekov's face went from angry to an explosive laugh which was cut short. He clutched at his side and exhaled through pursed lips. In a quieter voice he said, "It's like you know him for *years*."

I lifted his leg back onto the bed and resettled the sheet and blanket.

"Sergei has always wanted to go into space. Did you put him in space?" Grebenchekov looked hopeful.

"*Nyet*. Who *is* he?"

"He's . . . *avtoruchka*. Aieee. Sorry. I should not say that in front of you."

I had no idea what that meant.

Grebenchekov continued. "Sergei was in cosmonaut training with me, but he washed out so he became a . . . a pencil pusher. Also—the woman he wanted? She married *me*."

My eyes widened.

"She died five years ago. Cancer. My dear Nadya—ah, she was wonderful, but she would've screamed to see Sergei still grieving over another man's wife. And if she saw *me* still in mourning? Well, she would've *slapped* me upside the head."

He took the glasses off and ground the heels of his palms into his eyes "Ah, *devushka*, Sergei flew all this way . . . he couldn't wait to tell me . . . I will *never* go into space again."

I was beginning to see the merit of putting the man in orbit. "I'm sorry."

Grebenchekov, took a moment, polishing the lenses of the eyeglasses with a corner of his bed sheet. "What is the message from my Kate?"

I bit my lip. "Can I ask what *her* marriage situation is?" Rasmussen had told me she had a grown daughter after all.

"Divorced ten years."

I breathed out, relieved. Now I wanted to go find Sergei and take him *much* farther. What an asshole. "Kate said to tell you, 'Choose a date.' "

Grebenchekov's eyes lit up. "Ah—well, at least *that's* settled." He smiled. "She would not marry me until we were both off the flight rosters."

"I'm sorry I did not take Sergei farther away. He is only a few kilometers *that* way." I pointed. "I could take him to Australia but the weather is far too nice there."

"Are you sure you aren't Russian?"

"*Bol'shoye spasibo*. When do you leave here?"

"They want to transfer me back to *Zvezdny Gorodok* in two weeks." He looked at me and said, "That is—"

"Star City. The training center." I tapped my chest. "Huge fan."

"I always understood I would come back to Earth one day and never return to space, but . . . I had forty-five more days!"

I patted his arm. "Can Sergei hurt you? I mean, any more than he has?"

Grebenchekov shook his head. *"Nyet.* Just now I am heroic cosmonaut snatched from brink of death. *He* is *avtoruchka.*"

"Okay, that's the *second* time you used that word."

He looked guilty. "It means . . . pen. Like—" He held up his hand and twitched his thumb like he was clicking a ballpoint pen. "But—" He looked around, as if he expected someone to overhear him. "—it also means—" He frowned, clearly searching his memory. Finally Grebenchekov said, "I don't know American word. The British say 'wanker.'"

I covered my face and started laughing. "That works! That totally works."

You know, a *lot* of things don't turn out like you thought they would.

It was time for Tara to go to Paris, to meet up with Jade and her parents for the last ten days of their trip. I'd arranged to bring Tara to the Gare du Nord, by the Ludmilla Tchérina sculpture at the head of the stairs on the Eurostar platform.

We were early and I waited with Tara to make sure she connected with Jade. It's the busiest train station in Europe and there was plenty to watch. Also, while we waited, Tara told me the plot of *The Red Shoes* because Ludmilla Tchérina was in it.

"I thought she was a sculptor."

"And a ballerina, and a painter, and an actress."

"Wow."

Someone cleared her throat and I turned. Jade was there. Also her Dad. And her mother, Dr. Chilton, who held in her hands the *Guardian* newspaper. Guess who was on the front page, pulling a helmet from her head while cradling a Russian cosmonaut?

"Why, hello, Dr. Chilton. Mr. Chilton," I said. When they didn't say anything right away, I said, "Enjoying Europe?"

Dr. Chilton said, "The thing I've always liked about you, Cent, is that you are exquisitely polite, *even when you're putting my child's life in danger.*"

I looked at Jade. She was frozen, not looking at me, but at Tara.

Tara was frowning, looking from Jade to Mr. Chilton, to Dr. Chilton, and back to Jade.

Mr. Chilton was looking at Tara, then back Jade—not me.

Jade's mother was trying to glare at me, but she also kept shifting her gaze to Tara.

Tara shook her head, sad. "It's *not* about you, Cent. No matter what she's saying." She looked at Jade. "Is it?"

Jade opened her mouth to speak and her mother said, "Remember what we agreed on!"

Jade looked at the people streaming by. "Is this really the place to talk about this?"

Her father nodded. "I think Jade's right. We should find someplace quiet."

"No!" said Dr. Chilton. "We agreed."

Mr. Chilton said, "Not exactly, Misty. You just kept talking and *we* got tired."

Jade looked up at her dad, surprised. "I thought you were on *her* side."

"Honey," Mr. Chilton said. "We both want what's best for you. There's just some disagreement about what that entails."

Tara walked forward, stepping up beside Jade. In a harsh whisper she said, "I thought we were *beyond* this."

Jade sighed. "So did I." She put her arms around Tara and hugged her.

Dr. Chilton's face twisted and she stepped forward, her arms reaching out.

I jumped.

I didn't have to grab anybody. I was just instantly there, standing between Dr. Chilton and Tara. Dr. Chilton jerked back, gasping.

Mr. Chilton, wide-eyed, took his wife's arm to steady her. "Misty?"

"She's taking our daughter! They're both taking our daughter!"

As I said, sometime things don't turn out at *all* like you were expecting. This was not the European holiday *I'd* signed up for. I stepped away, returning to the railing and putting my back to it.

Mr. Chilton was whispering urgently to his wife. I only

heard a snatch during a momentary lull of the station's noise: "—but *you* might drive her—"

Jade was watching her parents intently, not letting go of Tara's arm.

"Rough trip?" I asked quietly.

Jade shuddered. "Not at first. But then as it got closer to the time when Tara was going to join us, Mom really had a . . . a *relapse*."

"Was it the publicity?" I gestured toward the *Guardian*, now being twisted and untwisted in Dr. Chilton's hands.

"No. Dad and I had almost got her reasonable—back to where I thought the trip would still be a *good* thing. But once she saw the picture, all her arguments came back, but now with *you* being the justification."

I looked back at her parents. Dr. Chilton was *not* calming down. In fact she was crying, harsh sobs and gesturing sharply toward us.

I looked at Jade, who was watching her mom with an almost detached air.

"You okay?" I asked. I would've been freaking out.

She rolled her eyes. "I was a wreck the first time, but there comes a point when it's just annoying, not heartrending."

I wasn't annoyed. I was acutely uncomfortable. "So what's the plan—leave Tara with you? Take her away? I mean, *I'm* not staying, so if you need something, this is the time to ask."

Jade turned to Tara and whispered fiercely, "Don't you *dare* leave me alone with her. Either we *both* stay or we *both* go. *Your* call."

Tara studied the skylights running down the peak of the station's roof. When she looked back down, she said, "Leave us in Paris—but get us away from *this*. Maybe she'll calm down."

Jade looked doubtful about the last phrase, but she said, "Please. Away from *here* anyway."

"Île de la Cité?" I suggested.

Tara's eyes lit up. "Oh, yes. Notre-Dame." She'd never been to Paris but she'd been reading up.

Jade nodded. "Yes. And it's close to our hotel."

"Cent sandwich," I said and they reached around me to hug each other, squeezing me in the middle like, well, like a lemon.

Her mother noticed, opened her mouth to say something, but I jumped.

It had just stopped raining and you could see the Rose Window reflected in the wet pavement in front of "our lady," Notre-Dame Cathedral. By the time Tara had taken several pictures we were *all* calmer. Jade sent her father a text saying that she and Tara were going back to Jade's room at the Hotel Melia Le Colbert.

As we walked over the Seine on the Pont au Double, Jade offered to teach Tara the "French tongue" and bobbed her eyebrows suggestively.

Tara said, "I think I taught *you*."

Jade to Tara: "Repeat after me, 'I am space girl: *Je suis fille de l'espace.*'"

Tara said *"Je suis fille de Spartacus."*

Jade laughed and said, *"Je suis Spartacus."*

And I said louder, *"No!* Je *suis Spartacus."*

And then a policeman, crossing from the Left Bank roared out, *"JE suis Spartacus!"* He touched his hat and walked on, without missing a step.

There was no talking after that. There was only laughing and holding onto the stone rail of the bridge to keep from falling over.

After the scene we'd fled at the Gare du Nord I certainly didn't expect *that* by the time I left Jade and Tara. A lot of things don't turn out like you expect them to.

# TWENTY-SIX

## Millie: Less Secrecy

Millie was curled up in the corner of the couch with her hands wrapped around a cup of tea, enjoying its warmth and the warmth of the fireplace, when Davy came in, frowning.

She tensed, unreasonably annoyed. She'd just finished brewing the tea and building the fire and it was the first time she'd been off her feet the entire morning. She watched him from the corner of her eye.

Davy flopped down onto the other end of the couch and stuffed his hands into his jean pockets, his head back against the cushion, staring fixedly at the upper reaches of the fieldstone fireplace.

"We're blown."

She nodded and sipped her tea.

"You knew?"

"We had the TV on in Mother's room."

Davy winced. "So, you saw the interview with Cent's biology teacher?"

"Yes. I loved his first line. 'I always knew she'd go far.' But they also made the connection all the way back to your adventures with hijackers before we were married, and there was a picture of me from New Prospect that one of my old family-practice clients identified. That led them to Mom and the 'Shots Fired and Multiple Arrests at Wichita Nursing Home' story."

Davy winced. "I saw the hijacking stuff but not the Wichita part."

"Well, it was inevitable."

"You're awfully *calm* about it."

Millie sipped her tea. "What's changed? Do we have to behave differently? More important, does this mean anything's changed upstairs? I mean, besides the talk I just had with Seeana, Bea, Jeline, and Tessa?"

Davy grimaced. "What did you say to them?"

"I gave them the opportunity to resign. But that if they felt they could keep our secret, we would give them a bonus at the end of employment equal to their total salaries. I mean, Cent's making money now, right?"

Davy nodded. "That was smart. The longer they work, the more money they get, but only if they maintain confidentiality to the, uh, end." He glanced at Millie, frowning.

Millie sighed. "Yeah. The 'end.'"

"How is Sam?"

"This morning was rough. We had to put her on the ventilator twice, but she's off it again. She managed to eat lunch and she's actually sleeping. When she's having trouble breathing, she doesn't rest at all."

"Hmmm?"

"She said that everything gets very simple. Her whole world narrows down to the next breath, all her concentration, all her effort. And she has this overwhelming feeling—fear—that if she doesn't give it all her attention, it will just stop." She bowed her head. "That's got to be just awful."

Davy opened his mouth but ended up just shaking his head. He slid his arm around her shoulders.

Millie leaned into him. "So, I am calm about the publicity thing. It's not my most *pressing* concern. And maybe this is a *good* thing."

"I don't see how."

"Remember when the NSA was tracking me and Mom? When my brother took them to court?"

"Yeah. It didn't stop them from snatching you and your roommate a week later."

"But they backed down. I think what we need is *more* publicity, not less. What would the press do with a story about Daarkon Group's real activities? What if we went public about all the disaster-relief aid we've provided in the last twenty years?" She put her cup down on the coffee table with a thump. "Maybe what we need is less secrecy, not *more*."

Davy's jaw jutted forward.

Before he said anything, Millie added, "Don't worry. I won't start sending out press releases." She jerked her thumb toward the upstairs landing. "Right now, all my energy is focused up *there*."

# TWENTY-SEVEN

## Cent: Safety Check

With Jade and Tara in Europe, I tried to do the rest of the satellite launches using just Dad and Cory, but Cory bailed on me.

"I've got to prep for the suit wrap, remember? We only have so much time before their semesters start and Joe, Tara, and Jade become unavailable. Then there's the *other* thing."

Dad and Cory exchanged glances and I nodded. "Right. Clearing out the suit and supplies." We didn't think it would be long before Cory's lab (and involvement) would be public knowledge. The plan was to move the operational supplies and the suit somewhere less accessible.

I looked at Dad and said, "Well, I guess you and I can do the sat prep while I prebreathe, then you could be ground crew."

Dad shook his head. "Don't you need a safety check for suit prep and donning? Use Joe. Then he can continue to prep the birds while I act as Capcom."

I felt my face twist and Dad looked at me, concerned. *"That's a sour look. Why doesn't that work? Is Joe not available?"*

*Was he?* That was the question, and not in the way Dad meant.

"Okay. I'll see if he's free."

Dad took me to the interior of the vault, 650 feet under the Kansas prairie.

"This is it?"

Fluorescents lit an ordinary ten-by-eighteen-foot room, Sheet-rock walls, concrete floor, metal rafters supporting a corrugated metal roof. There was a garage-style fiberglass door at one end with a folding table set up in front of it as a temporary work space. Heavy steel file-box shelves lined the remaining three walls.

"It's a big open cavern. These units are like warehouses built across the floor." He pointed at a set of eight boxes on one end of the right-hand shelf. "Those are the records I started with." He gestured at the rest of the room. "But we're paying for future capacity and not to have our boxes mixed with other customers'."

The rest of the shelves contained specialty boxes, many of them custom cases. A third of them were empty, but the rest held the satellites I still needed to launch.

"How did you get the jump site?" I asked. "Do they let non-employees down here?"

Dad said, "If you're spending enough, you get an escort down here when you're storing your stuff. Do you have this?"

I inhaled the cool, dry air and got whiffs of minerals and cardboard. I jumped away to the Eyrie, then back again. "Yeah. Got it."

Dad opened one of the cases and tapped a sheet of paper on top of the satellite. "Here's the prelaunch procedure. Every bird has one." He pointed at a tank of nitrogen in the corner. "There are some that need to have their cold-gas thrusters charged—I'll show Joe how to set the regulator and do the connections."

"Oh? So you have to have a penis to do that?"

Dad's mouth dropped open and I felt my face go hot.

He blinked and said, "Well, where did *that* come from?"

I stammered, "I'm just saying that *I* could charge the nitrogen reservoirs, too."

"Well, yes, I know you could. But I thought since Joe can't put *satellites in orbit*, he might handle the sat prep while you're taking care of *that* little chore. Did you think I was saying you were incapable of handling this?"

"Sorry, Daddy. I . . . it's not you."

"Joe? Does he say you can't do this kind of thing?"

I shrugged. "He doesn't *say* it. It's the college thing."

Dad winced. "He holds that over you?"

I waved my hands side to side, palm out.

"Or are *you* holding that over you?" he asked. "I'm sorry the high school thing didn't work out. I'd have said you probably could still do college *somewhere* right up until Space Girl's face became the international symbol for OMG and WTF."

I had to laugh at that.

"I know about missing college. I always wanted to do that. Know what else I always wanted to do?"

I shook my head.

"I always wanted to be an astronaut." He stepped closer and put his arms around me. "I know about a lot of kids who go to college. I only know *one* who has her own space program."

I leaned into him and wiped my cheeks on his fleece.

Dad rested his chin on my head. "If I were Joe, I'd be jealous of *you*."

I started prebreathing oxygen after breakfast and, during the next two hours, I moved the suit and supplies to the vault, organizing everything in checklist order.

Halfway through this Dad showed up and started doing satellite prep, turning on power switches, connecting batteries, charging nitrogen reservoirs.

I picked up Joe from behind Krakatoa and brought him straight to the vault.

Dad had his hands full but nodded. I pushed the clipboard into Joe's hands and he blinked, then cleared his throat and said, "Right. Procedure one-A, air processing unit. Step one, release latches on rebreather chamber—"

We'd done it enough times now that we had suit prep down to twenty minutes even *with* the rigorous double-checking every step that Joe was insisting on.

"I just don't want to be the one to fuck this up," he said. "I fuck up, *you* have to live with the consequences."

*Or die with them*, I thought, but I didn't voice this. "I'm good with being careful," I said, my voice muffled by the prebreath mask.

Joe snorted. "Could have fooled *me*."

Dad laughed, I think, though his face was still when I turned to glare at him.

Joe went down to the next item on his list. "Okay, go hit the bathroom." It was on the list, the last step before squeezing into the suit.

I jumped to the cabin for that step, checking in with Mom. This wasn't on the checklist, but *she* considered it a *critical* part of the process—knowing when I was about to go up.

"And don't forget to check in after, too!"

Back in the vault Joe relaxed the suit and I pulled off the fleece and sweat pants that I wore over my undersuit base layers. He made a show of turning away but he was watching out of the corner of his eyes.

I jumped into the suit. Through the oxygen mask I said, "There, you can stop pretending not to look."

He dialed down on the rheostat, shrinking up the suit. "Got news for you, girl. Without the coveralls, the suit is just as, uh, *contour faithful* as your long underwear is." He handed me the neck gasket.

I held my breath while I forced my head through it. And I mean "forced." Cory compares it to being born. Once it was snug around my neck, I snapped its collar ring into the inner seal on the helmet flange and Joe doubled-checked that it was fully engaged. We'd only got it wrong, once, back during testing, and that became immediately obvious the second we tried to pressurize the helmet and air rushed past my collarbone.

Fully dressed—coveralls, boots, gloves, helmet, backpack— I turned to Dad.

Dad looked at his watch and then back at me.

I shrugged. We were done early. When you don't make small talk, you go through the checklist at a pretty good clip.

Dad opened his mouth to say something, but then shut it again, pointing at his ear and then at the door to the vault. The last thing we wanted was for one of the storage-facility employees to hear someone speaking loudly in one of these units.

He turned to the laptop perched on one of the empty shelves and clicked through some options, then wrote a line on a piece of cardboard, handed it to Joe, and pointed at the screen.

Joe leaned forward and read from the screen, then the cardboard, then back to the screen again. He held up his thumb, and gave the cardboard back to Dad who stuck it in the top of the milk crate sitting on the folding table.

I stepped closer. The box held ten cubesats, and a chart of coordinates with times of insertion corresponding to the "empty" parts of our orbit. The first one on the schedule wasn't for another thirty minutes, but the scrap of cardboard had an insertion point scheduled for four minutes from now.

I held up my thumb and jumped.


I no longer had to look at the GPS to reach my standard "Yuri" orbit over the Marshall Islands, which was good, since in the vault my GPS wasn't getting any signal. I had to float above the Pacific for thirty seconds before the unit acquired enough satellites for a fix. Once it was working, I counted down to the insertion time and shifted to the new coordinates.

Got it in one try. That is, within the limits of error for my instruments and the CelesTrak software.

I tossed the cubesats in different directions to keep them from clipping each other. We probably didn't need to be too picky. The circumference of our orbit was 41,318 kilometers. If you laid out the 345 satellites end-to-end across their longest deployed dimensions, they would measure less than a hundred meters— a tenth of a kilometer. Distributed evenly in that orbit, each one could have a 120 kilometers of elbow room.

And, of course, this didn't count the inevitable drift as I added slight differences of velocity when I deployed them, or how atmospheric drag affected the units with different cross sections differently, or how the actual shape of the earth (not really a sphere, you know) caused perturbations in the orbits.

My phone was set to dial USSPACECOM but not, this time,

to General Sterling. Technical Sergeant Agatha Mertens was now our official liaison into the U.S. Space Command satellite catalog. She answered on the first ring.

"Good morning, Agatha. Apex Orbital here." I felt funny calling her by her first name but she'd insisted.

"Good morning, Cent. What do you have for me?"

"I have sats five three seven three two thru five three seven four one deployed. Mean anomaly at thirteen hundred Zulu today is fifteen point eight degrees." Since we were using the same orbital plane for all these nonpolar satellites, the only information they needed was where in the orbit the satellites were at what time. They already had the names of the satellites, transmitting frequencies, and operators.

"I copy fifteen point eight degrees at thirteen hundred Zulu. Sats seven hundred thirty-two through seven hundred forty-one. Ten sats in all."

"Correct."

"The list says those are all one-unit cubesats."

"You got it."

"Uh, the list here says you're putting up some more today."

"Yes?"

"It says *seventy-five* more."

"At least. Need to finish by Friday and I've got two hundred thirty-five more to go."

"Affirmative. I take it you'll be calling me back shortly?"

"Roger that, Agatha. Cent out."

We deployed 127 before we quit for the day.

Dad tried to do the Capcom thing for a while, but it just slowed things down and I convinced him that it would be a better use of time if he helped Joe prep satellites.

It got so that I could move directly into the new orbit before the GPS had lock and I would just adjust the mean anomaly as a secondary jump. After lunch, as a test, I rendezvoused with one of the earlier deployment points—that is, to its current location—and was able to eyeball seven of the ten birds I'd dropped off there a few hours before.

By the end of the day, Joe was ready to get out of there. "It doesn't look like a cavern," he said, "but it feels like one."

Even though it was only 6 P.M. local time when I jumped him to the alleyway behind Krakatoa, it was full dark.

"Jeeze. It was barely light when you picked me up, too." He raised his hand to wave goodbye.

I'd seen the sun today. I'd seen it rise and set several times, but he'd been down in the vault.

I wanted to say, *Do you want to see the sun?* I could jump him to Queensland where it was three in the afternoon and summer to boot.

"See you tomorrow," I said.


We launched *all* the remaining satellites the next day.

It was another long day in the vault for Joe, but Dad and he got into a rhythm on the preps and they easily kept ahead of me as I inserted sats into our orbit. It got to the point where I was spending as much time on the phone with Tech Sergeant Mertens as I spent deploying the birds.

"The tracking guys tell me you're getting a little clumpy around thirty-seven degrees mean anomaly," she told me.

"Define clumpy, please."

"You've got seventeen of your birds in a cluster one hundred fifty klicks long. It was the third set from yesterday and the twelfth set from today."

"That doesn't sound very clumpy to me. That's almost nine klicks per satellite."

"Just clumpy by comparison to the rest of the orbit. FYI and all that."

"Right-oh. We'll avoid that section of the orbit. What is that, less than a third of a percent?"

Sergeant Mertens laughed. "Something like that."

At the end of the day she reported, "Yesterday's one hundred twenty-seven was a record. Today's two hundred twenty obviously beat it. You took operational spacecraft in low Earth orbit from six hundred seventy-two to one thousand twenty-seven in less than a *week*."

"Nothing succeeds like excess. Most of them will reenter in the next three months. None of them should last past six. *Your* guys told us that."

"Not complaining. Just saying. Any more going up this week?"

"Coming down. I'm deorbiting at least fifteen hundred kilos of debris this afternoon."

"Oh, yeah. You do the three-to-one thing? Three kilos down for every one up?"

"Affirmative."

"What are you taking down? Do you have a target yet?"

"Yes and no. We're going to do some experimentation to figure out the upper limit of m . . . our capacity. We'll let you know as soon as we do."

"Well, don't drop anything on Denver. We just finished paying off the house."

"You name is Lottie Williams, is it?" I said.

Sergeant Mertens said, "Not following you."

"She's the only human who's ever been hit by reentering orbital debris. Tiny piece of a Delta second stage that bounced off her shoulder."

"The only human that's been hit by orbital debris *so far*. Keep away from Denver."

"I didn't realize you were bringing us *here*," Joe said. He'd been on this remote beach before. We'd surfed there, and swam, and we hadn't always worn swimming suits.

I just spread my hands and pointed at the rising sun. It was early morning here in Queensland. I was still on oxygen for the planned afternoon operations and I used the mask as an excuse not to talk.

Joe took off his shoes and socks and shirt and lay on the sand until Dad arrived with a bag of fish tacos from San Diego.

Eating while dealing with an oxygen mask kept my side of the conversation nonexistent. Dad and Joe discussed the different choices the cubesat clients had taken in how they powered up.

"I understand the problem," Joe said. "They had to consider

multiday holds on the launch pad with no sun hitting their panels, so they had to come up with remote procedures or a process that was initiated by the acceleration of the launch or being kicked out of the deployer. But jeeze, I prefer the guys who gave us a simple on switch or a cable to plug in."

Dad nodded. "I wonder how many previous satellites failed, though, because their batteries were depleted before their panels saw the sun."

Joe sucked on his lip and said, "There's awful waste in the way they do it."

He glanced at me as he said it. I raised my eyebrows and bobbed my head in encouragement.

He went on, "Power, attitude control, and communication are all duplicated on most of these birds. A few of them need to do stuff that requires autonomous motion, but most of them are either doing some of kind of Earth-pointing science or measuring various aspects of the LEO environment."

He drew a rectangle in the sand.

"If we put up a frame of some kind with a shared high-bandwidth radio—preferably some sort of beamed Ethernet—plus a robust power system . . ." He drew a dish antenna and added two sets of solar panels off each end. "And we added a mast, like the one on *AOS-Sat*, for attitude control." He drew a mast with a counterweight down below. "You could hang all sorts of experiments from it, changing them out as needed. You could do a six-by-eight grid of connectors allowing us to fly as many as forty-eight experiments."

"The control circuitry for that would be *very* complicated," Dad said.

Joe shook his head. "Doesn't have to be. Each experiment would still be its own computer. The hosting frame would be providing power and a network connection into a space qualified router connected to the main radio. Each experiment would end up with its own IP address and the researchers could communicate with their project's cpu over the Internet, removing their need for a ground station."

Dad looked at me and I nodded. It made sense. I took a deep

breath and lowered the mask to say, "If we used locking multi-pin connectors like the ones we used for the headset through ports, they could be the package's electrical *and* physical connection to the frame. Once in place, they don't have any."

I stuck the mask back on.

Dad said, "I remember Cory screamed at the price of those."

Joe said, "*Those* connectors have to hold pressure between the inside of the helmet and vacuum. We don't need to worry about that for this, since neither the network or power circuits in our frame, or the circuits in the client's package, will be pressurized. We could run—" He started counting on his fingers. "—twelve pin connectors? That would give us ground, twelve, five, and three point three volts, and then eight connectors for the Ethernet. Or we could just run four and handle the network with wireless."

I shook my head and held up the ten fingers, then two.

Joe nodded. "Yeah. Makes it simpler. Some of the experiments might incorporate radio sensing and we wouldn't want to interfere with those. Also, fewer circuits to get messed up by radiation. You could get that lady from Texas A&M to design it."

Dad said, "Roberta Matapang?"

I nodded but lowered the oxygen mask and said, "You should take a run at the design first, then you can work with Roberta to refine it. But it's your idea, so—" I shrugged and took another hit from the mask.

He got that deer in the headlights look and I added, "It'll look good on your resume."

"I didn't think it was safe for me to admit I had anything to do with Apex Orbital."

"Have you been watching the news?" Dad said. He looked sideways at me. "I'm not sure it's avoidable at this point. Maybe if you cut off all connection."

Joe said, "Not going to happen." He looked at me. "At least not from my side."

I studied the sky.

Dad sighed.

Payload Assist Module version D was a Delta third stage intended to raise a communications satellite into geosynchronous orbit fifteen years before. I say "intended" because the solid fuel which comprised most of its mass failed to ignite.

They were able to save the mission by jettisoning the PAM and using the satellite's hydrazine station-keeping thrusters to slowly move the bird into its intended orbit over the next two months. It killed a few years off the satellite's operational lifetime, but was better than a complete write-off.

The PAM-D tumbled along in a highly elliptical orbit with a perigee of only 187 kilometers out to an apogee of 6,743. Normally a perigee that low would degrade the orbit pretty quickly, but with the unburned fuel it was quite dense for debris so it punched through faint bits of atmosphere on its closest approach. Current estimates were that it would take another twenty years or so to deorbit.

It wasn't that large—a bit over two meters long, but it weighed over twenty-one hundred kilos and I had serious doubts about my ability to move it, but it *was* in free fall and I decided it was worth a try.

I intercepted it as it passed above Santiago, Chile, moving east-southeast toward the Argentina Pampas. It was headed into perigee, still four hundred kilometers above the surface but destined for a low point of 187. It was slowly tumbling, taking the large rocket nozzle in and out of shadow, so I thought it was cool enough that I could grab it without bursting into flame.

Well, unless the solid-rocket motor finally ignited fifteen years late.

I decided not to even think about it. I looked at my GPS readout. I only wanted to change one parameter, but the size of the motor still daunted me—like a midsized car. I could push one of those on Earth, easily, if it were in neutral. In micro-G, if I had something to push *against*, I could easily move it.

Wouldn't know if I didn't try.

The altitude readout dropped 140 kilometers—400 to 260— and the Andes, already in sharp relief by the low sun, became more spectacular. Instead of heading down into a perigee of

187 kilometers and whipping around the earth, the current trajectory would take the module down to forty-seven kilometers, through the mesosphere and into the upper stratosphere.

I pushed off the bell and killed my vertical speed. The module seemed to shoot down toward the earth, but I was still matching its progress across South America. It quickly became too small for me to see but then it reappeared, a glowing bright speck. Then, as it began ablating material, a sharp streak across the Pampas.

The flare as the aluminum/ammonium perchlorate fuel exploded over the Atlantic coast was probably visible as far away as Buenos Aires and southern Uruguay.

That night when I checked my e-mail there was an emergency message from Tara. I was scheduled to pick her up in three days, in Amsterdam, but she was emphatic. "Need you NOW." Fortunately she and Jade were someplace I'd actually been.

The new dam across le Couesnon rivière and the replacement of the old causeway with a bridge had done much to scour away the sediment from around the base of Mont Saint-Michel. The hill town was still dressed in its crown of medieval and Gothic architecture, but now it climbed out of the sea instead of the mudflats, an island once more.

I remembered the old parking lot along both sides of the causeway, crowded and noisy and stinking of exhaust, with buses parked almost to the old walls themselves. Now only pedestrians and public transport trolleys moved across the new bridge, which curved across the water on thin pilings. All of the tourist cars and busses were at the new car park, inland, two and a half kilometers away.

I met Tara and Jade in the tiny reception area of their hotel, La Mère Poulard, on the Mont itself—seven in the morning for them, eleven at night, for me.

I looked around for Dr. and Mr. Chilton and Jade said, "Dad took her to Saint-Malo for the day to see the aquarium and the chateau and the Palais de Justice. He really did it as a favor to us."

They offered to buy me the famous wood-fired omelet in the restaurant but added that it was astonishingly expensive.

"Ate a late supper," I said. "I'm good. Hope you've been enjoying the sights. Your e-mail made it sound like things are . . . difficult."

Tara shrugged. "Harder on Jade. Mr. Chilton is being good, but her mom . . ."

Jade made a sour face. "We want you to get us out of here. Today."

There were several people in the lobby, coming and going. I jerked my head toward the door and la Grande-Rue.

Fortunately it was still early for the tourists because the "Grand Street" is more of a walkway, a narrow, bricked path overshadowed by shops and hotels and cafes, all shoehorned into buildings older than America. Later in the day it would be too crowded for privacy.

We headed away from the Porte de l'Avancée and I stopped between the hotel and the town hall, where the stairway let us see the abbey crowning the top of the hill.

"Both of you?" I asked. It was never the plan for me to bring Jade back from Europe—just Tara.

Jade nodded emphatically. "Both of us."

"Do they know?"

"Dad will not be surprised. I'll text him once we're back in New Prospect."

"Uh, what will Tara's mom say?"

Tara and Jade exchanged glances. Tara said, "She's been calling. Turns out I probably shouldn't have used the Diné message."

I raised my eyebrows. "Was that bad? Did someone think that was cultural appropriation?"

Tara shook her head. "If anyone is upset, I haven't heard it. The Diné I have heard from are pleased the language got so much exposure. The problem is that, along with *your* photos, it led the press to someone *you* know who is part Diné. The reporters started calling my mother."

"Damn." I looked at Jade. "Uh, what about you?"

She shrugged. "*We've* been in Europe."

Tara glared at her and Jade added, "All right. There were some messages left on the home voice mail. You know what's *really* annoying?"

"From everything I've heard so far, you've both set a *really high* bar for annoying. I'm kind of afraid to find out."

"This is still my mom. She *likes* that I'm associated with an international celebrity. She thinks I can leverage the publicity to tremendous job prospects and a great future. So I should be *really* careful about the sort of relationships I have. Because, you know, press."

I winced. "I don't suppose you pointed out that Tara is equally associated with Apex?"

Tara sighed.

Jade sounded positively bitter. "She's fine with diversity in the *workplace*. Just not in the *family*."

"What about Joe?"

They both looked at me, eyebrows raised. Tara said, "Isn't that *your* family's issue?"

"Not *that*! Has Joe's name been coming up in the news? Has the press been after him and his family?"

Jade spread her hands. "Uh, not that I know."

Tara bit her lip.

I grabbed her arm. "What?"

"I probably shouldn't have used him for all the voice-over work. They were asking my mom about him, too."

He hadn't mentioned that to me.

I turned to the nearest wall, closed my eyes, and leaned my forehead against the cold, damp stone.

"Cent?" said Jade.

"Let's go get your suitcases."

# TWENTY-EIGHT

## Davy: Rumblings

Davy jumped into the backseat of Hunt's Toyota, on the passenger side, so his face would be visible in the rearview mirror. Fortunately, Hunt had hadn't put the car in gear yet, but he did spill his coffee.

"It's too early for this shit."

"Sorry. How's the ankle?"

"It's back. One hundred percent. How's the space business?"

Davy sighed. "Well. It's going well. A little more *public* than I'd like."

Hunt nodded. "Yeah. I was surprised you allowed it."

"You had a photo of a girl in your wallet."

Hunt's eyes narrowed. "Yeah?"

"Daughter?"

Hunt nodded.

"Doesn't live with you?"

"Divorce. I have her some holidays. Usually a month in the summer."

"How old?"

"Seventeen."

"Does she do everything you tell her?"

Hunt chuckled. "Okay, I got it. Though with mine, it's more

like posting stuff on Facebook she shouldn't—not visiting the International Space Station."

Davy looked away. "I have a choice of helping her or being excluded, but I've learned not to give orders that are going to be ignored or, worse, reacted against. Your daughter probably has a choice about how involved you are in her life."

Hunt nodded seriously. "Yes."

"Then you know. I just wanted to check in on Daarkon. Wondering if they are reacting."

"Well, Apex Orbital Services probably got their attention but instead of monitoring Daarkon as much as I should, I've been spending most of my time sitting in meetings."

"About what? Or is that classified?"

"I'm sure it is, but you know more about it than *I* do. We're evaluating the national-security implications of a private company with the ability to put hardware in orbit and, *especially*, remove hardware *from* orbit. Forget NASA—it's the NRO that's having fits about you guys."

Davy blinked. "I don't know that one."

"National Reconnaissance Office."

"Ah. The spy sat guys. They worried about the competition?"

Hunt shook his head. "No. Half of them are afraid you will start deorbiting their working assets and the other half wants to use Apex Orbital to put up specialty birds on short notice, to deal with developing situations. They were less worried when your daughter seemed to be limited to fifty kilograms, but the thing she deorbited two days ago weighed forty-two times that and I ended up in a whole other set of meetings as a result."

"We aren't interested in messing with your satellites. We *might* be interested in the short-term, specialty-satellite delivery gig, if we can figure out safeguards. The paranoid side of the NRO might use such a mission to take us out."

Hunt clucked his tongue. "Who's paranoid?"

"Paranoid *with a reason*. So, nothing from Daarkon?"

"Not *nothing*. We got some intercepts on messages to Stroller and Associates, but they're code words. There seems to be some activity there. Lots of personnel returning from overseas assignments but very few departing."

"Nothing from or to the Retreat?' "

"No."

"Damn. I don't even know what continent it's on."

Hunt put the car in gear. "When Gilead surfaced for his daughter's wedding, there wasn't any sign of him leaving or entering the country. Even private jets have to go through passport control. Doesn't mean he didn't, but there wasn't really a good reason for him to evade border control and a penalty for getting caught evading it. I'm pretty sure we're talking U.S., and probably continental U.S. at that."

Davy sighed. "That's something."

# TWENTY-NINE

## Cent: Yes, *maxime asperum*

When Cory heard that Tara and Jade were back three days early, he said, "Oh! Can they start this afternoon? I was really worried about getting everything done before they had to start classes."

"Jet lag, Cory. Be reasonable. But they are all prepared to start tomorrow. Are *you* really ready?"

He looked at his office ceiling and his eyes blinked rapidly. "Um, yes. I will be."

"Then that still puts you *three* days ahead of schedule. What time, tomorrow?"

"Nine sharp."

"I'll get them here. Did you and Tara come to an agreement about the name? I want a patch for the coveralls."

Cory spread his hands. "An agreement? No. But I did capitulate."

I allowed myself a small smile. "Well, Matoska Mechanical Counter Pressure Spacesuits was a pretty big mouthful."

"I *said* I capitulated. Space Activity Systems will be fine. The original Paul Webb design was called a Space Activity Suit anyway. I've got a lawyer working on the incorporation."

"What about the patent lawyer?"

"That application was filed last year. By the way, I had lunch with Dr. Seck."

I shook my head. "Where did I hear that name?"

"Joe mentioned her. She's the material-sciences professor who was funded for her work on hydrogen-rich polymeric nanocomposites for radiation shielding."

"Right! How'd that go?"

"When I heard how good her results were, I told her I had an application for a full-body underlayer radiation garment and she said she had some thoughts in that direction, but her primary interest was spacecraft shielding that didn't require flex."

"Disappointing, though I suppose we could do rigid torso panels and helmet pieces."

Cory licked his lips nervously. "I told her if she'd reconsider the flexible application we could test her work in situ."

I just stared at him.

"I said it in confidence."

"Did you at least have her sign a nondisclosure agreement?"

He shook his head. "I figured with *your* publicity it was going to break soon enough."

"Dad won't like it, but you're right. Your connection will probably break soon. The intelligence guys may have already cracked it. Did she bite?"

"I think so. Besides testing the undergarment, I said I just might possibly be able to place a test package with interior and exterior dosimeters in a circumlunar free-return orbit."

"Circumlunar!"

"I think you reached the velocities needed for that on your very first orbit. We'd have to retrieve the package, too."

"Oh. Of course. What was it that Tara said? No more freebies?"

Cory shrugged. "This isn't exactly a freebie. With good radiation shielding, who knows *where* we can go."

*We*? Ah, well, there was that.

"Okay, Cory. I wouldn't mention it to Dad just yet. Also, start thinking what you're going to do when the press starts camping outside your apartment."

He laughed. "I'm not worried about that. *I'm* not Space Girl."

"Well, don't say I didn't warn you. I have my own ideas about radiation shielding, too."

"Yes?"

"I'm thinking three feet of water."

He laughed. "That would do it, all right, but do you know how much water weighs?"

"Depends on the temperature, but call it eight and a third pounds per gallon."

"And you're just going to jump into orbit with three feet of water around you? We're talking about several cubic yards at sixteen hundred pounds per yard."

I shook my head again. "You're still thinking like NASA, Cory." I wasn't going to mention twinning just yet. "What happens if I get the suit wet?"

Cory blinked. "Uh, how wet? What kind of wet?"

"Fresh water, immersed."

"Why?"

"Three feet of radiation shielding."

"You're serious about that? We could work in the high orbitals with that!"

I nodded.

"Well, the suit itself is exposed to moisture all the time: your sweat. Immersing shouldn't be a problem for the *suit*. I wouldn't expose the suit to vacuum after that, though, until it was dry."

"Why?"

"You want to freeze to death? When you sweat it cools you down, but then the pores shut down when they're cool enough. If the suit were soaked in water, it would flash to vapor carrying a *lot* of heat away from your skin. Probably full-body frostbite at the very least."

Well *that* didn't sound very pleasant. "Let's say I *wasn't* in a vacuum at the end of the process. Would it ruin any of the equipment?"

He stared blankly at the ceiling. "I wouldn't want to immerse the portable power supply in water. It wasn't designed for that, but if you left it off the suit it would be okay. I *think* the satphone antenna would be okay. We could use some silicon sealant on the exterior headset connectors, but if it were *fresh* water, I'm not sure we'd have a problem even if we didn't. But we'd want to make sure it was well dried after.

"But you're not going to immerse yourself in the water as shielding. That isn't very—"

"No. It's just during transfer that the suit would be exposed to water." I twisted my outspread fingers around an invisible sphere. "Water in an outer compartment."

"An outer compartment made of *what*? You going to haul up a pressurized module in fifty-kilo pieces and assemble it in orbit?"

"I'll get back to you on that."

Joe was followed from his house but it was openly: three marked news trucks and two unmarked cars.

*I guess they did make the connection.*

I was waiting upstairs at Krakatoa and he ran up the stairs, ignoring the barista. I jumped him away to the vault before the first reporter made it through the door of the coffee shop.

I was prebreathing oxygen, which didn't make conversation easy, but I took the mouthpiece off long enough to say, "Why didn't you tell me the press were onto you?"

He looked down and said something inaudible.

I wanted to whack him. "What?"

"I didn't want to give you *another* reason to keep me away!"

It wasn't quite a shout but it was loud and I flinched. I took a few more breaths before I said, "Okay. I understand that. How are your parents taking it?"

"Mostly relieved. It explained some things for them—like how I got a surf tan in the middle of winter and swimming trunks in the laundry that were wet with *saltwater*. Also, where I've been spending my days the last two weeks."

"What about the press?"

He grimaced. "Mom bought an answering machine so they can screen their calls. Dad posted no-trespassing signs and called the sheriff's office when the reporters started straying across the lawn.

"My brother keeps saying he's willing to be bribed. He goes out to the sidewalk to talk, but he's just messin' with them. He doesn't know anything that isn't already out there and he has to go back to school, too."

"Any sign of interest from parties who *aren't* the press?"

He shook his head. "No."

I raised my eyebrows skeptically.

"I know," Joe said. "I won't necessarily see them coming, but I've been looking."

*I could keep him safe by having him stay at the Eyrie.*

I had a reaction to *that* thought that had nothing to do with any danger to Joe.

I motioned to the checklist and we moved on to the suit prep.

I'd purchased several reusable ice bags, the kind you see pressed to characters' heads in countless old movies because they were in a fight or had a hangover. These were made of rubberized cloth with a gasketed aluminum screw top.

We filled the first one completely with tap water so it looked more like a ball, and Joe cranked down on the lid extra hard before patting its exterior dry.

The rest of the experimental equipment was my chest-mounted video camera, an ice pick in a wooden sheath, and a thick-bladed hunting knife in a leather sheath.

"Ready?" he shouted, to be heard through the helmet. I held my thumb up and jumped to my standard "Yuri" orbit, 350 kilometers above the Marshall Islands.

The whole central Pacific was socked in by a tropical storm and I had to stare for a moment before tearing my eyes away from the cloud patterns.

I felt the sides of my test bag. It had been taut below but now it was drum tight. I'd half expected it to leak around the aluminum lid or explode, but it was holding fine, so far.

I gripped the lid firmly in my left hand and stabbed the ice pick into the opposite side. When I pulled the pick back out, water drops, vapor, and tiny ice crystals fountained from the hole and, as I'd hoped, stopped almost immediately.

I pushed at a nonpierced area of the bag and felt it flex. When I pressed against the area under the hole, I felt a stiffness in the immediate area. It was hard to feel the exact dimensions through the suit and gloves, but the stiff area was between the size of a nickel and a quarter.

I stabbed the bag nine more times with the ice pick, careful to get the entire process on camera. In each case, the leaks stopped within seconds.

Just like my own sweat, the evaporating water cooled down the region by the hole. My sweat glands stopped producing moisture when the temperature dropped to a comfortable level. The fountaining "pore" in the bag only stopped when it became blocked by a nice plug of ice.

I slipped the ice pick back into its wooden sheath and retrieved the hunting knife. The ice pick was an eighth of an inch at its thickest, but the holes it punched were less because of the stretch of the rubberized cloth. The hunting knife's cross section was half again as thick and three quarters of an inch from back of blade to cutting edge.

When I stabbed the bag with it, the resulting gash spread open like lips of a mouth opening to say "oh," and the jet of ice crystals fountained out without stopping. I felt the bag vibrate as more and more of the water within boiled. The outgassing jet spread into a broad cone shape and the bag actually pushed against my arm, pivoting my body on my long axis. As we spun, the spreading cloud became a spiral of brilliantly lit crystals.

I waited it out, careful to keep the jet pointed away from any part of the suit. When the jet finally stopped, the bag was less than an eighth of its original size and solid as a rock.

The bag dropped to the table in the vault with a *thunk* that I could hear even through the helmet, and vapor immediately formed around it.

Joe pointed my cheap automotive infrared thermometer on it and showed me the readout: minus twelve degrees Fahrenheit.

"Yeah," I said, speaking loud through the helmet. "Small holes sealed. Big hole didn't."

"Right," said Joe, handing me the next ball-shaped bag. "Try this."

I took seven more ice bags into orbit.

All of the ice bags contained tap water, but now they also had various additives. We tried chopped cellulose, cotton, wool, fiberglass, superabsorbent polyacrylamide beads, and various synthetic fibers.

"We have a winner," I said, later, helmet off.

The best mixture featured chopped bamboo fiber mixed with longer lengths of a wool-like synthetic fiber that entangled with itself and the bamboo. The combination rapidly formed a mesh across the punctures, freezing from the edges and building across the gap, forming a fiber-reinforced ice patch even when I sawed a hole three inches long through the cloth.

Joe was more cautious. "Maybe. Works well in the *short* run. We'll have to see how well it handles cycles of warming and freezing."

"It *should* be self-healing. If it melts to the point of leakage, rapid evaporation will freeze it again."

"It's got potential. Better to test it, right?"

I nodded and unstrapped the life-support pack. Joe automatically supported it as I shrugged off the straps and, as he set it on its shelf, I did the same thing with the connected helmet. We went through the rest of the postmission checklist, right down to scanning for micrometeorite impacts.

"You're getting good at this," I said.

"*We* are," he corrected. "I've always worked well with you."

*Except when you chose to* work *with another.* My face must've shown what I was thinking, because his closed up again.

"It's true," I said. "Works well with others. Achievement unlocked."

Joe muttered, "Works and plays well with—" He shook his head angrily. "Let's get the rest of the suit off."

I took off the coveralls and hung them. We were now using the new portable power supply and it remained attached to the suit for the entire mission. I flipped the interlock and turned the rheostat. The suit expanded away from me, letting go, and I took a sharp inhalation of breath that was half pressure release and half surprise.

Joe automatically supported the flange while I jumped out of the suit, then hung it on the rack, carefully averting his eyes.

When he finally turned back toward me, I stepped forward and put my arms around him.

He gasped and then his arms tightened around me with desperate—almost suitlike—pressure. He lowered his face into my hair and breathed deeply.

I stood there for the space of three deep breaths. When I let go, he did too, his mouth half open, his eyes questioning.

"Cory is going to work you like a dog for the next ten days," I said. "How would you like to go surfing?"

We hit the waves for three hours at Laniakea on the north shore of Oahu. When I jumped him and his short board back to his house, the press population on the curb had doubled, probably because of how he had disappeared on them earlier in the day.

The reporters didn't note the arrival, though, because I delivered him directly to his bedroom and, carefully not looking at the bed, kissed him lightly on the lips. As his arms closed around me, I jumped away.

In the morning I met Jade and Tara at Jade's house. "There's no press here?"

"We've kept low. *We* weren't scheduled back from Europe yet."

"When do your parents get back?"

Jade looked at her watch and made a face. "Two days, seven hours. On the bright side, Dad texted that Mom is relaxing and actually enjoying the last bit of their trip when she isn't haranguing me all day."

"Well, that's something." I jumped them to Cory's lab and went back for Joe.

He was dressed and ready, but he didn't look very rested.

"You look like shit," I said.

"Trouble sleeping," he said. "When you go to hug someone and they vanish . . ."

I'd experienced some of that myself but I said, "Well, you'll probably sleep well tonight."

We joined the others at Cory's lab and he led us down to the temporary work space off of the machine shops that he'd arranged to use for the work.

"First things first," Cory said. "The press calls started. Joe's status as a student working for *me,* a researcher in mechanical counterpressure suits, leaked out of the Cardinal Careers center. My cell and voice mail directs reporters to call university communications. They have the press release Tara helped me prepare before her trip, but we are definitely in that *next* phase."

I nodded and looked at their faces. "Everybody is still good with continuing?"

Cory said, "You're definitely covered by the university's privacy policy. The campus is private property and media reps are not authorized to enter academic or residence areas unless specifically invited."

Joe said, "That's better than what's happening back at my parents' house. I'm good."

Jade said, "We're in."

Tara said, "Right."

I looked back at Cory and raised my eyebrows. He nodded firmly in return.

"Right, then. I'll bring in lunch, as arranged. Work hard. *Ad astra per aspera.*"

Cory laughed. "Yes, *maxime asperum.*"

For my next appointment, I wore the Nomex coveralls and the Merrell boots I usually wore over the suit. Both were a little loose, but I wore a bright blue turtleneck under the coveralls and wore doubled socks on my feet, and they looked and felt fine.

The receptionist was looking down at her computer when I appeared before her, but she must've caught some movement because her head jerked up and her mouth dropped open.

"I have an appointment," I said.

"You *certainly* do!" She picked up the handset on her phone and pushed a button. "Fran, she's here." She put down the handset and said, "Ms. Wilde will be right down to get you." She pulled a piece of paper from her top drawer. "While you're waiting, would you mind autographing this? It's for my daughter."

It was a color printout of the photo Flight Engineer Rasmussen had taken of me from the observation cupola of the ISS—side lit by direct sunlight and front lit by light reflected off the ISS, floating in front of a mostly dark Earth.

"Uh, what's your daughter's name?" I finally managed, taking the marker she held out.

"Alisha."

I wrote, "For Alisha, Welcome to the Womaned Space Program! Best wishes, Space Girl. p.s.—this is my first autograph *ever.*"

When she read it, the woman said, "Ever?"

I nodded. "How old is she?"

"Eleven."

I reached up and ripped the Space Girl patch off of the Velcro on my shoulder and set it on the desk. "Give her this." I tapped the shoulder of the figure in the photo. "It's the one I was wearing then."

She reached out blindly to the tissue box and blew her nose.

A woman with short dark hair came down the stairs and said, "Welcome to BlimpWerks. We are *thrilled* to have you here, Space Girl."

I shook her hand. "Pleased to be here. Nice to talk to you in person." Fran Wilde was the person in the firm's R-and-D department who'd first told me about their new nylon/Kevlar fabric over the phone.

Ms. Wilde noticed tears in the receptionist's eyes. "Is everything okay, Audria?"

Audria nodded, tried to speak, then just tapped the photo and showed the patch.

Ms. Wilde read the inscription and said, "Oh, my." She squeezed Audria's hand before saying to me, "If you'll just come this way."

There were four other people in the conference room.

"She gave Audria the Space Girl patch off her shoulder."

"For her daughter," I said.

She introduced the people, though I'd already met Mr. Papadopolis, the sales engineer Joe and I had talked with before. Mr. Eaton was their president, Ms. Quincy was their manufacturing supervisor, and Ms. Adouki was their chief of marketing.

Mr. Papadopolis had been doing some reading. "I'm surprised you aren't talking with Bigelow Aerospace. They've actually put inflatable habitats in orbit."

I shrugged. "Their modules are too heavy. Even their smallest unit is three thousand pounds and it's air-lock sized. I want a bit more room."

Ms. Quincy, the manufacturing supervisor said, "We do not make habitats. We make blimps. Aerostats. We certainly don't have anything tough enough to survive micrometeorites and space debris."

I nodded. "*I'm* working on that. I just need envelopes that can handle ten psi. You've done twice that with the smaller test sphere, correct?"

Ms. Wilde said, "We did it with all the spheres. We needed to confirm the degree of deformation."

"Good," I said. "I want those and I need some modifications. How much for the spheres as they are?"

Ms. Adouki's stepped forward. "How public is this project?"

"What do you mean?" I asked.

"It's not a secret, is it? Would you post video of the spheres in orbit?"

"I suppose so. These are too big to *hide*."

"Would you object to logos painted on the spheres?"

"That's one of the modifications *I* wanted. Our Apex Orbital Services and Space Girl logos. Possibly an Iridium Communications logo. Did you want to sell ads to someone else? Or did you want a BlimpWerks logo?"

Mr. Eaton and Ms. Adouki exchanged glances and Ms. Adouki said, "We would love to sell ads to others."

I shook my head. "No. Our brand. Our advertising platform."
Tara had been very specific about it. She'd said, "Buy them if you
have to, but I don't think you'll need to."

Mr. Eaton said, "We would settle for BlimpWerks logos and
an endorsement on your part. We would provide the spheres
and modifications, within reason."

Tara is always right. I continued from her script.

"We would also add a BlimpWerks logo to my coveralls or
life-support backpack. We would provide video and stills of the
spheres deployed, with the BlimpWerks logo prominent. If you
wanted me to deploy one of your special designs, that could
also work—you'd just need a bit of gas to inflate it. Without the
Mylar, it wouldn't last very long in that intense ultraviolet, but it
would make a fantastic photo and video shoot."

Mr. Eaton looked at his team and nodded firmly.

"What are the modifications you need?" asked Ms. Wilde.

"I need to add some aluminum flanges. Also, have you ever
seen *matryoshka*—Russian nested dolls?"

Dad and I both changed into swimsuits before he jumped me to
a tiny strip of beach in a north-facing, cliff-bracketed cove, the
only beach on a tiny lava island sticking out of the Pacific off
Costa Rica. The cove's inlet was filled with sharp rocks, shel-
tering the beach from the northern swells but making a boat
landing extremely dangerous.

The only inhabitants on the island were seabirds and they
weren't thrilled with our presence. Fortunately, they stuck to
the higher rocks and didn't use the beach which, Dad told me,
was underwater several times a month during the higher spring
tides.

"So how did *you* find it?"

"I saw a picture in *National Geographic*. They were out here
shooting the Blue-footed Booby rookeries. I liked the privacy
so I paid a pilot take me on a flyover."

"A pilot? How far off the coast are we?"

"Seventeen kilometers. When you look at Google Earth it

doesn't even show up. It's on the charts as a marine hazard because those—" He pointed at the teeth-like rocks at the mouth of the cove. "—are all around the waters."

"I don't recall you ever bringing *me* here before."

Dad smiled slightly. "That's correct."

"Or Mom?"

"You mother has been out here more than a few times." Dad's smile got bigger.

I blushed. "Privacy, you say."

He nodded.

"So, like this," he said.

Dad twinned between the beach and one of the taller rocks just outside the cove. As I watched, he moved his "beach self" into the low surf and water began pouring out of his "rock self," flooding outward in all directions. As his "beach self" moved deeper into the surf, the water pouring out of his "rock self" rose higher and higher. When he was up to his neck, he didn't go any deeper, but in the cove so much water was flowing toward and through him that the water level in the cove was a good yard lower than the water outside.

He jumped away, back onto the beach, one "self" only, and the waters sloshed violently against the rocky arms of the cove and up onto the sand as the water poured over the "teeth" at the mouth of the cove to rebalance the water levels.

"Is that what you did to Lawrence Simons?"

His hand went reflexively to the scars just below his left collarbone, lighter than the rest of his skin. "Yeah. Last resort. I was chained to the floor and they had guns out and the next time your mother came into the room they were going to shoot her."

"So I could've done that when they had that wire around my neck?"

"What you did worked better. The guy still could've choked you even if you flooded the room."

My turn for a reflexive touch. The abrasion hadn't scarred, but the memory was still there.

"You do it," Dad said.

I walked out into the water until the water was waist high

before I started, but I didn't use the rocks outside the cove. I twinned to the beach, up the slope from my father. The water knocked into him before he realized it was coming, but he did jump away before it washed him all the way into the cove.

I stopped almost immediately, my one self up on the beach by the cliff face.

Dad reappeared on the sand, ten feet off to the side.

"Where'd you go?" I asked.

"Up there." He jerked his thumb up at the lava cliff behind us.

There was a deep cut in the beach where the water had eroded sand into the cove. Dad pointed at it and said, "You want to be careful. Running water can be a powerful force. If you're going to move earth or knock things over, make sure it's what you *wanted* to do."

I felt guilty. "Will that take long to fill in?"

He held his hand out and rocked it side to side "One way or another."

I eyed the cut doubtfully. "You said you had one more trick to show me, about twinning."

Dad nodded. "Okay. Watch this."

He twinned again, one self by me, the other five feet away. Then the one five feet away disappeared but I could tell Dad was still twinning because I could see faintly through him, the ocean horizon in the distance. I walked around him. When I was on his west side, I could see a distant coast.

"Where are you?" I said.

His twinning figure pointed up and I tilted my head back.

His other self was standing in midair, at least a hundred feet in the air. *Stationary.* It wasn't my velocity trick. He was just twinning to that place and sticking there.

He stopped, his one self still in the air, but no longer motionless. He dropped. Before he reached the level of the cliff faces above, he jumped back to the beach, beside me.

"Okay. *That* was different," I said.

"It has applications." He walked out into the water as I had, but continued until he was neck deep. Then he turned back to me and grinned.

The deluge dropped from above like a hammer, but I'd been expecting *something*. I jumped sideways to the far end of the narrow beach and shook the water from my hair.

He was still twinning. I couldn't even see his airborne self, but the water was rushing out of a spot twenty feet above the beach and pounding into the sand. Then it stopped and he was standing beside me as the last water fell.

The eroded beach cut was even bigger, now.

I had no words at first, but then I said, "I guess I deserved that. But look at the beach!" I jumped to the edge of the cut and had to step back as more sand collapsed into the water.

Dad joined me, wincing. "Yeah. I should fix that. Get back."

I took several steps back. Dad jumped to the bottom of the cliff, at the head of the cut. He twinned again but *dimmed* and I realized that wherever he stood, the sun wasn't shining. Then sand started flowing out of him, only knee high at first and then higher, his legs pumping up and down. His local self moved along the cut and sand poured out of him chest high, into the water and then rising above it, wet, then dry. He moved out from the cliff face and by the time he stopped twinning, sand was mounded three feet above the precut beach surface.

He plunged into the water, completely immersing himself and staying under long enough that I was starting to be concerned, then his head reappeared. He walked out of the water like normal people do. "Sand gets *everywhere*."

"Where did it come from?"

"The Isaouane-n-Tifernine sand sea."

I blinked.

"Algeria—in the southeast. I dropped down the face of a three hundred-foot-high dune causing it to slide. Then it was just a matter of keeping my head up."

"You brought African sand to a Central American beach?"

"Well, I wanted it to match. How do you think this beach got here in the first place?"

"You *made* it?"

He shrugged. "It was a rocky cove but I really liked the privacy and the 'teeth' keep out any big sharks. But it's a safe place to practice moving water, eh? Just don't carve the beach too much."

"Sterling."

"Good morning, General."

"Cent." I heard him cover the mouthpiece and say something to someone in the room, then he said, "What can I do for you today?"

"I need an orbit that has a higher incidence of micrometeorite and small debris collisions."

"Excuse me? Don't you mean lower?"

"No sir. We're putting up a test, uh, platform to see how it handles microcollisions and, while we've already tested the material with deliberate punctures, none of them were at orbital velocities."

"I see, I guess. How big is this platform?"

"It's a twelve-foot diameter sphere."

"Oh! An *inflatable*. You are okay with microimpacts, but you don't want anything big hitting it, right?"

"Right. Nothing trackable. Just the smaller stuff."

"Unfortunately, you could probably do that anywhere inside a thousand kilometers. Well, you don't want the orbit too low, though. A low-mass satellite with that cross section would deorbit pretty quick."

"Low mass? I wouldn't call twenty-eight tons low."

"You said it was an inflatable."

"Yes. But we're inflating it with thirty-three cubic yards of water."

"Water? You're putting twenty-eight tons of water in orbit?"

"For the experiment, yes. Is that a problem?"

"That's over seven times what the Dragon capsule can deliver to ISS."

"Oh? Cool."

"How many trips will it take you?"

"That's proprietary, General. Is there a higher incidence of microdebris in any particular orbit?"

"The stuff we know about also has the bigger debris mixed

in. Trackable. That's why we *know* about it. Twenty-eight tons? That's *huge*."

"It's a little bigger than your average spy satellite, but not *much*. What are those, twenty tons?"

"You know this from direct observation?"

"Wikipedia. Look, I'd like to put up my test sphere tomorrow. I was thinking out about five hundred klicks. Above the ISS but below the Iridium constellation. Perhaps a straight equatorial, zero-inclination orbit. You want to check that out and I can touch base with Sergeant Mertens before I begin?"

"Twenty-eight tons of water?"

"And change. I'll check in with Agatha tomorrow."

"Right. Jesus. Twenty-eight tons?"

# THIRTY

## Cent: 4,800 Joules

I picked up the twelve-foot sphere from Fran Wilde of Blimp-Werks. The porthole's aluminum frame was only ten inches across but they had it sealed and clamped into the fabric.

"We tested it at twenty PSI," she said. "It was tight as a drum after twelve hours."

I hefted the entire roll. "How did you get it so flat?"

"We pumped it out, down to a couple of psi. Compared to out here—" She waved her hand through the air. "—it's a 'vacuum,' but when you're up there it will probably expand without you doing anything."

I hefted the bag. By my calculations, the cloth alone weighed forty-seven pounds. The stainless steel inflation valve and the porthole with its half-inch-thick polycarbonate window and aluminum frame added another seven.

"So the flange anchoring system worked out?" They'd been worried about that. Apart from fill valves, they had no experience in bonding metal fixtures into their envelopes. Luckily lots of work on that problem had been done by others.

Ms. Wilde said, "Between our fabric reinforcement and this combination of toothed grips, compression gaskets, and sealant, I think we've got it solved."

"How's the big guy coming?"

"We don't take delivery of the outer port until the end of the week, but we did a full-assembly low-pressure inflation test with an aluminum hatch in its place."

"Oh? All the ports in?"

"Every one. We pumped the inner sphere to three psi over and the outer at two psi."

"Not exactly a leak test."

"No. Just an alignment test to make sure the inner flanges all matched up with the outer ones and that we had a uniform gap all the way around."

"And?"

"Three feet plus or minus three inches and we think the variability will shrink once you get gravity out of the mix."

"Very nice." I slapped the bundle in my arms. "Let's see how it flies."

Agatha confirmed that a five-hundred-kilometer equatorial orbit with a thirty-five-degree mean anomaly at midnight Zulu would be clear of any operational or derelict spacecraft *and* would cross the fringe of the Kosmos 2551/Iridium 33 cloud in a week.

Ms. Wilde was correct about the sphere's behavior once I got it into orbit. It may have only had a few psi of air in the tightly rolled folds but it was several orders of magnitude more pressure than was outside.

To keep it manageable while I refined the orbit to match Agatha's parameters, I'd wrapped the bundle several times around with a nylon cargo strap. As soon as I was in orbit, the cloth bulged out at the ends and from between the straps, but stayed mostly contained.

Once I was in the groove, I pulled open the Velcro closure and let it loose.

It expanded, quickly at first, then slowing as the pressure dropped with the volume increase and the stiffness and mass of the fabric became a factor. By the end of a minute, though, it was a sphere, though there were still wrinkles in the fabric and it easily dimpled when I pushed a finger into it.

I backed off and admired the whole. It was highly reflective silver with an almost painful highlight at the angle of maximum reflection. The occluded side, in shadow, was still lit by reflected earthlight.

The Apex Orbital Logo incorporating Space Girl predominated, with the zeppelin-shaped BlimpWerks logo above and off to the side. Both were repeated on the opposite hemisphere. They'd done them in gold Mylar with a black trim and fused them to the aluminized Mylar outer coating with an adhesive they said would survive wide temperature swings.

Right. Time to see inside.

I moved to the porthole, flipped up the sun visor, and looked within. No surprise, I saw nothing but black, but I'd brought a flashlight, an upper-end disposable that we *thought* would survive vacuum. I pressed it against the polycarbonate and switched it on.

The interior nylon layer was an unremarkable gray, but I could see well enough to jump within and I did.

The automated pressure valve on my oxygen feed didn't react because the interior was so close to vacuum as to make no difference. The port was pointed toward Earth and, after my eyes adjusted, it provided all the light I needed.

I jumped away.

I appeared in a defunct drilling yard in South Texas where we were renting a brand-new, never-used frac tank, a large open-topped, rectangular steel tank with a five-hundred-barrel capacity. This was the equivalent of seventy-seven cubic yards, twice what the sphere could hold.

Dad was standing on the catwalk landing at one end, dumping bags of chopped bamboo and synthetic-wool fibers down into the tank. He was wearing a wet suit and a dust mask and I could tell he was sweating up a storm because the fibers were sticking to his forehead and neck.

I jumped up onto the catwalk and he threw his last empty bag onto a pile on the ground, saying loudly, "That's the last of that."

The tank was three-quarters full, filled earlier when he twinned to the local municipal water tower, but the fibers were floating on the surface, matted.

"Time to mix. You should try and twin to your target."

He vaulted over the railing, splashing down into the water, then twinned from there to five feet above the surface of the water at the other end of the tank. The tank went from calm and matted to a roiling torrent as the liquid flowed through him to plunge back down, sucking the fibers under the surface and thoroughly mixing them into the fresh water.

Right. My turn.

My first attempt at twinning was several meters away from the sphere. The helmet purge valve buzzed from the pressure drop. I was immediately surrounded by fog as the hot, humid air rushed through me into space, the moisture flashed to ice crystals, and the BlimpWerks sphere was actually blown away from me.

I stopped twinning in orbit, and the helmet vented all the way down to 4.9 psi.

I jumped closer, and then into the interior of the sphere and twinned again. The walls moved away slightly and I heard a thump as they fully inflated, pressurized to one atmosphere. The pressure valve on my oxygen buzzed, bringing my relative helmet pressure up, and I stopped again, still in the sphere.

It was weird. I knew that I could actually take off my helmet in here. Well, until the walls started getting punctured by micrometeorites. I twinned again, but to vacuum, to outside the sphere, and my helmet buzzed again, venting.

My first thought was that the sphere would collapse, like it had when the BlimpWerks people pumped the air out in their factory, but it didn't. It wasn't the vacuum pulling in that had caused that, but the greater air pressure outside *pushing* in. When the outside vacuum matches the inside the sphere stayed "inflated."

I jumped back to Texas, tank side. Dad was back on the catwalk, dripping, but he'd taken off the dust mask.

"All mixed," he said, and held up a glass jar filled with liquid.

It was mostly clear but white and gray fibers floated uniformly through the mix.

I held up my thumb and he dumped it back in. I took a good look at the tank below before returning to the interior of the sphere.

I twinned to under the surface, crouched at the bottom of the tank, wondering how long it would take the water to flow into the interior of the sphere.

It was practically instantaneous, water flowing through the Cent-shaped hole (in all directions) with an orbital vacuum pulling it through. I untwinned, still in the tank, and jumped up to the catwalk. I felt the water draining out of the weave of the suit, out of my long underwear, but, in this heat and humidity, there was hardly any cooling.

Dad raised his eyebrows at me and I raised my thumb again.

I wanted to see how it was doing. I was half afraid it had split open as the water rushed in, but I was mindful of Cory's warning about not taking the suit into orbit while it was wet.

Dad went back into the tank, and twinned, draining out the last of the water/fiber slurry.

I went ahead and shut down my oxygen, purged the helmet, and took it off.

"Where'd you put the leftovers?" I asked him when he re-emerged.

"The input side of the local sewage-treatment plant. They'll filter it and the fiber will end up in compost."

I didn't get back to the sphere for twenty-four hours. Cory wanted the suit to dry thoroughly, and he hadn't done a close-up examination for wear and deterioration in over a month.

When I appeared in orbit, the sphere was *not* split open. It was *not* a spreading cloud of water vapor and ice crystal.

It was tight, the wrinkled cloth smoothed out, the logos more prominent. When I pushed against it, to test how taut the fabric was stretched, there was hardly any deformation. *I* moved away and it seemed to stay there. Okay, Newton's third law—equal and opposite reaction—but twenty-eight tons was 350 times more mass than me and the suit, so I moved 350 times faster away from our point of contact than it did.

The sphere was spinning slowly, about five revolutions per minute, and I positioned myself in its shadow and studied the rim, looking for any jets of water vapor and ice backlit by the sun.

After several moments I concluded there weren't any. A close examination of the surface didn't yield any obvious impacts, so I moved to the aluminum and polycarbonate porthole and installed the monitor.

The package was a used four-inch Android cell phone, fully charged, but with all the radios turned off. The only thing it was doing was running a seismometer app that used the phone's accelerometers to monitor vibration and displacement. I attached it to the port using a spring bracket that hooked into opposite sides of the aluminum frame and pressed the back of the phone firmly against the polycarbonate. To finish, I shaded it with a tent of ordinary aluminum foil, anchored around the perimeter of the port's aluminum frame with a twisted piece of copper wire.

Lastly, I took some video, myself in the foreground. This wasn't one of those selfies at the end of my arm. I now had a "tripod" to use when I wanted a stationary vantage point. In this case it was an extra mounting bracket to snap the camera onto. That, in turn, had two collapsible fiberglass cross pieces snapped into it. I could position this "cross" in space, pointed in the direction I wanted, and let go. Just like the ice skater spreading her arms, this slowed down any tendency of the camera to rotate.

It wasn't perfect, but it was easy to get the camera pointing in the correct direction for minutes at a time, and the poles folded down to store in a thin pocket on my left outer thigh.

Tara groaned and fussed when I asked her about the appropriate language for a press release, then took it over, using up her evening off to edit the video and post it and the press release.

It took five days to weave the first suit, but Cory was being extremely careful, triple checking every step and documenting everything. They went through several powered/relaxed to unpowered/clenched cycles before they put it on the life-mode simulator.

Cory was quite pleased. "Consistent and sufficient. Variation is under four hundred pascals and nothing less than twenty-nine point nine kilopascals."

"Let's try it in orbit," I said.

Cory said, "*No!*" It was almost a shout.

I blinked.

He cleared his throat. "I mean, we are a long way from that step. We need to check the performance with the pressure-sensor unitard, we need to cycle it at least a hundred times to make sure it's behaving consistently." He looked at me sideways. "This time we're doing it *properly*. No *shortcuts*."

My lips twitched.

"Can you get another suit made in the remaining time?"

"I have material for four more."

"This one took five days."

He said, "We were being very careful with the first one. Actual construction is about seven hours per suit. We'll go ahead and finish this batch."

"Five new suits? And the life-support backpacks? Helmets?"

"We ordered the helmets from the original manufacturer, but I've outsourced the visor assembly and the life-support backpacks. We're adding some safety monitors for oxygen and carbon dioxide partial pressures and an ear clip for blood oxygenation and pulse. Oh, and helmet pressure."

"Display? Audible alarm?"

Cory nodded. "Both, I think. Telemetry if I can arrange it, but that depends on what comms we end up with. All the sat-phone providers can handle data but I don't think we can use Iridium outside of LEO."

"Don't forget local comms. We have more than one suit, we can start doing multiperson missions."

"*Exactly*," he said and tapped himself on the chest.

I shivered. I'd been thinking Dad—maybe Mom. The people

who could survive a catastrophic failure of the suit. If I were in orbit with someone who couldn't teleport away at need, I'd have to stay *very* close. "Better make that redundant comms."

By the end of the week amateur astrophotographers were posting pictures of the sphere, a tiny shining speck just big enough to see as circular, with phases of illumination like the moon.

I'd found one point of impact, a frozen plug sealing a triangular hole a half inch across. According to the seismometer app, we'd had fifteen impacts total, but one had been clearly larger than the others, a sharp spike and movement that lasted for some minutes as the shockwave bounced back and forth through the watery interior of the sphere.

The other collisions registered as smaller spikes and, despite substantial searching, I couldn't find the holes.

At the end of the second week, we'd registered another twenty-five impacts, but really hadn't lost any appreciable water, though one of the impacts produced a hole nearly two inches across. You could see the fibers matted in the icy plug and I spent extra time watching how it behaved in full sun, even going so far as to halt the rotation of the sphere to keep it in full sun at least forty-five minutes.

It *evolved*, changing shape slightly and though I detected some vapor streaming away after its longest solar exposure (fifty-two minutes, terminator to terminator) it hadn't let go, but seemed to grow thicker, melting and refreezing on the outside like a scab that keeps getting picked at.

I went back to trying deliberate punctures but it took a *lot* more force to stab the icepick through the BlimpWerks fabric than it had the ice bag, probably because of the Kevlar layer. I finally managed it by adding sixteen-feet-per-second motion toward the sphere, about the speed you'd get from falling off a four-foot ledge on Earth, and punching the icepick into it at impact.

Only did it once. It hurt.

The only advantage of this deliberate hole was I could *find* the point of puncture. The hole still sealed immediately and it didn't tell us any more than the earlier experiments with the ice bags.

*What else could I try?*

Dad stared at me. "You want what?"

"A gun. Well, a bullet, but a fast bullet. Just *one*. And something to shoot it with."

"Ah. This is for the sphere?"

"Yeah. It will give us a known velocity and we can video the impact."

"Uh. But you'll fire it in a vacuum."

"Yeah."

He went off and talked to someone. When I next saw him he had a rifle and a box of ammo. "This is about as fast as it gets, for commercial off-the-shelf. The consensus seems to be that, as long as the rifle doesn't have time to heat up or cool down too much, it will be just like firing a rifle in the atmosphere."

"Ah. Expansion and contraction of the metal?"

"Yeah. Also, too hot and the primer or propellant might ignite on their own."

That was a scary thought, but it would definitely take time for either to happen. "How fast is it? How much mass?"

He handed me a sheet of paper. "One thousand four hundred two meters per second. Seventy-five grains."

"Grains? What's grains?"

"Grains. Wheat, barley. One of the oldest measurements." At my expression, he got out his phone and Googled it.

*"An English Penny, which is called the Sterling, round without clipping, shall weigh Thirty-two Grains of Wheat dry in the midst of the Ear."*

"Great. How many cubits a second does this bullet go?"

Dad relented. "Fifteen point four three two three six grains to the gram." He used the calculator app on his phone. "Round it to four point nine grams."

I did the calculations later while I was killing time prebreathing. The bullet's energy of impact would be north of forty-eight hundred joules. A more typical orbital collision was nine times faster. Kosmos 2251 collided with Iridium 33 at over 11,699 meters per second. At those speeds, the 4.9 gram bullet would impart over 335 thousand joules, the energy of a third of a stick of dynamite exploding.

Premission, I set the camera at a lower resolution to enable a higher frame rate: 120 frames per second, to capture as much of the event as possible. Once I was suited up, I took the rifle out to West Texas and fired it a few times from different positions. With the helmet on I couldn't hold it against my shoulder *and* aim down the sights but I could still roughly hit the center of my target, an eight-foot stretch of arroyo wall, from thirty feet. It kicked a bit, but the weight of the rifle and the rubber stock recoil pad on the butt absorbed much of it.

In orbit, I set the camera up on its "tripod," pointed obliquely at the center of the sphere on its fully lit side. It was cross lit by earthlight with a stretch of black space in the background.

I backed off thirty feet, put the gun's stock to my shoulder, and fired.

I didn't get to see the impact. The off-center thrust of the rifle spun me around. By the time I stopped the spin and returned to the sphere, the new leak was plugged, though there was a cloud of dispersing ice crystals in the vicinity.

I broke down the camera stand and returned the rifle to Dad, who was sitting in the warehouse in Michigan, standing by with our base-station cell phone, just in case I needed to check things from orbit.

"Did it work?" he asked, loudly.

I gave him the thumbs up. He looked at the rifle and said, "I'm going to leave it in the Eyrie until we're sure you don't need it again. All right?"

I nodded.

"Okay." He looked down at his laptop. "Your target just passed four hundred twenty-two kilometers over Vancouver

Island, headed east." He gave me the rest of the coordinates and speeds. I gave him another thumbs up and, picturing a very particular location, jumped.

The helmet purge didn't activate like it normally did in orbit. And I wasn't having to flip my visor down in the harsh glare of direct sunlight.

I was floating in the middle of the Tranquility node, International Space Station.

*Ha!*

I *thought* it was possible but trying it without the suit on had seemed a bit *risky*. I shut off my oxygen, purged the helmet, and popped it off. Good old noisy ISS.

I was unstrapping my life-support backpack when Rasmussen and Nagata floated into the node from Unity. Rasmussen was dressed in workout clothes. Nagata carried a DSLR camera with a huge telephoto lens. Rasmussen was talking but it was hard to hear her over the whine of the ventilation fans.

"Hey," I said about the time they noticed me.

Their eyes went wide and Rasmussen grinned. "If I knew you were coming, I'd've baked a cake."

Nagata brought her camera up automatically but then looked down at the telephoto lens. She shook her head. "Too close. Could you back up about six hundred feet?"

I hooked the helmet and backpack into the bungee cords of the treadmill behind me, then looked at Rasmussen. "Oh— sorry. Are you about to use that?"

She dismissed my apology with the wave of her hand. "Later. Right now we've got a visitor."

"Why didn't the depressurization alarm go off?" asked Nagata.

"Well," I said. "I came, uh, *directly.*"

Nagata blinked. "Directly. You mean from ground side? Say, California?"

"Ground side. Not California, though. I was about five hundred feet above sea level so air pressure was probably pretty close."

"Why'd you wear the suit, then?" asked Rasmussen.

"Well, I wasn't *sure* if I could do it. Last thing I wanted to do is end up in my shirtsleeves three meters *that* way." I pointed at the closest bulkhead.

Nagata said, "I'll tell Commander Elliott you're here."

Rasmussen put her hand on Nagata's arm. "Wait a minute, Alis. I want to talk to her about Misha. *She* could solve it."

Nagata blinked. "Kate, uh, the director would completely flip—"

"Maybe it would be better," said Rasmussen, "if you didn't *know* about this conversation."

Nagata exhaled through pursed lips, then said, "*What* conversation?" She turned to enter the observation cupola. "What visitor?" To no one in particular she said, "There are no activities scheduled for Leonardo today."

Kate gestured at my helmet and backpack. "Better not leave that in sight."

I raised my eyebrows. "O . . . kay." I unhooked the straps and followed her into the Unity module and she motioned me *down*, toward Earth, into the Leonardo PMM. Even with all the bags and storage racks, it felt *huge*, more than twice the volume, at least, of my twelve-foot sphere.

Rasmussen looked both directions and followed me, then pulled me sideways into a gap behind a large, lumpy, white storage bag, automatically hooking her foot under a cargo strap.

"What's going on, Flight Engineer?"

She grimaced. "It's Kate. And they tell us your name is Millicent? Millie?"

My turn to wince. "Just Cent. Named for my mom and she goes by Millie."

I was drifting back toward the open middle of the module and Kate snagged my coveralls sleeve to pull me back. "It's Misha—Flight Engineer Grebenchekov."

"Complications from his surgery? He looked great when I dropped his glasses off."

"Complications from politics. He's in D.C. I understand you met his, uh, associate, Sergei."

I nodded. "The wanker? Yes. Did I get Misha in trouble with my little . . . pest-control procedure?"

"Well, *I* nearly busted a gut laughing when I heard about it." She shrugged. "Hard to say how much of it was that, how much of it was Sergei and Misha's history, and how much of it was Misha's insisting on a formal announcement of our engagement."

"But Misha is well?"

"Physically? Yes. He requested taking convalescence in the U.S., using that time and accumulated leave so he can be there when my Dragon capsule lands in a month. Between Sergei and some conservatives in Russia, permission was refused. He was ordered back to Moscow and the orders didn't come from Roscosmos, but somebody in the parliament. Misha refused and the Russian ambassador was told to confine him to the residence. It's an epic FUBAR situation."

"FUBAR?"

Kate blushed. "Military acronym. You're seventeen?"

I nodded.

"Well, you've heard the word, I'm sure. Fucked up beyond all recognition."

I laughed. "That's very useful! What can I do to help?"

"With Misha?"

"Sure."

"It would be good if you could get him out of the residence so they can't hustle him onto an Aeroflot flight. He doesn't need the stress right now, postsurgery and all. It's bad enough he's still in postmission recovery, too."

"Will they even let me see him?"

She rocked her hand back and forth. "They said he was too ill to meet with NASA's interagency relations lead, but the ambassador is one of Putin's old cronies and he has that same publicity lust. I bet *Space Girl* could get access *if* there was a photo op with the press."

"Gotcha. I'll see what I can do."

---

Tara liked the idea but then, she's a romantic. She made the call to the networks first and, once she had them on board, she conferenced the embassy's press office in.

When she was done she said, "Worked like a charm. Since the networks have committed, the ambassador will give us fifteen minutes in the late afternoon in front of the residence." Tara laughed. "The optimum timing to make the five o'clock news."

I'd prepped so I could show up *my* way, appearing a hundred feet above the street and dropping to a clear space inside the wrought iron fence. It was overcast and dark already.

The D.C. cops were keeping the press from crowding the fence or blocking Twenty-fifth Street NW, but when I dropped from the sky in my highly visible white coveralls, the camera strobes lit up the street like lightning.

I stood up fully and waved to the press, ignoring the shouted questions.

Embassy security, spaced ten feet back from the fence, closed in on me and I turned toward them, smiling. When it looked like they weren't going to stop short of grabbing me, I jumped past them to the landing at the head of the stairs, where a microphone had been set up on a stretch of red carpet.

The ambassador, bracketed by two large men in suits and trailed by Grebenchekov in his Russian Air Force uniform, was just emerging from the residence. The two security men practically threw themselves between me and the ambassador, but he said something abrupt and they stopped, hands inside their jackets.

I stood still and tried to look harmless. I was a full head shorter than any of them, even Grebenchekov, the shortest.

Grebenchekov, who'd been frowning, smiled when he saw me. The ambassador took one look at his face, then stepped forward past the security men and held out his hand, timing it so we met directly before the microphone. "Space Girl, I am very glad to meet you!" His English was good, only lightly accented, and the PA made it audible to all.

He gestured to the embassy security people at the fence.

They opened the gate and allowed the press to push in as far as the bottom of the steps.

I shook the ambassador's hand and said "*Moye udovol'stviye*" and his smile increased. I held my hand out to Grebenchekov but he used it to pull me into a hug, followed by air kisses on both sides of my head.

"And you clearly know Colonel Grebenchekov," the ambassador continued. "We are pleased to welcome *Kosmos Devushka*— Space Girl—and to have this opportunity to thank her for her recent rescue mission."

I ended up sandwiched between the two of them, and the ambassador motioned at the microphone. Luckily, Tara and Grandmother prepped me for this, too.

"Apex Orbital Services was delighted to be of service during the recent emergency. We hope to be of further service to the Russian Federal Space Agency." I reached out and pulled the Apex Orbital Service patch off its shoulder Velcro. "I'd like to present this patch, which I was wearing during Misha's medical evacuation, to Ambassador Pimenov."

The ambassador and I did the standard graduation-photo pose, right hand's shaking, left hand passing the object, faces turned to the cameras.

"And I would like to present this patch," I ripped off the Space Girl patch from the opposite shoulder, "to Flight Engineer Grebenchekov, as a memento of that event." It wasn't the one I'd worn then. That one went to the BlimpWerks's receptionist for her daughter. When I held the patch out to Grebenchekov, I was careful to tilt it so that he could read what I had written on the back.

*Standby for liftoff.*

He blinked, then we did the pose. He leaned forward to speak into the microphone. "I owe great debt to Space Girl. When she rescue me, it was *launch* of lifetime friendship."

*Ah, he got it.*

The ambassador looked at his watch and said, "We can take a few questions." He gestured to one of the reporters.

"Is it true that you go into orbit without a spacecraft, Space Girl? And, if so, how?"

"Yes it's true. As to how . . . I think happy thoughts."

The other reporters laughed but the reporter opened his mouth to pursue my nonanswer. The ambassador cut him off, though, calling a different reporter by name.

"Colonel Grebenchekov, when are you marrying Flight Surgeon Kate Rasmussen?"

Grebenchekov licked his lips and then said, "We are still working on the details." The ambassador cleared his throat and Grebenchekov added, "No further comment."

The ambassador flicked his finger to another reporter, who said promptly, "What kind of services does Apex Orbital perform and which of them are you offering to Roscosmos, Space Girl?"

The ambassador looked at me, eyebrows raised and apparently quite interested.

I said, "Besides our recent medevac from the ISS, Apex has delivered over three hundred satellites into orbit in the last month alone. We have also removed over twenty-four hundred kilograms of orbital debris and have done preliminary orbital tests on habitat-construction techniques for our own permanent facility in orbit."

"Is that to be a manned facility?"

I rolled my eyes. "It will be a *human*-occupied facility. I *guess* we'll let some of the boys in, if they *behave*."

More laughter, especially from the women reporters.

"In any case, we hope to offer both NASA and Roscomsos astronaut and cosmonaut transfers to and from orbit." I put my arm around Grebenchekov's waist, glanced at my watch, and said, "Beginning . . . *now*."

I jumped.

I was a *little* worried about Grebenchekov, especially when he started crying.

"Are you all right?"

He blinked and shook his head to toss the tears away. "It was the microgravity. I never thought I'd feel it again."

We were floating in the Leonardo Permanent Multipurpose Module. I heard someone shouting, "Misha! MISHA!"

Kate Rasmussen shot past the opening to Leonardo, looking in, then snagged the doorway stopping herself. With a shriek, she launched herself into the module. Misha gave a low, intense, "Ha!" and met her halfway.

I was afraid they would collide painfully, but they clearly had it down, grabbing each other in a way that absorbed most of their motion and turning the rest into a spinning hug followed by a truly heroic kiss.

When they'd backed off to stare hungrily at each other, I asked, "How did you know?" I hadn't told her what I was going to do since I wasn't sure I *could* do it. I'd just committed to getting him away from the residence.

She said, "I was watching the press conference. You said it. Then you did it." She blinked tears away.

She tugged at Misha's collar. "What is this crap, Colonel?" They both laughed.

It was less than a minute before the entire crew was in there and Misha looked like he was *accreting*. Even Commander Elliott was grinning like a fool, though he was the first to break away and confront me.

"Did you okay this with the ISS flight director?"

"No."

"Are you going to take him back down?"

"Later. When *she* goes. It's probably still not a great idea for him to pull five Gs, so I'll get him down gently."

He pursed his lips. "They're probably going to want you to take him back down *now*."

"Aren't you shorthanded without him?"

"He *should* be convalescing."

"He's had fifteen days. And surely the micro-G will help. In any case, it will be good science. Postsurgical recovery in a microgravitation environment."

Elliott shook his head.

"How was the fudge?" I asked.

He laughed. "Are you reminding me that you're *benevolent*?"

I grinned. "Face it. I'm *handy*. Remember how he got to the surgical team in the first place. If he has a relapse I *will* come back."

I was back in two days, but not for medical reasons. I offered to bring a justice of the peace, but Navy Captain and Spacecraft Commander Ken Elliott said there was plenty of precedent—*he* presided over the ceremony. Flight Surgeon Kate Rasmussen gave *herself* away. Flight Engineer Alis Nagata was matron of honor, Flight Engineer Oleg Astakhov was best man, and I brought the flowers, which I floated down the aisle.

First flower girl in space.

An estimated seven million people watched the live stream. A lot more caught it on the news.

Grebenchekov said, "*Now* let them try to separate us."

# THIRTY-ONE

## Millie: Alarm

The radio-frequency alarm went off in Millie's closet in the middle of the night. Davy sat bolt upright next to her with a gasp. She pulled the pillow over her head, but felt the mattress rebound as Davy *jumped* away.

She sat up. Davy was standing in the walk-in closet, looking at the upper shelf, his face lit by a screen. "Four hundred six megahertz. Huh." He grabbed the portable sweeper, powered it up, and vanished.

"You could turn off the alarm!" Millie blinked. *Something is transmitting from inside the house?*

She got up and pulled on her robe, shuffled her feet into her sheepskin slippers.

She didn't know how to shut off the alarm. It was intentionally loud enough to be heard all over the house, though the door to the bedroom was closed and also, she hoped, the door to Sam's room across the hall. She pushed the closet door shut, which helped and, rather than open the bedroom door, jumped across to Sam's room.

It wasn't Seeana's shift but she was in the room by Sam's bed, helping Jeline do something with the Resmed positive pressure ventilator.

Sam wasn't using the Resmed—she was awake, using an

oral-nasal oxygen mask. This was better than having to use the positive pressure ventilator, but not as good as her baseline—supplementary oxygen through a nasal cannula.

*Though the ideal would be to get her off* all *supplementary oxygen.*

The door to Sam's room *was* open and Millie could hear the high-pitched tone of the radio-frequency alarm even through the closet and bedroom door. When she pushed Sam's door shut she could *still* faintly hear the alarm.

She went back to the bedside and took Sam's hand. "How are you feeling?"

Sam rolled her eyes and weakly tapped her collar bone. "Same-oh, same-oh." She pointed at the oximeter readout which read 91.2.

Millie nodded. If it dropped much lower they would have to put her back on the Resmed.

Seeana said, "What's that noise?"

"One of Davy's gadgets."

If there was an illicit transmitter in the cabin, *somebody* brought it. She didn't distrust Seeana or *any* of the health staff, but it couldn't have gotten here by itself. "He's trying to fix it."

The door opened suddenly and Davy was there, holding the portable sweeper. Millie laid Sam's hand down on the bed and patted it, then went to him, raising her eyebrows.

He said quietly, "I thought it would be in their quarters but it's up *here*." His face was blank, utterly blank, and the only times Millie had seen him like that were moments of extreme danger.

"Could it be some of the medical equipment?"

Davy's eyes were shifting between Seeana and Jeline. He took a step forward and lifted the sweeper, swinging it from side to side. He stepped forward and now the sweeps took in the bed end of the room, where most of the equipment was.

In a neutral voice he said, "Hey, Seeana, did you do anything special to the ventilator?"

Seeana said, "We changed out the air path. It's part of the normal maintenance and—" She lowered her voice, turning away from Sam. "—I'm afraid we're going to need it for a pro-longed stretch."

Davy pointed the sweeper at the ventilator and frowned. Then he pointed it at the remote oximeter display. When he swept it back to the bed he said, "Damn. It's in the mattress, I think."

Sam was frowning now. "*What's* in the mattress?"

Davy kept his eyes on Seeana and Jeline as he said, "A radio started transmitting from this room at midnight. Precisely at midnight, like it was on a timer."

Seeana and Jeline looked at each other with a do-you-know-what-he's-talking-about? expression on their faces. Millie didn't think they were acting.

Davy dropped to his knees and lifted the edge of the fitted sheet. "Don't see anything. Can we move Sam temporarily? Put her in our bed?"

Millie nodded. "Yes. Do we have enough time?"

Davy said, "I don't know. Perhaps we should just go."

Seeana blinked. "Go? Does this mean someone ratted you out?"

Jeline said, "Does this mean we don't get our bonus?"

"Help me move her," said Millie. "Let's figure out what's go-ing on first." To Davy she said, "Turn off that friggin' alarm!"

She dashed across the hall, back into the master bedroom, and pulled back the covers and top sheet. She didn't see Davy kill the alarm but the shrill tone stopped abruptly, then Davy appeared holding Sam and set her down on Millie's side of the king-sized bed.

"Still warm," Sam said.

Seeana rolled in the oxygen cylinder they'd been using and reconnected it to Sam's mask.

Davy's eyes locked with Millie's and she said, "I'll wait here with Mom."

He jumped away.

Thirty seconds later he walked back through the door, the sweeper in his hands, staring at the readout.

"Was it in the mattress?" Millie said.

Davy shook his head. "It moved. In here. Seeana, could you stand on that side of the room?"

Seeana, frowning, stomped over to the far side of the bedroom.

Davy shook his head. "Not on Seeana. Millie—move over there."

Millie joined Seeana.

Davy said, "It's on Sam." He made adjustments to the sensitivity and moved it down her body.

"There." He pointed at her hip. "Millie?"

Millie pulled the covers back. Sam was wearing a flannel nightgown and underwear. Sometimes she resorted to adult diapers but lately she'd been managing with a bedpan. "Excuse me, Mom." She ran her fingers over the cloth but could feel nothing but cloth, skin, and bone. "Are you sure, Davy?"

Davy picked up Sam and moved her over to the other side of the bed, then ran the sweep again.

"It's not *on* Sam," he said.

"It's *in* her."

# THIRTY-TWO

## Cent: Soot and Ashes

The night before, I'd built a fire in the Eyrie's stove to fight the chill. I had been fighting the urge to go get Joe, to let *him* warm me, but I was still afraid, still . . . cold. I overdid the fire a bit—nothing dangerous, but I made the Eyrie so warm that I ended up sleeping in the buff. When Dad shook my shoulder I snatched the covers up to my chin.

"I thought we had an agreement about privacy!" I couldn't see his face in the shadows.

"Get dressed. I need your help."

Adrenaline flooded through me. He was dead calm, but something about his voice was wrong and I smelled something that reminded me of last night's fire, but with a chemical component.

I reached out and hit the light switch.

His face was streaked with soot and his hair had ash in it.

"What happened!"

His expression looked numb. "Everyone is all right, but the cabin is gone."

"Fire?"

He shook his head. "Missile. Probably a Hellfire II with a metal augmented charge for an extended pressure-wave kill."

*"Is Mom all right!?"*

"Yes. Everyone got out. I went back for an oxygen tank and I saw the exhaust trail out of your grandmother's window. Nice clear night. Thought it was a meteor at first, but it curved in toward the cabin and I jumped away." He blinked. "Came back after two minutes. The only part still standing is the springhouse. I'm not positive but I think I saw a drone complete a circle and head south."

"Turn around and keep talking! *Where* is Mom? Grandmother?" I jumped out of bed and pulled clothes from the dresser.

"Sam's in the vault and so is your mother. Seeana's with them. I dropped the other girls at the Vito Cruz train station." At my blank look he said, "On the Manila Light Rail. It's a good thing they were sleeping in their scrubs."

I dressed for the cold, my base layers and then my snowboarding boots, pants, and jacket.

"You got them all out *before* you saw the missile? How did you know?"

"The radio frequency alarm went off. There was a transmitter in the house. 406 megahertz. Digital signal. Data. Probably GPS coordinates."

"Who brought *that* in? One of girls?" I really didn't think that was likely, but I suppose somebody could've planted a tracker on them.

"Sam."

"That doesn't make any sense."

"It's in her hip. It's still in her hip. It's still transmitting. That's why I took her to the vault."

"Her hip?" I still wasn't getting it.

"Her hip surgery. Looks like they added a bit more than plates and screws when they went in to fix it."

I was dressed now. "What do you need?"

"Your mattress, to start. Sam's lying on a comforter spread on the table. We've got the Resmed and a portable oximeter but we're using one of the small $O_2$ bottles from the spacesuit and we'll need more, soon. I figured you had a source, yeah?"

I nodded.

"Right. I'm gonna take the mattress and bedding there, then

go get a screen and a portable toilet. You get oxygen, right? And if it's a medical supply grab some adult diapers and a bedpan."

"They won't be open now," I said.

"*Look into my eyes*," he said. The remainder went something like "You have clearly mistaken me for someone who cares."

I winced, then nodded. "Okay. It's an emergency, I get that. We can pay later."

He began stripping the bed.

"*Someone* is going to pay."


Oxygen first.

I showed up with the first tank, setting it down in the corner of the room with a *clunk*. Dad had obviously been there because the table was up against the wall and Grandmother was lying on my mattress. Mom and Seeana both looked over at the noise I made and Mom burst into tears.

I stepped forward. "Is Grandmother all right?"

Seeana was looking at Mom, surprised. So was Grandmother.

"Sorry," Mom said. She was using a disposable wipe on her hands and I saw they were streaked with soot. I looked at her feet. Her sheepskin slippers were caked with more soot and ash.

"You've been to the cabin," I said.

She looked at my clothes. "You haven't."

"Not yet. What's wrong?"

"I just . . . you were conceived in that house. You were born there. You were raised there. When I saw you—" She looked away.

I worked my mouth for a moment. I guess it hadn't sunk in yet. Perhaps it would be better if it didn't sink in until I'd finished gathering supplies.

"I'll be right back. This tank holds ten times as much as the ones we had, but it uses a different regulator."

I returned with the regulator, the bedpan, and a box of adult diapers.

Mom had stopped crying. Her face was calm and she was even laughing at herself a little. "Things. They're only things. You're okay. Dad's okay. Mom's okay."

I hugged her. "Right. Just things. I'm grabbing some more *things* right now—cylinders, okay?" I ferried three more from the gas-supply warehouse. "What else do you need immediately?"

Mom said, "Dad's taking care of the critical one and *I* can deal with the others. We could use some more room, though." She jerked her chin toward the suit rack and the life-support pack supplies.

I nodded. "Right. I'll put them in the Eyrie. That way I can access them without disturbing Grandmother."

"Ah. Good thought."

I looked down at her ash-and-soot-covered slippers. "Some of my clothes will fit you."

She nodded, "So they will."

I ferried the suit and supplies to the Eyrie, filling up some of my empty bookshelves.

*Okay*, I thought. *Time to see for myself.*

I didn't go directly to the cabin. I'd seen the state of Mom and Dad's clothes. I appeared on the ridge above, in the shelter of the pavilion that overlooked the valley and marked the start of my snowboard run.

The wind was still for January and it was cold and clear, at least five below zero. Even dressed for snowboarding I wasn't dressed warmly enough, but at least there wasn't windchill on top of it.

I could smell the cabin: smoke, something metallic, and something sour. And parts of it were still burning. I could see embers and a bit of flame at the corner of the foundation and, in the light of the moon, I saw what looked like dark straw scattered across the snow, but I realized the straw had to be at least wrist thick.

*Shattered logs. Those were the walls of the house.*

As my eyes adjusted I made out jagged pieces of metal roofing in the mix, and less-identifiable scraps of furniture.

*They were targeting* all *of us.*

I remembered six-year-old me running around the living

room pretending I could jump. Mom would close her eyes and I would run into another part of the cabin.

"Where did she go?" Mom would say.

And I would pop up and say, "Boom, I jumped!"

*Boom.*

The smoke was making my eyes water. I think it was the smoke. Anyway the tears were freezing on my cheeks.

"You shouldn't be here."

I jerked, but it was Dad's voice so I didn't jump away. I couldn't even see him until he moved, and even then I had trouble telling what was snowbank at the edge of the pavilion and what was him.

"What are you *wearing*?"

Dad sighed. "Layers. You're going to freeze."

"I'm surprised you didn't twin to someplace warm."

He said sarcastically. "If I wanted to show up on their instruments like a blazing torch, I would do that."

I looked back out at the valley. *"Whose* instru-m-m-m-ments?"

*"They* aren't here yet," he said. Then, less firmly, he added, "I don't think."

"What are you ga-ga-ga-going to—"

He jumped to me, grabbed, and we were in the Michigan warehouse.

Now I could see why I had so much trouble seeing him. He was wearing an arctic camouflage ghillie suit over a white arctic parka, overmitts, insulated pants, and musher boots. Beneath the parka hood he was wearing a thick white balaclava and goggles, which he pulled down around his neck as the lenses fogged in the warehouse's heated air.

"Warm up," he said pointing at one of the building's electric radiant heaters. "I'll be back in a minute."

I dropped to my knees in front of the heater and unzipped my jacket. The heaviest shaking stopped almost immediately, and then Dad was back, dropping boots, overmitts, an insulated bib overall, a balaclava, etc. Everything was white. The goggles and boots were still in their boxes. Everything else was on store hangers, with the tags still attached.

"Join me when you're dressed for it," he said, and then he was gone.

I had the feeling he hadn't gone through checkout. I glanced at the tags and was sure he hadn't—it was 2:30 in the morning in Edmonton, Alberta, so the store in question was definitely closed.

I was still chilled, but I moved away from the heater. By the time I was dressed, I was overwarm and it was a relief to feel the icy cold of the ridge. Dad was back in his snowbank, tucked at the side of the pavilion but well under the roof.

"We're still much warmer than the surroundings," he said. "But there has to be three feet of snow on the roof, so keep it above you and I think we won't stand out."

I joined him in the snowbank, kicking out a niche and letting it shape to my butt.

"Why haven't they arrived? Why didn't they arrive immediately after?"

"They didn't know where we were. Not until their transmitter began broadcasting."

"How long after that did the drone fire the missile?"

"Twenty minutes? I'm thinking they already had it in the air, prestaged, ready for the transmitter to come on."

I frowned. "Isn't that a *little* like throwing a dart in the dark while blindfolded? How many drones did they put up?"

"You're thinking they already knew where? At least roughly?" He was silent for a bit. "Everybody *I* brought to the cabin was checked for electronics."

"Except for Grandmother."

He cleared his throat. "Yeah. You made sure that Joe, Tara, and Jade never had their cells, right? Or any other electronics?"

"Right."

"You're positive?"

I wasn't. I remember once grabbing Joe and taking him directly to my bedroom for some exceedingly satisfying sex. I didn't bother making sure Joe didn't have his phone and I'm pretty darn sure he was too busy to be looking at the GPS readout, but I didn't want to get into that level of detail with Dad.

"Pretty positive," I said. "Consider this—what if Grandma's tracker didn't go off because of a timer? What if it went off because the drone was broadcasting some sort of command?"

I couldn't see his expression, but he went, "Hmmm." After a minute, he said, "I prefer that. That would be less scary."

"Less scary? Somebody put a tracking device in my grand-mother's hip so they could shoot a missile at my house and you think that's not scary?"

Dad clucked his tongue. "*Less* scary. Less scary than people we trust giving up our location. Less scary than the thought that they put lots of drones up at the same time. That scenario would pretty much indicate the full cooperation of the air force."

"You don't think this was the NSA and the CIA?"

"I don't *think* so. It doesn't feel right. You've been working pretty closely with USSPACECOM. They know your capabilities and they'd be a lot more cautious about going after you. I mean, you take out *one* keyhole spy satellite and, with launch, that's two *billion* dollars out of their budget." He shook his head. "No. I think it's the Daarkon Group—Hyacinth Pope's people. They have the resources to field *one* drone—to get hold of one or two Hellfire missiles. I'm already after them, which they know, so they probably know it's not like I'm going to change that if they miss me. They've been hiding from me. I think they're tired of hiding, but they don't dare come out unless we're all dead."

"You think they'll come check for bodies?"

Dad nodded. "It was a few minutes between the time we moved Sam and the missile hit. They *might* think the signal stopped transmitting because of the explosion. But they'd want to be sure."

"Dad, what if they just call Yukon Search and Rescue? The Mounties would look through the wreckage and count the bod-ies. Those assholes wouldn't have to expose themselves."

Dad frowned. "It's *possible* I suppose, but they can't count on the Mounties to finish up. I guess we'll just have to see who shows up."

I peeled back the cuff of the overmitt to check my watch. "It won't be light until ten eighteen, but of course they could time their arrival for first light."

"You think they won't come tonight? It's clear weather and you know how rare that is."

"What's the weather forecast?"

"High-pressure ridge until tomorrow night. So, yeah, clear during the day, too."

"I have no idea." I yawned suddenly and felt my jaw pop.

Dad said, "We'll take it in shifts, then, until morning. How does ninety minutes on, ninety minutes off sound? Off shift at the Eyrie. On shift comes and gets the other if there's action."

I gritted my teeth. "Are you *really* going to come get me if I'm the off shift?"

Dad sighed. "Unfortunately."

"What does *that* mean?"

"You were awfully handy when we extracted Sam from her nursing home. I don't know what will happen, but your Mom would feel better if we were *both* here."

"Promise?"

"Promise."


I was right about first light. I'd only had my eyes closed for fifteen minutes when Dad shook me awake at 10:30 Pacific time.

"What?" I said.

"Helicopter. Coming up the valley from the south. It's *not* yellow and red. You awake?"

"Go!" I said. "I'll be there."

I'd been lying on the platform bed sans mattress, but adequately padded in the insulated bib and unzipped parka. The boots, gloves, overmitts, balaclava, and goggles were in a pile beside me and I scrambled into the boots and gloves, zipped up the parka, and carried the rest of the gear with me. Dad was crouching low behind the snowbank at the front of the pavilion, only his head above it.

I pulled on the rest of the gear, cinched my hood closed, and joined him.

The Canadian Search and Rescue aircraft, helicopters *and* fixed wing, are all painted high-visibility yellow with red trim. This large helicopter was gray with bright orange highlights. We got a good look at the lettering on the side as it did a pass over the cabin foundation before settling out in the valley, where winds kept the snow from piling too deep.

"CHC?"

Dad said, "They're a transport provider for the oil industry. They have lots of heavy, all-weather equipment like that Super Puma."

The eight figures who jumped down from the starboard-side cargo door were dwarfed by the helicopter. It was twice as tall, landing gear to the top of the rotor, as the tallest of them. They began moving across the flat in a familiar shuffling motion and standing taller than I expected in the snow.

"Snowshoes," I said.

Dad said, "Yes. Somehow I don't think these guys are my boys from Costa Rica."

"What's the plan?"

"We watch. I'll probably grab some of them—scare them a little, but we want to leave someone capable of running. Can you follow them? See where they go?"

"The helicopter? I guess. Hardly orbital velocities. Now?"

"No." Dad shook his head. "First we watch."

I felt odd when they started picking their way through the debris field, and Dad actually growled when the first of them climbed over the remnants of the front door. I knew how he felt and I expected him to move then, before they walked in our home, but he put his hand on my arm as if *I* might go after them.

"Don't."

"Project much? I wasn't going to."

We were whispering. They were about a thousand feet away, but with the air as still as it was, sound carried. We'd already heard some of *their* spoken words and now I heard something else—a small-plane motor, like a small Cessna.

Dad pointed.

It was circling, perhaps two miles out. It *wasn't* a Cessna. It was hard to see against the lighted sky and I bet it was invisible with even a small amount of overcast.

Dad vanished and I searched the ground below, looking for him to appear, or, more likely, several of *them* to disappear, but Dad was back beside me in seconds, his hands holding Mom's fancy image-stabilized binoculars.

He studied the drone and swore.

"Are you upset that it's back?"

"It never left. Look."

He handed me the binoculars and I studied it. The long narrow wingspan, the inverted-V tail, the pusher prop. "What am I looking at?" I asked.

"Under the wings."

"Uh. One missile. On the port side."

"But not two. It fired the other one last night and it's been circling wide, waiting for these guys."

I lowered the binoculars.

"They could fire the other missile if they see us."

He nodded. "Yes they could." He looked at me. "I don't suppose you can crash it?"

The drone was doing about eighty-one miles per hour, an economy "loiter" speed, and it was easy for me to match velocities. I'm sure the sensor suite in the pod suspended beneath the forward fuselage wasn't looking toward its own wingtip, but as soon as I latched my mitts onto the very end of the port wing, twenty-five feet away from the drone's body, I'm *sure* the operators noticed.

My weight rolled the plane sharply over on its side and the asymmetric drag from my parka-thickened cross section yawed the nose toward the ground. I felt the wing buck and flex as the automatic onboard stabilization systems fought to right the craft and the engine went to full revolutions as they goosed the throttle.

I was about twenty-eight feet away from the prop and the last thing I wanted was to be thrown into it. That was *not* my preferred way to crash the vehicle.

*Enough.*

I held on hard and dropped my relative velocity fifteen feet a second. My drag had been introducing yaw before, but this threw the craft into a flat spin, perpendicular to the ground, and threw me out, too much centripetal force for me to keep my grip.

Still conscious of the prop, the minute the wing slipped out of my hands, I flinched back to Dad at the ridge top. The drone's flat spin turned into a tumble as the pilot and the autonomous systems struggled to stabilize the craft. For a few seconds I thought that between the remote pilot and the onboard systems they'd succeed and I'd have to go back, but then the outboard half of the starboard wing snapped off and spiraled away. Five seconds later the drone smashed into the thickly forested slopes on the far side of the valley.

"I hope *that* cost them a pretty penny," said Dad. "Good work."

The men below hadn't reacted to the drone but they reacted to the sound of the crash with calls of alarm, and their postures shifted. Then I heard a faint yet familiar sound.

"That's an Iridium satphone handset!" I said.

Dad nodded, lifting the binoculars. "Tail-end Charlie, there," he said. "Hold these."

If I'd tried to use the binoculars I would've missed it. The farthest man, the one who loitered at the edge of the debris field, had one arm held up in the classic talking-on-the-phone pose, and then he was gone.

That seemed fast, even for Dad, but then I realized it was the camouflage. He'd been there but I hadn't even registered him against the snow before he'd snatched and left.

He appeared beside me five seconds later, the Iridium handset in his hand, studying its display.

"Where'd you drop him?"

"The beach."

"Australia?"

"Oh, no. *My* beach. That one I made off Costa Rica."

Ah. The little rocky island where I'd practiced twinning.

"I didn't have time to sweep him for electronics but at least I have *this*—" He held up the handset. "—and there's no cell service out there."

"I'd have thought you would use the pit."

He shrugged. "It's too close to the Eyrie." He gestured below, at the remnants of the cabin. "If you haven't noticed, we're running out of space."

I smiled sadly, but of course he couldn't see it under the balaclava. *Space is the one thing we* aren't *running out of.* "Was he armed? Are they?"

"He *was* and waving it around as soon as he fought his way out of surf and that wet parka, so let me deal with him. Don't know about *them*. I suspect they're just temps, especially the way *this* guy—" Again he held up the satphone. "—was hanging back."

"Huh?" I thought the guy was just squeamish, worried about finding bodies or pieces of bodies. "How do you figure?"

"Well . . . he was at the edge of the debris field, right? If they had found something—a survivor, opposition—he would have been outside the blast radius of the other missile."

"Seriously—they would've fried their own guys? You're not just being . . . you?"

"I am being 'me.' But I'm still serious. How do you think I got so paranoid in the first place?"

The day before I would've thought he was crazy, but that was before someone implanted a tracker in my grandmother's hip and then fired a missile to kill her and everyone in her vicinity.

"It's sad that I agree with you," I said. "What are you going to do with *them*?" I gestured at the men below."

He considered them.

"I think your Royal Canadian Mounted Police idea has merit. I really think these guys are day labor, hired for this." He vanished and reappeared a few minutes later with a five-pound sledgehammer in his hands.

"You just said they weren't the bad guys!"

He acted hurt. "It's not for their heads, it's for the tail rotor on the helicopter! I just want them to still be here when the RCMP arrive."

"Ah."

"I've got this," he said, gesturing at the valley, the helicopter, and the men standing among the pieces of the cabin. "But you might want to check on the others."

"Mom and Grandmother?"

He shook his head and held up four fingers.

"Joe, Tara, Jade, Cory."

The suit team had finished the fifth suit two days before Joe's semester started. Tara had another week before dear old Beck-wourth High School resumed, and because Jade wasn't doing the Smith interterm minicourse in January, she wouldn't start for an-other two weeks. Cory tentatively suggested they could use Joe's last two days for testing, but this offer had a uniform response.

"Fuck no!"

Cory took the revolution good-naturedly. When I phoned him after finding his office, lab, and apartment empty, he said, "I'm reading at a coffee shop. Why?"

I didn't want to panic him but I also didn't want to leave him dangerously uninformed. "They made an attempt at me and my parents. Keep your eyes open, okay?"

"An attempt? Like they tried to kidnap you?"

"Something like that," I said.

"Well, which was it? They did or they didn't?"

I sighed. "They blew up our house."

I heard his chair scrape across the floor as he shifted abruptly. "Is everyone all right? Your parents?" I decided not to mention that Grandmother was back on the respirator, weaker than ever. "We got everyone out first."

"That's *not* how you kidnap someone."

"Thank you for pointing that out. I think they've given up on trying to *use* us."

"I thought they didn't know where you live?"

"We are *not* having this conversation over the phone. I need to check on the others."

"Yes! Sorry."

"Eyes open."

Jade and Tara were at Krakatoa, hiding from both sets of parents, but not, unfortunately, the press who were camped out downstairs.

"Why aren't they up here with you?" I asked. Jade had warned me over the phone so I'd arrived back in the corner, out of sight of the first floor.

"The management put a 'mezzanine reserved for private party' sign up. That's us. Wish it would work for our parents," said Tara.

"I thought *your* mom was okay with this," I said to Tara, gesturing between the two of them.

"It's not the relationship," Tara said. "It's the publicity. The press keep pestering her and—" She glanced at Jade and rolled her eyes toward the ceiling.

Jade finished for her. "Tara's dad resurfaced, awful as ever. She and her mom tried to renew the restraining order, but Tara turned eighteen last month so it's no longer a child protective services issue."

Tara shook her head. "We should've pushed for prosecution back *then* but Mom thought that getting custody permanently revoked and that restraining order was hard enough. Since the domestic-violence charges weren't made *and* the incidents were more than five years ago, the judge we saw only wants to consider current behavior in justifying a restraining order."

I hadn't told them about the cabin but my anger about that bled over easily. "He would have a hard time bothering you from *Perth*," I said. "Say the word."

Jade smiled, but Tara said savagely, "Why should *he* get to go to Australia!"

"True," I said. "Um, how would you guys like to spend a week there?"

Jade's eyes lit up. I could tell *she* liked the idea.

"How's *your* Mom?" I asked.

She held out her hand and rocked it. "She's trying, but that's almost worse. She and Dad are seeing a therapist and it's bringing up . . . stuff. I'm really glad they're doing it, and I *think* it will be really good when they're further along, but just now . . . it's a bit painful. Especially when they drag me along for 'family' sessions."

Tara put her arm across Jade's shoulders. "Fun times, eh?"

I bit my lip. "You have no idea."

They looked at me. Tara said, "A breakthrough with Joe? A break up? *Something*?"

I almost smiled. "No. Joe's the next call, though, because they—" I blurted it out. "They tried to kill us last night. They *did* blow up the cabin." I leaned forward and told them the whole thing.

"Wow," Jade finally said after the silence that followed my story. "That makes *my* troubles seem petty."

"These might *be* your troubles," I said. "They could still come after you. I was serious when I said you could spend a week in Australia. Or France. Or how about St. Martin in the Caribbean? They speak French there."

Tara said, "Is this on the company? I kinda blew my savings on France."

"Yes. A cottage with a kitchen, say?"

"What?" said Jade. "No room service?"

Tara elbowed her in the ribs and said, "A cottage would be lovely. What's the weather there?"

My phone connected to the coffee shop's WiFi. "This week, high of eighty-two, low of seventy-five. And unless you're going to hang out at Club Orient, you'll only need swimsuit bottoms."

Tara's eyes got big. "What?"

"French—all the beaches are topless." She looked like she was rethinking her answer and I said, "Topless isn't *required*. Just allowed."

I jumped them to each of their bedrooms, but waited with Jade.

Since the secret of how Joe had managed frequent travel back and forth to Stanford was out, he was spending the last two days of vacation in New Prospect with his family. Well, with his family and some trailing press.

I was worried about the press. It was a good way for *them* to get close.

*Them.*

I was starting to sound like Dad.

On the other hand, unless *they* replaced all the reporters with operatives, the pack of journalists were also witnesses.

I used Jade's phone and texted him.

Me: ¢ here. WRU@?

Joe: Luncheon Junction w/fam 4 post-fb feast.

Luncheon Junction was the restaurant in the old converted train station where we'd had our first date. They had really good pie.

Me: Watch out.

Joe: WTF?

Me: Old Friends.

Joe: ?

Me: Like Jason

Jason ran the local drug ring and had been used by *them* to try and catch us. He'd snatched Jade and Tara to pull me in and he tortured one of his own gang members when she wanted to quit.

Dad broke his arm and jaw.

He'd deserved it. He was serving twenty years for aggravated assault in the first degree.

Joe: FFS

Me: (.)(.)

Joe: Tits?

Me: Try again.

Joe: Eyes open?

Me: Yes. Or I can extract you. J&T taking that option.

There was a pause. Was he distracted? Was he wondering if I was inviting him for something more? *Was* I inviting him for something more?

Joe: No. Mom pissed about bn gone last 2 wks. Making up4it.

I thought about telling him he was putting his family in danger *by* hanging around them, but I didn't know. *I* was probably the one putting them in danger. *They* could be monitoring his phone or Jade's phone.

Me: OK. B4N

Tara called her Mom and told her she was going out of town. Jade left a note.

The one-bedroom cottages on Rue de Grande Caye normally ran fourteen hundred dollars a week but that was with an advanced reservation. I figured we would have to pay double on such short notice, but a tropical storm near Miami had disrupted flights and there'd been several cancellations.

We secured a cottage away from the beach for seven hundred dollars. I left Tara and Jade with all the unused cash, for groceries, shopping, and restaurants.

"No plastic, right? And no cell phones. Not only will they track you with it, it's expensive as all get-out. Stick to e-mail. The WiFi's free."

"Yes, Mother," said Jade.

"You think you can survive this?" I was looking out the louvered windows at the palm trees. You couldn't see the ocean from this side but the Baie du Cul-de-Sac was less than a hundred yards away.

Compared to the icy bite of New Prospect's air, the breeze which pushed the curtains was like a caress—warm, slightly humid, and laced with the scent of tropical flowers. Inside, the cottage was tile floors and wicker furniture with brightly colored cushions and a king-sized bed.

Hell, why wasn't *I* staying there?

Tara said, "We'll tough it out."

I hugged them and jumped.

Things were not so good in the vault.

"—awfully weak," Seeana said as I appeared.

Mom nodded at me, acknowledging my arrival, but turned

back to Seeana who was kneeling on the mattress next to Grandmother.

Grandmother was on the Resmed ventilator and seemed so small, curled up in the middle of the mattress.

Seeana used her thumb to pull up Grandmother's eyelid. "I don't like the color of her sclera."

Mom said, "A bit yellow, yeah."

I didn't like the fact that Grandmother didn't flinch or even seem to notice that Seeana had pulled the lid up. "Unresponsive?" I said.

"She's exhausted," said Mom.

"Should we take her to a hospital?"

Mom said, "It may come to that. We drew some blood. Your father is having her levels checked. We're a little concerned about liver function."

" 'A little?' " I said.

Mom looked away. "This has not been a good day."

Dad popped in, a sheet of computer printouts in his hand. "Liver enzymes are slightly elevated but it's looking more like a flare up of the polymyositis. Her CK and aldolase levels are up. Do you want me to fetch her neurologist?"

Mom bit her lip. "If we hospitalize her, sure."

"What's CK and aldolase?" I asked.

Seeana said, "Muscle enzymes. More muscle damage. Not good. She was responding so well to physical therapy before the last break. I was hoping to move her into aqua exercise but there's no way she'd handle that now."

"Swimming?" I said.

"No. You wear floats that keep you upright, with your head above water. You can walk, jog, and do other exercises without putting any weight on your bones. But the water pressure pushes in on your chest and makes it harder to breathe. *Later* that's great. Helps you exercise your diaphragm and chest muscles, but right now—" She shook her head. "Even with the respirator she's having trouble fighting gravity."

Mom and I locked eyes.

Dad said, "Son of a BITCH!"

Seeana was looking around, confused. She was the one who'd said it but she didn't get it.

I said to her, "It's the one thing I can do something about."

Despite his initial reaction Dad said, "It's an *insane* idea. It could *kill* her."

Mom said, "She's not exactly safe down *here*. Up there she could *fly*. Well float, but become truly mobile instead of pinned to the mattress like . . . like an insect mounted for display!"

It was odd, but I'd done the most pertinent research and I hadn't even been aware it applied to Grandmother.

"Microgravity actually *encourages* osteoporosis," I said.

"Sure." Mom said, "We're not trying to cure the osteoporosis. We're trying to ease the pulmonary distress and allow non-impact exercise."

I felt I should make the whole case. "Yes, but the bone loss does other things. The calcium ends up in the bloodstream and can cause other problems. Renal stress and kidney stones."

Seeana nodded. "Perhaps, but the Fosamax she's been taking has really dropped her blood calcium levels and she could take potassium citrate supplements to reduce the chance of stones."

"There's other negative effects of microgravity," I said. "Nearly everyone throws up initially. The otoliths float up and start banging off of parts of your inner ear that they would normally only hit if you were lying on your side or upside down or flat on your back. Your brain compensates after a few days but vomiting is a pretty common result of the vertigo. Also from the fluid moving into your upper body. Your head gets puffy and your sinuses feel stuffed up and your body senses there's too much liquid and it tries to get rid of it—sometimes by vomiting. You definitely pee a lot the first two days."

"Is this fluid dangerous?"

"Well, it's not pleasant. The longest time I've spent in orbit was ninety minutes and I could feel it. On the other hand, I've never stayed up the forty-eight hours or so where things start adjusting."

"Have you thrown up?" Davy asked. "You never mentioned being space sick."

"I came all the way back to Earth more than once for nausea-related reasons but I've apparently been up enough that my brain no longer interprets the vestibular input as being caused by some toxin that needs to be removed from my stomach ASAP."

"Are the fluids in the head dangerous for someone as old as Mother?"

I raised my hands and shrugged. "The closest thing we have is John Glenn's flight on STS-95 back in '98. He was *older* than grandmother, seventy-seven then, but he was in excellent health.

"I do know that there was some question about whether higher intercranial pressure could increase the chance of strokes or retinal bleeding, but it's never really been tested. You don't spend that kind of money sending people up who *might* not survive it."

Dad said, "We could get her into a really *good* hospital. We can afford it. They're not going to order a drone missile strike on Johns Hopkins or the Mayo Clinic."

"Maybe not, but she would still be a hostage—a target. Someone could still do something in one of those settings, like the awful tracking device they put in her hip."

"We need to get that out," said Davy.

Seeana said, "We need to get her *healthy*. The last surgery nearly killed her. I don't know if putting her in orbit will help, but I do know this underground storeroom of yours is pretty bad. I'm worried about the ventilation down here. It was designed to hold records, not people."

"Don't you think you should at least *ask* a doctor?" said Dad.

"No."

We all looked down, shocked. I don't think any of us realized Grandmother was awake, much less listening. Her voice was weak but she'd pulled the oxygen mask off to be heard.

"Mother? How much of that did you hear?"

"Enough."

"But you said no?"

"I said no to *asking a doctor*. They don't know if it will help but they'd be crazy to say yes. What a malpractice suit. So *don't* ask them. Just do it."

"You *want* to?"

"Of course I *want* to, even if it doesn't help." She looked at Dad, "Even if it's an insane idea and kills me dead." She took two deep breaths with the mask back on before adding, "I want a chance to be Space Girl, too."

# THIRTY-THREE

## Davy: Columns On the Board

It was *taglamig*, the cool dry season in the Philippines, though both the "cool" and "dry" were relative since the temperature and the humidity were both in the seventies. One of Tessa's younger brothers answered the door of her parents' house next to Muntinlupa City Technical Institute, where her father taught.

Tessa was right behind him, shrugging into a light jacket. "Coming, Mr. Davy. Go on, Ferdy."

Behind Tessa, a man walked into the hallway as the boy retreated back into the house. He was Tessa's height but stout, with gray temples and bifocal glasses "Tessa?"

She turned around, an exasperated expression on her face. "*Ama*!" She sighed loudly, then gestured to Davy. "Mr. Davy, this is my father, Professor Adolfo Lapena. He has been wanting to meet you. *Ama*, this is my employer, Mr. David."

"David Rice," Davy said, and shook the man's hand.

Tessa looked embarrassed. "We can go now!"

Davy raised his eyebrows. "Ah. We *are* in a bit of a hurry but did you have a concern, sir?"

Professor Lapena was studying Davy's face. "You are paying my daughter more than *I* make as a senior faculty member at my technical college."

"Oh?" *Great.* The man thought his daughter was doing something immoral or illegal to make so much money. Davy supposed that he *was* taking her in and out of the country illegally, but he didn't see how to reassure the man. "Don't you trust your daughter?"

Tessa flashed an expression at Davy that told him this was how *she* was seeing this.

Professor Lapena said, "I am told you have a daughter. You can understand, then, that I want to make sure my daughter is not being taken advantage of."

*Dammit.* "It's because we've asked her not to divulge certain things about her employment, yes? Is that what worries you?"

The man nodded.

Davy turned to Tessa. "You definitely earned the bonus. I can go ask Jeline or Bea if this is causing you trouble at home."

Tessa's eyes went wide. "No! You asked *me*. *Ama* should have more faith in me!"

*I don't have time for this.* He turned to Professor Lapena and said, "She is employed as an experienced geriatric-health aid to care for my mother-in-law." He turned back to Tessa. "Have we ever asked you to do anything that isn't part of that job?"

Tessa shook her head vigorously. "No!"

Davy looked back at Professor Lapena and raised his eyebrows, then jumped past him, into the house. The man staggered as Davy vanished from his field of view but Davy didn't have to catch him, though he'd been ready to. Now he said, "We have secrets, though, that your daughter has been asked to keep."

This time he *did* have to steady Tessa's father to keep him from falling.

"Easy there. We're going now."

"How did you do that? Wait. Your daughter—she's the one in the news?"

Tessa looked at Davy and said, "Well?"

Davy nodded at her.

"Yes, *Ama*. I take care of Space Girl's grandmother. Okay? We're going now."

Davy jumped Millie to Cory's lab since she'd never been there, and she went back for Seeana. Cory led them all down the hall to a departmental conference room, where Cent was waiting for them.

"Been here before?" Davy asked her.

"Oh, yeah. When we brought Joe, Jade, and Tara into the suit-assembly gig, we had our first scheduling meeting here." She looked down at her watch and blinked. "That was only a month ago."

Cory said, "Are you guys sure about this?"

Millie said, "Yes."

Cent said, "Come on, Cory. We're not going through this *again*." She looked over at Davy, who'd raised his eyebrows. "Just play back *our* discussion of five hours ago and you've already heard all this. Just different speakers."

Davy said, "We have a much better chance with your help, Cory, but with or without, we're proceeding."

Cory sighed and turned to the white board. "Right. Cent is in charge of getting our—" He wrote *STRUCTURE: CENT* at the far-left top of the board. "—in orbit and assembled. Which consists of—?" He looked at Cent.

Cent held up a hand and began ticking things off on her fingers. "The inner and outer sphere, the view-port assembly, the gas-pressure purge, the cooling exhaust, the DC power conduits, and the bundled coaxial-antennas feed. All of these have already been delivered to BlimpWerks or are expected within the next two days. Once assembled in orbit, we need to add the initial atmosphere and three hundred twenty-one tons of water/fiber shielding."

Cory listed each of them as separate items below the heading.

"Right. Orbit, as discussed?" He started a new column.

"Yeah," said Cent. "We want to be away from the worst of the debris, in the so-called 'safe' radiation zone between the two Van Allen belts." She looked down at a sheet paper. "As circular as we can get it, ten thousand three hundred ninety-three kilometers altitude or an orbital radius of sixteen thousand seven hundred seventy-one kilometers. That's as close to a period of six hours as we are likely to get—four orbits a day and enough out to be stable for decades."

Cory wrote the details down under the heading *ORBIT.* "You know that the radiation zone fluctuates wildly, right?

Cent nodded. "Three feet of water, remember?"

Cory nodded back. "Inclination?"

"What did you decide about the need for time in eclipse?" Cent asked.

"It's going to be hard to say. The albedo on that fabric is quite high and the thermal mass of the water is going to stabilize things considerably, but really, it comes down to how much heat we generate internally. We don't absolutely *need* the shading since we've got other ways to dump heat. It's really more about ground track than anything."

"Right, then. Fifty-one degrees, like the ISS. That will take our ground track as high as Canada and down to the edge of Antarctica."

"Okay." He started a new heading. *LIFE SUPPORT: CORY.* "We're scaling up our suit life support which means—" He began writing down components in the column: *$CO_2$ absorption, moisture absorption, oxygen storage and release, pressure purge and controls, ventilation, cooling.*

Davy said, "Power?"

Cory started a new column headed by *POWER.* Underneath it he wrote, *PV panels, batteries, charge controllers, inverters, lights, breakers.* "We're still going with off-the-shelf equipment?"

"Long as we can handle the fire danger. Pure oxygen and all. Add fire extinguishers and emergency self-contained breathing apparatus. And lots of training."

"Smoke detectors?" asked Millie.

"A full suite of atmospheric monitors," said Cory, scribbling away. "$O_2$ and $CO_2$ levels, pressure, carbon monoxide detectors, smoke and particulate detectors, temperature—air and water. Oh—radiation monitors. We should be good even with a solar storm, but we should be checking inside and out and know when to stay away from the view port."

Cory looked dismayed about the growing number of things listed under life support, then moved all of the sensors into a separate column labeled *ENVIRONMENTAL MONITORING*.

"I'll take a run at that," said Davy. "I know some people who excel at that sort of thing."

Cory looked relieved and added Davy's name to the heading.

The next column heading simply said, *TOILET*. He turned back and said, "I understand you've discussed this?"

Davy, Cent, and Seeana looked at Millie.

"Everybody wears diapers?" Millie said.

"*No*," said Cent. "And it would be best if we didn't have to ferry people back and forth for restroom breaks. Shift start and end will be difficult enough."

Millie raised her hand. "Okay. Put me down for that. I'll work on it. I've been reading Mary Roach's book. We'll need to replicate the negative-pressure ventilated units on the ISS but ours will be less complicated. *We* don't need to recycle the urine and we don't have to wait for resupply missions to transport accumulated feces."

Cory went back to the *LIFE SUPPORT* column and added: *Odor-absorption: activated charcoal. HEPA filtration.* He said, "We can look into the Apollo-type fecal-collection bags for the short run. Adhesive, stuck to your bum. *Really* unpleasant and messy."

Millie sighed. "So I hear. Not the NASA holy grail of 'good separation.'"

Almost desperately, Davy said, "Comms?"

Cory grinned and started a new column: *COMMS*. Underneath it he wrote *Iridium Sat phone? Imarsat or Globalstar phone and Internet data, and suit2suit vhf radio.* We're not sure about whether the Iridium phones will work at that altitude but Inmarsat and Globalstar should." He looked around. "Okay, what's the most critical? What can wait the longest?"

Cent said, "Most critical: life support. As important as the structure itself. Proceed in parallel."

Davy said, "What about power?"

Cent shook her head. "Power *generation* can wait. We can

ferry charged battery packs up until the panels and charge controllers are on line."

"What kind of batteries?" asked Davy.

Cory said, "I would prefer lithium iron phosphate. Orientation doesn't matter, and they're energy dense, especially when you compare them to lead acid. While they're not as energy dense as lithium ion, they're safer. More thermally and chemically stable—don't heat up as much during recharging and they last longer: two thousand recharge cycles versus one thousand to fifteen hundred for lithium ion." He spread his hands. "But they *are* pricey."

"But safer?" asked Millie.

"Yes."

Millie said, "Cost is not a factor. Not for safety."

Cory nodded.

Cent said, "We might get them donated, anyway, for an endorsement."

Cory waved his hand at her acknowledging the point. "We'll want explosion-proof switched connector harnesses to avoid sparks. We want to test all the electrical systems in pure-oxygen environments, and we definitely want to keep the humidity low to prevent water condensing in electrical devices."

"But not too dry, please," said Seeana. "If you could keep it above forty percent relative humidity, please, for lung health."

Cory blinked. "Okay. In the suit we just pulled most of the moisture out and let Cent hydrate by mouth. We didn't have an intermediate target—no active sensing."

"Can't we just use an off-the-shelf dehumidifier?" asked Millie.

"They depend on gravity to collect the condensate," Cory said. "I'm confident we can pull the water out of the air. It's turning the process on and off that's the problem. The unit on the ISS uses a centrifuge and is quite complex."

"Split the airflow," Cent said.

Cory scratched his chin. "Gotcha. Switch it back and forth. I can figure that one out."

Millie looked at her watch. "Right. We'll need some of the

medical equipment replaced that we lost in the missile attack—mostly monitors. And we'll need an infusion pump with enough volume to handle fluid replacement, not just drug administration, but I'll work with Seeana on that. Seeana and I need to get back to our future resident. Any other questions for us?"

Cent was staring at the board, sucking at her upper lip, looking a bit overwhelmed.

Cory laughed "Your own space program, you said? NASA employs over seventeen thousand people." He turned back to Millie. "No questions for now but *there will be*."

Davy picked up Hunt from D.C. and started the briefing while they both looked down on the destroyed cabin. When Hunt's shivers became constant and his lips were positively blue, Davy jumped him to a baking-hot lava flow in the middle of the tiny islet off the Costa Rica coast.

Now Davy was overdressed, so he took a moment to shed some layers in the Eyrie while Hunt lay down on one of the smoother stretches of lava, soaking up the heat.

"Better?" Davy said when he returned to the island in the only pair of jeans he now owned.

Hunt was sitting up. "Yeah."

Davy led Hunt over to a cliff top overlooking the tiny cove where he'd left the "person of interest."

"Head down, okay?" he said. "He had some sort of automatic when I dropped him here."

Hunt peeked carefully over the edge, then ducked back. "Well, that's interesting."

"What? He didn't off himself, did he? He was okay fifteen minutes ago."

Before Davy stuck his head over, Hunt shook his head. "Not that. I recognize him."

Davy raised his eyebrows.

Hunt said, "Your daughter—I presume it was your daughter—launched Mr. Doe thirty feet down the hallway outside your mother-in-law's room in Wichita."

"I thought those guys were all still in jail."

"Oddly enough, so did I. There haven't been any reports of releases or escapes. Mr. Doe there never gave his name, and there was no match on his picture, fingerprints, or DNA, but that didn't stop the judge from sentencing him."

"Substitution?"

"Maybe. Daarkon Group could afford to pay someone to do the time for his weapons charges."

"I was going to question him, but because of his employer's missile, we're scrambling to come up with new facilities. Do you guys want him?"

Hunt nodded. "Sure. If nothing else, it will be interesting to see what kind of strings get pulled when the Kansas Department of Corrections ends up with *two* prisoners when they should just have one. But that's dessert. Let me have him in D.C. for a few days, first."

"Good. Where would you like him delivered?"

# THIRTY-FOUR

## Cent: If You Build It . . .

We didn't tell USSPACECOM *what* we were putting 10,393 kilometers above the surface of the earth, but they did confirm that their computer projections showed remarkably little chance of collisions or orbital perturbation in the long term.

I'd moved the major structural components into orbit and was dealing with the fiddly bits, shifting the inner and outer spheres so that all the connectors lined up, then carefully engaging their clamps and seals, when the phone rang.

"Hello?"

"Sterling here."

"General. I didn't think my Iridium phone would work out here."

"Iridium rotated one of their spares to point out. You just entered its cone. Since you're over nine thousand kilometers away from it, its 'footprint' is a lot bigger than on Earth, but you're heading northwest and it's heading south so we've got about four minutes to talk.

"Your current altitude is another nonlunar record, isn't it?"

"Huh. I guess so. But really, there should be a separate category for me. I *cheat*." And, to tell the truth, I'd been more worried about Grandmother than space records.

"We got a good return on your, uh, project there. They're telling me it's about eleven meters across."

"The outer hull has a diameter of twelve yards, so, yeah. That pretty good shootin', Tex."

"What is it?"

"Our new digs. We had a problem with the old one."

"Ah. I heard."

My stomach clenched. "You *heard*? Who told you?"

"The CIA told the DIA who told me."

*"Did they have something to do with it?"*

"Whoa, there. No! I was told they learned about it from your father. Didn't he turn over a person of interest to them?"

I exhaled. That made sense. This project was demanding too much from *all* of us for Dad to be off conducting interrogations, so I guess he outsourced it. "Ah. Good. I didn't want to think they did, but it *was* a drone strike after all."

"I heard. The U.S. provided a four-man team of RPV experts to the Canadian Security Intelligence Service. They'll be helping with the debris analysis."

I didn't know which was worse. People who wanted to kill us pawing through the wreckage, or people who wanted to help us doing it. "They better dress warmly."

"Your family is all right, though? My liaison got that part correct?"

"At least so far." I didn't want to go into the tracker-implanted-in-Grandma story. I didn't know if Dad had told them about that. "We hope our new place is beyond their reach. We hadn't planned on starting Kristen Station for a few months."

"Kristen?"

"It was Sally Ride's middle name. Sally Kristen Ride."

"Station? A ma . . . womaned facility?"

That was remarkably clueful of him. "General Sterling, I *like* you. Yes, it's to be an *occupied* facility. Apex Orbital headquarters plus some space-medicine research and a guest room or two. Technically, it's Apex Orbital Services Kristen Station, but Kristen Station for short."

"Yes. Round. So we're seeing an outer hull. Does that mean there's an inner?"

"I'm sure we'll do a video tour for the website when we're done but yeah. Ten yards inside diameter—over fourteen thousand cubic feet of pressurized habitat. Less than half of the International Space Station's shirtsleeve space but one has to start *somewhere*."

"You're doing this by yourself? That's a pretty big project for one small company. Do you need any assistance?"

"With Kristen Station? Got a spare microgravity toilet?"

"I don't know. The two in the ISS were made by the Russians and NASA paid nineteen million for one of them."

"Well, we'll let you know. We're new at this so we're probably going to make a *bunch* of mistakes." *Hopefully without killing anybody.* I bit my lip. "You could get the assholes who blew up the house I was born in. I mean, I know that's not what *you* do, but you could encourage all those security and intelligence people who do."

General Sterling cleared his throat. "Right. I honestly believe that there's substantial pressure to do so, if just to prove to Canada that *we* aren't conducting drone missile strikes within their national borders."

"Need to get back to work, General. I've still got three hundred twenty-one tons of water to bring up before I can put my interior assembly crew to work."

"Three hundred twenty-one tons? What do you need six hundred forty-two *thousand* pounds of water for?"

"Shielding—micrometeorites and radiation. Also thermal mass. It goes between the hulls—one yard of water all the way around. It's better than metal since it doesn't generate secondary radiation."

I think I could hear his mouth working but he wasn't managing actual words. Finally he said, "I was aware of the benefits. But we don't do it because it costs too much to move water into orbit in *those* quantities."

I grinned. "You can't afford to do it without somebody like *me*. I would gladly trade you twenty tons of water, *delivered*, for a working microgravity toilet. What's your best lift cost right now? One thousand dollars per pound? At forty million that would be worth two, yeah? See what your friends at NASA would say to *that*."

I tested all the connectors and flanges by twinning from the inner sphere to sea level, filling it pretty much instantly to 14.7 psi of normal mixed-air atmosphere. Then I did the same between the two of them.

Both balloons—hulls—felt tight as basketballs. By the light of a chemical glow stick I navigated the space between the two spheres, going from connector to connector, but I couldn't *see* anything wrong.

I jumped to the interior. Our view port was pointing away from the sun and the earth and it was dark inside.

The view-port assembly consisted of an aluminum pipe, three feet in diameter and three feet long, that connected flanges on the outer and inner spheres. The inner hatch was clear polycarbonate and opened 180 degrees, up against the fabric of the inner hull. This was to let people enter the cylinder and reach the outer window, the most expensive part in the station's structure so far: two panes of aluminum silicate glass with an insulating layer of vacuum between them. There was an exterior optical coating to filter ultraviolet light and an exterior shutter made of Kevlar over an inch-thick layer of Dr. Seck's experimental radiation shielding, which pivoted out of the way using an interior lever.

I'd left the inner hatch open so I didn't end up with a vacuum holding it shut. Again, I couldn't tell anything from just looking. In any case, the suit was acting like it should at sea level so the spheres weren't leaking so fast that they were causing my purge valve to bleed helmet air to match.

I shut off the oxygen, purged the helmet, and took it off.

My excuse was that I wanted to hear if there were any leaks. Truth was, I wanted to see what it was like. I flung the chem light away from me and watched it fly across the open interior of the station, then ricochet tangentially off the tight fabric again and again until it worked its way back to me, losing some energy with each collision.

Out loud I said, "We have *got* to bring some tennis balls up here." My voice seemed to vanish into the space, not inaudible, just not echoing. I wondered how the acoustic qualities would change once the exterior volume was filled with water.

I'm sure when I pushed off the inner wall that the station moved significantly in the other direction, but the feeling was like sailing across a dark space, free as a bird.

*A bird that is currently being exposed to radiation and, if the right meteorite came along, vacuum.*

"Get on with it, girl."

I did spend some time listening at each through connection, but I couldn't hear or see any signs of leaks.

I put the helmet back on.

Time to put the shielding up.

We didn't premix the fibers into the water this time. The frac tank wasn't anywhere near big enough and we didn't want to have to mix multiple loads.

After just few experiments, I found I could jump directly to the station, just as I'd made it into the ISS, without having to hit vacuum first.

I twinned from between the hulls to outside, in orbit, evacuating the volume. As with the earlier sphere, it didn't collapse on itself because there was no outside pressure to push *in*.

We wanted as little air as possible in the shielding, so before I put the fiber bundles between—even direct jumps leaked a little—I left the bundles floating outside. I was glad they were bundled—plastic bags would've popped like balloons as soon as we arrived in orbit. I jumped them, one bundle at a time, between the inner and outer hulls and shook the fibers out of the bundles, raking them apart with my fingers.

There was an electrostatic thing happening and fibers seemed to be accumulating on the fabric. When I'd shaken out all twenty bundles (ten bamboo fiber, ten synthetic wool) and disposed of the packaging, I returned to the interior and twinned to the Rosemont water reservoir in Montreal, five feet under the surface.

I'd been thinking about using a swimming pool, perhaps an Olympic-sized pool, to keep down bacteria growth, but the people at BlimpWerks had nixed that.

Fran Wilde said, "Bad enough that you have all that ionizing radiation up there. Chlorine is an oxidizer—that's how it kills germs—and it will react *badly* with the nylon and the coatings. Please—no chlorine!"

I thought Dad was crazy when he suggested a reservoir in Canada *in the middle of the winter*, but he'd said, "It's completely underground and runs above sixty-five degrees. Very clean water—they renovated the entire reservoir in the last decade."

It *felt* freezing, but these things are relative. The water filled the space in less than fifteen seconds.

When I untwinned, I stayed with the shielding. I was hoping that none of the fiber ended up in the reservoir. When I cracked another chem light, it was apparent that the fibers had thoroughly mixed through the liquid. I could barely see the light at arm's length.

Cory let me use one of the new suits to return to orbit in twenty minutes, rather than requiring me to wait for twenty-four hours while the original suit dried.

No geysers of ice crystals were spewing from the outer hull of Kristen Station. When I jumped into the interior, the reaction of my helmet's oxygen feed to the inner sphere's pressure told me we still had *something* close to one atmosphere.

Grabbing the view-port frame and adding tangential velocity, I rotated the structure so the window pointed toward Earth. This was far easier than I'd expected, leading to the realization that the water wasn't moving; the hulls' fabric was sliding across it. The largest amount of resistance was where the water was flowing around the view-port cylinder as it dragged through the liquid.

The inner coating of the sphere (a light gray so pale it was almost eggshell) reflected the bluish earthlight from the side opposite the window, diffusing it throughout the interior. This time when I kicked off the wall it felt far more solid than it had before, and I watched the surface ripple away from the point of contact, a slight pulsing wave more imagined than seen.

I nearly vomited as the circular interior destroyed my sense of up and down. Well, that and my attempt at a quadruple somersault, wall-to-far wall.

I returned to Cory's lab and took off the suit and then, sure it was a stupid thing to try, I jumped right back to the station, arriving inside (GOOD!) beside the view port, in my long underwear.

I knew we needed to get the life support going but I was more worried about $CO_2$ accumulating around my face than running out of oxygen. I knew if I kept moving, it would be a long time before the air reached toxic levels.

I gulped, suddenly scared.

*Come on, girl, it's time.*

I appeared inside the front door of Joe's house. I could hear the TV going and called out, "Hello?"

Ms. Trujeque stuck her head into the hall from the living room and said, "Oh. Cent! I didn't hear you knock. I could swear that door was locked."

I shook my head and jerked my thumb over my shoulder. "I didn't come through the door. Some of those reporters are still out there."

She blinked. We hadn't talked since I was still attending Beckwourth High School back when I started dating Joe. That was before we had to leave town in a hurry. Joe and I had still dated after that, but secretly, to keep Joe from becoming a target.

Then we'd had our breakup and there was even less reason for me to be hanging out with Joe's mother.

She gave me a doubtful look like, *You look like a nice girl and not a demon from hell but you never can really tell.* At least that's the interpretation my imagination provided. "The reporters. Right! That's *why* we've been making sure the door was locked. Come in! It's just me and Joe. His brother and father are off shooting pool."

Joe was on the end of the couch closest to the TV and I guess he hadn't heard my voice over the television because when I came into the room he shot to his feet and looked confused.

*There's a lot of that going around.*

"Hey," I said.

"Hey," he said.

"I wanted to show you something."

He raised his eyebrows.

I turned to Ms. Trujeque. "Do you have a couple of gallon ziplock bags and some paper towels?"

"Sure. What for?"

I said, "A quick science experiment."

We followed her into the kitchen. I folded four sheets of nice, thick, absorbent paper towels into each bag, tucked one into my back pocket, and handed Joe the other. "Keep it open, just in case."

"In case of what?"

I smiled at Ms. Trujeque and I hope the smile didn't *look* as weird and nervous as it felt. "I'm going to show Joe the construction on our new office. We'll be gone about ten minutes."

Ms. Trujeque suddenly looked nervous. "You're going to do that thing, like when you give him lifts to Stanford?" She'd never seen it. She'd only heard about it after Space Girl made the news and Joe was outed as one of the narrators on our satellite's audio loop.

I nodded. "That's right."

"Where is your new office?"

I looked at my watch. "Right now? It's over Greenland."

I don't think Joe's eyes could have gotten any bigger. "Already? I thought the habitat was *months* away."

"Well . . . circumstances. We had to change the timing."

Ms. Trujeque looked from me to Joe and back again. "You mean *space*?"

"Ten minutes only," I said.

"Won't you suffocate? Or explode?"

"Oh, no. It's inside our station. A shirtsleeve environment."

She stared at Joe and I wondered if she was going to tell him not to. You could see it, a sudden terrorized expression coupled with the realization that he *would* do it no matter what she said.

"What are the bags for?"

"Space adaption syndrome."

She looked puzzled and I added, "Joe might vomit."

"Hey!" Joe said. "I will not!"

"Better men than *you* have, but hopefully not," I said. "*Especially* if you hold your head still. Do not swivel it around, do not indulge in vigorous motion. This trip is for *looking*, not doing, okay?"

He started to nod but stopped himself. "Okay," he said, instead. "No motion."

"Good. Treat your neck like it's a rigid post. It doesn't turn or tilt. Move your whole torso when you want to look at something. *Slowly.*"

Ms. Trujeque tried to smile, but it came across as resignation. She said, "I'll start some peppermint tea for when you get back. When I was pregnant with Joe I threw up *every* morning for four months, but peppermint tea always brought me around by lunch."

"That sounds great," I said. I locked eyes with her. "We'll be *right* back."

Joe didn't throw up when we first appeared in the middle of Kristen Station, but he yelled.

"Sorry," he said, breathing rapidly. "It's not the jumping," he explained. "It's the falling." The *feeling* of falling, he meant.

We were pretty much dead center in the sphere, the view port was "beneath" us, since our feet pointed at it. The port was no longer pointed directly at Earth, but a substantial amount of earthlight was still coming in the window and the giant, round room still looked amazing.

"Eyes on me," I said. "Up is away from the viewport. Down is toward it."

"Wow."

"Look, I didn't want to say this in front of your mom and it's a trillion-to-one shot, but just suppose we lost *both* hulls at once and you found yourself exposed to vacuum. *Don't* hold your breath, okay?"

He blinked and his eyes moved from my face to the sphere's wall. "Would it really make a difference? We'd be dead in ninety seconds."

"*I* can have us back in the atmosphere long before that. But if you hold your breath you'll rupture your lungs, right?"

He took a deep breath, exhaled. "Embolism. Right. *Don't* hold my breath."

I jumped in place, adding a foot-second toward the view port, and snagging his ankle as I drifted "down." We settled, gripping the inner frame of the view port, on opposite sides. "Okay, now you're lying on the floor looking *down* through the window."

He was clenching the improvised barf bag tightly but his color looked okay.

I wasn't used to looking at the earth from this altitude, or through a window for that matter. I'd been concentrating on the work: deploying the outer sphere, then the inner, hooking them together, and filling them. I'd been a good, hardworking Space Girl and I felt justified taking a moment now.

It was late afternoon over the North Atlantic and we could see the terminator creeping across central Europe as the sun set. "Pretty cool, eh?" I said.

Joe didn't say anything and when I looked at him, my heart melted. He was using the paper towels from the improvised barf bag, but not to vomit. He was wiping the tears from his eyes.

I swallowed. "I did that the first time, too. No matter how many times you look at it in magazines or TV or even on an IMAX screen, the real thing beats it all hollow."

His voice was hoarse. "How high?"

"Orbital radius or altitude?"

"Uh, both."

"The semimajor axis is sixteen thousand seven hundred seventy-one kilometers. Varies about ninety klicks between apoapsis and periapsis. Ten thousand three hundred ninety-three kilometers above sea level."

He was holding his fist at arm's length and using it to measure the earth's disk from edge to edge. "Forty-five degrees?"

"Just under. Forty-four point seven degrees. Call it ninety full moons. The first time I did the calculations I was three degrees low."

He tilted his head up to look across the view port at me. His hand darted to his mouth and he began breathing rapidly through his nose. After twenty seconds, he said, "You weren't kidding about sudden head movements."

"No." I eyed the bag he was holding. In the astronaut corps they make the "emitter" clean up any "emissions," which is fair, but I pictured vomit splattering against the view port and almost had to use the spare bag I'd tucked in my back pocket.

"Why were your calculations off?"

Thank god for distractions. "Turns out the earth is *not* a flat disk. If it were, the edge we'd see would be farther away than the tangential edges of the sphere we're actually seeing. When you're this close, it makes a difference."

"I wouldn't call over six thousand miles *close*."

"Well, I wouldn't want to *walk* it, but we're less than the earth's diameter from the surface." I edged clockwise around the frame, moving closer to him. "Sometime I'll show it to you from *two hundred* kilometers. That's a whole different treat."

"Why didn't you put the habitat down there?"

"Not safe."

"Oh? Orbital debris? Or atmospheric drag?"

"That. And intentional efforts." I didn't want the mood shattered but I hadn't told him what happened to the cabin, yet. "Hold still."

I eased up behind him and put my arms around his chest, resting my chin on his shoulder so I could look past his head down through the port. I pressed my body against his.

He covered my hands with his and groaned. "Oh, girl." We started to drift away from the view port and he grabbed the frame again.

"Shhh. No head movements." I took a deep breath. "Remember when I texted you—told you to keep your eyes open?"

"Yes. Have those guys come back to New Prospect?"

"Not that we know. But . . . they destroyed our home—the cabin."

His body spasmed and he jerked his head around to look at my face, and then he had to curl up and use the bag.

I backed off and let him get on with it, breathing through my mouth. I kept an eye out for "escapees," but he captured it all and the paper towels did a good job of keeping it *in* the bag.

Once he sealed the mess inside, I pulled him away from the smell and opened the other bag to get an unsoiled section of paper towel to wipe his mouth. Then I gave him the unused bag, still open, still ready.

"Good capture," I told him. "You were *definitely* going to clean it up if you got the window."

His color was already bad, but when I said that he spread the mouth of the bag and moved it closer to his head. He kept it together, though, taking two careful breaths before saying. "Everyone's okay? Your parents? Your grandmother?"

"Yes." Remembering that distractions are good, I told him about the missile and the drone and the embedded tracker and finally about our plans for Grandmother.

"Christ! Why didn't you tell me this two days ago?"

I gestured expansively, indicating the sphere around us. "Busy, you know?"

"I could've been helping Cory with the life support!"

"You will, Joe." I hugged him, front to front this time. "He's going to need help both down there and up here, installing it. *Experienced* help."

He *almost* shook his head, but stopped himself in time. "Ha. *Some* experience," he said bitterly. He wasn't letting go of me, though.

"More experience than *Cory* has."

Joe's mouth dropped open. "He hasn't been up here yet?"

"No." I kissed his cheek. "Only me. You're the first."

This time the tears came with sobs and incoherent apologies and we both had to use paper towels on our eyes.

"I want to kiss you a little more seriously," I said. "But there's no way I'm going to do that until you've rinsed your mouth out. And if I don't get you back, your mom is going to be *sure* that you're dead."

He held up his hand. "And I want to kiss you but . . . are we back? You've forgiven me?"

"The short answer is yes."

"And the long answer?"

"The long answer is there's too much shit happening in my life right now for me to give you the long answer."

"Why now?"

"Because there's *too much shit happening* in my life right now. I need you."

Returning to gravity settled Joe's stomach immediately and he was able to stand without falling over after a few moments. I let him take the used bag outside to the trash. When I left him, the goodnight kiss was delightful and he tasted divine.

Ms. Trujeque's was right—peppermint tea was *great*.

# THIRTY-FIVE

## Cent: You can't fall

I replaced the air in the station before I brought up any more visitors, twinning between the lower end of the station (next to the view port) to a snow-covered stretch of ground next to another "station," the upper Pikes Peak Cog Railway station, fourteen thousand feet above sea level. I only held it a few seconds, but my ears *hurt* from the sudden pop.

I should've worn my spacesuit.

When I untwinned, the air in the station was full of fog.

Oops.

To avoid as rapid a change when I repressurized, I twinned from lower altitudes, working down two thousand feet at a time. The water droplets disappeared almost immediately, reabsorbed as the pressure increased. I adjusted the view port so it directly faced Earth again and went for my next visitors.

Next was Dad, of course.

He was the one who introduced me to the ideas, the one who made me turn my attention to space in the first place.

He didn't jerk or yell when we appeared in the middle of the sphere, but I know he'd experimented with skydiving in the past, so the sensation wasn't alien.

I'd given him *and* Mom the same lecture I'd given Joe about sudden head movements. I'd advised them to jump to move around the volume, something Joe couldn't do.

Dad popped around, feeling the inner hull, pushing off and drifting through the middle, then he settled by the view port, his mouth open and his eyes wet. I handed him a handkerchief.

So far, we were a hundred percent on deeply emotional initial reactions to being in space. At least this time I was prepared for it.

I went back for Mom.

She *did* yell.

The first time Mom ever jumped, she'd been falling off a cliff. It was a wonder she didn't flinch away, but she didn't. She breathed out and her muscles untensed and she held her head still.

"It's *huge*," she said.

"Like an empty house. We'll see how it feels after we move in." I pointed down at Dad and the window. "You should see the view."

I gave them ten minutes while I floated nearby with a small battery-operated fan, pushing the air (and to a lesser degree, myself) around to keep our exhaled $CO_2$ from accumulating around us.

Then I asked, "Can you guys test if you can jump back to the Eyrie?"

Mom said, "Surely you mean the vault?"

"No. I want you to go straight to sitting on the bed. Your balance will be off. You certainly don't want to fall over on Grandmother."

"No," she agreed. "We don't want that."

Mom vanished. Then Dad.

I looked at the stack of makeshift emesis bags in my hand, relieved. I was really glad I didn't have to clean up anything. More important, my parents' ability to jump back to ground side meant I could depend on them to evacuate others in an emergency, a *big* load off of my mind.

And then Mom was back.

I blinked, surprised.

When *I* jumped into Kristen Station or the Leonardo pressurized module of the ISS, I'd been looking up the orbital parameters and using the GPS as part of my destination visualization. In the ten minutes Mom had been looking through the view port, Kristen Station had moved almost three thousand kilometers. Even during the five seconds she'd been gone, it had moved almost twenty-five kilometers.

"How did you do that?" I sounded accusatory, and I softened my voice. "Jump back, I mean."

Mom said, "Shouldn't I have? There's a certain smell—I think it's from the coating on this fabric," she said, tapping on the inner hull. "That's what I was concentrating on, anyway."

I didn't know what to say. Finally I went with, "That's good." I certainly didn't want to go into all the reasons she *shouldn't* be able to. "You can help ferry people and supplies up."

"Of course." she nodded. "You were right, by the way. I was *really* dizzy for a moment there when I got down. Your father should have listened. He arrived standing and fell *right* over."

"Is he okay? He didn't throw up on the bed?"

She vanished. I checked my watch, staring at the seconds. A full minute went by and I thought, *maybe it* was *a fluke*, when she appeared again, frowning.

"Is Dad all right?"

She waved a hand. "He's grumpy. He said I shouldn't be able to jump back here and we had an argument about it. And since he *knows* one couldn't possibly jump here without the precise orbital parameters, he *can't*."

I laughed. "Sometimes a little knowledge is a dangerous thing."

Mom snorted. "Someone should tell him that it's impossible to jump from Canada to Texas, too."

"I'm going to go get Cory. Since you *can*, would you go get Mr. Grumpy Pants? Cory will have some specifications and questions about sensors and monitors."

Mom grinned. "I would be *delighted*."

Cory brought a measuring tape as well as five different kinds of Velcro and three different kinds of closed-loop hooks all with adhesive mounting pads. Down on the ground he'd been all business, talking about what he needed to find out on this trip. He thought he was all in ready-to-get-things-done mode, so when he spent several minutes at the view port tearing up, it caught him by surprise.

"Handkerchief?"

He accepted it silently.

When he did get back to his to-do list he said, "Your Ms. Wilde at BlimpWerks said that all of these adhesives are safe for the fabric and its coating, but she's not sure which ones will stick best or stink the least."

So we got down to finding out.

First thing Velcroed to the wall was the zippered nylon-mesh bag holding my emesis kit.

(Take one forty-count box of gallon-sized ziplock bags and five rolls of extra-absorbent paper towels. Assemble four towels each into each ziplock for forty space-sickness bags. Use the one-plus roll of leftover paper towels, an extra-large container of unscented, hypoallergenic baby wipes, and an extra-large container of medical sanitizing wipes for additional cleanup. To keep from adding to the mess, include one twenty-count package of odor-blocking disposable face masks.)

All of the adhesives seemed to stick with equal vigor, but one of the hook's pads had an odor which caused both Cory and then Dad to snatch for, and use, their barf bags.

(Most important thing to know about space-sickness bags? Keep them within reach at all times.)

We promptly disqualified *that* brand.

"To be fair," said Cory, "if we had the ventilation running and the activated-charcoal filters going, we *might* not have cared."

"It's still off the list," I said. "We need the hooks to *anchor* the ventilation system. If it makes us throw up while we're installing it, it's not doing its job."

And on the second day I said, "Let there be light," and there was light.

And Joe said, "Ha, ha."

*If* the view port was pointed in the right direction, you could get a lot of light through from earthlight and a huge amount from the sun, but until we had some form of attitude control, we couldn't count on it.

The first three batteries brought into the station were attached to three superbright LED work lights. We moved them around, sticking adhesive Velcro patches to the fabric of the inner hull wherever we needed them, but most of the time the lights sat on the "equator" equispaced 120 degrees apart and swiveled ninety degrees "up," away from the view port. This lit the "upper" surface of the inner hull and flooded the entire volume with soft, indirect light.

Once we had light, I put on my space suit and we took the pressure down to 2 psi, then brought it back to 10 psi (about ten thousand feet on Earth) using straight $O_2$, a process which required me to ferry forty size-H oxygen tanks up, one at a time, empty them into the volume, and return them to the medical-gas supplier.

Next came the QDLS (quick and dirty life support) system, strictly for dealing with $CO_2$ and oxygen.

Cory took a plastic thirty-gallon barrel and mounted a sixteen-inch, twelve-volt car radiator fan in a hole cut out of the bottom. Using the removable top as a mounting bracket, he created a cylindrical mesh basket to hold soda lime pellets that took up most of the interior. The unit stood on three spread wooden legs, ending in circular pads anchored to the inner hull by, you guessed it, Velcro. A three hundred-amp-hour lithium iron phosphate battery strapped to the cylinder and a simple explosion-proof switch (no spark) completed the unit.

The fan blew air straight out, a column of air that hit the opposite wall and circulated back along the inner hull to be sucked back in the other end of the barrel.

To replace depleted oxygen, we had two MM-sized oxygen tanks yoked together with a settable automatic valve to kick the ambient pressure back up to 10 psi when the excess $CO_2$ was pulled out of the air.

Cory floated throughout the volume, spot-checking with a

portable $CO_2$ detector. There were areas in the volume where the levels rose above our targeted five hundred parts per million, but most of the interior was fine. Cory wanted to perfect it but I said, "That's the job of our permanent installation. If necessary, I'll refresh the atmosphere, but this is good enough for construction. When?"

Cory stared off into the distance before saying, "The machine shop should be done with the last of the access hatches this afternoon. We can do our trial assembly and test tomorrow. If that works out, we can install it two days from now."

It took four days.

There were six attempts to assemble it. The first three times, design and machining errors turned up. The fourth trial was the first time all the parts fit. The fifth one included a three-hour electrical-and-mechanical test run, and the last one was the rehearsal for orbit.

Mom and I ferried the sections up in the order they were needed and no faster. Cory, Dad, and Joe assembled them. Everything *did* fit, but microgravity added wrinkles, easing some tasks, complicating others. When I wasn't ferrying assemblies I was chasing fasteners and tools drifting away at precisely the wrong time.

Joe named it "the stack," which made sense, since it was stacked sections of three-foot-diameter tubular aluminum ventilation duct covered in open-cell acoustic insulation. Assembled, it stretched from high noon (the "top" of the sphere, directly opposite the view port) to four feet short of the view port frame.

The air entered the stack at the bottom, just above the view port, through a washable blanket filter designed to catch crumbs and particulates and parts and *anything* else not tied down. Just behind the blanket, it passed through a disposable HEPA filter capturing particles down to .3 microns.

Next it hit the first of the cartridges, as we called them, pretty much like the cartridges in the suit's pack, only these were three feet across instead of three inches.

First up was the soda lime cartridge, holding an entire forty-four-pound keg of $CO_2$ absorbent. Its access hatch had a transparent port so you could examine the color of the absorbent, important because we were using soda lime with ethyl violet, which changed color from off-white (low carbonic acid: fresh) to purple (high carbonic acid: depleted.)

Then the air took one of two paths through the desiccant section: the empty passage or the passage with a mesh half cylinder filled with silica gel. A solenoid-activated flap diverted the return air through the desiccant when the relative humidity rose above 60 percent and bypassed it when it was below 40 percent.

After moisture control, we came to odor control: two cylindrical cartridges filled with activated charcoal, with a combined length of four feet.

After odor control, came temperature.

Our initial calculations showed that we probably wouldn't need to heat the interior, but we probably would have to cool it.

The three-foot-thick layer of water shielding came in at sixty-five degrees Fahrenheit, all 321 tons of it, and the Mylar outer layer of our outer hull was reflecting a lot of the sun's heat away. However, vacuum is a great insulator. Heat can radiate away, but not very fast. Water is famous for cooling systems, but not in free fall. Without a gravitational gradient, one of water's most effective mechanisms for heat transfer, convection, doesn't work, since expanding water and contracting water don't rise and sink relative to each other. This left conduction, and water is seventy times *less* conductive than carbon steel. State changes of water, though, are good for heat transfer, even in free fall.

The cooling section of the stack held a heat exchanger, twenty meters of two-centimeter-inside-diameter stainless steel tubing spiraling through aluminum fins. It ran from a thermostatically controlled valve connected to a 250-gallon bank of water bladders, to the coolant exhaust, a pipe that led through both hulls and opened into open space.

When the thermostat in the return air vent went above seventy-five degrees Fahrenheit, the valve opened a three-millimeter hole and vacuum sucked water from the water bladder into the heat exchanger. The water boiled and flashed to vapor, rapidly cooling the stainless pipe, which in turn cooled the air rushing past it. When the air reaching the air intake dropped below seventy degrees, the valve closed.

Since the cooling module didn't require ready access to the heat exchanger, our bank of five water bladders, each eight inches in diameter by almost four feet long, were bundled around the stack at that point, along with our oxygen bank, twelve size-H cylinders holding almost eighty-three thousand liters of $O_2$.

After the cooling module, the air finally hit the fans, or more specifically, the fans sucked the air *through* all those other modules. Two inline counter-rotating eight-bladed props ran off separate permanent magnet motors and separate batteries (for redundancy), six feet from the very top of the stack, providing five hundred cubic feet per minute of airflow, with an option to bump it up to nine hundred, if we were willing to put up with the noise.

The fact that they counterrotated caused more turbulence and a bit more noise, but it canceled any tendency for the motors and props to impart rotational energy into the structure itself

The last four feet of the stack had the outlet vents, sixteen directional ports aimed tangentially, shooting out streams of air in a spiral that spun the station's entire volume of air around the stack like a slow, thick-waisted tornado, leaving no part of the interior in still or stagnant air.

The stack was anchored to the station at the top end with a circle of closed steel rings attached to the fabric with adhesive patches. Four bright-colored ropes ran from the intake end to similar rings mounted around the view port frame.

This would've been enough to secure the unit if it hadn't become immediately clear during its assembly that the stack was jostled in several directions by people kicking off, gently colliding, and pulling along the unit. We added twelve more ropes: four at the equator, running out like X and Y axes to the stack's Z axis, and at four each at the thirty-fifth parallels north and south, vertically in line with the others, but running perpendicular to the surface of the sphere.

Cory, still in his weight-saving mode, had suggested parachute cord, which was structurally sufficient, but I said, "Thick enough to grab comfortably and neon bright so people *see* it."

"Ah. Yes." He doubled the size of the attachment patches and doubled up on their number, too. "I hadn't quite thought about them as pathways and handrails." Two days later we added two ropes running down the length of the stack as well.

Since we were buying rope, I hung three fifty-meter-long pieces of white sheathed, Kevlar-reinforced climbing line from the mooring rings fastened around the outside equator of the station and clamped the ends of all three to the handle of a 103-pound kettle bell, a piece of exercise equipment.

Like the AggieSat Lab's conductive tether, this "fell" down the local gradient and put tension on the three ropes toward Earth. Unlike the other tether, ours was *not* conductive, so it didn't interact with the magnetic field and slow our orbit, but it did keep the view port pointed consistently at Earth. Since the kettle bell's inner orbit sought a faster path around the earth, there was a tilt so the kettle bell didn't even hang in our view of Earth, but off to the side.

Dad's rocketry friend, Wanda, in return for expenses and the promise of an hour in the habitat within the next month, built an entire suite of sensors that reported their states wirelessly (Bluetooth 3) to multiple laptops (for redundancy). When acceptable parameters were exceeded, the computers sounded appropriate alarms through attached speakers, ranging from quiet beeps for maintenance reminders to screeching Klaxons for life-threatening events.

We monitored air pressure, since that would be the first indicator of a leak, using four of Wanda's remote sensors and one stand-alone unit with its own siren.

There were six $CO_2$ sensors reporting parts per million: four of them spread through the volume and one each in the stack before and after the absorbent.

Four $O_2$ sensors reported overall oxygen percentage (98.9 percent). Six sensors reported air temperature: four in the volume, and one each in the stack before and after the heat exchanger.

Two humidity sensors sat in the stack, in front and behind the desiccant module.

There were four *sets* of sensors in between the inner and outer hulls, reporting water temperatures at six inches, eighteen inches, and thirty inches from the outer skin.

Six accelerometers glued to the inner hull measured shock waves traveling through the water, either because an occupant kicked off the interior (a low-amplitude blip on the graph from one or two sensors) or a micrometeorite slammed into the exterior (a sharp spike detected on multiple sensors within microseconds of each other).

Two smoke and two carbon monoxide sensors sat just inside the air intake, as did off-the-shelf, battery-operated models with their own alarms.

We had yet to start on our own power generation. I rotated alternate banks of batteries down to the Michigan warehouse for charging every other day. We had two separate battery compartments, gasketted airtight chests mounted at the equator, which also reported draw rates and voltage states through Wanda's sensors.

We had three radiation sensors, one outside, one in the viewport cylinder, and one inside, out of direct line with the window.

We had fire extinguishers and emergency self-contained air units and fiberglass fire blankets.

Seeana, Tessa, Bea, and Jeline had spent sixteen hours on ground-side training, working on microgravity emergency and medical procedures, but there's only so much you can simulate in gravity.

We moved the sessions to orbit.

Bea washed out. She was psychologically unable to detach microgravity's feeling of falling from impending death, going into adrenaline-fueled panic attacks. She tried multiple times, once with a sedative, and, finally, begged to be excused.

But Seeana, Tessa, and Jeline spent eight hours in Kristen Station practicing procedures: injections, vacuuming aspirated fluids, and intravenous fluid administration with the infusion pump, using each other as test subjects. They also got really good at emesis cleanup, but that wasn't simulation.

Though Mom was the most fervent proponent of this project,

she was also the one with the most concerns and worries, but even she finally ran out of questions.

"Let's do it."

"This might be the last bath I ever take," Grandmother said.

I'd brought the portable bathtub into the vault and ferried several five-gallon buckets of hot water from the Michigan warehouse.

Mom, washing Grandmother's hair, said in a carefully neutral tone, "What do you mean?"

"The gravity thing. How would you, up there?"

"We can bring you down here if you get *too* stinky," Mom said.

"Perhaps. But I've been putting up with just sponge baths for a while."

Grandmother got the *good* drugs, a scopolamine prophylactic dermal patch for motion sickness, and Seeana had promethazine standing by. The drug made Grandmother a bit woozy, but she understood about not moving her head.

She wore an adult diaper and her cotton flannel nightgown with warm socks and we tucked her into bed for travel.

Not my mattress. We'd made our own NASA-type sleeping gear, taking a tropical-weight hooded sleeping bag, putting armholes at the shoulders, and sewing Velcroed anchor straps top and bottom, to "hang" it.

Dad had selected five progressively higher altitude locations, all indoors, to transition Grandmother to the air pressure of Kristen Station. He'd made the run four times as a rehearsal.

"Shortly after I start, *they* are going to get location information, so I'm not going to linger at any of these stops longer than it takes Sam's ears to clear."

"Understood," said Mom. She was adjusting an oronasal mask on Grandmother's face. Dad already had the small, connected oxygen tank in a bag slung over his shoulder. Mom zipped up the sleeping bag and helped Davy lift Grandmother, only stepping back when Grandmother's head was leaning on Dad's shoulder. "Ready?" Mom asked.

"See you in space," said Grandmother.

She and Dad vanished.

Mom and I looked at each other and jumped.

Jeline and Tessa were at the view port and Seeana was checking over her medical supplies and equipment in "sick bay," a section of the inner hull halfway between the equator and the view port. Small items were stored in zippered bags and large items were by themselves, all Velcroed to the wall.

Over the last week the amount of fuzzy-loop Velcro patches and strips had proliferated across the inner hull like some odd fungus, growing in squares, circles, and lines.

Seeana turned her body (not her head) to look at us, raising her eyebrows.

"Any minute," I said.

Jeline and Tessa heard and pushed off the view port frame, floating up to us along the stack.

We waited, an expectant pause that was too short to say anything, yet an eternity to endure, and then . . . Dad and Grandmother appeared above us, next to one of the stack's equatorial anchor ropes.

Grandmother didn't yell, but I saw her body twitch, that involuntary reflex, like dreaming you're falling and jerking awake in reaction. Dad left one arm under her and put the other across her waist, giving her some sense of support.

Mom jumped to their side, her eyes anxious. I pulled myself up, pushing from rope to rope, hoping we weren't going to have another Bea-type reaction.

When I could see Grandmother's face, I relaxed. Her eyes were big, but she wasn't panicked. She was looking around, moving only her eyes. "It's *bigger* than I pictured," she said. "And boy, that breeze on my face feels good after all that time in the ground."

*In the ground.* I hadn't thought about the vault as a metaphor for burial. I certainly knew what she meant about still air, though. The ventilation in the vault was passive and it had gotten pretty stuffy before Dad started doing some daily atmosphere exchanges by twinning to the tropics.

Mom said, "First things first—let's get rid of *that*." She pulled the strap from behind Grandmother's hair and lifted the oronasal mask off.

Grandmother looked a little alarmed as the mask came off.

Mom handed it to Davy, who tucked it into the bag with the oxygen tank. He pushed it down toward Jeline, who snagged the bag out of the air and shut the regulator off, then passed it on to Tessa, who went to put it with the medical supplies.

In the time she'd lived with us, I don't think I'd ever seen Grandmother without some sort of oxygen feed on—a nasal cannula at the very least. She took a breath, then another and the corners of her mouth twitched up. "It's *easy*. It's . . . enough."

Seeana floated up next to us, a ghastly smile on her face.

I said, "Are you all right, Seeana?"

She dropped the pretend smile. "Sorry. I tilted my head up too fast. I'll be okay in a minute." She said to Grandmother, "Get your arms out of that bag, Sam."

Grandmother threaded her right hand out of the bag's armhole and stared at her fingers. "I haven't lifted my hand that high in months," she said.

"You're not lifting it *now*," said Seeana. She clipped a small portable oximeter to the end of Grandmother's index finger. Her eyebrows went up as she looked at the readout.

Mom twisted to see and laughed out loud. "Ninety-seven, and you only just arrived."

Grandmother freed her other hand, and was holding both of them out, moving them up, higher than her head, then down, almost to her waist. I wondered if she'd noticed that Dad was no longer holding on to her.

Seeana reached up to her own neckline and unclipped something from the cloth of her scrubs. She leaned in and reached over to the side of Grandmother's head. "Here—just like a clip-on earring."

"What's this?" Grandmother asked feeling the centimeter-wide piece of plastic clipped to her earlobe.

"Wireless oximeter. There's no point in taking you off oxygen tubes if you have to trail wires around, too."

Grandmother licked her lips. "I can go anywhere in here?"
Mom and Dad nodded.

"I'd like to look out that window."

Dad reached toward one of the sleeping bag straps and Mom smacked his hand. He pulled it back, shaking it and glaring at Mom.

Mom ignored him and said, "That's an *excellent* idea, Mom. Go *do* that."

Seeana's smile came back, only this time it was genuine. "Yeah, that's right. You *go*, girl."

Dad made a silent "ah" shape with his mouth and he pushed off the rope, drifting back, followed almost immediately by Seeana and Mom.

Grandmother's eyes got really big and then twitched down, looking at the empty space under her, suddenly aware that no one held her—that no one was supporting her.

"Here, Grandmother." I held out my hand and, when she gripped my fingers, I moved them to the closest rope.

She reached out with her free hand and tentatively felt the texture of the sheathed line, smooth, almost silky, then closed her fingers around it.

I pulled my arm back from her other hand, and she resisted, gripping my fingers harder. I stopped, waited.

With a firming of her mouth, she released my fingers and took hold of the rope.

I smiled and said, "It's just for common convenience, but we consider the view port is *down*. That lighted end is *up*. You *can't* fall and it takes very little force to move you anywhere you want to go."

# THIRTY-SIX

## Cent: I'm kind of a mushroom myself

"The surgeon died in a car accident about eight hours after the missile took out your residence in Canada, but I expect the more relevant event was when you snatched Mr. Doe and the drone crashed."

Hunt and Davy were in Maclean, Virginia, sitting in the back of Hunt's favorite sushi restaurant. Davy had ordered tea but wasn't touching it.

He'd made *that* mistake in the past.

"Not an accident?"

"No witnesses. The car hit a light pole at high speed but there were impact marks on the driver's side where another vehicle forced it off the road."

"They wouldn't have killed him if he didn't know something."

"Or some*body*. We talked to the anesthesiologist and the scrub nurse. The surgeon told *them* that the device was an experimental electrical bone-growth stimulator."

Davy gritted his teeth. "Electrical, anyway."

"Is it still transmitting?"

"Not currently, but it could be back in sleep mode, waiting for a triggering transmission. Not that that would do them any good."

Hunt laughed lightly. "I suspect that moving her into orbit was the last thing they expected you to do."

Davy nodded. *And that had a positive benefit.* But there was still a smoking ruin where their home of twenty years stood. "What's the story on the drone?"

"It *was* a Predator. It wasn't one of *ours*."

Davy looked very skeptical. "Not one of the CIA's?"

"Not one of the U.S.'s. It was one of several MQ-1s sold to Italy. It reportedly went down in the Adriatic Basin west of Montenegro, twelve hundred meters deep."

"And here it is scattered across a Canadian hillside."

"Tell me about it. The DoD is, to say the least, livid. That unit has U.S. technical advisors."

"So it *was* one of yours?"

"There was U.S. personnel around. Investigation ongoing. Diverted or stolen."

Davy remained stone-faced. "Doesn't mean it wasn't black ops of some kind." He relaxed a little. "Okay. I don't believe it was you guys for lots of reasons. But just so you know? If I find a reason to change my mind, you guys are going to start losing orbital assets right and left."

Hunt jerked his chin sideways, neither denying nor affirming. "Predators are operated long range through a Ku-band satellite link and I've been told that this bird *wasn't* using our . . . orbital assets." He paused. "Now, I'm kind of a mushroom myself," meaning he was kept in the dark and fed bullshit, "but if true, this means they were using the C-band line-of-sight data link which is limited to one hundred fifty nautical miles."

Davy frowned. "That would reach into Alaska, barely, but it was in the mountains—line of sight would've been interrupted from a ground station. If it wasn't being controlled by satellite, it had to be controlled locally."

Hunt shook his head. "You have one other possibility: an airborne asset controlling it from a distance. It would have to be high, but it could be almost out to one hundred fifty miles if it were high enough."

"But the drone loitered overnight!"

"It could do that on automatic. The human pilots and their aircraft could've spent hours on the ground, then gone back up when the helicopter you disabled reached the area."

"Seems like an awful stretch. Why are you bothering?"

"Because we found that aircraft."

# THIRTY-SEVEN

## Cent: Live From Kirsten Station

Jade and Tara were furious with me. Tara said, "We would never have gone off to the beach if you'd told us you were doing this!"

Turns out being furious makes you move your head a *lot*. Tara got most of her ejecta into the bag, but Jade blasted her emesis sack right out of her hands with just the sort of results you might imagine.

Thank god for Tessa. She was there with the clean-up kit in seconds. I got another emesis bag into Jade's hands, then Tessa and I donned odor-blocking disposable masks and chased globules down with wads of paper towels.

This is the sort of thing that really stops a conversation, but ten minutes later, at the upper end of the sphere, we resumed it.

Quietly (Grandmother was napping) Jade said, "Have you posted any video? There wasn't a hint of this on the news when I was scanning the channels in St. Martin."

"Not yet. We've had other priorities. We're still a construction zone, you know."

"Yeah, but this is *huge*. Your grandmother is *living* in space. She's the only one, right?"

"Technically. The rest of us are commuters so far."

Jade said, "I'm surprised you aren't up here all the time!"

I looked at her, eyebrows raised, and she blushed. "They say you get over it in a week!"

"*You* haven't tried our microgravity toilet. *Some* things work better down there." To be fair, we had the pee part working pretty good. The other system still had problems but at least I could jump the entire unit down to Earth and steam clean it when necessary.

Tara, turning a little *more* pale, said, "But you should definitely let us do an interview with your *resident*. Not only is it historic, it's the best way to reward our sponsors and to get more."

"Okay. We'll talk about it."

We did. Dad hated the idea, Mom was neutral. I was iffy, myself, but when Grandmother was all for it, I chimed in on the pro side.

Tara skipped an entire week of class to set up the interview.

All the networks were interested, but when they discovered it wouldn't be one of those remote interviews, where the interviewee was talking from space and the reporter ground side, they went crazy. Millions were offered for an exclusive, which was reasonable, given that the Russians charged over twenty-five million to send a space tourist up.

We said no.

After all the back-and-forth we agreed to one reporter to be selected from the different networks by lottery *after* the candidates had passed microgravity testing in a commercial parabolic aircraft. We would broadcast live through satellite link in equipment provided by the network pool, and we would keep the equipment after.

The only thing any of the networks fought us on was that we specified it be a woman reporter.

Dad didn't trust them, of course. Before he allowed the equipment in the station, he had it examined carefully by Wanda and her friends.

It turned out to be an unmodified off-the-shelf, high-end

mobile-reporting setup that used satphone technology to provide live HD video and stereo audio from anywhere in the world. It had the added advantage of functioning *as* a satphone, letting a news anchor ask questions, studio to frontline.

A thirty-second clip of our equipment test ran on most networks.

"Space Girl here. Welcome to Apex Orbital Services Kristen Station, currently—" Pivot to viewport. "—ten thousand three hundred eighty-three kilometers over the Gulf of Aiden. Please join Pulitzer Prize-winning journalist Connie del Olmo when she tours this new facility and interviews the people who live and work here, this Saturday evening, ten P.M. Eastern, seven P.M. Pacific." Cut to exterior shot provided by me, and the chorus of Wilson Pickett's version of "Mustang Sally."

Pulitzer Prize or not, Dad was sure *they* might use this to get at us. However, since he was trying to keep his face unknown, he gritted his teeth and agreed I should be the one to get Ms. del Olmo at her home station, WETA-TV in Arlington, Virginia.

It was a good thing Dad didn't go—he would've have had a fit. Though they promised not to publicize the "launch" before the fact, they'd asked permission to tape it. People must've been telling their families because almost half the forty or so people in the courtyard between WNET's two building were too young to work there.

Most of them were looking up, including Ms. del Olmo, probably expecting the sort of arrival I'd done at the Russian embassy.

Instead I walked up the few stairs from the South Quincy Street sidewalk and threaded my way through the crowd. Since I was wearing my Nomex coveralls with all the patches, old and new, the crowd parted after my first "Pardon me." I should've jumped directly to her side because out came pictures, autograph books and pens, handshakes, and cameras accompanied by desperate pleas: "Could I just take one quick picture with you?"

*Oh, god.*

It didn't take *that* long and at least I was prepared for the girls who pushed forward for a handshake or a picture or just to look with large eyes.

I'd taken our entire store of Space Girl patches and put them in a bin up in Kristen Station. They'd been up there for over ten days so I could say, each time I took one from the cargo pocket on my leg to give to another girl, "This patch has traveled over four million kilometers through space. What will you do?"

I thought Ms. del Olmo would be irritated at the delay but she was grinning when I finally got up to her. Then I realized the cameras were live and probably had been as I made my way through the small crowd.

She shook my hand firmly. "Call me Connie. I mean it. It's the only thing I'll answer to."

She wore a blue NASA flight suit, *not* new, with her name on it and a patch for the Journalist in Space program on the shoulder. I gestured toward it and she said, "When I was younger. I was one of forty on the final list before the program got scratched when . . . when it got scratched." Her smile faltered.

"When Columbia broke up over Texas."

"Yes." She looked at her feet. "Miles O'Brien was picked, though he didn't get to go either. We all got flight suits."

"So you'd done the vomit comet before? That must've given you an advantage."

"Hey! Who's conducting this interview?"

One of the crew laughed.

I said, "Are you ready?"

"I am. What do I—"

"—do?"

Tara was already pointing the camera and she got Connie's whole-body spasm as we appeared. I released Connie but held on to her arm until I was sure she'd adjusted.

"Not . . . much, apparently." Connie lifted her wrist to look at her watch. "We go live in four minutes." She was blinking rapidly. For a moment I thought she was disoriented but I caught on.

"Handkerchief?"

Jade and Tara had declared themselves our AV crew. Jade pulled herself across on one of the stack's guide ropes and said, "Here's your mic." She placed it in the air in front of Connie and carefully let go so it hung there, barely drifting, no rotation. (I knew for a fact that she'd practiced that for over thirty minutes.)

Connie looked at Jade, bemused. "Thanks—" She looked at the embroidered name on the white Nomex coveralls. "—Jade."

The handheld wireless mic had come with what Tara told me was a "flag"—a box that fit over the body of the microphone so you could put a decal for station ID on each of its faces. Jade created an abbreviated Apex Orbital Services logo for it, AOS, where the 'O' was a tilted ellipse, like an orbit. Connie stared at it as it floated in front of her, then grabbed it like a lifeline.

With the mic her hand, her whole posture changed. "Right. Who's on the line with New York? Is my feed live?"

Tara, also in Apex coveralls, lifted her hand and pointed at the headset she wore. "Ready at the networks." She held up her thumb. "Video and audio feed are A-okay."

Connie looked at Tara, then Jade, then very slowly tilted her head forward, looking down to take in the lower half of the volume. She said, "Who *are* all these people? *Scratch that.* Where are we starting?"

"From ten thousand kilometers above the surface of the earth, I'm Connie del Olmo reporting live from Apex Orbital Services Kristen Station!"

I'm sure most of you saw the tour and interviews. Our sponsors certainly let us know that *they* did, which is why I added all those patches at the last minute, especially the green $3MedO_2$ for Tri-City Medical Oxygen. (Not only were they providing our oxygen, they'd forgiven me for "borrowing" two tanks after hours the night the cabin was destroyed.)

You didn't see Dad or Jeline, who decided not to become a public figure, in the show. Cory and I decided we would create a separate event later, specifically about Matoska Counter-Pressure Spacesuits.

But didn't Grandmother look great?

She wore that elegant chiffon puff-sleeved blouse in off-white, black bootcut slacks, and black slipper socks. Because of microgravity she was still carrying some extra fluid in her upper body, puffing her face slightly and reducing wrinkles. "And my jowls don't sag!" she'd said to Seeana while doing her makeup.

"This is my grandmother, Samantha Harrison. She's our permanent resident." I was eager to get Connie pointed at someone else. The woman was very nice and all, but after five minutes of having the microphone pushed toward me, I was ready to jump over to the ISS until she was done.

Okay, it was me, being tongue-tied.

Connie looked quite a bit younger beside Grandmother, but Grandmother looked more graceful, more at ease floating in midair. Fifteen days of practice will do that.

"I understand you're the reason this is all here?"

Grandmother smiled. "Well, I'm the reason it's here *now*. They were already planning it, for later, but my medical issues made it more urgent."

"Tell us about that."

"I was bedridden on Earth, on oxygen full time, often on a positive-pressure respirator. Besides severe osteoporosis—I've broken *both* hips—I have neuromuscular issues that interfere with my breathing and, especially after my last hip fracture, make it hard to do physical therapy."

"You certainly aren't on a respirator *now*," Connie noted.

Grandmother took a deep breath, spreading the fingers of her hands as she did so. "Indeed. We're breathing ninety-eight percent oxygen at ten psi and I'm *not* pinned to a bed." She leaned closer to Connie and said conspiratorially, "Gravity *sucks*. Up here, I'm free as a bird."

I was in the frame for most of the show but I stayed in the background as much as I could and handed off questions to the others.

Connie asked about food and Grandmother said, "No, we aren't cooking yet. We keep fruits, bags of nuts, granola, tortillas, peanut butter, and honey, but meals are all takeout—or more specifically, brought up."

"Is that food prepared especially for zero gravity?"

"No, though I'm eating spicier food than usual up here," Grandmother said. "We had take-out Mexican food for supper. Enchiladas in red sauce, with rice, refritos, and lettuce-and-tomato garnish. It came in the restaurant's clamshell box, but because Millie—have you met my daughter yet? Anyway, she gave the rice, beans, and garnish a quick stir before bringing it up. It all stuck together and to the container. To a spoon," she smacked her lips, "it was good."

Mom said, "It sure was."

"This is my mother, Millie Harrison-Rice."

Connie said, "Quite the resemblance, there, Space Mom."

Mom rolled her eyes. "It was only a matter of time. Now that the words 'Space Mom' have been uttered, let's *never* do it again. *I'm* Millie, thanks."

We floated down to the food-and-utensil section and Mom said, "Even a fast-food burger works all right if it's in a paper wrapper—though Tessa here had an inflamed eye for a day and a half after an unplanned collision with a French fry."

I said, "Tessa Orcullo is one of our mission medical specialists."

Tessa shook hands. "I used to *like* French fries."

Connie asked, "Ouch. Any foods that don't work?"

Tessa said, "Some *forms* of food. I had a black pepper-inhalation incident that was pretty nasty. We like spicy foods up here and I thought it would be okay to open one of the paper packets that came up with some takeout." She glanced over at Mom and grinned. "Now 'Space Mom' has banned all particulate spices."

Millie groaned.

Connie said, "I don't think I could live without some salt and pepper."

Seeana said, "Food is either seasoned down *there*, or suspended in liquid up here."

I said, "Seeana Walker, supervising mission medical specialist."

She shook hands with Connie. "From Wichita, Kansas. Hi, Mom!"

Connie laughed. "In liquid?"

Seeana plucked a clear squeeze bottle from a mesh pocket. "Hold out your finger." She squeezed a tiny drop onto Connie's finger, where it clung.

Connie touched it to her tongue. "*Salty.*"

"Yep. *Really* salty water. Don't overdo it. We've got hot sauce in packets, too."

I handed Connie a water bag—a liter plastic bladder with a screw top from which emerged a drinking tube. We were trying several, from bladder canteens designed for backpacking to disposable bags of water intended for survival kits. This was our favorite so far, washable and refillable. "Need a drink?"

She had a sip and then we did the obligatory water globule floating in air, and she bit it out of the air. The scene was spoiled slightly when she got part of it down the wrong pipe, but she recovered quickly.

Mom showed Connie a Japanese bento-style lunch tray with individual snap-on covers for each section. "Sometimes we actually do cook down there and sometimes the meals come in leaky containers so we use these."

Connie said, "Soup?"

"If it's not chunky, *these* work." Mom tapped Connie's water bag. "If it's thick, like stew or chili con carne it works fine in one of these," she tapped the bento tray. "Surface tension and surface wetting forces hold fairly well.

"You *can* actually use a bowl to hold liquids, but mostly drinks come in bags. Hot drinks in *insulated* bags. And we bring up bulk water in this." She tapped a ten-gallon collapsible bladder with a squeeze-bulb hand pump attached. "We can fill small bags or use it for washing."

Connie took another sip and put the bag out in midair, but it almost immediately headed "south" with the ventilation breeze.

"Where's it going?"

"Where *everything* goes," said Joe.

"Joe Trujeque, Mission life-support specialist—our Stanford University engineering intern," I said. He glared at me and I stuck out my tongue, but not on camera. I'd made up the titles that afternoon but I hadn't told Joe. "Tara Bochinclonny, behind the camera, is our marketing and public relations director. Jade handles some of our communications graphic design and is our Smith College intern." I'd suggested adding "Beckwourth High School intern" to Tara's title but she'd said she would kill me if I did.

Joe led Connie down to the intake end of the stack where we were able to find a French fry, a pea, and several smaller pieces of less identifiable food sitting on the outer blanket filter, along with a collection of hair in various colors and shapes.

"Most of it ends up here, which is good, 'cause you don't want it in your lungs. We swap this out daily."

While he talked, I demonstrated, taking off the nylon strap that cinched the filter to the stack's end and rolling the blanket inward, from the edges, enveloping the debris and exposing the HEPA filter underneath.

While I stuffed it in one of our laundry bins, a Rubbermaid container with a snap lid, Joe got out another blanket filter. "The blanket filters go to the laundry for cleaning, but we haven't decided yet how often we're replacing the HEPA filter." He tapped it. "Probably once a month."

Joe led the way up the stack, identifying each module and answering questions.

"Cent takes the desiccant and activated-charcoal cartridges outside so the moisture and stinky volatiles evaporate off in the vacuum."

Connie asked, "Do you process the carbon dioxide absorbent that way, too?"

"No. We just replace it, something *we* can do because our cost to station is so low." He looked at me.

I said, "Eventually I'd like to replace this section with an amine or zeolite swing-bed system so we can regenerate our absorbent and do away with disposable."

"What about oxygen?"

"Like so much of our stuff, it's takeout. We bring it." I tapped the 3MedO$_2$ patch on my coveralls, then pointed up the stack where the tanks clustered around the heat exchanger. "Our total bank provides over a hundred person days of oxygen, but rather than let it run low, I swap out two of those big guys every other day."

"Same thing for power," said Joe. "We are—well—Cent is, transferring batteries ground side every other day for charging."

"Busy girl," said Connie.

"For now. When we add solar, I won't have to. Then we'll investigate oxygen-generation methods using electrolysis. We've got quite a bit of water up here, after all."

Connie frowned and looked back down toward our "kitchen." "Those little bags?"

Joe laughed and pointed, shifting his finger as he spoke. "There, there, there, there, and there. *Everywhere* but at the window, you're looking at a wall of water three feet thick. Three hundred twenty-one tons of it."

"For drinking?"

"Heck, no. For radiation shielding," said Joe. "For micrometeorite armor. And for thermal mass. It's why this station is even possible and you aren't receiving any more radiation in here than you would in a typical airliner."

"You know," said Connie. "I quite like three feet of water."

We did five minutes at the view port and then Tara stuck the camera to a patch of Velcro and all eight of us gathered, floating behind Connie as she said, "From ten thousand kilometers above the earth, this has been Connie del Olmo from Apex Orbital Services Kristen Station."

Our Singapore server cluster crashed again, but we'd *warned* them about the show and they were able to swing extra capacity in fairly quickly.

Coverage was mixed.

We were dilettantes and amateurs. We were insane space squatters. We were bold pioneers. The whole thing was the biggest hoax since the moon landings. Space Girl's Space Mom is *hawt* and Space Granny wasn't so bad either.

There were thousands of inquiries about moving all variety of invalid relatives into our facility. There were hundreds more decrying our privileged ability to move one invalid relative into space.

There were a substantial number of people willing to pay fantastically large sums for relatively short visits.

"Omigod," Tara said. "This could be a *much* more lucrative sideline than the satellites."

"Who cleans up after them?"

"For this kind of money? I will!"

"Greedy."

"Charge that much money, give three quarters of it to *charity* and it's *still* a lot of money."

"*That* has some merit. Let me think about it." My phone beeped and I glanced at it. "Time for some station maintenance. Batteries and $O_2$. And Cory's first trip into vacuum."

"Yeah? His first EVA?"

"How can it be an EVA if there's no vehicle? We've been calling it EAO, exoatmospheric operations."

"Has he tried it on?"

I laughed. "The actual question is, has he taken it *off*. I don't think I've seen him out of it in the last three days,."

I wasn't storing my suit in Kristen Station because there was always the possibility I'd have to arrive there after a disaster, for some kind of rescue or evacuation work. But for planned vacuum work I moved it there first, since it was the perfect place to purge nitrogen from my system.

Nitrogen levels were creeping up in Kristen Station. Every time someone came up, even if they'd emptied their lungs before the jump, their bodies would outgas it for several hours.

Cory had a solution though. Oxygen concentrators are designed to strip nitrogen out of normal air so we had plans to adapt one for the purpose when we could get to it.

It was on the list.

The list was growing.

*How many employees does NASA have?*

I dropped off my suit and charged life-support pack, sticking them to a wall, then picked up Cory's equipment (except for his suit—he *was* already wearing it.) Then I took him up.

There was *some* nervousness.

"Grandmother, talk to this boy. He needs distraction."

The plan was for Cory to spend the next forty-five minutes purging nitrogen while visiting with Grandmother and running through the station's recorded environment data on the computers, while I put on a portable $O_2$ mask and started my maintenance list.

Two laundry bins were dropped off at a cleaners and three bins of clean laundry returned to the station.

Five doubled bags of trash dropped into a random Dumpster in Fort Worth.

Two wire-mesh cartridges of depleted soda lime emptied and then refilled with eighty-four pounds of new pellets in the Michigan warehouse. Cartridges sealed in plastic bags and then parked in the station until needed.

A portion of the list required suiting up, like the weekly inspection of Kristen Station's outer hull, looking for damage and signs of fabric deterioration. There'd been a few impacts recorded by the accelerometers, but small ones, and there was a good chance that we wouldn't even be able to find where they'd gone in, but it was a perfect job for Cory's first space-walk.

Also, perfect weather. And by weather I mean solar weather; the Van Allen belts were still behaving, which still put our orbit in the sweet spot, radiation wise.

Also on the list were retrieving rejuvenated activated charcoal and desiccant cartridges, and checking the measurements between our outside mooring rings, destined to anchor a framework for solar panels.

When we could get to it.

It was on the list.

But we still weren't done flushing nitrogen, so I turned to the last nonspacewalk task on the list, swapping out oxygen cylinders.

There are lots of tri-cities in the U.S., but the three that Tri-City Medical Oxygen served were Fremont, Newark, and Union City on the east side of San Francisco Bay, down near San Jose.

I always made this trip empty-handed first, to make sure I could arrive without falling over. The H-sized tanks weigh about as much as I did and the last thing I wanted was to fall over with one on top of me.

The loading-dock doors were down, which was not normal, and I wondered if I'd mistook the day, but it wasn't the weekend and it was normal hours. I walked around to the office door and saw a hastily scribbled sign taped to the inside of the window.

**Closed because of IDIOT PLUMBER. We have gone to hire a DIFFERENT PLUMBER and the water should be drained by tomorrow. Deliveries will still be made.**

**(SG, your tanks in usual place.)**

It made me smile. *They should try dealing with leaking water in microgravity.* But it also made me worry.

We'd been awfully fortunate so far.

The worst leak we'd dealt with was when the computer-controlled solenoid valve on our cooling water failed open, resulting in a twenty-degree drop in air temperature before Mom manually closed the feed from the water bladders. She also could've closed the shutoff valve where the exhaust port went through the inner hull (which we had to do when we swapped out the bad valve).

I wasn't worried about the air integrity of our inner hull as long as the water and outer hull stayed in place, but that outer skin, despite the Kevlar and the outer Mylar, hadn't been intended for space. The water inside helped protect it from massive temperature swings but it was still getting hit with fierce ultraviolet and vacuum.

It was why we tried to keep at least one jumper up there at all times.

Yes, we'd chosen a low-debris orbit, but that didn't mean we couldn't take a hit from some chunk from outside the Earth-Moon system, zipping in at *real* speeds. My worst scenario involved a hit from something big enough or fast enough to penetrate both hulls—resulting in rapid decompression. The jumper would have fifteen seconds, tops, to get everyone out before she passed out.

And there wasn't a jumper up there right now.

I jumped into the building, back to "my" rack near the "filled" side of the cryogenic charging tanks.

My feet splashed through an inch of water. It was everywhere, and smaller pieces of equipment were stacked on cinder blocks or each other, to keep out of the wet. Even my rack, a floor stand that held four H-sized tanks with a laminated sign that said, *APEX ORB SVCS: Full Tanks Only. 2 person sign-off!* had been raised up on a set of four-by-four lumber blocks.

I jumped back to the station and looked around. Everything was fine. Cory was at one of the control/monitor computers and Grandmother floated nearby, saying something. Jeline was the mission medical specialist on duty, which wasn't very onerous—she was playing solitaire using a magnetic board and a deck of metal-core cards that we'd brought up so Grandmother could continue playing and teaching them contract bridge.

Grandmother looked up at me and said, "Everything all right?"

I exhaled. "Yes. Everything's fine."

The two depleted tanks had already been uncoupled from the pressure manifold, but were still held against the stack by individual straps. I unclipped the first strap and let the tank float out to where I could get my arms around it, then jumped it back to Tri-City, putting it with the dozens on the "empty" side of the filling stations, then repeated the process for the other one.

I splashed through the water to my rack. When I took hold of the valve of the first filled tank, I got the biggest shock of my life.

Electrical.

It seemed as if every muscle in my body seized (including my grip on the valve) and I blinked, blinked, bli—

# THIRTY-EIGHT

## Millie: Do you know where Cent is?

Davy was not thrilled with Millie's proposed house-hunting areas but he had to admit his choice of wilderness isolation hadn't worked out so well.

"It worked for a *long* time, dear. I loved that house and *we're going to rebuild there*! But meanwhile, we need a ground base with a little more scope. Trying to make do with the warehouse and the Eyrie just isn't working."

"But . . . but urban blight?"

"Yes. Fewer questions. Cheaper properties. *We* don't need to drive through those neighborhoods. People won't question security shutters and really heavy doors."

"Anybody could drive right up to it!"

"The best place to hide a needle is in a bunch of other needles."

He got an odd expression on his face. "Huh. I hadn't thought about that."

"You hid in New York. You hid in Stillwater."

"I didn't mean *me*. That airport that Hunt found? The base for that drone-control aircraft the CIA found?"

"Yes. I thought that didn't lead anywhere useful?"

"Well, not *yet*. They were operating out of Hayward Executive Airport in the East Bay area. I've been looking for a ranch or remote estate in central California. Maybe I should be looking in the cities."

"Those are *not* small cities."

"Needles. A lot of needles."

"Good luck with that. Meanwhile, I'm going to try and find a house."

She wasn't bothering with a Realtor, or even doors for that matter. She didn't care about the state of the neighborhood or the yard. She wanted a large kitchen, multiple bedrooms, a large utility space and garage, and good electrical mains.

And bathrooms. Large bathrooms with showers, bathtubs, toilets. While she didn't have to use the microgravity toilet in Kristen Station, she had tried it. After that she'd jumped to the small bathroom in the Michigan warehouse whenever necessary.

She was looking at a boarded-up hotel in Detroit, twenty rooms, a room-service kitchen, and an indoor (drained) pool and hot tub, when the satellite pager went off.

Expected Cent back 50 min ago. Cory here for their spacewalk. Not responding to page.

—Sam

Millie jumped to Kristen Station by way of the Michigan warehouse and the Eyrie.

She said, first, "Did you text Davy?"

Her mother said, "Not yet. Next, if you hadn't responded."

Cory was frowning. He was wearing the suit, but he'd relaxed it partially. "It's not like her, but I thought maybe something came up that you would know about."

Millie shook her head and regretted it. "No. She wouldn't leave the station without transport this long without arranging for Davy or me to cover. When did you last see her?"

He pointed at Cent's spacesuit, backpack, and helmet Velcroed near the equator, where Cent kept it when on station. "We were both prebreathing for my first spacewalk, but she'd just taken two empty $O_2$ tanks down to swap them out." He gestured toward the oxygen-tank bank where the gap was obvious. "Do you suppose the replacements weren't ready?"

Sam shook her head. "They keep four filled tanks prepped for us at all times. Cent says they've been very reliable."

Millie went to video uplink with the built in satphone. "I'm texting Joe, Tara, and Jade." She sent them all:

Do you know where Cent is? —Millie @ station

Then she took a deep breath and said, "And now I'm texting Davy."

Tara responded before Davy arrived. Jade's response came almost immediately after, while Millie was filling Davy in.

"I'll check the regular places again," Davy said. "While you wait to hear from Joe." He was back in under a minute with snowflakes in his hair. "I hit the warehouse, the Eyrie, and even took a quick look at the cabin site, up on the ridge and the springhouse. Nothing."

When five minutes passed and Joe still hadn't responded, Millie rang his cell phone, but the call went directly to voice mail.

Millie jumped Cory back to his lab so Cory could use his faculty clearance to get Joe's class schedule.

"Huh. Two of these lecturers post attendance and Joe wasn't in either class today."

"Well, he wasn't with Cent *then*," Millie said, pointing at one of the class times. "She was still doing station maintenance."

They tried Joe's phone again using the landline. No response.

"I'm taking you back to the station," said Millie.

"Why? They might call here or something."

"It's the 'something' I'm worried about. You don't have to go to the station but I'd feel a lot better if you weren't in your usual haunts right now."

"You think they've been grabbed?"

Millie didn't say anything. Instead her cheek twitched and the corners of her mouth pulled down.

Cory said, "I'll go back to the station."

# THIRTY-NINE

## Cent: Oubliette

I could hear someone talking. No, two someones, but I was really confused. I hurt all over and it was like my brain wasn't working properly.

"—yes, they have that trick with water we discussed, but they really can't get away when you secure them like this."

The hairs on the back of my neck stood on end. I *knew* that voice, but I'd only heard it the one day, less than a dozen sentences almost two years before.

*Isn't she supposed to be in prison?*

The second voice had a different quality about it, slightly electronic.

I tried to jump and it was like being grabbed by vice grips at my wrists, ankles, elbows, and neck.

"Ah—she's awake."

I was in a steel chair in the middle of a concrete room. There were steel cuffs over my wrists and forearms, anchored to the chair arms. A steel band around my neck was anchored to something behind me. Something equally firm held my ankles back against the chair legs.

I jerked once, to see if the chair itself would move, but it felt like it was fastened down.

No, actually it felt like it was set into the floor.

The floor, the walls, and a ceiling about twelve feet above me were smooth, cast concrete. Not bricks, not precast panels. It looked like it was all one piece relieved only by a large drain grate in the floor, a steel-framed, mirrored window in front of me, and a door that looked like it belonged on a submarine off to my right.

Oh—and the lights. Bright lights above the mirror pointed into my face. Less-bright lights mounted high on the walls and shining up to the ceiling for indirect lighting reminded me weirdly of the northern hemisphere of Kristen Station.

I tried to voice my earlier thought but it came out as a series of croaks.

Hyacinth Pope shook her head. "Didn't get that, sorry." She didn't look a bit sorry. There was something creepy about the way she leaned toward me, an almost hungry posture.

I swallowed and moistened my lips, then tried again. "Aren't you supposed to be in prison?"

"Ah! *Someone* is. The system thinks it's me and is satisfied. I certainly find it satisfactory."

The voice I'd heard earlier spoke. "I'm glad to see you survived your little shock." It came from the direction of the window and I finally located the speakers. They were close to the high-intensity spots above the mirror and had been hidden in the glare.

"I don't feel like I survived it. I feel like I was put in a sack and beaten with sticks, then died."

Hyacinth laughed.

The voice on the speakers said, "They did have to restart your heart. But it just took a little bit of epinephrine."

Now *that* was an unsettling thought.

"And of course you were also sedated until we had you . . . secure."

I looked around again. "What is this place *for*? It looks like something out of a Bond film."

The voice said, "It was made *for* your parents. That was before you entered the picture. Oh, by the way, in case you're thinking of trying your father's trick, the one with the water, it won't do any good. Simons's security detail told us all about that."

I blinked. It wasn't hard to look confused, I *was* confused. Maybe they were telling the truth about my heart stopping or maybe their sedative was still in my system. "If that's the case, why is Hyacinth in here with me?"

Ms. Pope looked slightly unsettled at that response.

"Hyacinth volunteered. She has an *unhealthy* fascination with your family. You've all had such a profound effect on the course of her life," the voice said. "But we shouldn't tempt you. Bring in *the boy*."

It felt like my heart *did* stop.

Joe's hands were cuffed behind him and he had a bruise on his right cheekbone and a split lip. The two guards holding him had hard faces and were wearing black, unmarked fatigues with sidearms in holsters.

Joe saw me, and threw himself sideways at one of his guards, but the guard just sidestepped and tripped him. Without his hands to check his fall, Joe went down *hard*.

I felt that pain again at the neck and wrists. Apparently I'd just tried to jump again and hadn't even been aware of the intention.

"Mr. Trujeque will be your guarantor."

One of the guards knelt by the large drain I'd noted and worked some sort of latch, then lifted the grating on unseen hinges. Hyacinth held it open while they wrestled Joe over to it and pushed his head and shoulders down through it, then held his legs and lowered him down in.

I pictured a huge fall, and Joe landing on his head, but when they let go, Joe's feet were still visible. They pushed the shoes down through the opening and shut the grate. One of them stood on it, while the other operated the latch. When the grate was secure, they parked themselves in the rear corners of the room, just enough on the edge of my vision that I could tell they were there when I turned my head.

"It's not a *large* oubliette," the voice said. "Only four feet deep and four feet across, but I assure you that your boyfriend cannot possibly reach the latch from inside and, should you decide to flood this chamber, even to the tippy-tippy-top, it will be Mr. Trujeque who drowns first.

"Even should you decide that that is *worth* it to get at Ms. Pope and the guards, it will not touch *me* at all. The chamber was built to contain a phenomenal amount of pressure. More pressure inside just makes it stronger, forces the door and windows more firmly onto their gaskets."

He paused. "Frankly, I'm dying to test it, but that would be hard on the staff. And, in the long run, I think we'll get more cooperation from you if we leave Mr. Trujeque alive. *Mostly*, alive."

"Cent! Don't do anything for them!" Joe's voice echoed weirdly, seeming to come from above me as it bounced off the ceiling.

"Are you all right?"

"Fine. But even if I weren't, don't cooperate with them!"

This was where Dad was supposed to show up, or, if I really wanted carnage, Mom. I wondered if there were clues for them to follow, for them to find us. "Joe, where did they get you?"

Hyacinth looked at the window to see if she should stop my questions.

"Coming out of my dorm room this morning, heading for the library."

The speakers remained silent, so Hyacinth settled back.

"Witnesses?" I asked.

Hyacinth looked amused. "*I* work clean. The boy came out at the crack of dawn. His roommate was appalled, but apparently little Joe here has been neglecting his schoolwork for *your* project and has some catching up to do. I assure you no one saw or heard us bag him."

"You bugged his room." I was outraged, which was pretty hypocritical considering I'd almost done it myself.

Hyacinth yawned.

"Is that right, Joe? No witnesses?"

"Well, it *was* pretty early."

There were certainly no witnesses at Tri-State Medical Oxygen. "What did you do with the people at Tri-State?"

"Their owner was 'induced' to send everyone home for the day. We were so pleased how well this worked that we've reset the trap. Do you think your parents will come looking for you?"

# FORTY

## Davy: Trap

They were on the roof of a specialty-welding shop across the street and two businesses down from Tri-City Medical Oxygen.

"Trap?" said Millie.

"Trap. What kind, though?" Davy was terrified he'd find his daughter in there, dead. "*You* stay clear, right?"

Millie said, "You're not the only one who's terrified. Don't be a jerk."

"I'm *thinking* about your Mom."

He saw that that got a reaction.

If all three of them were captured or killed, Sam (and currently Jeline and Cory) would be stuck out there beyond the reach of anything short of an emergency Falcon Heavy launch.

"Okay. Understood." She held up her radio. "I'll wait here, then."

Davy looked at her steadily and saw that she meant it. "Right. Give me ten minutes then call the police and say you heard gunshots at this address."

Millie shuddered. "At least they'll send an ambulance with the response. Huh. Maybe *that* one."

Davy turned his head to see what she was pointing at. It was an ambulance, parked between a self-storage business, and a floor-tile wholesaler. "I remember another ambulance, once. Do you?"

"One with an angel on the doors?"

Davy nodded. Back when he'd been captured, before Cent was even born, they'd drugged him and carried him off in an ambulance.

She lifted the binoculars. "It's pretty generic for an ambulance. All the universal symbols but nothing about an affiliation. Not seeing a town or a city or a county on it."

"Right."

He jumped, appearing behind it, and peered in through the smoked glass of the rear doors. Nothing. He jumped inside, looked around, and returned to Millie.

"No driver, no paramedic. The gurney isn't in there, either."

"Trap," she said. "But they wouldn't have the ambulance unless they wanted to carry away a *living* person."

Davy took a deep breath and blinked hard.

"Trap. Let's trip it."

He entered the building through the office. It was the only room that had a window, giving him a sight inside. The only noise he could detect was running water and once he left the office, it was everywhere, giving credence to the note left in the window.

He walked to the cryo fill tanks, gliding his feet along, not splashing, not lifting his feet and dripping. The rack with *APEX ORB SVS* on it was set back slightly. He noted the blocks of wood lifting it from the water and stopped, looking around for any sign of *them*.

He took out his cell phone and used the light. The cable running up to the rack was nearly invisible, but once he spotted it, he saw where the copper conductor was grounded to the frame with a screw and a freshly drilled hole.

Suddenly he was less sure that his daughter was all right, and absolutely furious. Were they watching? Or did they have something rigged to the current, so they could detect when the trap was sprung that way?

He went back to the office and grabbed a blue-plastic recycling bin that looked sturdy enough. He quietly emptied it onto the floor and, as he returned to the trap, he grabbed one of the dozens of chains used to secure bottles together so they wouldn't topple.

Back by the rack, he inverted the recycling bin in the water and climbed up onto it, then tossed the chain over the rack, letting the other end drop into the water.

The spark was big enough to make him want to jump away. *They did this next to full oxygen bottles?* But then he heard a beeping noise from the back and the lights went out.

There were just two of them, dressed for the ambulance. One of them had an orange EMT trauma bag and the other one had a bright flashlight.

*Screw it*, he thought. *The old ways are best.*

He took the one with the flashlight first, and was back for the second one so fast that the first one hadn't hit the water yet when his partner also appeared fifty feet above the water of the pit.

Back at Tri-City, he ripped the cable off the rack and followed it back to where it was hooked to some kind of power supply plugged into the wall. On a piece of masking tape, someone had written *5,000 volts pulsed ECD.*

He returned to the rooftop across the way. "All clear," he told Millie.

They found the ambulance gurney in the employee break room. Right behind it, the owner was tied up in the closet.

"They came in before any of my employees. One of them stood beside me, smiling, as I sent them all home. None of them realized he had a gun in my kidney." The man was shaken. "He took great pains to tell me I'd die slowly. 'I'm a trained paramedic,' he said. 'You'll bleed out before they can save you. It will really hurt.'"

"Have you seen Space Girl today?" Millie said.

"I've been tied up in that closet for five hours. I haven't seen *anybody.* Bathroom," he said. "NOW."

Davy got out of his way.

# FORTY-ONE

## Cent: Nothing

Partway through the "interview" I decided I really owed Connie del Olmo an apology. Compared to the "interviewer" on the other side of the mirror, Connie was an angel from heaven.

Don't think I wasn't scared.

I was.

I was terrified they'd pull Joe back out of the oubliette and start cutting pieces off of him. This wasn't fanciful imagination on my part. The possibility had already been discussed by the voice. Hyacinth had pulled out a knife clearly sharp enough to do the job and pointed her thumb toward the guards. "I have *all* the help I need."

I looked past Hyacinth to the mirror. "What do you want, Mr. Gilead?"

I saw the Hyacinth's eyes widen ever so slightly and knew I'd hit it on the nose.

"Who?" said the voice. He did it well, really, but I didn't buy it. I just looked in the direction of the mirror and raised my eyebrows.

There was a sound like something brushing the mic, and muffled speech, then the mic was uncovered and a different voice came on, deeper, older, not frail exactly, but definitely not young. "So my name is not unknown to you."

"Yes."

"That explains a few things. What are your father's intentions? Toward me and my organization, that is."

"Two years ago? He was just following the strings. More recently it's been getting a little bit more personal. And really, Mr. Gilead, if you'd just ignored us, you could've gone on pulling your strings and running things from behind the curtains. But you couldn't leave well enough alone, could you?" I hadn't realized how much anger I'd been holding. "All in all, it would've been better if you'd just sent an e-mail."

"I doubt your father would have answered. I have quite a few more questions. For instance, where are your other bases? Who has your father been working with at the CIA? And is it really true that you could destroy any satellite currently in Earth orbit?"

I would've pinched the bridge of my nose if I could reach it. My face must've shown something of this.

Gilead said, "What would you call that expression, Ms. Pope? Disdain? Disbelief?"

I said, "Disbelief is pretty close. Do you really think you have any chance of getting my cooperation?"

Hyacinth said, "Disbelief and a little bit of contempt, apparently."

I smoothed my expression. Contempt was too strong. I remembered Dad's scars and the story of his time in these people's hands. I thought Gilead was insane, but that was not a comforting realization.

He waxed philosophical. "I've always found it *fascinating* that young people have such a sense of immortality. It's probably—"

"Evolutionary?" I said. "Oddly enough, I've had this exact lecture from my mother."

"I don't think she took it in quite the same direction I'm going," Gilead said. "Ms. Pope, let's have Mr. Trujeque up again. I think we could benefit from a *practical* demonstration."

*Damn.* "You really don't want to do that."

"Oh, I really think I do."

"Let me rephrase that then," I said, watching the guards

unlatch the grate. "I don't think the results you will get are the one you are expecting."

They pulled the grate open. It was a lot harder, apparently, to get someone out of the oubliette than to put them in, especially if you wanted them conscious. The guard reaching down had to pull back up, one hand to his face. His eye was swelling shut.

Mr. Gilead was not pleased. "What happened?"

"Lucky kick," the guard said. "Should've cuffed his legs. I'll get 'em."

He bent back to the grate and Mr. Gilead said, "Wait." The volume of the speakers increased. "Mr. Trujeque, if you do not stand up and cooperate I will have Ms. Pope cut one of your girlfriend's ears *off.* Either one, Ms. Pope. Lady's choice."

"Joe," I called. *"Both hulls."*

"Huh?" he said. "Down *here?"*

"Trillion to one!" I took three deep, fast breaths.

"What is *that* supposed to do?" Hyacinth said, taking the knife back out of her front pocket. She was making a show of it, using her thumb to swing the blade out slowly until it locked open with an audible "click."

Over the speaker Gilead said, "Mr. Trujeque, your girlfriend is about to lose an ear. Don't you think—"

Hyacinth took a step closer and I twinned.

To space.

The air rushing out of the chamber staggered the guards and Hyacinth, though she kept her knife. Sound was leaving with the conducting medium and the last words I heard over the speaker were "Kill her n—" I was holding my throat open, letting the air leave my lungs.

Two seconds.

I suppose they could have built the window to withstand pressure from *both* sides. They'd been so busy making sure it could withstand *anything* that they'd failed to consider what happened when it was up against *nothing.*

The steel frame and mirror pulled away from the wall, bolts tearing from the concrete, and the frame folded along the lower left corner where bolts still held. Papers and books and *a per-*

*son wearing a tie* blew through the opening, falling to the floor around me. An older man clung to the counter just inside the other room, his face constricted with rage. He was screaming words, I think, but I couldn't hear them and I was pretty sure I didn't want to hear them.

Five seconds.

The far room was full of fog that streamed toward me revealing wainscoting and wood panels, built-in bookshelves, a mahogany bar. There was a brief rushing sound as the air from that room rushed through me, temporarily raising the local pressure, then the sound hissed away again. Hyacinth pulled her hand back and lunged toward me.

Seven seconds.

The door visible in the far wall of the next room was steel in a steel frame and probably opened out. *It* withstood the pressure, but the wall next to it did not. Books, shelves, paneling, metal studs, and Sheetrock blew toward me. Another wave of air hissed by. Hyacinth's blade flashed forward, reflected intensely bright sunlight, then passed from sight, followed by her arm, her head and shoulders, and then the rest of her, disappearing into silence.

Nine seconds.

One guard was on his knees, fighting to stay up, and the other was lying on his side, blood streaming from his mouth and nose. He'd let go of the grate to the oubliette but the rush of air had been keeping it open. Now it started falling.

Eleven seconds.

I could feel water boiling off of my tongue and my head swam, but all my concentration was on the twinning, on maintaining this hole into vacuum. The grate slammed back into its frame and though I couldn't hear it, I felt it distantly through the chair.

Thirteen seconds.

My sight was tunneling in and I saw the last upright guard fall forward onto his face, definitely unconscious, making no effort to catch himself with his ar—

"—ent. Cent!"

Joe had his hands on both sides of my face, looking into my

eyes. His hands were still cuffed but clearly not still behind his back. I tried to lift my hand and realized I was still locked in that damn chair.

"Hmmm?" I said.

"Are you okay?"

"How . . . long?"

"Uh, long? Oh, how long were you out? It's only been a minute or two since you . . . you did that thing."

I shook my head, trying to clear it. I was still having trouble thinking but I couldn't tell if it was from the depressurization or the earlier electrocution or whatever they'd drugged me with to transport me here from Tri-City.

Wherever *here* was.

I scanned the room. There was one guard lying on the floor, bloody mouth, clearly dead. The older man—Gilead?—lay across the counter with his head partway into *this* room, staring fixedly at nothing. I didn't see the other guard or the man who'd blown into the room.

Or Hyacinth.

"How'd you get out?" I asked.

He pointed with both hands at the grate. "I got the cuffs under my legs and in front of me as soon as those assholes dumped me down there. I don't *think* I ever lost consciousness, but I sure got dizzy."

"I saw the grate shut!"

"Yeah. Saw that, but thank God, it didn't latch."

"Where's the guard and that other guy?"

"When I popped up out of the hole, the other guard was just coming around, so I snagged his collar and pulled him down headfirst while he was still groggy and used him as a step stool to get the rest of the way up. He was just getting turned around when I stuffed the guy in the suit down and they got tangled. I got the grate latched before they could get unstuck."

"Unstuck?"

"Unwedged. It was tight down there with just *one* of me. What happened to that Ms. Pope? Did she book?"

"She did leave," I said. "Can you get out of those cuffs?"

He bent down and picked up an automatic pistol. "It was on the floor. I guess the guard drew it but passed out before he could decide what to shoot. The dead guy still has his." He put the grip in my hand.

"I was going to try and shoot the chain myself but it was really awkward." He pulled his hands apart stretching the handcuff chain taut. "I figured you could fire and I'd hold the chain in front of the muzzle."

Did this idea sound bad because I was still dizzy or even though I was still dizzy?

*Even though*, I decided. "Why don't you go look for a handcuff key in the guard's pockets?" I said.

Joe stared down at the gun, his mouth open. "Or maybe I could go look for a key in the guard's pockets," he said brightly.

It was not in his pockets but it was on a key ring clipped to his belt. Fortunately, this included a key that fit the massive padlock on the back of my chair. Once that was off, Joe twisted the released lever and all seven restraining cuffs—ankles, wrists, elbows, and neck—opened.

I nearly fainted when I staggered upright, but a few deep breaths and Joe's hand on my elbow steadied me.

I checked both men's pulses just to be sure, wrist and throat. These weren't the first dead men I'd ever seen, but Gilead and the guard were the first ones I'd *killed*. I didn't know how to count Hyacinth.

"Stroke maybe? Looks kind of old," said Joe peering at Gilead. "The guard . . . well, he held his breath, clearly. Embolism."

"I think so. Don't know about Gilead." I shut away the view of both corpses by burying my face in Joe's chest and putting my arms around him.

He squeezed back. "Let's get out of here," he said.

Oh, I wanted to, *so bad*. I shook my head. "Not yet." I gestured at the guard and the grate. "There could be people out there who got caught in this."

Joe looked at me like I was crazy, but when I didn't say anything else, he picked up the automatic pistol again.

"Do you even know how to fire that?"

He pointed at the trigger, then the muzzle. "It's a Glock. You squeeze that part, things come out of that part. Very fast."

At least he wasn't pointing it at me or himself, but my face was expressing doubt.

He pulled the slide half back and showed me that there was a bullet in the chamber. When he held the gun down and to the side, he did *not* put his index finger in the trigger guard, but held it straight along the frame above.

Maybe he wouldn't shoot himself. "Okay."

"Do you want the other gun?" He tilted his head toward the dead guard.

"Not really," I said.

He took the magazine from the other gun and the two spare clips from the guard's belt.

We couldn't open the door, the one that looked like it belonged on a submarine. "Maybe they do it remotely," I said, pointing my chin at the observation window.

Joe eyed Gilead's corpse and said doubtfully, "We could climb through."

I shuddered.

I jumped us past the body into the paneled room. There were files and books and papers and a computer workstation. I knew Dad would really like to see this stuff, but I couldn't be bothered. I didn't open the door into this room, but walked through the torn wall into a hallway.

There were three cells, empty, no bars, just steel doors with reinforced-glass inspection windows and pass-through slots for meals.

"I woke up in one of those," Joe said. He rubbed his right buttock. "They stuck me with a needle when they grabbed me."

We found an elevator. There was only an "up" call button. Joe pushed it and it opened immediately. I glanced inside—three floors G1 to G3. We were G3. Joe moved to enter and I blocked him, shaking my head.

The stairs weren't marked, but the door to the stairwell opened outward and the catch had ripped during the "evacuation," so it was open.

On the next level up, there was a dining room and a kitchen and three bedroom suites, luxurious, in the manner of the observation room below. Two of the suites showed signs of occupancy. Several containers had exploded in the kitchen, and flour and dry cereal and some sticky liquid were sprayed across the floor.

On the top level there was another kitchen, more institutional, a dining/TV room and several small rooms that screamed servants' quarters. Things were scattered up here, too, and we heard voices from the other end.

Two paramedics came up the hall, one pushing a gurney and one carrying a trauma bag. The uniforms looked all right but their faces looked demented.

Worry will do that.

I stepped out into the hall.

"We were just leaving," I said.

Mom jumped the five yards to me, her arms on my shoulders, peering at my face. The uniform she wore was too big, the pants cuffs were rolled up and the shirt bunched at the waist. "Are you all right? What did they do to you?"

"Why is your uniform wet?" I asked.

Dad saw me and his knees buckled before he caught himself and leaned heavily against the gurney.

When Joe heard Mom's voice, he stepped around the corner, Glock no longer held at the ready.

Mom took in his split lip and bruised face. "What did they do to *both* of you?"

Joe grinned. "You should ask what Cent did to *them*!"

Dad straightened. He looked like he'd aged ten years, I thought, but in a light voice he asked, "Okay. What *did* you do to them?"

"Nothing," I said. "A *lot* of nothing."

Mom wanted Joe and me medically checked, but I was reluctant. I'd probably feel different by tomorrow, but after the day I'd just had, there wasn't a doctor on Earth that I'd trust. Fortunately I knew one off the planet.

Flight Surgeon Rasmussen-Grebenchekova heard our stories, shook her head, and checked us over for barotrauma, paying special attention to our ears, sinuses, and lungs.

We had our exam in the Destiny module so she could use the ultrasound unit to give our sinuses, lungs and, in my case, heart a look.

"The voltage went from arms to legs? Yeah, you could have had fibrillation." She did an electrocardiogram and a neurological assessment, too. "For a person who should be dead twice over," she said, "you're looking all right, but there could be delayed effects."

She gave us a both a stern look and said, "For the barotrauma I recommend a high-oxygen environment for the next forty-eight hours." She grinned. "I happen to know you have such a facility available."

"Yes. And when you've got an hour or two," I said, "we'd love to have the newlyweds over for dinner."

"The newlyweds would be delighted. I've been curious about your resident."

"Really? We're looking for someone interested in monitoring her long-term progress. It would help, I suppose, if that person knew how to handle themselves in microgravity and just happened to have a specialty in space medicine."

She stared at me, her face still. "Don't say that if you don't mean it. Misha and I are slated for retirement. Our chances of another mission from either of the space agencies is exactly nil."

"I *do* mean it. I'd love to get Misha's input on our upcoming solar-panel installation."

"Well then, I think we could say that once Misha and I are officially retired from our respective agencies you will find us very interested in your future *endeavors*."

The restaurant was in Stanville, Ohio, and the *spécialité de la maison* was the soft-serve ice cream dipped in a chocolate coating that seemed more like wax than cocoa, but Dad insisted.

"It's the perfect time. They're deserted the hour before school gets out."

We sat in the corner booth on hard, laminated seats.

Joe got the red-plastic basket of popcorn shrimp, though he was having an adventure finding actual shrimp in the breading. I got a small chocolate shake. Mom had a diet soda. Dad got the dip cone.

"Your father played bad cop and I played—"

"Good cop?" asked Joe.

Mom looked embarrassed and I groaned. Joe hadn't seen Mom the *last* time I was in Hyacinth Pope's control.

Dad shook his head. "That's not exactly how I would put it."

I asked, "Did you get out the baseball bat again?"

Mom looked prim.

Dad said, "We had the box they wired to the oxygen rack. She never actually touched one of them, but—" He held his hands a foot apart. "She could get sparks *this* big."

"Okay," I said. "So you played bad cop and Mom played insanely scary cop and you got them to tell you where the Retreat was?"

Dad shook his head. "It was in the recently found addresses in the ambulance's GPS. Mother just got really creative with her questioning to make sure that's what it was."

"And made sparks," Mom said. "*Big* sparks near their heads. Their hair stood up; I never intentionally zapped them."

"Wait," I said. "*Intentionally?*"

"It wasn't on *purpose!*" Mom looked a little guilty. "There was a learning curve. The guy was wetter than I thought. Grounded."

Dad said, "She took advantage of it. She screamed, *How many guards monitor the video cameras facing the entrance at thirty-seven thirty-two Montrose Avenue!* He nearly wet himself."

"He may *have* wet himself," Mom said. "It wasn't that long after you dropped him in the pit. How would you *tell?*"

"What did he say?" I asked.

Dad cleared his throat and "screamed" softly, "How should we fucking know? That *woman* at the tunnel took the girl and sent us back to reset the trap! We've never been in their stupid bunker!"

"You believed him?" Joe asked.

Mom said, "We played variations on the same theme with his partner a little bit later. Similar results. He actually provided enough description for us to find the stupid door. We'd never have figured out that it was down there in the parking garage. Then it was just a case of finding the crowd of people trying to escape a sucking maw of death."

Between them, Mom and Dad had dropped over eleven guards and staff into the pit by the time they found us.

"They were still pretty shook up," Dad said. "All but the two outside guards got caught in your, uh, low-pressure system."

"So, whose idea was it to call the FBI?"

The San Francisco FBI office fielded the agents who went into the scene. The Retreat was built into the foundation of a commercial bank in Silicon Valley, accessed from a gated section of the lowest level of the adjoining parking garage.

"That was Hunt. *One* prisoner he was willing to bend the rules on, but he thought the rules against domestic operations would, uh, snap rather than flex when it came to concealing the death of a billionaire and the covert imprisonment of his security staff."

"You put them all back before they came, right?"

Dad nodded. "They had those handy cells downstairs. I hope the FBI found the keys. I didn't use 'em. They certainly found plenty of other stuff.

"Daarkon Group is going down hard. This was their very unpublic records. Offshore accounts, payment schedules to more than a few purchased congressman and senators, some interesting blackmail video and photos starring various highly placed officials, foreign and domestic.

"And there was one hundred thirty-five million dollars' worth of Euro bearer bonds, a half million in gold, and two Picassos in Gilead's closet."

I blinked. "Wow. The FBI told you about the bearer bonds?"

Dad scratched his nose. "The FBI found an empty closet."

"What?" I looked at Mom.

She was looking at the ceiling and shaking her head. I had the feeling this was not a revelation to her.

Dad said, "Bastard blew up my home. Subverted my mother-in-law's surgeon. *Tried* to kill my entire family. Kidnapped my daughter and her boyfriend." He ground his teeth together, then visibly unclenched them and rubbed at his mastoids with his fingers. "Look, the U.S. government is seizing the offshore accounts. We're talking three billion plus. I think they can afford to leave some for us. They wouldn't have any of it if not for our efforts." He raised his glass to me. "Our *joint* efforts. I just wish I knew what happened to Hyacinth Pope."

I cleared my throat.

"General Sterling called me up this morning about a new cloud of orbital debris."

"Why?" Mom said. "Does he want you to remediate it?"

I shook my head. "He called me because its point of origin was my standard orbital insertion over the Marshall Islands."

"Is *that* where you were twinning?" Dad said.

"Yes. He's seeing a bunch of books and papers and office supplies that ended up there. And one elongated object between one and two meters, approximately sixty-five kilos."

Joe blinked. "You said Hyacinth booked."

"She did. She is *still* booking—seven thousand seven hundred twenty meters per second." I sipped from my water, staring down at the table. "I *think* she was trying to stop it—the depressurization. Anyway, she stuck a knife in me and it worked so well she just kept going."

Mom said, "She tried to stab you?"

"Whoa." Joe shifted back in his chair, eyes wide. "Insanely scary cop, I presume?"

"Mom, she's in orbit. She wasn't exactly dressed for it."

Mom took a couple of deep breaths. "So she's not coming back?"

"Sometime near the end of next month she will burn up in the upper atmosphere. Call it cremation."

Dad reached over and patted the back of my hand. "Wasn't your fault."

I glowered at him. I knew he was right but *she passed right through me*. It was . . . unsettling.

"She'll go out as a shooting star," Dad said. "It's more than she deserves. I'm not exactly sad, but I promise you, if I see any meteors next month I won't be making a wish."

I exhaled, puffing out my lips. "Okay, then. Does the FBI want to talk to me? For murder?"

Dad shook his head. "They're not sure you were there. The guard who survived isn't talking, or Gilead's assistant—what can they say? 'We were torturing this seventeen-year-old girl we kidnapped and she hurt us?' "

Joe raised his hand, "I helped a *little*."

Dad smiled. "Okay, 'and she and her boyfriend kicked our butts?' So if it's not a kidnapping/torture investigation, it's also not a murder investigation. Gilead wasn't exactly shot—autopsy says cerebral aneurism. The guard's embolism is also not a regular murder method."

"Hunt knows we were there," I said.

"Hunt is the guy who encouraged us to stay *out* of it."

Joe said, "What are they saying happened, then? Like when *all* their air went away?"

Dad said. "Suspected gas leak."

I did have to laugh at that. "Ow. Literally true, too."

"If that's settled, I want dessert," said Joe. He looked at Dad. "Do they take bearer bonds here? I think *you* should buy."

# FORTY-TWO

## Cent: The List

The list is a monster that never dies.

Two weeks after our visit to the Retreat, Cory finally got his spacewalk, thirty minutes of tethered inspection work clambering around the outer skin of Kristen Station. I took him out and delivered him to his first tether ring, then backed off. He did the rest himself, with three ten-meter pieces of climbing line with snap-on carabiners at each end. The only time I had to intervene was when he lingered over our cooling-exhaust port.

Dad followed, eager.

Mom went next, reluctant, but she understood that we needed jumpers out there with the "spatially normative" for both normal and emergency transport. I cheated—after five minutes of tethered work on the station, I jumped her to 160 kilometers altitude with the earth spread across her entire field of vision. We spent the rest of the spacewalk pointing out beautiful clouds and identifying landforms to each other. Her attitude about wearing the suit was greatly improved by the time we returned to the station.

Joe went next. Grandmother declined and Seeana said, "Maybe later." Jade and Tara said, "Spring break, for sure!" but Jeline and Tessa leapt at the chance.

This led up to the famous photo on the cover of *Wired*. Six spacesuited figures (Dad, Mom, Cory, Joe, Jeline, and me in all the working suits) arranged round the exterior frame of the viewport with Grandmother, Seeana, and Tessa inside. The sun was behind the station and we were all lit by full earthlight, all but Dad's visor open, all but Dad's face visible. All of our heads pointed toward the center of the view port, a white coveralled snowflake with triaxial symmetry.

We needed every one of those suits a month later, when the station's outer skin began delaminating in earnest. We'd already noticed the tendency and, though it was expensive, we were ready.

We didn't replace the outer skin—we enclosed it with a thicker version, with more Kevlar, more layers, a heavier deposition of aluminum on the Mylar outer layer and space-rated bonding agents.

The new skin had to go up in two halves because we didn't have the option of jumping the entire station *within* an intact sphere. Thank goodness, we hadn't started the exterior geodesic framework for the solar panels, so we just had to deal with through ports for exhausts, wiring, and, of course, the view port. Seams and through ports were sealed with exotic adhesives and shielded with Mylar overpatches.

The suit video recorded during this project, edited by Jade and Tara and narrated by Grandmother, went to PBS, which filled it out to a full hour by having Connie del Olmo do split-screen questions and commentary with Grandmother, ground to orbit.

With the proven capability of their equipment, Matoska Counter-Pressure Spacesuits received contracts from NASA, SpaceX, Orbital Sciences, ESA, and Roscosmos, with additional interest from the China National Space Administration and the Indian Space Research Organisation. Venture capitalists were trying to *throw* money at Cory, but thanks to a substantial influx of Euro bearer bonds from an unnamed investor, he was able to turn away all offers with the information that the fiscal foundation of MCP Suits, Inc. was sound.

Apex Orbital entered into formal agreements with NASA, ESA, and Roscosmos for orbital emergency transportation and limited routine transport of personnel and cargo. We, too, had an influx of anonymous capital, and were able to shift Earth-side support, research, and development to a set of employees selected by our new director of ground-side operations, Wanda Chappell. She was a regular visitor to Kristen Station to "properly assess her division's performance in meeting station needs."

Cory resigned his Stanford teaching position—there was just no time—but MCP Suits, Inc. entered into a formal research relationship with the university.

Joe and Jade got full-ride scholarships from their respective schools. Their appearance as Stanford and Smith "interns" in orbit during the first Connie del Olmo interview had generated huge press for each institution and general increases in alumni donations.

When Jade let "slip" that the Apex Orbital Services director of public relations was considering Smith College, Tara's test scores were reviewed by admissions and, in a "coincidental" meeting outside one of Jade's classes, the dean of financial aid told Jade that there was a "great deal of assistance available for diverse students with high academic potential and a precollege engagement with their career of choice."

Dr. Rasmussen-Grebenchekova had Grandmother start some weight-bearing exercises involving elastic bands. "You should put in a treadmill. She should walk and, maybe later, run."

To everyone's surprise Grandmother started jogging without the treadmill, clearing a path around the inside of the inner hull that was slightly inclined off of the equator of the station to avoid the stack's support lines.

"I had Seeana find me these shoes with tacky rubber soles," she explained.

She would start with a good tangential tug on one of the stack anchor lines and then begin pushing with her feet. As her forward speed increased, the force against her feet became greater, like a skateboarder or a stunt bicyclist doing a complete loop inside a cylindrical concrete tunnel.

A month later Rasmussen tested her on a reduced oxygen mix, monitoring her blood oxygenation resting and exercising, then had us reduce the station's oxygen content to 50 percent. This forced us to go back to mask prebreathing, but we were glad to.

One day Grandmother floated up to me and said tentatively, "I've received an offer, but I don't think I should take it if *you* think it's a bad idea."

"Did one of those marriage proposals hit the spot?" I said. I was only half joking. She'd gotten about four hundred.

She twitched her hand, flicking away the great mass of love-lorn humanity with a flip of the wrist. "No. I've been offered a half-hour show on the Retirement Living cable channel. I'd have a guest on for most of the show and take audience questions and do some sort of personal essay at the end."

"Do they want the guests to come up here?" I said, alarmed. I was against that, and not just because of security. I didn't want someone bringing anything communicable and getting her sick.

"No. We'd do them split screen, guests on Earth, me here. The producers and I were talking about one-third medical, one-third lifestyle, and one-third celebrities over sixty." She bit her lip then said in a rush, "I was just worried it was exploiting the station and you and everything you're working on up here for *my* ego."

I hugged her. "Nonsense. Go for it."

"You're sure?"

"Absolutely! Is the satphone rig we have up here good enough?"

"They want to use the satellite they lease capacity on but they said they would provide all the equipment we needed. We just have to schedule the show for when we're not on the wrong side of the earth from that satellite."

"I had to calculate that when we were looking at geosynchronous-based satphone providers. We're blocked from any particular geosync point for about seventeen minutes every six-hour orbit. Surely they can find a good slot in the other almost-twenty-three hours."

Everyone knows the opening credits of the show: Cue catchy

music, title over station exterior, tracking shot to the view port
with Grandmother gesturing the viewer in, and the jump cut to
the interior with her floating forward to say the show's catch-
phrase, "Welcome to my world."

It rapidly became the channel's most-watched show, drawing
viewers from outside its target demographic. When they took
the format to an hour after five weeks, there was pressure from
corporate to move it away from the "old folks" channel, but
Grandmother refused.

After it went to an hour, I made one five-minute appearance,
for her sake, but mostly I kept a low profile.

The damn list was not getting any smaller.

We got the framework and the panels and the charge controllers installed. We didn't do active pointing but distributed them
uniformly across the perimeter of the sphere. This meant that a
large percentage of them were pointing away from the sun at all
times, but enough were in sunlight that I got to stop running
batteries up and down.

Wanda's people, working with Misha and Stanford, came up
with a zeolite swing-bed $CO_2$-absorbent system that also absorbed moisture, keeping me from having to haul soda lime or
swap out the desiccant.

Still on the list was a system that would electrolyze oxygen
from water, a system for automatically reactivating our charcoal
filters, a food freezer, a food heater, and, always, an improved
microgravity toilet.

The list is a bitch. No matter how many things you take off
of it, it grows and grows.

Still, one day I jumped down to the relatively new offices of
Matoska Counter-Pressure Spacesuits, Inc., and walked into
Cory's office.

He looked up from his computer, an annoyed you-have-
disturbed-important-work look on his face, but it vanished when
I set the plastic-bagged jar on the desk with a *clunk*.

His hand's darted out and I said, "Don't open it! I promised
it would arrive uncontaminated."

"I *know*." He held the package up and tilted it, watching through two layers of plastic and the thick glass as the fine, dark gray sand slid and shifted.

He looked back at me, his mouth parted. "You *said* you could," he said finally. "How did the Tyvek work?"

"Good. A little dust made it onto the surface of the radiation layer and the tiniest bit onto the Nomex coveralls, but I didn't see anything on the MCP suit, and I used a magnifier."

"You were warm enough?"

"Mostly. We're going to need better boots—my toes were getting numb by the time I left. The overgloves were good, though."

He looked back at the jar. "I was expecting reddish brown."

"Basaltic sands from the dunes in the Melas Chasma. I've got pictures. The bluffs north of there are *astonishing*."

He set the jar down carefully. "So," he said. "Mars."

I nodded, "Mars."

So that's *one* thing off the list.

# Acknowledgments

Special thanks to Cory Matoska of Lubbock, Texas, whose generous contribution to the Con-or-Bust charity (http://con-or -bust.org/) won him the right to be a named character in this book. That this character's first name also matches my good friend Cory Doctorow's, that part is only a fortuitous coincidence. Really.

More thanks are due to my family. I have Frankensteined my daughters for parts of Cent, and Millie owes a great deal to my loving wife, Laura J. Mixon.